Praise for the *Tales from the Riven Isles* series

'Simpson sticks the landing with an epic conclusion. Fans of Andrea Hairston's *Master of Poisons* and other secondary world fantasy will enjoy this expansive magical adventure.'
Publishers Weekly on *Tinderbox*

'This promising debut features strong world building and well-developed systems of magic.'
Booklist on *Tinderbox*

'*The Hatter's Daughter* is an action-packed adventure of a retelling, and fans of the original story will love seeing the appearances of many reimagined characters – even as their seemingly perfect world of Wonderland is taken over by new and very dangerous forces that threaten heroine Faith and her entire Underneath. This book takes you on a wild ride down the rabbit hole and all the way up again, and it won't let you off until everything you've ever thought was impossible in this world becomes compellingly curious.'
Kelly Ann Jacobson, author of *Tink and Wendy* and *Lies of a Toymaker*

'*The Hatter's Daughter* is a fun and fresh adventure through a land of magic and encroaching decay. This fast-paced, magical tale is filled with charm and surprises, and features a world at once familiar and unique.'
M.H. Ayinde, 2021 winner of the Future Worlds Prize and author of *A Song of Legends Lost*

'With protagonists you can root for and a supporting cast of characters both old and new, this book will charm fairy -tale readers of all ages!'
Elana A. Mugdan, author of *The Shadow War Saga*, on *The Hatter's Daughter*

W.A. SIMPSON

STEELBOUND

Tales from the Riven Isles

Book Four

Following *The Hatter's Daughter*

This is a **FLAME TREE PRESS** book

FLAME TREE PRESS
6 Melbray Mews, London, SW6 3NS, UK
flametreepress.com

US sales, distribution and warehouse:
Simon & Schuster
simonandschuster.biz

UK distribution and warehouse:
Hachette UK Distribution
hukdcustomerservice@hachette.co.uk

Thanks to the Flame Tree Press team.

Cover art by Nick Wells/Flame Tree Studio from sketches and layered files created using new photos and a stock images from FlexDreams, Karol Moraes and Peyker (Shutterstock.com) combined and crafted in Photoshop. No AI, AGI or LLM was used in this process.
The font families used are Avenir and Bembo.

Flame Tree Press is an imprint of Flame Tree Publishing Ltd
flametreepublishing.com

A copy of the CIP data for this book is available from the British Library and the Library of Congress.

1 3 5 7 9 8 6 4 2

HB ISBN: 978-1-78758-982-7
ebook ISBN: 978-1-78758-983-4

Printed and bound in the UK by CPI Group (UK) Ltd, Croydon, CR0 4YY

Represented in the EU for product safety and compliance by Authorised Rep Compliance Ltd, Ground Floor, 71 Lower Baggot Street, Dublin, D02 P593, Ireland. Contact at www.arccompliance.com

W.A. SIMPSON

STEELBOUND

Tales from the Riven Isles

Book Four

Following *The Hatter's Daughter*

FLAME TREE PRESS

London & New York

CHAPTER ONE

Well, John Henry was a little baby
Sitting on his daddy's knee,
He picked up a hammer and
A little piece of steel
And cried, Hammer's going to be the death of me!

"Burn, witch!" The echoing cry prophesied the end. Ursa understood the weight of her destiny with unshakable determination. Expectation, not fear, made death seem commonplace. The fiery and violent arrival of death held no importance. Future uncertainty also played a part. If all went well, she could leave her current problems behind and begin again elsewhere. Her refusal to forgive condemned her to eternal torment in the nether-hells.

She spent centuries roaming those dreadful places, much like a vagabond. A single fatal error resulted in the loss of her home, family, and title.

Flames danced around the pyre and licked the wood and kindling. Sweat and dust combined on her skin, obscuring the villagers in a blurry haze that stung her eyes.

Don't they have anything more worthwhile to spend their time on? Silent, private mockery taunted the mounting pain.

The attention of the crowd suddenly focused on her laughter, a defiant sound in the face of pain. A condemning voice rose above the din of the crowd. "See how she mocks us? I will eradicate the witch and return her to her wicked master." Condemned to death by the self-proclaimed Archdeacon Barnabas, she received the jeers of the unlearned masses.

The curses and jeers were continuous. Humanity's fear and ignorance created a deafening noise. She had grown tired of them. Sick of it all. She showed no remorse, even as the end drew closer.

People believed the boundary between life and death revealed the complexities of existence. Ursa saw the flickering flames, splintering wood, and shadowy figures of executioners disappear.

* * *

As the ship neared Lark Harbor, serving Joringel, Bale, and Avynne, Ursa trembled with anxiety. Or at least, that is how she remembered it. Over five hundred years had passed since Ursa last visited the Riven Isles. Ursa hated her own fear, a senseless, irrational terror. The probability of her being recognized was low. Ursa realized she had to face her haunting nightmares to overcome them. The unrelenting torment forced her to retreat. Summer heat in the Isles varied by location. This morning resembled all the others.

Ursa remained unperturbed by the surrounding commotion. The situation baffled her. Her safety was guaranteed unless she went Underneath. She recalled that first day. Four guards, led by their commander, escorted Ursa from her home, gave her a sack of food for a week, a waterskin, and five silver crowns. She considered humbling herself and seeking their pardon. She would offer them anything, including herself, to remain.

She walked away instead.

The ship docked with the captain's expert navigation. With the familiar backpack, Ursa experienced a sense of muted comfort. She tossed it over her shoulders with practiced ease, knowing her day's travels would soon be over with the setting sun. She had already found an affordable place to stay. Ursa's ingenuity had carried her through good and tough times over the years. To put it mildly, her beginning in Above Ground had proved chaotic.

The return to the pier seemed dreamlike. She softly whispered, "Obligation, not desire, brought me here."

A journey through numerous southern cities immersed her in an environment filled with recognizable sounds. To Ursa, fey and humans mixed. From a respected fey, she became a wandering dokkalfar woman.

Ursa proceeded on her journey and arrived at the inn. She paid and went upstairs. Besides bedding and a dresser, only a mirror, decanter, and bowl filled the room. Ursa removed her pack and boots. The rest of her clothes stayed on. When she'd first arrived in the Southern Kingdoms, she'd taken a room at a boarding house which she paid for by doing grunt work. One night a fire broke out. The result of a resident's negligence with a pipe showed her the consequences of carelessness.

Ursa relaxed on the bed, reaching for her pack strap to lift it. After digging, she found what she looked for. It was her most cherished item. A map of the Riven Isles. Almost nothing seemed familiar.

Finding refuge in nearby lands after exile proved impossible. Out of deference to her mother, not a single dokkalfar would harbor her. Wishing to be anonymous, she explored the fey realm, meeting fairies and dwarves before meeting the serpentine naga in Bhagavati. Though she aimed to fit in, her unique qualities stood out among the varied fairy folk. Despite her attempts to integrate with lesser fey – brownies, gnomes, kobolds, and fauns – she failed. With her heritage exposed, expulsion or rejection followed; she found no sanctuary. No one dared to provoke her mother, fearing her wrath.

All of that held no significance now.

She had returned for one thing. Her ancestors expected her to use a talisman to fight a mysterious enemy. Ursa ran her index finger over the map surface until she came to the name of a village. Farrowden.

"This is your final resting place?" Ursa muttered aloud. "Some pissant human dunghill?"

It did not surprise her very much. Humans cared less about their dead than they did their living. The trip would take several days. "Very well."

* * *

Ursa arrived in Farrowden after dark, believing the townspeople were already resting. The houses, with their sagging roofs and tilting walls, appeared on the verge of collapse. An odor of dung and animals permeated the air.

An unnatural quiet had descended upon the area. Animal sounds filled the night here. The faint sounds of voices from nearby cottages should be discernible, at a minimum. But silence reigned; night waited expectantly.

Ursa crept along, staying in the shadows cast by the buildings. She found the cemetery beside the decrepit church. A small window threw a pale square of light into the night. Ursa hesitated, unable to tell whether anyone moved within. The burial ground itself was kept tidy, paths raked and headstones upright.

Her sight remained sharp in the dark, and after a short search she found the grave. The Southern Kingdom's intricate magic system encompassed various disciplines, including elemental magic, spirit magic, alchemy, runecraft, divine magic, arcane knowledge, as well as both dark and light fey – all recorded in written spells.

A decade of research interrupted because she was forced to complete this laborious task. The Riven Isles were no longer her home. She doubted her ability to regain her magic. Its vibrancy had faded since she left. If she couldn't make use of it, she would have to search for a shovel or pickaxe.

With her hands on her knees, Ursa crouched down to the earth. Did she remember how to do it? How to connect with the Celestial Vine? Would it grant her request? Ursa quelled her doubts by taking deep, even breaths and clearing her mind. With mastery achieved, she fell into the darkness's soothing hold.

The Vine rested there in the warm earth, but now that she connected, she didn't know what to do next. It had been so long that the memory of speaking to the Vine had faded. Should she plead? Barter? She discovered that she didn't need to do anything further. The Vine's tendrils entwined with her, a tender caress. Contact with it unleashed a torrent of emotion, reopening wounds she thought closed – but healing was far from complete.

A wave of fury and solitude crashed over her, threatening to break her composure. A scream, a denouncement of the day that shattered her life, lived within her. Her tears fell unnoticed. Ursa calmed herself, raising her hands over the earthen mound.

The earth yielded beneath her, flowing like water. A dark geyser leapt, splitting the soil, while the land heaved and a jagged mouth opened, revealing...

"Sinner!"

The spell fractured. A thunderous crack flung a curtain of soil over her. The abrupt interruption and Ursa's vulnerable position left her unprepared and unable to defend herself in time. She glimpsed a man towering over her just before his blow landed.

★ ★ ★

Ursa's awareness returned, spurred by a relentless headache and the painful dryness of her throat. Standing proved too difficult for her.

Time ceased to have meaning; then consciousness returned, bringing with it the bitter, acrid taste of something unpleasant. Firm, impersonal hands pressed a cup to her lips, tilting her head back. As the liquid seared its path downward, her body spasmed in rejection, yet her mind sharpened in response. However, clarity proved short-lived, and she drifted away once more.

Ursa awoke for the third time, her limbs heavy with grogginess. Panic fluttered in her chest as she realized she could not move. Rough ropes bit into her wrists and ankles, binding her to a chair. She scanned the room, seeing many faces focused on her. A man stood at the front. His intense gaze sent a shiver down her spine. Anticipation filled the air, and Ursa knew her ordeal continued.

"I am glad to see you awake."

Her eyes burned, the sourness of the liquid staying in her mouth. Ursa peered through watery vision at the old man who addressed her.

"I am the Archdeacon Barnabas. The Netherborne Enclave blesses me to preach their word unto the flock and lead their children on the

Holy Path." The Archdeacon Barnabas, with his gaunt frame, wore luxurious robes that highlighted his status, the fabric rich and opulent. The villagers' tattered rags only stressed the disparity between them. His visage, marked by passing time, was sharp and severe.

Ursa's thoughts stayed a jumble. She struggled to understand the unfolding events. "Free me, you maniacal whoreson!"

A woman in ragged homespun stepped forward and approached her. She drew her arm back and slapped Ursa across the face.

No one had slapped her that hard since—

"Hold your tongue, fey bitch!" Barnabas roared. "I discovered you violating the sanctity of a grave. Deny it if you wish, but I saw you with my own eyes!"

How could she deny it? And they would question her tale of her ancestor showing up in her dreams, requesting she recover the goods buried in his grave. Ursa remained silent. This caused an angry murmur to spread through the crowd. Barnabas continued speaking, scolding her for being a lawless child of the demon Arroth, whoever that was. Ursa tried to block him out, to call on the Vine. She sensed its presence there, but something kept it from reaching her.

Ursa soon found out what. "What have you done to me?"

"We have fed you the blood of the Enclave, which rose from deep within the earth as proof against the demon's power." Barnabas moved from behind the lectern and strolled toward her. "Because of your filthy crime, I sentence you to death!" As he uttered the final syllable, they faced each other closely. His crazed expression was obvious, and his foul breath polluted the air between them. "You will burn!"

The villagers erupted in cheers, while others hurled oaths and curses. They swarmed around her, akin to a flurry of agitated hornets, hoisting her aloft – chair and all. Outside, more villagers had gathered, torches in hand. Yet amidst them, a peculiar light pervaded – a glow both dark and chilling, enveloping every being present.

Ursa did not move. Her limbs were leaden, indifference settling like iron, yet a thin, stubborn thread of hope trembled beneath her ancestor's hand. If he did not come, she would die tonight.

CHAPTER TWO

Ursa's homeland, the realm of Underneath, was a marvel of splendor and riches. A cavern so vast, its ceiling shrouded in mystery, visible only by the grace of light magic or during the ethereal ballet of wil-o'-wisps as they engaged in their enigmatic mating rituals. With each equinox they came, and the cavern ignited with their luminescent love. The walls were alight with gemstones, casting prismatic colors in a dazzling display.

People spread rumors about the palace, said to be a monumental structure carved from a single, massive pearl at the center of this underground kingdom. Though many debated the truth of such tales, the palace's surface gleamed with the unmistakable luster of that precious gem. Enveloped in the Celestial Vine's embrace, the sight was mesmerizing as purple blossoms released their intoxicating scent.

Then came the humans.

Although allowed, their presence was rarely received favorably. But the trio that stumbled into their domain bore the scars of a perilous journey. Their wounds, hidden beneath tattered bandages, spoke of recent battles, and their clothes – torn, soiled, and bloodstained – revealed a desperate flight. Among them was a woman, the assumed leader, who lunged forward, begging for mercy and an audience with the queen.

From the circular window of her chamber, Ursa watched them navigate the path to the palace until they vanished from sight.

"There you are!"

Ursa was startled by the familiar, beloved voice. She spun to find Tantia, her closest companion, her kindred spirit. The palace had become a sanctuary for Tantia after the satyrs claimed her parents' lives. Together, they had weathered the storms of youth, their bond forged in the fires of countless escapades.

Tantia's beauty was a testament to her faun lineage, her lower half cloaked in fur that glinted like threads of gold. Her attire – a waistcoat and shirt in regal teal and gold – complemented her radiant hair. A dagger hung at her side, but it was the flute, wrapped in cloth and slung over her shoulder, that was her true weapon. Carved from the sacred branch of the Celestial Vine, it held the power of enchantment and song.

"I see we have visitors." Ursa closed the window with a soft click. "Is Mother meeting with the humans?"

"I thought you may have seen them already." Tantia's grin was mischievous as she folded her arms with a flourish. "Her Majesty requests your presence." She nodded toward Ursa, a silent urging to prepare.

Ursa, with a haughty lift of her chin, walked past Tantia, who laughed in her wake.

* * *

Chaos erupted as Ursa walked through the halls. Guests and palace nobles hurried to secure positions on the palace floor. "What is all this fuss?" Ursa muttered to herself, but Tantia heard.

"Humans from Above Ground, how often do they come here? Who knows what their purpose is?"

"Why should I care?"

Tantia did not respond, but Ursa could guess what her friend was thinking. Despite their friendship, Tantia thought Ursa was a snob. She was, but her life taught her about her specialness as a dokkalfar royal.

As Ursa entered the throne room, she found the humans already pleading their case, while someone had positioned the seat of power at the center of the circular space on a raised dais, unlike most throne rooms. Courtiers, distinguished by family and rank, stood along the walls next to carved pillars, each adorned with their respective family crests. Ursa seated herself on a cushion on the lower steps, near her mother's feet. Her height restricted her leg extension, making this unusual. Her mother seldom summoned her to take part in royal decisions.

"When did this happen?" the queen said.

"Five days ago." The group were all on their knees, and they kept their eyes downcast. "We could barely fend them off."

"And what of your own leaders? Are they not willing to help?"

"Not the villages. They focus their resources on the larger towns and cities."

"You are still their people, and they find your safety of no import?"

"We have sent for help many times." The woman reached inside her tattered coat and withdrew an envelope smeared with dirt. "This was their response."

"Ursa."

Stepping down, Ursa approached the woman. Her nose wrinkled at smelling blood and human odor. She picked up the envelope, holding it at the edge with her thumb and forefinger. As she carried it back to the throne, she noticed someone had already broken the wax seal.

"Read it."

Ursa gasped, her eyes widening at the unbelievable sight of her native tongue. The message was straightforward. "The message states they refuse to offer any help. They should either make their way to the capital or seek help elsewhere at their discretion." Ursa frowned at the kneeling humans. "Why haven't you done so? Emigrate to the capital?"

"Your Highness," the woman said, "we are born and raised in our communities. They comprise our world, our hard-earned creation. How can we abandon them?"

"Homes and possessions are worthless if you are dead." Ursa looked at her mother for confirmation. "Isn't that correct, Your Majesty?"

The queen nodded twice. "Yes."

"Please, we beg of you!" the woman continued. "Help us save our homes. We will be your grateful servants."

The queen tapped her chin with her index finger. "What say you, daughter?"

"The concerns of humans are not ours. They come in with their cowardice and filth and expect us to rescue them? If you live in this world, you must defend yourselves. Life will be cruel otherwise."

"These are the dark fey," protested the woman. "We lack strength and resources."

"Is servitude the only thing you offer?" Her mother leaned forward, gazing at the woman with her fingers steepled.

"Yes, Your Majesty."

The queen leaned back into the cushions. "Very well. We will protect you."

Ursa whipped around in astonishment. "Mother, you can't agree to this?"

"Not only will I agree, my dear," the queen said, "but I want you to lead our forces."

"With all due respect to Your Majesty, I see no reason to do so."

A collective gasp filled the hall with her words. Even the three humans raised their gazes in shock.

The queen's tone held a clear warning as she asked, "Why not?"

"We are dokkalfar. We are perfect and greater than humanity. Humans are not worth saving."

Murmurs increased in volume. The humans were looking at her mother.

"You will do this." Her mother's words held an air of finality.

Ursa crossed her arms. "Yes, Your Majesty."

Ursa watched with a sense of loathing as her mother ordered the three to be given rooms, new clothes, and food. Ursa was to have them lead her to their village early tomorrow morning.

Tantia fell into step beside her as the throne room emptied. "Why are you so against humans?"

"I'm not concerned with humans either way."

"Then why refuse?"

"Because they are here. They have invaded our kingdom and disturbed our peace."

"Three humans are an invasion?" Tantia said.

Ursa could not help but chuckle. "Yes, I know."

Silence filled the air before Tantia's pensive demeanor shifted and she requested a decrease in hostility toward humans.

Ursa halted, irritated. She turned to stare Tantia down. "Are you forgetting my father? Your king, His Royal Majesty?"

"You know I haven't," Tantia huffed, "but there was no proof that humans—"

"Why are you defending them?"

"I am speaking the truth."

"What do you know as truth? Humans came asking for help. Father went to assist them but never returned. They claimed the manticore killed him and—"

Ursa had always had a catch in her throat since then. They built a memorial to him in their impoverished little village. Did they believe it sufficient compensation for losing her father and one of Underneath's greatest warriors?

Tantia placed her hands on Ursa's shoulders. She kissed her on the forehead. "I am sorry. I know this subject upsets you."

"Don't apologize," Ursa said. "I trust you to always be by my side, no matter the situation."

Tantia grasped Ursa's hands and squeezed. "Of course."

★ ★ ★

In Ursa's opinion, things were much too bright Above Ground. She was always squinting and holding her hand over her eyes. It put her in a sour mood as she rode her favorite hippogriff at the head of a squad of warriors and archers. Tantia was at her side. The faun was not a warrior, per se. Her weapons were a piccolo and a lute. Her music could lull an enemy to sleep or have them enslaved to her will, although she was loath to do that. The Celestial Vine had granted her Gift to her.

Someone adorned the humans with Gifted leather armor for protection. They were farmers and merchants, not fighters. They were at the back of the line. Their village was several miles to the south, only a half-day's ride away. The dark fey appeared before sunset, catching people off guard during meals and returning from the fields.

They arrived at dusk and reached the top of the hill, from where they could overlook the quiet village. Across borders, they glimpsed a distant town, similar in appearance. Ursa commanded her soldiers to spread out along the ridge and the humans to fall back into the safety of the woods.

There they waited.

As the sun sank low on the horizon, nothing occurred. Nightbirds called and crickets sang. Ursa grunted.

"Perhaps we scared them away?" Tantia offered.

"Perhaps." Ursa pursed her lips. Suspicion rose in her chest.

"Your Highness?" The human woman dared approach her. Ursa heard her name but then forgot it.

"What is that?" Ursa did not look at her.

"We don't— I mean to say, perhaps your presence here frightened them away?"

"We thought along the same lines, Mistress Crisynth."

Crisynth? What kind of ridiculous human name is that?

"You don't need to address her that way." With a slight tug on the reins, Ursa turned her mount around. "We're leaving."

"But Your Highness—" Crisynth began.

Ursa cut her off. "We came as we said we would, and nothing is amiss. Do you want us to camp on the hill all night?"

"Your Highness?" Tantia spoke up. "We should stay here tonight. Or perhaps – Mistress Crisynth, would your village be able to accommodate us?"

"We have no provisions to camp overnight," Ursa said. "And I'll not sleep in a bed that was soiled by common humans."

"Princess Ursa, this is not right."

Ursa stared at the human woman in utter disbelief. "What did you just say to me?"

"Ursa." Tantia's said in an urgent whisper. "She is correct. We must tread cautiously."

"If you would like, Tantia, you may take four guards and stay here. Return first thing tomorrow morning to report." Ursa turned her attention back to Crisynth. "Woman, dare not speak to me in such a manner or face dire consequences."

Crisynth paled. Her lower lip quivered, and she laid her fingers against it. Her ragged breathing and the fear in her expression gave Ursa a sense of triumph. "Tantia, choose your soldiers. The rest follow me!"

Darkness greeted them upon their arrival in Underneath, and Ursa longed for a simple pleasure – to slip into her cherished silk nightgown and embrace serenity. Though duty called for her to present herself to the queen, fatigue burdened her, and she trusted the queen would forgive her need for sleep. Choosing rest, she sent word via a servant. Settled in bed, Ursa indulged in a glass of wine from a gleaming goblet and the risqué verses of a ljósálfar bard, until sleep claimed her.

She did not rest long.

Hands grabbed hold of her. Initially, her sleep was so deep that she mistook it for a lucid dream, but Ursa regained her senses and discovered that unknown individuals were dragging her from her bed. Whoever they were, they brought no light, and only the spill of hallway illumination revealed their presence, enough for her to discern a minimum of five individuals.

"What in the nether-hells—!"

The sudden sharp pain of a rough hand striking her cheek left her reeling in shock. Such an affront was inconceivable. No one dared to touch the crown princess. Yet, as the realization settled, her royal training gave way to instinct. She thrashed her feet, finding their mark with a precision that elicited a pained grunt from her assailant. In the next breath, someone captured her ankles and hoisted her into the air.

Ursa's cries tore through the chaos, hurling threats and curses, vowing a swift and merciless retribution upon them all.

Ursa's singular focus had been escaping. Her every instinct honed toward slipping through the bonds that held her. When her captors dropped her onto the cold marble floor, she understood her surroundings. The extravagant throne room. She lifted her head, and there, upon the imposing throne, sat her mother. The expression etched on her face was a volatile blend of fury and disdain, a storm waiting to break.

"Mother?"

"Silence!"

The single shouted word startled her. Why was her mother—?

"Come forward."

Ursa's first assumption was that her mother addressed her, but then the movement caught her attention – a shift to her left. A crowd had formed. How had she not noticed before? Guards, citizens, and a smattering of courtiers who looked at her with equal disgust. Crisynth, who had appeared haggard during their first encounter, now stood before her. Crisynth wore her leather armor with many gashes, and blood splatters marked her like grim battle scars. Ursa's impulse was to speak, to question, but the room's charged mood silenced her. A cold sweat prickled her skin, a visceral warning that defiance would come at a perilous cost.

"Speak," the queen said.

Instead, Crisynth collapsed to the floor. Her slight frame heaved with sobs. One man, whose name Ursa had not bothered to inquire about, stepped forward and knelt. He pulled Crisynth against him.

"Our people are being slaughtered."

Ursa, for the first time, considered someone besides herself. An edge of panic pierced her chest. "Where is Tantia?"

The queen ignored the question, or her silence was the genuine response.

"No!" Ursa cried aloud. "Where is Tantia?"

"Speak of the battle," the queen commanded the gathering.

"There was no battle." He glared at Ursa before returning to her mother. "When the additional forces departed, a horde of dark fey set upon us."

They were waiting, Ursa thought. Until she left? Everyone knew about her hatred of humans.

"Some villagers had never seen those before. Despite being outnumbered, the warrior and her soldiers fought valiantly."

The villager continued his tale and recounted creatures draped in thorny cloaks of the darkest green. Winged horrors with eyes like smoldering coals haunted their nightmares, and the mere presence of the nightmares extinguished lanterns' light. Among them prowled the familiar goblins with wicked grins, lamias slithering to ensnare the unwary, Red Caps dripping with malice, and the Black Agnes, who snatched away children with their vile hands. Succubae and incubi haunted their dreams, descending upon their homes like a dark tide plague from some sinister realm.

As the man fell silent, fear and horror filled the hall. Ursa's mother fixed her attention on her daughter. "What do you have to say for yourself?" she demanded.

Ursa's mind remained foggy. She was unable to speak. "Mother—"

"Do not address me so familiarly!" The queen rose from her throne, striding toward Ursa. With a sharp slap, shock, anger, and pain converged.

The queen turned, robes sweeping, and returned to her throne. Crossing one leg over the other, she steepled her fingers. Her expression revealed a decision made. "Innocent men, women, and children died because you abandoned your duties," she spat with disgust.

"But I didn't!" Ursa protested.

"Infants snatched from their mother's arms. The sick murdered in their beds."

Footsteps interrupted her mother's words – boots striking marble. Someone strode past Ursa. Ursa realized the sound was hooves, not bootheels.

"Tantia!" Ursa tried to stand, but rough hands compelled her to stay down.

Tantia stood before the throne. She crossed her arms and bowed. Her expression lacked the love and admiration Ursa had once seen, replaced by something akin to her mother's disdain.

"Because of your crimes," the queen declared, "I banish you from this kingdom. Stripped of your title and family, you'll carry the weight of your treachery. News will spread across the realms. Others will decide your punishment."

Ursa's mind went blank. Tears streamed down her cheeks. She wanted to scream, to deny this reality.

"Take her from this palace, out of my realm."

Hands seized her, and Ursa lacked the strength to protest. They dragged her away, leaving her with nothing, not even her sense of self.

She was nobody.

CHAPTER THREE

Death loomed over her, an inevitable conclusion.

It seemed proper, she mused. To these unenlightened mortals, her actions were unforgivable, a sin of the highest order. They had not endured the torment of ceaseless nightmares. One can only endure so much before exhaustion.

The veils fell, shielding her from the memories she was all too eager to forget.

Yet the hush persisted. Ursa's eyes swept over the assembly, pondering if death had already claimed her, sentencing her to this perpetual replay. The onlookers stood paralyzed, resembling sculpted effigies caught mid-tirade and curse.

Ursa looked down and saw the fire also frozen in time. The flames performed a languid ballet, like foliage swaying in a soft breeze. The air held gilded embers suspended in a state of inertia.

Movement to her left caught her attention. Now, what was this madness?

Three figures appeared from the shadows like phantoms. Clad in military garb, they bore the unmistakable air of soldiers. Among them stood an elder, his demeanor exuding authority – a clear mark of his superior rank. Ursa couldn't hear his words, although he issued commands with a firm posture and decisive gestures.

The surreal became reality when one soldier neared her, and a radiant dome sprang to life around them. It didn't just glow. The air seemed to hum with the sound of a distant clock. Ursa, captivated by the spectacle, was unaware of the soldiers removing the logs with the villagers' tools. The ropes binding her wrists slipped away unnoticed.

The elder now positioned himself before her, extending his hand. Ursa, still in a daze, accepted it. He drew her to him. "Are you unharmed, miss?"

Ursa blinked, startled by his presence. "What's happening?"

"A rescue, it seems."

Guided by the old soldier, Ursa drifted from chaos. There, the mystery of the light unraveled.

A young woman, garbed like the soldiers. A similar luminous orb surrounded her, with its runes reflecting the ones Ursa had seen. The old man whispered to the woman – words Ursa couldn't catch – and the runes stilled, the light dimming until it vanished. The woman came close to collapsing, but the elder's prompt support saved her.

"Lucea, are you all right?"

"Yes, I'm fine."

Without the orb's brilliance, only the suspended fire lit the surroundings. The older man took hold of Ursa's elbow, and they escaped into the darkness of the woods. They reached a road with a covered wagon, brightened by three lanterns. Ursa's vision, tinged with the sphere's afterglow, adapted to the dim light.

It took a few moments, but Ursa regained her composure. "Who are you people?"

The young woman calmed herself and stretched to her full height. She traded glances with the older man. "I am Lucea."

"Isengrim."

Ursa's attention shifted to the soldiers, who seemed nervous.

"Go ahead," Isengrim encouraged with a nod.

Now they shared a look. Ursa realized by their appearance they had to be brother and sister.

"Aoki."

"Rei."

"We shouldn't stay too long," Isengrim said. "Lucea's spell will wear off soon. Into the wagon."

Ursa saw Aoki and Rei approach the front and climb onto the seat. Rei took the reins. Isengrim lowered the back gate and helped Lucea in.

"Climb aboard, miss."

After centuries of exile, Ursa was wary of everyone. Even someone who saved her. Which she'd not asked them to do. "No."

Confused, Isengrim stared, and Lucea leaned out the back. "Why not?"

"I don't know you," Ursa said. "You have my appreciation and someday I hope to return the favor, but for now, I have my journey." Ursa didn't want them to think her mad about what she planned, but she couldn't leave the village just yet.

"Once they realize what happened, they will pursue. We must be away," Isengrim said. "And if they discover we helped you—"

"Fine." Ursa climbed into the wagon and halted in complete shock.

She found herself in a space that defied the ordinary. Evidently, a potent spell caused the interior to exceed the limits of possibility. Her ability to stand at full height proved this.

The inside was a cozy, welcoming abode much larger than the modest exterior suggested. A plush seating area was adorned with cushions embroidered with protective and comforting sigils. The seating area, which was arranged in a semicircle, created a sense of community and warmth, perfect for sharing stories or enjoying the company of fellow travelers.

On either side were soft beds with thick, feather-down mattresses. The spell masked the movement of the carriage to ensure peaceful sleep. The far end served as a kitchen, equipped with a compact hearth that flickered with ever-burning flames. Here, one could brew a pot of tea or cook a hearty meal.

"Make haste, miss."

The whispered words urged her to move forward. Isengrim followed, pulling up the stairs and closing the door. The wagon showed no signs of moving. Ursa perched on a cushioned seat and crossed her arms and legs. By focusing on the wall, she sought to evade their curious glances.

"Lucea, would you mind making some tea?"

"Of course, Isengrim."

Ursa's curiosity led her to look at Lucea. She opened a cupboard, which was full of foodstuffs, and withdrew a small wooden box. Ursa had another shock, however, when Lucea could draw water from a pump in the kitchen sink. Obviously, a deflection spell. Whoever created the coach was a powerful magician, indeed.

Lucea poured tea into three cups on a silver tray. Isengrim chose first, then Lucea showed with a nod that Ursa should take one. She did so.

Lucea continued. "Introductions complete. Who might you be?"

"Nobody." Ursa knew she was being unreasonable, and it was unlikely that these people would recognize her name. But why tempt fate? Besides, it wasn't a lie. She was nobody.

"Well, I will not call you nobody." Isengrim grinned, and it was the first time she saw his smile of pointed teeth. Ursa moved to draw her concealed dagger before realizing she didn't have it. Did those damnable villagers put their hands on her?

"Problem?" Isengrim titled his head. "Oh, my teeth! My apologies, you needn't worry. I'm a shapeshifter. We all are." He made a sweeping motion with his hand.

Lucea smiled, also with pointed teeth. "Some can hide our teeth, but the process is unpleasant, so we don't bother most times." She sipped her tea. "But if it troubles you that much—"

"It's fine," Ursa said.

To Ursa, the silence was awkward, but Isengrim and Lucea seemed quite comfortable.

"Would you like to travel with us?" Lucea said. "Our destination is Jack-In-Irons."

"No thank you," Ursa said. "In fact, if you would let me out here, I would appreciate it."

A quick look passed between them. "That's a good idea. We should camp anyway," Isengrim said. He reached behind him and rapped on the wall three times. Rei opened the door and tugged down the steps. They paused in a clearing at an abandoned campsite probably arranged by merchant travelers. When she was away, Ursa had seen similar setups, except they often included a tiny cottage with bunk beds. If beds were insufficient, people could resort to using their bedrolls on the floor. The expectation was that those who stayed would clean up after themselves, although not everyone did. Ursa always did.

She stepped out of the coach but didn't move any closer, choosing to lean against it. While Aoki and Rei set up camp, Ursa noted their teamwork with their Gift. Because her power had waned, it had taken some time for the familiar power of knowing a Gifted. Aoki vanished into the forest and returned with a stack of wood. She arranged it in the pit, then with a gesture, set them on fire.

So, she's a witch. Elemental, Ursa thought.

Rei lifted his hands toward the heavens, and within moments, a single spark ignited into a brilliant orb of white. From this radiant heart, slender tendrils of energy unfurled, weaving a lattice of light that blossomed into a dome, mirroring the one conjured by Lucea. Ursa's brow creased in confusion. Despite their shared bloodline, their Gifts diverged. Rei was a sorcerer. This was a unique event.

Despite Ursa's desire to question them, other priorities arose. Only when Isengrim called, "Come and join us," did she become aware of them gathered around the fire.

"Again, no thank you."

Ursa straightened away from the coach. "I'll leave you now. Safe journey." Ursa was relieved when they said no more and didn't stop her.

Ursa made her way back through the woods, letting her senses and instinct guide her. She knew when she'd reached the village again because of the smell, including that of burned wood. When she exited the forest, the quiet caught her attention once more, but it had changed. All homes remained in darkness, devoid of any light. Even when she passed the church, the single light was gone.

Were they lying in wait for her to return? No, that made little sense. With extra care, she returned to the gravesite, kneeled again, and called on her power. Fortunately, her earlier attempt had worked somewhat, so it didn't take as long to reveal the decaying coffin. After a final look around, Ursa descended into the open grave. As she prayed, she opened the coffin.

The legend said that anyone trying to steal this scared talisman would face the wrath of its wielder. But the Steel Driver himself had chosen her to come here, for reasons known only to him, to commit the vile sin of grave robbing. There it lay, positioned beneath the corpse's crossed arms.

The Steel Driver's Hammer.

As Ursa's fingers wrapped around the cold metal of the shaft, a sudden jolt coursed through her. The hammer seemed to acknowledge her touch, awakening from a deep sleep. Her eyes fluttered closed, and a torrent of visions swept her away.

She saw a figure, towering and purposeful, standing atop a craggy peak. She was descended from the original wielder. The knowledge came to her. It had a name – Iron Reaver. With each swing of the hammer, mountains trembled, sending cascades of rock and earth tumbling down. The landscape obeyed, reshaping as he commanded with his powerful hammer.

Amidst the chaos of shattering stone, dark fey beasts emerged, their forms twisted and malevolent. But they were no match for her ancestor's fury. Iron Reaver moved like an extension of his own arm, crushing the creatures under its relentless assault. Every strike created a symphony of destruction, dispelling darkness with sparks from the hammer's impact.

The visions faded as quickly as they had come, leaving Ursa with a newfound sense of purpose. Iron Reaver served a purpose beyond being just a weapon. With the hammer in her grasp, an unbreakable bond to her ancestor and a fierce determination to live up to his legend possessed her.

Ursa climbed from the grave, her fingers clutching Iron Reaver. As she stood, she stretched to her full height, the weight of the hammer a comforting presence in her hand. She claimed ownership. She cast a cursory glance over the town. The hush pressed down on her. She noticed the emptiness. A chill ran down her spine. Surely, not all the villagers had—?

"Shite." Ursa's breath came in sharp bursts as she sprinted toward the woods, the Iron Reaver's weight a constant reminder of her purpose.

CHAPTER FOUR

The face Lucea saw in the mirror was not her own.

She was supposed to be healed after using her power to the point of having her life shortened by five years.

"It was necessary." How often did she say those words to the unfamiliar image? But a fiery rage simmered within her, poised to burst forth. That was enough, but she wanted to direct her anger toward that person. To someone she loved and admired, and she hated herself for it.

Lucea worked to dampen her feelings. She seized her hairbrush and combed it through her hair, which again had unruly curls that resisted taming like before. Lucea huffed in frustration and slammed the brush down on her dressing table.

The sound of rapping at her door caused a groan of annoyance. "Who is it?"

"Lady Lucea?" an unfamiliar voice said. "His Royal Majesty desires your attendance."

Despite her royal position, Leonine had allowed Lucea ample time to recover. Well, she supposed that time was over. Memories flooded Lucea as she faced the door, dragging her into the past.

"Dear Vine! Lucea!"

"If I'm understanding – she is keeping me – us and this room at the same time. It doesn't go forward or backward. Did you sense something here just now?"

"Gods be damned. Forgive me if this is a mistake, Lucea."

They didn't realize she was aware of everything. Her power not only controlled time but transcended space. They were the same. This knowledge was only for the chronomancer. Lucea recalled Harper breaking her spell and the pain she suffered. The frost of time numbed Harper's arm.

Lucea was in agony too. Not only that, but she also found fury burning despite her spell. Anger at Harper and Eica, for whom she'd cast the spell. Lady Eica was her dear friend and when Lucea saw the Rot was trying to influence her, Lucea acted, casting her most powerful spell even as Lady Eica told her not to.

I knew what would happen to me, but I cast it anyway.

I'm furious with Lady Eica for making me do it!

However, Eica was the one accompanying her. Who cried for her? Lucea cried too.

Reynard the Fox and the diviner Harper tended to her and visited her. It brought her joy. However, when alone, she realized that five years of her life were the cost.

New clothes, including her uniform, footwear, coats, and jackets, were available. And of course, undergarments to secure her – burgeoning – assets. Many of the young men had a sudden and sometimes unwanted interest in her. Which only made her self-conscious. That is why she chose to stay in her chambers when she didn't need to be present. But the king had summoned her, and she must obey. As she walked into the grand hall, King Leonine and his first queen sat on their thrones, but to her surprise, Lord Isengrim the Wolf was also present.

Lucea kept a respectful distance as she kneeled, her fingers entwined and her eyes downcast. "You summoned me, Your Majesty?"

"Yes, my dear." Leonine rose and extended his hand to his wife. They stepped down from the dais. "Would you mind coming with us, please?" He turned to Isengrim. "Lord Isengrim." They moved through the Royal Entrance to the left of the thrones. Lucea scrambled to her feet and hastened to follow. In this room where the king received guests, he bade Lucea sit, and a light repast was served.

"The fight against the Rot continues." The king took a sip of tea.

"Yes, Your Majesty."

"The Triumvirate's members each have a mission. Finding and routing the instances of Rot."

The witch Isbet. Lucea's dear friend Harper the diviner and, although they hadn't met yet, Lady – no, Princess Faith.

"May I ask a favor?"

A favor? The king is asking me for a favor?

"As you understand, we've been warning Jack-In-Irons about the Vine Root's peril." The king set his cup down and balled both hands into fists on his knees. "I can't fathom why they have not responded. Word of the upheavals concerning the Rot must have reached them by now."

"I am at your command, Your Majesty. Tell me what you need from me."

"I would like you to travel to Jack-In-Irons and request an audience with Praesidere Dhidihn Farstride."

"Me, sire?" Lucea's brows shot up. "But why?" Lucea drew in a sharp breath and clamped one hand over her mouth. Such outbursts were not becoming in front of the king and queen.

Leonine didn't seem to notice. "Because you are the one I trust to perform this task successfully."

But why? Why me? I'm no diplomat! I don't want to leave home!

"And Lord Isengrim will accompany you."

"Then why do you need me?" Lucea flinched at the question.

"Lord Isengrim will ensure your safety, but you will represent the royal family and Vale."

"I won't know what to say." *Lucea, you're always chattering!*

"I will provide you with paperwork to present to her. Make certain you speak to her alone. She has several children who may try to bar your way. Isengrim will see that they don't."

Her uncle was a formidable fighter. Lucea needed to settle a score with the Rot, but wondered how.

"I have faith in you, Lucea."

His words made her breath catch. "Your Majesty."

"I receive constant reports from the Triumvirate. We need Jack-In-Irons to prepare for—" Leonine halted.

"We don't wish to frighten you," the queen said.

Lucea drew in and released a deep breath. "I'm not afraid. Yes, sir, I will accept this task and complete it to the best of my ability."

"Thank you." The king rose and helped the queen up. The meeting was declared over. "I will have the paperwork delivered to your chambers. You will leave on the morrow."

"Yes, Your Majesty."

⋆ ⋆ ⋆

"You seem troubled," Isengrim said as he escorted her.

"Of course." Lucea chewed her lower lip. "Why me, Uncle?"

Isengrim chuckled. "Leonine preferred someone who wouldn't storm the palace with bluster and threats. You have taken care of his household since you came out of diapers."

Lucea smiled and blushed. "I was older than that."

"At any rate," Isengrim continued, "it is not ours to question the commands of our king."

"Of course not."

Lucea had a few surprises ahead of her. This was not the first time she'd traveled, so her preparations raced ahead. She was just leaving her chambers with her backpack across her shoulders when a familiar voice called, "Lucea?"

Lady Eica approached from the opposite end of the hall. Lucea smiled once. When the anger tried to rear its ugly head, Lucea forced it down. "Eica, how are you this morning?"

When she reached Lucea, she gripped her hands. "I'm glad I caught you before you left. I finished a reading for you."

"Oh?"

"This journey is significant. You need to be in Jack-In-Irons."

"Can you tell me why?"

"I'm sorry," Eica replied, "but the cards predict your journey will bring great success. You will also meet someone who will be very important to your task."

Lucea understood she shouldn't press further. The reading yielded no specifics. And as to this meeting with someone? The who and why eluded her. "Thank you, Lady Eica. Please take care of yourself. I will see you when I arrive home."

Lucea discovered Isengrim awaited her outside the palace with two young soldiers who were siblings, Rei and Aoki, and who both possessed the Gift. What astounded her was the sight of a covered wagon, something they didn't use in Underneath. The construction was polished dark-brown wood, giving it a plain appearance, while the covering remained pristine off-white.

"We'll be using this to travel? How will we transport it Above Ground?" Lucea asked.

"King Leonine made this possible. An exit lies across Belltide. Reaching the destination will take time, but we'll be comfortable in the coach."

Lucea doubted that until she saw the interior. Rei opened the coach door and lowered the steps. When Lucea approached, she wasn't certain if what she was seeing was real. She approached and leaned in.

She squealed in surprise. "Look at this! It's amazing." Lucea was unable to stop grinning in delight. It resembled a small cottage, with beds, cushions, and a tiny kitchen equipped with cupboards and an unexpected fireplace. Behind her, Isengrim chuckled.

"Quite comfortable."

Lucea was familiar with spatium expansion magic. Some sorcerers possessed an acquired Gift. And like chronomancy, it was very rare. "What about horses?"

Isengrim nodded to Aoki and Rei. And before her, they both shifted into draft horses. Brabant, in particular. Aoki was a beautiful, dappled gray with a black mane and tail, while Rei had a similar look but roan coloring.

"They'll take us until we reach Above Ground, and we'll buy horses there." Isengrim grinned. "It will cause a scene if a coach is driving by itself."

Lucea chuckled.

"Climb aboard while I hook up the team."

"Yes, Uncle."

Lucea flopped on a cushion and surveyed her surroundings. It lacked luxury but amplified rider comfort. Her uncle climbed onto the deck, pulled up the stairs, and closed the door. Before sitting, he rapped the wall with his knuckles. Lucea noticed the absence of movement.

Isengrim made tea and removed a package of cookies from one cupboard. Lucea was certain that they were freshly baked right out of the oven. This was another type of magic, related to spatium expansion, called provisio conjuring, also under sorcery. Both needed near godlike magical power.

"I'm assuming Rei didn't do all of this?" Lucea mused.

"Oh no, I guarantee you that."

"Can you provide any information about the creator of this coach? It was impossible for anyone to live in Vale."

"I wish I were able to tell you," Isengrim said. "I desire to learn, but Leonine did not inform me."

Lucea sat back with a huff. "If I had to guess, it would be someone from Jack-In-Irons."

"They live near the Vine Root." It made sense. The Vine Root held the greatest concentration of magic.

"Perhaps someday—"

The door opening interrupted them. Rei stuck his head in. "Lord Isengrim?"

"Yes, Rei?"

"There appears to be turmoil in the nearby human settlement that's frightening our brethren into fleeing. There's a small hamlet named Farrowden, with few residents. I thought, perhaps—"

"We should investigate?" Lucea said.

"If you both wish it."

"Why not have a look together?" Isengrim stood and held out his hand for Lucea.

Upon leaving the wagon, they indeed found something was frightening the animals. Too panicked to communicate in their flight, Lucea and the others searched for the source.

"I hope it isn't a forest fire," Lucea said as they made their way through the trees.

"Oh no, we would have known that," Isengrim said.

Lucea came to a halt. "Oh no."

"What it is?"

"Don't you sense it? Smell the stench?" Lucea shivered.

Isengrim raised his head and sniffed the air. "No. It can't be."

"Milord? Milady?" Rei inquired.

"Keep moving forward with caution," Isengrim said. "And pray that we are mistaken."

But Lucea knew they weren't wrong. The unmistakable miasma of the Rot permeated the air.

They emerged from the shelter of the woods, their eyes widening in shock at the scene before them. A cacophony of voices, raised in anger and fear, filled the air; a single, venomous shout cut through the tumult as the villagers, faces twisted in rage, formed a half-circle around the bonfire.

Amid this madness stood an old man, his words as vile as his intentions, inciting the crowd to violence. Someone tied a dokkalfar woman to the stake. She did not scream or struggle. Through her cat's eyes, Lucea saw someone resigned to their fate. The old man gave a nod, and the torchbearers stepped forward, igniting the kindling beneath her feet. Flames devoured the wood, casting a sinister glow on the faces of the onlookers.

But before the fire consumed its victim, Lucea stepped forward and summoned her power. Time warped around them, freezing the villagers like painted figures. The flames flickered and froze, their dance suspended midair. Lucea's eyes closed in concentration as she observed the images, or rather auras, enveloping each person.

"Hurry!" Isengrim ordered.

The three rushed forward. Rei and Aoki cleared the logs away and released the woman. Isengrim led her away from the horrific scene, holding her hand, to where Lucea waited. Isengrim whispered with satisfaction, knowing they had succeeded.

As they escaped into the shadows, the spell's hold waned. The villagers stirred, confusion etched on their faces, as they tried to understand the sudden stillness and the disappearance of their intended victim. The bonfire crackled, alive with movement, as if it hadn't been an instrument of death just moments ago.

CHAPTER FIVE

A shrill cry shattered Lucea's nightmare, jolting her into wakefulness. She bolted upright, her mind still tangled in the remnants of sleep, making the world appear blurred as if shrouded in mist. The campsite became overrun as figures ravenous as locusts swarmed in. The protective barrier – Rei's creation – where had it vanished? Iron grips encircled her, cutting short her thoughts as the stench of decay and sour spirits invaded her senses. As her consciousness still drifted in the haze of slumber, she offered no resistance as someone lifted her off the ground. The chill of metal pressed against her neck.

"Stop!"

Time itself seemed to obey the command, as if Lucea had cast her spell anew.

"Make one more move, and I'll cut her throat!"

The assailant's words resonated in the air, mingling with his foul odor, paralyzing Lucea in a vise of fear. Isengrim, in his lupine half-form, snarled, his fangs dripping crimson as he gripped two foes aloft. They fell like rag dolls. Rei and Aoki were unconscious at the feet of two of their attackers.

An elder pushed through the throng, his eyes locked on Isengrim. "Heathen scum!"

"You've no right!" Isengrim growled, the sound more animal than human.

Lucea's mind screamed for action, yet her body refused to heed the call. Where was her magic?

"I am Archdeacon Barnabas, of the Netherborne Enclave. Reveal the witch's whereabouts, and we shall trouble you no further." He intoned each honeyed syllable as a veiled threat.

"What witch do you speak of?" Isengrim snarled.

"Archdeacon!"

"What is it, Brother Jeshiah?"

"We found a wagon on the road, empty except for some provisions."

"And her trail?" Barnabas turned back to Isengrim. His impatience palpable. "Surely you aided her escape, though I confess, the method eludes me."

"How could we assist anyone when we're as lost as you are in this chaos?" Isengrim's frustration echoed Lucea's own.

"Very well, let us entertain this charade," Barnabas conceded. "They condemned a necromancer who defiled graves and got caught in the pyre."

"Such savagery..."

"I note your opinion," Barnabas dismissed with a nonchalant wave. "Yet ignorance of her location does not absolve you. We cannot allow sorcerers to wander unchecked."

"And what are you implying?" Isengrim maintained a defiant posture.

"Absent the witch to purge, you will serve as our offering. A sacrifice to the Enclave, to quell their thirst for the damned!"

"Have you lost your mind?" Isengrim demanded.

"Please!" Lucea spoke out. "Our king bids us to confer with the leaders of Jack-In-Irons concerning a matter of grave importance!"

Barnabas ignored her. "You will face judgment in Farrowden."

"You will not!" Isengrim roared. He leaped for the archdeacon, shape-shifting as he did so to the full wolf.

"Heathen, son of a bitch!" the one who held Lucea captive screamed. "She's dead!"

Just as Lucea expected the sharp pain of the knife, her captor choked and collapsed. The knife clattered to the ground. His body pulled her down with him, and she landed hard on the forest floor. Then, something huge rushed by her in a blur.

With a thunderous roar, Ursa burst through the underbrush, a massive hammer in her grasp. She charged the unsuspecting villagers with a ferocity equal to Isengrim. The air crackled with energy as she swung. Each attack was a whirlwind of motion that left her adversaries disoriented.

Isengrim, in his wolf form, fought beside her. Every muscle in his body was tight, ready to strike his enemies. Their movements were synchronized in a deadly dance. The villagers, overwhelmed by the sudden onslaught, scrambled to defend themselves, but the pair's skill and determination overpowered them.

The chaos before her snapped Lucea out of her daze. Her tone, firm and resonant, cut through the clamor of their skirmish. With deliberate motions, she traced spell circles in the air, each marked with ancient runes. Time itself bent around her, responding to her will. She cast a cautious spell, potent yet precise, to avoid ensnaring Isengrim and Ursa in its effects. The spell circles materialized beneath her foes. Their movements slowed as if moving through molasses, while her allies found their speed and strength magnified.

The balance of the fight shifted with every word she spoke, every rune she invoked. And in that turning tide, Lucea's eyes caught the archdeacon, a wraith in the shadows, making his escape. The ferocious might of Isengrim and Ursa dispatched his followers, those who hadn't already scattered.

When her spells faded, Lucea pushed herself up and ran to Isengrim. "Uncle?" Lucea kneeled where he lay. Isengrim regained his human form and was clutching his side as blood seeped from between his fingers. "Oh, dear Vine!"

Ursa kneeled next to her. Aoki and Rei were awake and stood nearby, looking anxious.

"Don't fret," Isengrim said through clenched teeth. "This is nothing."

"Don't play the grizzled warrior!" Ursa scolded. "You need a healer, or a surgeon." Her gaze shifted toward Aoki and Rei. "Is a curative spell familiar to either of you?"

Both shook their heads.

"Uncle," Lucea said, "we should take you home."

"No!" Isengrim growled. "Our king has tasked us—"

"Where is home?" Ursa interrupted.

"The town of Vale Underneath."

"I am familiar with it," Ursa said. She didn't explain the specifics.

"Another town lies ahead, a few days of travel." Isengrim's voice weakened. "We can—"

"No," Ursa said. "I may locate an entrance to Underneath."

"How?" Lucea asked.

It worked before. It would work again. Ursa set the hammer aside and sank to her knees, her fingers delving into the rich, dark loam. She cleared her mind, allowing her essence to flow into the depths of the earth. With a humble heart, she called upon the Vine, her thoughts a gentle plea. Yet, when the Vine answered, a dissonance echoed through its response. Ursa sensed a multitude of beings, their presence invasive, striving to drag the Vine into an abyss of darkness. An inexplicable fury ignited within her. Fueled by her anger, she drove the intruders away. In a fleeting vision, she glimpsed a towering mound of earth and stone rising from the forest floor. Silently, she offered her gratitude to the Vine and ascended back to the waking world.

"Are you all right?" Lucea was kneeling beside her. She reached out a tentative hand and touched Ursa's shoulder. "You seemed in a trance, but then your expression became angry."

"I am fine." Ursa explained as best she could about what she experienced.

"That was the influence of the Rot," Lucea explained.

"What is this Rot?" Ursa demanded.

Lucea turned to stare at Ursa in confusion. "Are you unfamiliar with the Rot?"

"I've heard the term whispered," Ursa said. "But I thought it was some superstitious fairy tale."

"It isn't!" Lucea was aware she shouldn't count on Ursa being informed about the Rot, but after her own experience, Ursa's dismissal angered her. "I faced the Rot. I have friends who experienced violation by that filthy thing!"

Ursa inclined her head. "I apologize."

"Fine." Lucea still wasn't quite ready to forgive. "Uncle, we are going home."

Fear filled Rei's voice as he asked, "Won't that take us back within reach of those villagers?"

"We will take the chance." Lucea refused to encounter the fervent archdeacon once more.

"I am aware of a new opening nearby," Ursa said. "Many have occurred. Would this Rot be the cause?"

"Yes," Lucea said. "Would you be willing to escort us? We can pay—"

Ursa's expression hardened and Lucea realized she had insulted the dokkalfar woman.

"Listen, I didn't mean—"

"We'll need to get him into the coach." Ursa picked up the hammer and straightened before setting it over her shoulder.

Lucea's eyes widened at seeing the hammer for the first time. Its formidable presence was unlike anything she had ever seen. The intricate runes etched along the haft glowed with an ethereal light.

Lucea stepped forward, her hand trembling as she reached out to touch the cool, dark metal. Lucea sensed a bond with the weapon, as if it acknowledged her as a fellow survivor, strong and enduring.

"What are you doing?" Ursa took a step back.

"Is that—?" Lucea withdrew her hand. "The Steel Driver's Hammer?"

"Yes," Ursa said to Lucea's shock.

"You!" Ursa pointed at Rei, asking, "Have you mastered levitation?"

"Well – I – that is—"

"Speak!"

"Yes," Rei said. "However, I'm uncertain—"

"No!" Ursa said. "You have to do this, understand?"

Rei looked at Lucea in desperation.

"Please, Rei, do what you can."

"Yes, milady."

Lucea watched as Rei stood still and focused. The surrounding air moved, forming a spinning force underneath Isengrim. With arms raised, Rei levitated the wolf. Rei confronted a tough challenge as he progressed with Isengrim's body floating ahead of him. Lucea could see the strain in his expression and the sweat that ran rivulets from his brow.

Despite his struggle, he placed Isengrim into the wagon on the bed. Rei passed out soon after. They deposited him on the opposite bed. As they gathered inside the coach, Ursa retrieved a map from her pack and pointed out thc location of the entrance to Aoki.

Lucea found bandages and wrapped Isengrim's wound. "He requires stitching, even if we can take him to a healer. We may have to take him to the nearest settlement." Lucea moved to the kitchen to wash her hands. "Perhaps I can help further." She kneeled before the bed. She again used her Gift to weave another rune circle. Lucea pressed her palm to the ragged wound, pulled the moment inward, and watched the cut unstitch – blood retreating, skin knitting as if time ran backward – until flesh lay whole and warm, a bitter rewind leaving her breath shallow and the room a fraction older. Lucea's body teetered on the brink of collapse from exhaustion, yet she exerted herself to shift her focus to Ursa. The dokkalfar reclined against the opposite cushion. She seemed to doze off. She extended one leg and flexed the other at the knee. She held the hammer across her thighs.

Lucea was on the verge of speaking when she noticed Isengrim muttering. She shifted her focus. "Uncle?"

"Lucea?" His voice trembled and carried little strength.

"Yes, Uncle?"

"Where is the dokkalfar woman?"

"She is right here, Uncle."

"Woman, come here."

Ursa didn't move, but she was looking at Isengrim. "I'm fine here."

"Don't disrespect—" Lucea began.

Isengrim took her hand and squeezed it. "It's quite fine, my darling."

Lucea didn't agree, but she held her tongue.

"Ursa," Isengrim said. "I have a favor to ask of you."

Ursa lifted one brow. "Yes?"

"I'm unsure if you heard Lucea speak with that madman," Isengrim said. "Lucea tried reasoning with him so he may understand our mission."

"I heard her words while I hid in the underbrush."

"His Majesty, King Leonine, tasked us to travel to the capital and beg Praesidere Farstride…" Isengrim went to adjust his body to sit up. Lucea pressed both hands against his torso.

"Stop, you shouldn't move. I have a spell keeping your wound from getting worse."

Isengrim cast a quick glance downward and smiled. "I see."

"It will slow down the time surrounding the wound and keep it from getting worse."

"Can you just speed up the process, so he's healed?" Ursa asked.

Lucea glared at her. "It might worsen matters if I did. What if the wound doesn't heal? What if—" She couldn't continue. Lucea refused to entertain the thought.

"Lucea." Isengrim's tone was firm. "I must tell her. Lady Ursa, our world is at stake. The Rot is more than a danger. A malevolent being, capable of enslaving or killing those with weak minds or profound sadness. There are three young women who are engaged in separate battles against them." He coughed and a trickle of blood came from his lips. Lucea rose and retrieved a washcloth from the cabinets. Wetting it, she returned to Isengrim's side and wiped away the blood.

"We need to warn the praesidere that Jack-In-Irons will need to prepare for war."

"You sent messages?" Ursa stretched her bent leg out but held on to the hammer.

"Yes," Isengrim said. "But the king received no response. It's crucial not to leave it like this."

"Hence this visit?"

"Yes." Isengrim took Lucea's hand that held the washcloth. "I am charging you with escorting Lucea to the capital. Ensure that nothing hinders Lucea's progress or causes her any injury."

"Uncle—!"

"I am certain you can manage independently." Isengrim grinned. "However, this task should not be pursued alone. Lady Ursa, if you agree to do this, I ask that you do not underestimate my dear Lucea. She will greatly assist you."

"She is a talented witch." Ursa directed the words at Isengrim, but her attention was on Lucea, causing her cheeks to warm.

"That she is," Isengrim said. "So, Lady Ursa, do I have your word?"

Ursa seemed to be pondering the request. She was silent for a long time.

"Very well," Ursa said and grinned. "As long as you don't offer me money."

Lucea scowled and Isengrim chuckled.

"I want your word!" Isengrim was serious again.

"You have it, Lord Isengrim," Ursa said. "I will accompany her to the city gates."

"Thank you." Isengrim's tone was one of profound relief.

"Rest, Uncle." Lucea covered him with the folded coverlet. "You'll be home soon."

Isengrim did not respond, slipping into unconsciousness again.

"He'll be all right," Ursa said.

This brought her attention back to Ursa. "The truth," Lucea demanded. "I want the truth from you. You've said it is the Steel Driver's Hammer. How did you get it?"

Ursa said, evenly. "From the Steel Driver."

"Don't insult me!" Lucea said. "You claim to have got it from the long-deceased Steel Driver."

Ursa tried to change the subject, raising Lucea's suspicions even further. "I agreed to take you to Jack-In-Irons out of respect for your uncle." Ursa nodded at Isengrim. "I owe you no further explanation."

"The nether-hells you don't!" Lucea said. "What treachery have you dragged us into, grave robber?"

CHAPTER SIX

Ursa gripped the haft of the hammer. Lucea's words were like a knife in her gut. She'd been accused of many things in her life, yet grave robbery was the ultimate insult. But wasn't the girl, right? Ursa had retrieved this from a grave, unwillingly.

"You know nothing about this situation." Ursa forced the words through clenched teeth. "So, I'll ask you to keep your opinions to yourself."

Her face flushed, Lucea said, "I'll not travel with someone of questionable morals."

"I gave your uncle my word."

"He wasn't aware of the situation. You are free to leave."

She could go. Who cared what this peasant girl thought of her? Ursa recoiled at the thought. It was the same arrogant attitude that had caused her banishment. Ursa was about to respond when Lucea spoke first.

"Please accept my apologies."

Ursa's eyebrows shot upward, and her eyes widened. "What?"

"You came to our aid when you didn't have to." Lucea's eyes were downcast and her smooth, pale skin held a hint of a flush. Ursa realized she was lovely. "You fought for and protected us." Lucea raised her gaze to meet Ursa's. "You are correct in saying I know nothing about your situation." Lucea nodded at the hammer. "A simple grave robber, I presume, wouldn't bother doing that. You could have used the attack as cover to escape."

Ursa was impressed. "Apology accepted."

"You're not obligated to tell me anything, but please continue to travel with me."

"I will." Ursa agreed. She exhaled. "The Steel Driver appeared to me, he revealed the location in a dream."

"Ah – I see."

An uneasy silence fell.

"What made you recognize this as *the* hammer?" Ursa asked.

Lucea laid a finger on her cheek. "I like to believe I am a scholar of history." She motioned to the hammerhead with a nod. "Can you read those runes?"

"Yes."

Lucea drew in an eager breath. "The hammer's name remains unknown to most. I found an obscure reference tome that mentioned it and the spells attached to it."

"Iron Reaver," Ursa said.

Lucea beamed. "Yes, very good. And you know of the spells?"

Ursa cleared her throat. "Well—"

"You haven't looked at them, have you?" Lucea clucked her tongue. "May I?" She reached out her hands.

"Careful, it's heavy," Ursa warned. She turned the haft toward Lucea's hand, setting it down on the floor. Lucea kneeled next to it and leaned over. "Hmm… This appears to be in different languages. I suppose that makes sense if you don't want anyone to learn all the spells." Lucea's brow furrowed. "But then again…" Lucea reached out one slim finger. Two things happened. The runes glowed with an ethereal light and when Lucea touched the etchings, she received a shock.

"Ouch!" Lucea put the injured finger into her mouth and sucked on it.

"I'm sorry!" Ursa reached out her hand.

Lucea removed her finger. Infuriation burned beneath her skin. "It's all right. I should have known that might happen." She looked at Ursa again. "This – it is yours – you're descended from the Steel Driver."

Ursa sighed. "It would seem so."

"You're uncertain?" Lucea's brow once again creased in confusion.

"No one ever told me this." Ursa recalled the tedious lessons her mother forced her to take. Her mother insisted on it. A ruler should always be knowledgeable about their history and the world they govern.

"That's—" Lucea began but didn't finish her thought. "Perhaps the kingdom library holds—"

"It doesn't matter." Ursa's words were sharper than she intended. She worked to change her tone. "As soon as I complete this task—" What? Would she return to that backward village and bury the hammer back with her ancestor? Send it to her former kingdom as a historical treasure? They would not accept it unless she sent it covertly.

"Ursa?" Lucea's tone was gentle. "Where were you just then?"

"Someone gave me a task." Ursa's eyes remained fixed upon the hammer. "I'll discard this once we're finished. I didn't want it."

"Someone forced this on you?"

Ursa saw no reason to conceal their travel plans. "My ancestor came to me in dreams." Ursa recalled him standing tall and proud. The hammer rested across his muscular shoulders. And that smug grin annoyed her to no end. What puzzled her was where the dreams transported her. They were never alone. Ursa always heard the clang of metal against metal. Fog-shrouded shapes, clanging, toiled – their purpose unclear. Ursa could see they were in a rocky, barren plain surrounded by mountains. The mysterious figures continued to work and for a time the swirling mass of fog would clear, allowing her a glimpse of long strips of metal connected by thick slabs of wood. Then a distant, mournful cry, not of human origin, pierced the air. The sound echoed, a lament for the lost.

"How strange," Lucea said when Ursa finished her description. "You seemed lost in thought."

Ursa couldn't say. Unfamiliar sights and sounds marked the place. "My ancestor tasked me to return to the Isles. He said a great evil threatened the land, and that it would destroy everything I knew."

Ursa crossed her arms and closed her eyes. Her jaw clenched, angry. "I ignored them at first, you see..." She wasn't ready to speak of her banishment just yet. "I've lived overseas for a long time, convincing myself I no longer cared about the Isles."

Ursa was thankful for Lucea's attentive silence. "Dreams persisted, morphing into nightmares."

Before she realized, Ursa was describing the nightmares that haunted her and forced her to act. About finding herself trapped in a dark, twisting labyrinth. Regardless of her path, she returns to where the hammer rests. The walls close in as she hears the relentless clang of metal, growing louder and more oppressive, until it jars her awake with her heart pounding.

Night cloaked Ursa's wanderings along the iron and wood path. The fog was a living entity, churning around her, obscuring her vision. Spectral figures of long-forgotten laborers appeared from the mist, their faces contorted in eternal torment. Their eyes, brimming with sorrow, implored her. The haunting wail of a distant, unseen creature echoed through the night, but the phantom never appeared, leaving her with an overwhelming sense of unresolved fate.

But the worst of nightmares had Ursa becoming one of the spectral figures, toiling on the ancient path of iron and wood. Regardless of her fervent efforts, the task stayed unfinished. Severe muscle pain and bleeding hands did not stop her working. The booming voice of her ancestor echoed in the background, a relentless reminder of the crucial task she was neglecting.

At some point Lucea had drawn her knees to her chest and wrapped her arms around them. Were her eyes glistening with tears? Had Ursa's words affected her that much?

"Numerous tormentors plagued me each night. I fought to stay awake, but of course, my body succumbed." Ursa trembled and her face went hot with embarrassment.

Lucea wiped away tears. She stretched her legs out and pushed her body forward onto her hands and knees and crossed the space between them. She settled beside Ursa and wrapped her arms around Ursa's shoulders and rested her head. Ursa stiffened.

"I don't care how dire the situation is," Lucea said gently. "Your ancestor had no cause to torture you like that."

Ursa's breath caught in her chest as her throat tightened. Lucea's touch was as gentle as her voice. Ursa had allowed no one to touch her – at all. Not since being forced from her home. Yes, some plotted her harm. Such bastards soon learned Ursa wasn't some defenseless maiden. One thing she practiced with fervor was her combat training. Since her father's death, Ursa was determined to protect herself. That had included her family until they'd cast her aside.

She'd not experienced a gentle touch since…

"It is no longer important." Ursa pulled away from Lucea's embrace and grasped the hammer, pushing it beneath the nearest cot. "You'd better get some sleep." She sat down and pulled off her boots. As she lay across the comfortable bedding, she turned her back to Lucea. She knew she was cruel, but the compassion Lucea showed her was more than she could accept. Years of mistrust had hardened her heart, making her reject any sign of genuine care.

As she stared at the dimly lit wall, Ursa's mind raced. She recalled countless betrayals, each memory a sharp reminder of why she couldn't lower her guard. The warmth of Lucea's embrace lingered on her skin, a stark contrast to the cold barrier she had built around her heart. She wanted to believe in Lucea's kindness, but the fear of vulnerability was too overwhelming. What if she allowed Lucea in, just to get hurt once more? The thought was unbearable.

Ursa sighed, her body tense with the internal struggle. She wished she could explain her actions to Lucea, to make her understand they weren't about her. But words failed her, and so she remained silent, hoping that sleep would offer a temporary escape from the turmoil within.

⋆ ⋆ ⋆

The sound of the coach door opening woke Ursa. For a moment, she was confused. Then she remembered where she was and realized she'd had a good night's sleep. No nightmares, no dreams, just restful sleep.

"We have arrived," said Rei.

Lucea had slept sitting up against Isengrim's cot. The rune circle was still active, so Ursa surmised Lucea had refreshed the spell overnight. Lucea turned and kneeled beside Isengrim. "Uncle?" she asked in the same tone she'd used with Ursa the night before.

He awoke, his eyes more focused than they had been. "Lucea?"

"We've arrived at the entrance."

"Very well." Isengrim tried to sit up, but Lucea placed both hands on his shoulders.

"No, let Rei levitate you."

"I can walk."

"No, you can't!" Lucea insisted. "Besides, any unnecessary movement may disrupt my spell."

Isengrim sighed in defeat. Ursa thought about how helpless and embarrassed he must feel. She was familiar with those emotions. No seasoned warrior emerges unharmed; the wolf rejected coddling. Ursa instantly knew Isengrim's protective duty. She stood and stretched her legs.

"Good morning," Lucea said, showing no sign of anger or upset.

"Good morning," Ursa replied, picking up Iron Reaver and slinging it over her shoulder before leaving the cart.

A low fog clung to the ground, thick as pipe smoke in a dive tavern. Ursa could barely see Rei and Aoki standing near what appeared to be a mound of dirt and rocks. Something disturbing floated within the fog. Ursa failed to recognize it, but as she approached the siblings, she saw their intended entry: a gaping hole. Twisting black vines covered the entrance, sealing it so one would need a machete to get through.

Ursa's only huge weapon, the hammer, would prove useless here. Those damnable villagers had taken her only other weapon, the dagger given to her on the day of her exile.

Footsteps behind them alerted Ursa to Lucea's presence.

"What's taking so—?" Lucea halted upon seeing the vines. "Oh no."

"I take it that is the Rot?"

Lucea nodded. Ursa's suspicions were confirmed when Lucea stepped closer, and the vines began to writhe like a nest of snakes. Lucea's eyes narrowed in concentration as she surveyed the vines. She took a deep breath, seeming to center herself, and raised her arms, palms facing outward. A subtle blue glow radiated from her hands, bathing her surroundings in an otherworldly light.

Lucea chanted, steady and rhythmic. As she spoke, intricate symbols and patterns formed in the air around her hands, resembling the delicate gears and cogs of a clock. The symbols rotated and interlocked, creating a complex, moving rune circle that hovered just above the ground.

The blue light intensified, and the rune circle expanded, its gears turning and clicking into place with mechanical precision. The air hummed with energy, and the vines reacted, twisting more violently, as if sensing the power being summoned.

Lucea's chant grew louder, her voice resonating with authority. The rune circle pulsed with light, synchronized with the rhythm of her words. Lucea thrust her hands forward decisively, and the rune circle surged toward the vines, enveloping them in its glow.

The vines shuddered and disintegrated, and the blue light dissolved them into nothingness. The entrance was now clear, the path ahead illuminated by the fading glow of the rune circle.

Lucea would have fainted away, but Ursa was quick to react and caught her, supporting her. Lucea's eyes were closed as her head rested against Ursa's shoulder. Still, she spoke. "Prepare two packs for us. Bring them first, then Uncle and the coach." Rei and Aiko rushed off.

"Thank you, Ursa."

"Just rest." Her curiosity piqued, Ursa walked on the uneven ground, each step a negotiation with the landscape. The stones –

stubborn and unyielding – lay scattered like forgotten chess pieces, their rough edges jutting upward as if daring anyone to pass.

The twins returned with two stuffed backpacks. They laid them at Ursa's feet. At some point, Lucea had slipped into unconsciousness. Ursa preferred not to lay her on the ground, opting instead to set up camp.

Isengrim picked his way across the forest floor, leaning on Rei's shoulder. Aoki walked beside them, carrying a carved and bejeweled wooden box.

"Damn it all." With Lucea fainted in her arms, Ursa wouldn't be able to help the wolf. But she didn't believe it was her place to scold him.

As they approached the entrance to the cave that led to Underneath, the air grew cooler, and the light dimmed. The mouth of the cave loomed before them, a dark, yawning chasm that seemed to swallow the forest's sounds.

Isengrim paused, his eyes meeting Ursa's with a mixture of determination and fatigue. "This is where we part ways." He managed a smile, despite his obvious pain. "Rei and I will continue to the healer's den. Aoki, you know what to do."

Aoki nodded, her grip tightening on the box. "I'll make sure it reaches the council."

Ursa shifted Lucea's weight in her arms. "Be careful," she said. "We'll meet again soon."

With a final nod, Isengrim and Rei turned and disappeared into the shadows of the cave, their figures swallowed by the darkness. Aoki lingered for a moment, contemplating Ursa in silent accord, before she receded into the abyss.

Ursa took a deep breath, steeling herself for the journey ahead.

CHAPTER SEVEN

Even in her entranced slumber, Lucea sensed the moment her quintessence surged back, restoring the full potency of her Gift. Awareness seeped in, layer by layer. First, the coarse fabric cocooning her, its texture abrasive against her skin. Then, the rich aroma of fire and wood smoke intertwined with the earthy scent of the forest. And the unmistakable sensation of another presence nearby.

"How are you feeling?"

Lucea pushed up on her elbow and smiled. "I'm much better."

"Your power is remarkable. No wonder many people covet it." Ursa sat with her knees raised, her chin resting on her folded arms.

Lucea's heart clenched at those words. She looked away, her fingers tracing patterns in the dirt. "It's not as wonderful as it seems," she murmured. "People see what they want to see. They don't understand the burden."

Ursa's expression softened. "I didn't mean to bring up painful memories. I just… I admire your strength, Lucea. Not just your power, but your resilience."

Lucea sighed, a small, sad smile playing on her lips. "It's hard to be strong when everyone wants a piece of you."

"What of your king?" Ursa asked. "Surely you don't believe he—"

"Oh no," Lucea amended. "King Leonine is a man of virtue and honor. He granted me my position and demands nothing untoward about me."

"I'm glad. You deserve to be treated fairly."

Her words surprised Lucea. Ursa had been so aloof, but now, the concern and admiration in her tone soothed her doubts. "Thank you."

★ ★ ★

They made good time, although Lucea had to call on her Gift every so often to keep up with Ursa's pace. Restoring her to a rested state involved reversing what had happened. Ursa's sudden halt in the middle of the road surprised her. "Are you all right?"

"Yes, why?"

"I've been walking at a rough pace. Not meaning to be insulting, but I wonder how you're keeping up."

Lucea found no reason to be secretive. "I have been using my Gift to refresh myself."

"Why didn't you tell me you were having trouble? Overusing your Gift might leave you unable to use it when needed."

Lucea hadn't thought of that. Her Gift came so naturally she didn't consider it. "I'll be fine, I promise. I want to put as many miles as possible between us and those zealots."

"Hmm." Ursa nodded. "Understandable. Let me know if you need to rest."

"I will." Lucea said. "And you will do likewise?"

This caused a genuine smile. "I will."

They continued and remained cautious whenever they heard people on the road. They encountered farmers and other travelers. Lucea hoped that perhaps the zealots had given up their pursuit, but she was doubtful.

When they started off again, Lucea noticed Ursa was slowing her pace, reasoned that she was doing so to make the journey easier on her. Lucea wanted to protest but she thought, *I may need my power soon enough.*

★ ★ ★

Darkness fell as they reached Grayfort, a sizable town. The town's stone walls loomed above them, casting long shadows in the dimming light. Each stone seemed to hold centuries of stories, worn by time and weather. A small, ancient tower stood vigil over the town, its silhouette stark against the twilight sky. The tower's narrow windows flickered with the faint glow of candles, hinting at the lives within. As they neared the gates, two stern-faced guards, their armor glinting in the dusky light, crossed their halberds to block the entrance, scrutinizing them.

"What business do you have in Grayfort?" one guard demanded.

Ursa stepped forward, speaking steadily and respectfully. "We seek rest and supplies. Our journey has been long, and we are weary."

Ursa's respectful tone impressed Lucea, who assumed she had to deal with guards before. Provoking them was unwise.

The guards exchanged a glance before lowering their weapons. "Very well," the second guard said, stepping aside. "You may enter."

"If you're lookin' for someplace cheap," the first volunteered, "there's the Rare Rose, straight down the avenue on your right."

"Thank you, sir," Ursa said.

As they passed through the gate, the sounds of the bustling town enveloped them. Ursa turned to Lucea. "Do you have any money for the supplies we need?"

Lucea nodded, reaching for the small pouch secreted beneath her bodice. "Yes, but I also have a letter of introduction and accommodation from His Majesty." Unease settled in her chest. The old town's twilight whispers sounded less like secrets, more like warnings. The cobblestone streets, inviting before, now appeared twisted and labyrinthine, casting shadows that seemed to dance with malice.

Grayfort's buildings, with their moss-covered roofs and ivy-clad walls, stood silent and foreboding. The comforting window glow transformed; it felt like unseen eyes. The air, thick with the scent of fresh bread and exotic spices, carried an undercurrent of something darker, something that made her skin prickle.

The ancient tower at the heart of the town caught her attention again, and Lucea couldn't resist gazing at it; her eyes were drawn to it. Its silhouette was stark against the darkening sky, like a silent sentinel.

Candlelight danced in the narrow windows, but the light felt false, trapping shadows that suggested unseen threats.

Despite the market's usual evening commotion, they walked undisturbed. The merchants cried their wares. The townsfolk rushed about their evening errands with the usual concentration. Workers walked, talking jobs and meeting for drinks. No one seemed to notice anything untoward.

"You're troubled," Ursa said.

"I—" Lucea rubbed up and down her shoulders. "There is something about this place. I'm uncertain why I feel this way."

"I've never been here, myself," Ursa said. "Let's find lodgings. It will be best not to be out in the open."

Lucea nodded. She resisted the urge to link her arm in Ursa's. The king's confidence supported her mission. Now was not the time for self-doubt.

It turned out that the Rare Rose was a shared hostel. Lucea had heard of these places, but she'd never slept in one. A deep sense of gratitude washed over her for the charm and care evident in its upkeep. The warm, inviting shade of the walls, embellished with delicate floral patterns, added a touch of elegance that Lucea couldn't help but admire. The subtle scent of fresh roses permeated the air, creating a welcoming atmosphere.

Behind the front desk stood a plump, cheerful old woman. Her warm smile put Lucea at ease. Her twinkling eyes spoke of kindness and experience as she greeted them with a friendly, "Welcome to the Rare Rose." The desk itself gleamed under the light, polished to perfection and adorned with a vase of fresh roses. "I am Ionneld, the proprietor."

At least here Lucea experienced a sense of calm. Inside the hostel, her unease vanished. Lucea questioned the area's defenses. It would make sense.

The shared areas were warm and pleasant. Comfortable seating arrangements and a few well-chosen books and games beckoned them to sit and stay awhile. Lucea found the Rare Rose charming, despite its small size, due to its carefully considered details.

Ursa was speaking with Ionneld, whom Lucea realized was a brownie. She stood on a stool, being just over a foot tall, her frame bent from countless years of diligent work. Although her wrinkled and weathered skin resembled the pages of an ancient tome, her age didn't reflect the lively mischief sparkling in her eyes. She pulled her gray hair back into a tight bun, covering it with a simple, worn cap, adding to her quaint charm.

Ionneld wore practical, earth-toned garments made up of a faded, patched dress with a tied apron that spoke of her meticulous nature. Her years of service and care manifested in every stitch. The air was filled with a light scent of fresh herbs and baked goods, cultivating a sense of domesticity and ease.

Lucea felt a mix of admiration and curiosity. Ionneld radiated warmth, promising loyalty and protection to her admirers.

"Lucea, the letter please," Ursa said.

"Of course." Lucea removed her backpack and opened the flap where she'd secreted the letter. She had wrapped it in oilcloth to keep it from getting wet. She presented it to Ionneld. The brownie woman's eyes darted back and forth across the page.

"This is acceptable," Ionneld said. "Please wait here a moment." She handed the letter back. "I've reserved a private room for you."

"Thank you," Ursa said.

With Ionneld's departure, the two turned to view the common room. Despite its modest proportions, it created a snug environment for travelers. There were five other travelers there now, enjoying the space, which was furnished with plush, comfortable chairs, and a couple of well-worn sofas arranged around a low wooden table. Someone had draped soft, knitted throws over the furniture, improving the cozy atmosphere.

A modest fireplace crackled in one corner, its flames casting a gentle, flickering glow across the room. Positioned above the mantelpiece, a wooden shelf displayed a compilation of aged books, board games, and various ornaments. One of the five was deep into a book. Another dragged on a pipe.

A small, circular table situated by the window was covered with a floral tablecloth. More visitors sat playing cards.

The scent of fresh roses, a signature of the hostel, and gentle conversation filled the air. Weary travelers found solace and respite there.

Ionneld returned and bobbed a curtsy. "Your room is ready. Shall I check your weapon?" She nodded at the hammer.

"No, thank you, I'll keep it with me," Ursa said.

"The Rose takes no responsibility for lost or stolen weapons and personal items."

"Of course."

"Please follow me."

Lucea liked the elderly brownie, despite just meeting her. Their room, though narrow, mirrored the inn's cleanliness and order. Lucea appreciated their privacy.

"The communal bathroom is at the end of the hall on your left. Help yourself to food; the kitchen is open to everyone. Many people bring their own food, but for a few extra coins, we will provide you with basic meal ingredients. It's up to you to cook them and to clean up after yourself. We will charge you a fee for any mess left behind."

"Your hostel is wonderful," Lucea commented. "Thank you."

Ionneld blushed with pleasure. "You're welcome."

When they were alone, Ursa said, "I believe we could both use a shower." The hammer went under the bed.

"Agreed," Lucea said. "Would you like to go first?"

Ursa's brow creased. "What do you mean?"

"Well—"

Ursa's grin was mischievous. "I take it you've never used a communal shower?"

"Well, no."

"Come with me."

Lucea followed Ursa down the hall. Two bathrooms, each door marked with a symbol unfamiliar to Lucea, lay beyond. Ursa flung open the left door.

The bathing room was a square chamber of polished wood. Two small tubs were centrally located. Two wash basins, each with an overhead showerhead, sat beside the tubs, allowing for brief rinses or complete cleansing. Nearby, someone had stocked the shelves with rough but serviceable towels. Near the towels, baskets overflowed with soap. Cedarwood, soap, and fresh linens perfumed the air.

Without explanation, Ursa undressed.

"Wait, what are you doing?" Lucea shrieked.

Ursa turned to her, puzzled. "What?" Then her expression became one of slight amusement. "You've never undressed in front of another woman before?"

Lucea's whole body flushed. "Not like this."

Her embarrassment gave way to irritation when Ursa let out an uproarious laugh.

Lucea crossed her arms and glared. "What is so amusing?"

"We have the same parts, true?"

"My parts are my business!" Lucea stood her ground. She spun around, ready to storm out, when Ursa wrapped her muscular arms around Lucea's waist.

"Oh no, you don't!" Ursa said. "Get over here."

The dokkalfar lifted Lucea off her feet and carried her over to one shower. "Let's get that gown off."

"No, wait!"

"Stop squirming!" Ursa chided.

Before Lucea could protest further, Ursa had removed her gown, and she stood there in her undergarments. "All right, off with the rest of it."

When Lucea hesitated, Ursa made grabbing motions with her hands. Lucea removed everything.

"Go on, hop under while I finish undressing."

Lucea reached out and let some of the water sprinkle across her fingers. It was warm. She couldn't help but step under the flow, enjoying the running water against her skin. Ursa stepped under the second shower.

"Here!" Ursa tossed her the soap and Lucea nearly lost the slippery thing. Still, it had a pleasant scent of lavender, which surprised Lucea, and she lathered up.

"Bet you have nothing like this in Vale, eh?"

Lucea didn't speak. She couldn't speak. Molten gold surged through her veins. It left her dizzy.

She'd noticed the beauty of Ursa's face and her striking green eyes. As the water ran down her body, it made a glistening sheen on her dark-brown skin. She had a lithe, yet muscular build that spoke of both agility and strength. Her coffee color caused the intricate runes painted on her body to stand out. Lucea remained captivated until Ursa turned to her. With a knowing smile, she winked.

Lucea faced forward. And here came the telltale flush. "No, we have nothing like this in Vale." Ursa roared with laughter. Lucea would not pout. She was much too old for that.

"Here," Ursa said. "I'll wash your back." She touched a finger on each of Lucea's shoulders and turned her around. Lucea expected Ursa to be rough, but it was the opposite. Ursa took great care.

"I – I'll wash yours next."

"Are you sure?"

"Yes."

While taking care of Ursa, Lucea asked about the runes.

"They are for protection," Ursa said. "In my travels I met people with their own Gifts. I had to – take on certain jobs and one employer was so appreciative he gave me the runes. He had similar ones all over his body that he could use for a variety of spells."

Lucea noticed her hesitation but did not comment on it.

Once they finished, they dried off. Lucea, having noticed their soiled garments, was reluctant to wear them once more.

"Gather them up," Ursa said. As Lucea stepped out, she saw a large basket in a wall niche. Ursa lifted the lid and dumped her clothes in. Lucea did so as well.

"They'll clean them for free in most places." Ursa said.

They returned to their room. Lucea had a change of clothes in her pack and a nightshirt. She opted for her clothes, which were a simple pair of brown trousers and a linen shirt. Ursa did the same thing. "Here." Lucea called on her Gift and used it to dry their hair. "You don't want to go to bed with wet hair."

"Thank you."

Overcome by sleep, Lucea stretched across the bed and pulled the coverlets over her. "Good night, Ursa."

"Good night."

A strangeness – Lucea could only describe it as such – struck her as she hovered between light sleep and wakefulness. The bed underneath her dissolved into nothing and she floated through a nothingness that carried her along. Lucea tried to fight, to wake herself, but whatever held her proved stronger. Darkness rendered her Gift useless.

She eventually rested upon something hard and cold. Whatever force held her in place released her, withdrawing a tendril of fog from around her. Lucea startled awake. She was no longer in the hostel. A giantess towered over her in a strange place.

"I am Lady Artemise Samara," the giantess said. "Welcome to my tower."

CHAPTER EIGHT

Ursa watched Lucea sleeping and couldn't help but smile at her innocence. She briefly questioned the wisdom of her decision. Was this world safe for her? Lucea possessed her Gift. However, how might she respond to a lethal threat? What if she found herself in the midst of battle?

Ursa whispered, "That explains your presence."

Her current predicament still amazed her. What kind of person would abandon a helpless girl? She possessed a pretty face but also skin of – she hesitated to use the word alabaster – of exceptional quality. Ursa laughed every time she heard or read that description of love in sonnets and songs. But Lucea did have smooth, flawless skin, pale though pink at her cheeks. And those amber eyes, a unique color, were likely because of her shape-shifting animal type. Ursa realized her ignorance of her shape-shifting options. It seemed obvious considering she and the wolf were from the same land.

She would persevere, despite the uncertainty of future events. Ursa learned from her travels that looking into the future was pointless. Diviners possessed limited foresight.

Ursa took a deep breath and pushed herself off the bed. She wasn't as tired as she thought. She needed a drink. Ursa exited the room, closing the door. Ionneld remained at the counter, writing ledger entries. Ursa asked about the nearest tavern.

"My cousin owns one. He'd appreciate the patronage. It's called the Mighty Hand Tavern. Head straight down the road, you'll see it on your left."

"Do I want to know what that name means?"

Ionneld winked. "Absolutely not."

Ursa couldn't stop the chuckle. "Thank you."

Cool night air, unburdened by the hammer, felt pleasant. Her ancestor couldn't begrudge her a few drinks. Not that it mattered to her. Ursa questioned her ancestor's power and the gods' indifference.

Despite its suggestive name, the Mighty Hand looked well-maintained and welcoming, much like the Rose. A warm, inviting glow spilled out onto the lively street scene, where patrons of all shapes and sizes mingled and laughed together. Some leaned against the wooden façade, while others sat on barrels or benches. The sturdy, ornate door stood open, beckoning anyone to step inside.

Ursa gasped upon entering the tavern. Earth's fey performed this simple spell. The bar to the left was a flurry of activity; a brownie with nimble fingers poured frothy ale for a group of travelers who swapped tales of their journeys. Across the room, a similar scene played out, conversation and laughter a soothing drone. Lively patrons occupied worn wooden tables and benches scattered throughout the room. Tapestries depicting heroic deeds and fantastical creatures adorned the walls. In the corners, small groups were congregated around tables, engaged in hushed conversations.

At the far end of the tavern, a stage bathed in soft light beckoned. A young minstrel sat playing a lute. His fingers danced across the strings. The cheerful tune enlivened the atmosphere. The air was filled with the tantalizing aroma of roasted meats and baked bread, a symphony of scents that danced on the senses.

As Ursa moved deeper into the tavern, she noticed a cozy nook tucked away in the shadows. A fireplace crackled, casting dancing shadows on the walls. The air was thick with the scent of pipe tobacco and aged whiskey. A few patrons lounged on plush velvet chairs, lost in their own thoughts or engaged in muted conversation.

"Welcome!" The voice drew Ursa's attention. The brownie man was grinning at her, his hands splayed on the bar top. "What may I help you with?"

"Ionneld suggested your tavern." Ursa moved to the bar and slid onto one stool.

"That wonderful cousin of mine, always sending me business." He thrust out his hand. "I'm Romhir. Welcome to my tavern."

Ursa grasped his hand and shook it. "I just came here for a drink. I've been traveling awhile."

"By yourself?"

"No, I have a companion. She was exhausted. Ionneld is taking care of her."

"Of course she is. My cousin is a treasure." Someone from the other end of the bar called for more rum. "Excuse me for a moment."

As he went to wait on the other traveler, Ursa scanned her surroundings. She saw that groups of lesser fey had gathered there. Ursa hated that term. She didn't use it after her exile. The Hand possessed a unique allure. Besides brownies, dwarves, gnomes, and pixies were there. A few greater fey, unequal to the dokkalfar, possessed unique power. A lycanthrope sat with a witch. She didn't seem unhappy. Witches often forced them to do their bidding. A dhampir and an ogre shared a table? And a pair of Cat Sith. Now, there was a surprise.

"Are you all ready?" Ursa was taken aback by the question. She hadn't even noticed Romhir had returned.

"Yes. I'd like a spiced rum, please."

"Coming right up! Would you like something to eat? We just pulled some meat pies out of the oven."

"If they're as delicious as they smell, you've found yourself a new regular."

Romhir chuckled. "That's nice to hear."

He delivered her drink in a metal mug, then went to take care of her food order. As Ursa sipped her drink, she continued to watch people, not allowing herself to focus on a particular group for longer than normal. Someone entered, and he drew Ursa's attention, as well as that of a few others. He wrapped himself in a plain brown cloak and clutched at the folds to hide his face. His cautious stance at the door fueled Ursa's hope for his safety. He took some hesitant steps past the threshold, and that was when Ursa saw his legs. Curly golden fur covered them, which ended in cloven hooves. Obviously, a faun, one of the lesser fey. Despite their size, they were often mistaken for satyrs. However, a satyr wouldn't bother hiding itself, not to mention satyrs were much bigger, and their hair was unkempt. Satyrs were not concerned with cleanliness.

The situation changed when the faun saw her and approached.

Ursa's stomach twisted. That couldn't be—?

"Excuse me." The voice was low and soft, unmistakably male. It eased her suspicions, but not by much.

"Yes?" Ursa said, somewhat annoyed.

"Welcome to my tavern." Romhir appeared to address the faun. "What may I get you?"

"Oh." The faun was uncertain. "You don't by any chance have dragon fruit wine?"

"Yes, we do. Have a seat."

The faun hoisted himself onto the stool with difficulty. Romhir soon returned, bearing a tray with a goblet and a pitcher. He set the goblet down first and filled it with the pale pink liquid. While still balancing the tray, Romhir deposited the generously filled meat pie, a fork, and a napkin. Ursa wasted no time digging in. It was delicious! The best—

"Lady Ursa?"

Ursa froze, gripping the fork, which would make the perfect weapon if needed. "How in the nether-hells do you know my name? Speak fast!"

"I – I'm sorry," the faun stammered. "I'm Callen Evermore. They sent me to find you."

"I didn't ask you for your name." Her tone was deadly. "I asked how you knew mine!"

"Please allow me to explain. I mean you no harm."

Ursa snorted a laugh. Callen Evermore posed no danger, despite fauns' lesser fey power. "Speak," she demanded.

Callen sipped his wine. "I would rather we spoke in private."

Ursa narrowed her eyes and stiffened her jaw. She acknowledged the shadowed table in the corner. "Hey, Master Romhir, mind if we take that table?" Ursa motioned with her fork.

"Go right ahead."

Once settled in the corner, Ursa continued to devour the savory pie. The minstrel began with a new song, which provided an additional cover.

"My people once called Farrowden our home."

Ursa found that hard to believe. "If you want to continue speaking with me, I expect the truth."

"It is the truth!"

"Fauns dwell in Underneath and in the Deep Woods." Ursa took a sip of rum and scrutinized him over the rim of her mug.

"We used to reside in Underneath!" For the first time, there was a spark of anger in his expression. "We were driven out by the Rot."

Before Ursa could respond, he continued.

"We are not higher fey!" Callen said. "We pleaded for help. A ljósálfar Vine offshoot existed yet provided no assistance."

Ursa wasn't surprised. The egocentric and arrogant nature of the dokkalfar made Ursa's people seem humble and reserved in comparison.

"We wandered, lost and without a home. We found other fauns, but the Rot pursued us everywhere. We couldn't understand why, but when others lost their homes, no one would permit us into their territories."

Just as rapidly as his anger rose, it fell into despair. "They forced us to make our new home Above Ground."

He drained his goblet. "When we came upon Farrowden, it seemed a blessing. The place seemed abandoned for a century. The lingering signs of human presence confirmed our safety."

"How long were you there?"

"Since before I was born," Callen said. "My grandmother told me the story of how we rebuilt our home and about the discovery of the graveyard. It was horribly unkempt. No one deserved to have their resting place in such a state."

"Thank you for taking care of it."

He grinned. "Upon discovery of the Steel Driver's grave, we recognized this as a hallowed site, and my family pledged to treat it with respect."

Callen fell silent and stared into the empty goblet.

"What happened?"

"Barnabas." Callen dragged his claws down the table surface unconsciously, leaving marks. "I hate him."

Ursa didn't respond, waiting for Callen to continue. He needed to talk. To release this ugliness into the air. "He came upon our home in the night and burned it with fire. Chaos reigned. The fire separated me from my mother and grandmother. Upon reuniting with my mother, I learned of my grandmother's death."

"I'm so sorry," Ursa declared.

Callen sniffed and wiped the back of his hand across his eyes. "Thank you."

Callen was silent for a few moments, and Ursa guessed he was trying to regain his composure. "It was clear to us what a dangerous man he is. A traveler's tale of capture and escape thwarted our plans for far-off refuge."

"They're just snatching people into the woods?"

"To Barnabas, everyone is a sinner and needs to be cleansed."

"That's a zealot for you," Ursa said. "When I was in Farrowden, Barnabas mentioned the name of his cult. The Netherborne Enclave? Do you have any information about that?"

Callen's furry brow wrinkled. "No, I'm afraid not."

"You didn't reply to my question," Ursa said. "How are you familiar with me?"

"My mother saw you in a vision. You and your companion, while you were escaping the archdeacon."

"She's a diviner."

"No, she has future-sight. Her connection to the Vine has always been strong, as my grandmother's was."

"What about you?" Ursa hurried to finish the pie, which was going cold.

"I have not found my power yet." Callen's expression was disappointment, but he brightened moments later. "But my mother and grandmother assured me in the past that I will. I have the Gift, no doubt."

"Lucea will be eager to meet your mother."

"Mother is eager to meet her!"

"Is this an invitation to your village?"

"Oh yes!" Callen grinned. "I suppose I should have said so sooner." His downcast eyes revealed his sadness. "You are still being pursued."

"Damn it to the nether-hells!" Ursa growled. "I was hoping he'd turned his attention to other things."

"My mother couldn't determine why he was still after you, but perhaps if you are near to her – if she can touch you, the connection will be much deeper."

"How much time do we have?"

"Barnabas will be here after sunup. Mother couldn't tell exactly when."

"Damn it again." She thought of Lucea, sleeping. Ursa didn't wish to wake her and hustle her out. "Callen, will you wait for us here? I'll bring Lucea and we can leave now."

"Yes, of course," Callen said. "Don't worry about paying for your food. I'll take care of it."

"Thank you." Ursa was beginning to like the faun. She left the tavern and rushed back down the avenue. When she reached the Rose, she flung open the door, much to the surprise of Ionneld, who sat behind the desk.

"By the Vine!" Ionneld exclaimed. "Are you all right, Lady Ursa?"

"I'm so sorry, Lady Ionneld," Ursa said. "Lucea is still in our room?"

"Yes, to my understanding. I remained at my desk."

"Thank you." Ursa dashed down the hall.

"Wait, what's wrong?" Ionneld called after her.

Ursa burst through the door, her heart pounding. "Lucea!"

But the room was empty, its stillness a chilling contrast to the panic surging through her.

"Lady Ursa?" Ionneld's voice, laced with surprise, pulled her from her shock.

Ursa spun around. "Where is Lucea?"

"S-she's not there?" Ionneld stammered, her expression distressed.

Ursa's mind raced. Perhaps Lucea was in the bathing room? She bypassed the brownie and sprinted to the bathroom; Lucea was nowhere in sight. An icy dread settled in her stomach.

"Is there a back way out?"

"It's behind the desk."

A disturbing thought struck Ursa. A vision of the archdeacon and Lucea as she fought against him filled her mind. She couldn't let that happen.

Ursa fled down the hall, out onto the street with pounding footsteps. She raced to the tavern, her heart slamming against her chest.

"Ursa? Where is—?" Callen said when she got there.

"She's gone!" Ursa slammed her hands down on the tabletop, drawing attention of the patrons, but Ursa didn't care.

"What? But how?" Callen's eyes widened in disbelief.

"Barnabas! Your mother was mistaken!" Ursa wanted to throttle him.

"No. That's impossible!" Callen protested.

Romhir approached. "Lady Ursa?" he said, tentatively.

Anger, a white-hot fury, consumed Ursa. The world around her seemed to blur, and she could feel her blood boiling.

"Lady Ursa." Callen chose his words. "There's no way the archdeacon could have taken her."

"Then how do you explain her disappearance?"

"Is someone missing?" Romhir asked.

"Her companion," Callen replied for her.

"She was back at the Rose?" Romhir raised his eyebrows in surprise.

"Yes," Ursa confirmed. Her eyes never left Callen. She felt an urge to scream, destroy, lash out. But she understood she needed to remain calm. An outburst wouldn't aid her search for Lucea. Nevertheless, she was unsure how to continue. Ursa was lost for the first time since her exile.

CHAPTER NINE

Lucea's eyes were fixed on the colossal figure above her. Lady Samara's presence seemed to swallow the dim light of the room, her shadow stretching long and dark.

"I know who you are, Lucea." Samara's tone was a low, resonant timbre that seemed to echo within Lucea's very bones. "I know what you are."

The sorceress was cloaked in a blood-red cassock, reserved for religious figures. It was split down both sides from waist to ankle. Draped over her shoulders was a black stole inscribed with archaic runes that hinted at dark and forbidden magic. Upon observing them, Lucea visibly shuddered.

Lucea's instinct screamed at her to flee, but her body seemed caught in paralysis. She considered asking why she was there, then Lucea loudly chuckled. The question remained, didn't it? Each romance – novel or play – featured a maiden taken to a handsome rogue's manor. Samara's reasoning wasn't as obvious.

With effort, Lucea stood. "How dare you take me by force!"

"You have squandered your Gift," Lady Samara said, with a tone of profound disappointment. "Such power, wasted. Five years – gone."

Lucea's eyes widened. How did she know about Eica? Her mind raced with the implications of Lady Samara's knowledge. She glanced down and noticed a tattoo on Lady Samara's leg – a black thorn vine, twisted and ominous. It resembled the mark of the Vine. The very symbol that her friend Harper and the witch Isbet bore.

"Those Beholden to the Rot bear this mark," Lady Samara explained, her eyes watching Lucea's every reaction. "Like those who serve the Vine."

Lucea's heart pounded. She knew of the Rot's sinister influence. She met Lady Samara's gaze with a mixture of anger and curiosity.

"You insult me, but align yourself with such filth?" Lucea demanded.

Lady Samara offered no response. She stood there, her silence heavier than any words she could have said.

"If you will not respond or explain yourself, I'm leaving."

Lady Samara's hand twitched, and a searing light erupted around Lucea, encircling her body in a painful embrace. Every nerve ending seemed to catch fire, and she was rooted to the spot, unable to move.

"What have you done?" Lucea gasped, her voice strained and trembling.

Again, Lady Samara ignored her question. Her fingers moved in an intricate dance, and Lucea found herself walking toward a nearby chair, compelled by an unseen force. She sat down, her body betraying her will, and stared up at the sorceress in defiant silence.

"The Rot has seen you," Samara said. "They know of your Gift, and you shall submit to their will."

Lucea's hands tensed around the ends of the armrests and she unconsciously leaned forward in her anger. "To the nether-hells with you and the Rot!"

"To begin, I need to determine the extent of your power," Samara said, ignoring Lucea's oath. The sorceress turned and approached a wooden table nestled against the stone wall. The table was crafted in the shape of a quarter moon, fitting snugly into the curve of the tower interior. Its dark, polished surface glistened faintly in the dim light, hinting at the secrets and experiments it had borne witness to over the years.

Samara worked at the table without speaking. Lucea took the opportunity to truly examine her surroundings. She could only assume she was on the top floor of the tower she and Ursa had seen when they had first entered Grayfort. Shelves laden with unsettling potions, ingredients, and unspeakable artifacts lined the walls. Tall, arched windows shrouded with weighty, dark curtains allowed only slivers of moonlight to pierce the gloom.

At the far end of the room, a cauldron bubbled ominously over a flickering flame, releasing foul, greenish vapors that curled through the air. Nearby, an assortment of cages and glass containers housed grotesque, writhing creatures.

The air was thick with the acrid scent of burning herbs and the metallic tang of blood, mingling with the whispers of ancient, forbidden spells. Samara's dark power and relentless pursuit of dark magic were evident. The room was a place light avoided.

Lucea's path to freedom lay behind a formidable iron door, its surface marred with the passage of time and reinforced with thick, sturdy iron bands. Large, round bolts punctuated the metal, adding to its impenetrable appearance. A rusted latch, intricately forged in the shape of a snarling dragon, glared mockingly at her. The jagged edges and ancient rust of the latch served as a cruel reminder that even if she managed to break free from her bindings, the mere touch of the metal could be enough to seal her fate.

Leaving the table, Samara faced Lucea. Three jars were lined up on the table surface. Lucea's hands trembled as her eyes fixed on them. Each one held an ethereal being, illuminated by the flickering candlelight that cast long, eerie shadows on the stone walls.

The first held a wil-o'-wisp. It floated within its glass prison, its form constantly shifting and shimmering with an eerie, spectral glow. The light danced in shades of blue and white, casting faint, ghostly reflections on the jar's surface. Despite its delicate appearance, the wil-o'-wisp's movements were quick and unpredictable, like a restless spirit searching for an escape.

The second held a fairy, its tiny body no more than a few inches tall. Typical of her type, the fairy possessed a small, delicate form and wings shimmering with every rainbow color. The fairy's long, flowing hair, glittering like strands of moonlight, cascaded down her back. Her large, expressive eyes were filled with a mixture of fear and defiance as she hovered restlessly within the confines of her jar, her fragile wings fluttering incessantly against the glass.

It was the occupant of the third jar that caused Lucea to tremble with a mixture of fear and revulsion. Within was a homunculus. A grotesque parody of human life, a small, twisted figure reaching a foot in height. Its skin had an unhealthy, grayish hue, stretched taut over a gaunt, emaciated frame. Its features were distorted and asymmetrical, with one eye larger than the other and a misshapen mouth that formed a permanent grimace. Its limbs were thin and spindly, ending in clawlike fingers that scratched and tapped nervously against the inside of the jar. A dark, malevolent aura seemed to emanate from its very being, a chilling reminder of the dark magic that brought it into existence.

"Come here." Samara gestured again, forcing Lucea to stand and approach. A second gesture propelled paper across the room, seemingly from nowhere, but Lucea knew it was levitation. The papers arranged themselves on the table. A pen came to rest next to them.

"You will begin with the wil-o'-wisp."

Samara took hold of her body once again, forcing Lucea to raise her hand and gather her Gift. Samara drew her power out like a leech sucking blood, and when Lucea tried to fight, the spell that bound her sent fire through her body. She hesitated, seeking an alternative.

Her Gift seemed to have no effect on the wil-o'-wisp. It persisted. Lucea expected to be punished for this but instead saw Samara scribbling on the sheets as she hmm'd and nodded, not surprised by the results.

"Very well then, next."

Lucea's heart pounded as she moved to the second jar. She hesitated, a sense of dread washing over her, but Samara's icy glare left her no choice. As she channeled her power once more, the fairy's form began to shift. Its wings folded in, and its tiny body curled inward. Before Lucea's horrified eyes, the fairy transformed into a radiant flower, petals glowing with an otherworldly beauty.

Samara's lips curled into a sinister smile. She wrote, her finger guiding the pen in a frantic gesture. "Now the last one."

With mounting fury and desperation, Lucea approached the jar holding the homunculus. When she released her power, the features of the homunculus contorted and aged, its body withering to dust in a matter of moments.

Lucea's breath came in ragged gasps as she turned to Samara, her eyes blazing with anger. "How dare you make me use my power for this...*abomination*!?"

Samara remained impassive, her tone a whisper. "This is only the beginning, Lucea. You will learn to harness your power to its fullest potential. Your wants are no longer of concern. I have been tasked with readying you to be consumed by the Rot."

Lucea's fists clenched at her sides, her fury a contained storm. Somehow, she had to break Samara's hold on her. But even that wouldn't solve her escape problem. Lucea could only hope Ursa was out there somewhere searching for her.

With a mere flick of her wrist, Samara silently commanded Lucea's body against her will, taking control once again and forcing Lucea back into the worn wooden chair. Lucea watched as Samara gathered the three glass jars with meticulous care. The sorceress crossed the room with an air of chilling purpose, approaching the cauldron, which bubbled and hissed with dark, magical energy. One by one, she dropped the jars into the swirling concoction; each sank with a sizzle.

But Samara wasn't finished. Raising her hands, she began an incantation, the words tumbling from her lips in a harsh, guttural cadence that sent shivers down Lucea's spine. As the spell commenced, the room was enveloped by a stifling and eerie weight, casting it into darkness. Samara's focus was entirely on the ritual, and as her incantation grew louder and more intense, Lucea felt a subtle shift in the binding magic. She sensed Samara's grip on her weakening.

As Samara's incantation reached its crescendo, the bubbling cauldron began to churn violently. From its depths, a thick, noxious mist began to rise, coiling and twisting like a living entity. The stench was overwhelming, a vile combination of decay and sulfur that filled the chamber with an oppressive, nauseating cloud. Slowly, the Rot emerged.

The sight was horrifying – a formless mass of decaying flesh and sinew, oozing black ichor. The shape was constantly shifting, grotesque limbs and distorted faces forming and dissolving within its foul substance. The Rot's surface was pocked with boils and festering wounds, from which oozed a sickly, greenish fluid. A cacophony of guttural moans and hissing whispers emanated from the creature, a symphony of agony and malice.

The air near the Rot darkened, seeming to recoil from its presence. Foul tendrils reached out, leaving trails of corruption on everything they touched. The Rot's malevolent aura seeped into the room, an overwhelming force of evil that threatened to suffocate all life within its grasp.

They conversed in a language that Lucea didn't recognize, yet she could understand the words. They were speaking about her.

Lucea's heart pounded as she sat there, the weight of their words pressing down on her. As Samara continued painting vivid pictures of how Lucea would serve the Rot, Lucea began to gather her strength, focusing on the energy that swirled within. Once their conversation ended, the Rot returned to its putrid form. Samara turned to face Lucea. Her pupils were full and swallowing the color of her eyes. "You are to be my student. I will be your master, and we will serve together."

"I will not!" Lucea screamed in defiance.

Samara's face twisted in an expression not unlike the Rot. She turned, quickly and deliberately, and turned back brandishing a menacing shale dagger. "It appears you need convincing," Samara forced the words between her clenched teeth.

As the sorceress began her strike, a powerful external force ripped the iron door from its frame, pulverizing the stonework. The disruption caught Samara's attention. Lucea released her power. The glowing blue bubble surrounded Samara. The runes and equations danced and shifted. The effect was immediate. Samara's features began to wither, her skin sagged and her hair turned white as the years caught up with her in an instant.

Samara's scream filled the room, a sound of pure agony. Then Ursa was there, her eyes wide with shock. She stopped dead upon seeing Lucea and the now ancient crone that was Samara. As Lucea tried to push herself from the chair, Ursa rushed to her side.

"I have you."

Samara's cries continued to reverberate around the chamber as she fought to maintain her balance. The stone floor beneath the sorceress shattered, sending shards flying, and thorny vines burst through the cracks, wrapping around her frail body. The sound of a beast devouring its prey filled the air, a gruesome accompaniment to the chaos.

Lucea grabbed Ursa by the wrist. "We have to go, now!" she shouted urgently. Together, they fled from the room, their footsteps resounding on the stone steps. They didn't dare look back. The sounds of Samara's transformation and the beast's feeding faded into the distance as they ran for their lives.

CHAPTER TEN

Earlier that evening they had met at the Rose.

"You're sure nobody entered or exited?"

"Certain."

"And that door behind the counter? You weren't at the desk—"

"That door is locked, and there has been no forced entry."

"Did you interrogate the other tenants?"

"No."

"By the nether-hells, why not?"

"I will not terrorize my guests." Ionneld's patience thinned; Ursa read it in her pinched face.

Romhir cut in. "You're being unfair and insulting."

She had wrecked their room under the guise of a search. No one had moved to stop her; other guests had noticed the noise, and Ionneld and Romhir had to calm them and coax them back to their rooms with promises of Romhir's finest vintage.

Now, as her energy bled away and the anger cooled, Ursa could not stay upright. She sank before the front desk, rested her head against the smooth wood, and closed her eyes, forcing the tears back – the sight of a weeping maiden was unpleasant. Maybe Lucea had left on her own. Who was she trying to convince? Even as the thought formed, Ursa knew it was a lie. Ursa wasn't certain how long she sat there, but after a time she sensed a glass being pressed into her hand.

"Drink," Romhir said.

It turned out to be whiskey. The scent was the sweet of honey and malt. Ursa drank it straight down. Oddly, the rush of warmth that spread through her body helped clear her head. With renewed attention, Ursa stood. "Please forgive me, Lady Ionneld."

Ionneld smiled with sympathy and took one of Ursa's hands, squeezing it.

Romhir pointed to Callen. "You, Sir Faun. What is your part here?"

"Callen. And I need to warn Ursa and Lucea that their enemy is in pursuit."

"Enemy?" Ionneld focused a questioning look at Ursa.

"What trouble are you bringing to my cousin's hostel?" Romhir demanded.

Ursa could have throttled Callen right then. She gripped the haft of the hammer tighter. A thought struck her as the runes began to glow and pulse against her palms. Ursa stood without responding and strode from the Rose. Once outside, she stopped. The cobblestones were her only obstacle.

"Sunder." Ursa raised the hammer and brought it down upon the cobblestones, shattering them into shards and clouds of dust.

"What in the nether-hells—?" Romhir said.

Ursa went to her knees and dug her fingers into the flattened earth. Her eyes closed as she gathered that part of herself to render an impassioned plea to the Vine. However, the response she received, if one could call it that, was unlike any Ursa had ever gotten before. Ursa saw a vision of the green, healthy Celestial Vine entwined with a black thorn vine, spiraling around the tower they'd seen upon entering the city. She felt a sudden, sharp fear, but knew she must rescue Lucea.

Ursa stood and brushed her hands down her trousers. "There." Ursa nodded toward the tower. "Lucea is there."

"Lady Samara's tower?" Ionneld said incredulously.

"Lady Samara?" Ursa asked.

"This is her town. She protects us. She is a powerful sorceress," Ionneld offered. "I can't imagine why she would want Lucea."

Ursa could. "Just how powerful is this sorceress?"

"She is not fey," Romhir said, "but I don't understand. You believe Lucea is in her tower?"

"The Vine told me as much," Ursa said.

"But why?" Ionneld said.

"Well..." Ursa laid the hammer over her shoulder. "I suppose I'll have to ask her." As she turned to go, she said, "I'll go alone. This doesn't involve you."

"I'd say we already are involved," Romhir spoke up.

Ursa hesitated. Her companion didn't go to the tower of her own volition. Lucea would have left word. Ursa could only assume that Lucea had been taken by force.

Ionneld approached. "We're strangers, yet I trust you; this is the approach we take. If— When you rescue Lucea you will return here. I will have horses waiting for you. From here you will ride for the West Gate."

"I can't— How will I repay you?"

"We have Lucea's letter, recall?" Ionneld said. "Wait right here."

"I would recommend, Sir Callen, that you ride ahead and wait for them at the gate," Romhir suggested.

"All right," Callen said.

Ionneld returned. "Here." She handed Ursa Lucea's letter.

"Thank you," Ursa said, "for your kindness and trust."

"You are welcome," Ionneld said. "Safe travels to the three of you."

"Callen," Ursa said, "if we do not return before the gate is ready to close, leave without us."

"But—" Callen began.

"No," Ursa said. "Lucea and I are on a mission. Lucea was to speak to the leader of Jack-In-Irons to warn them about the Rot. Will you be willing to do such?"

Callen drew himself up. "Yes, I will."

"Thank you."

Ursa doubted Callen would gain an audience. That would mean the city – all the Riven Isles – would fall before the Rot. But she would not abandon Lucea.

Ursa fought the urge to run. She didn't want to draw too much attention to herself. Despite the late hour, people still roamed the streets. Ursa chose a steady jog. The tower, the city's tallest structure, proved easy to find. Ursa circled it, shocked by the absence of an entrance.

Ursa gripped the haft of the hammer and laid her forehead against it. She felt the heat from the runes as they glowed with a light Ursa somehow perceived through her closed eyes. Runes flashed into the darkness behind her lids. Spells. Other spells. Ursa hesitated. A knot of worry tightened in her chest at the thought of the sound giving them away. Although she might not have a choice.

Forgeheart.

Ursa opened her eyes and drew in a breath. She examined her surroundings, hoping no one would see. She laid the hammerhead against the stone, which glowed a deep red, the color blooming across its surface. The hue then shifted to a vibrant orange as the heat intensified. Ursa watched in fascination as the color continued to change with the rising temperature – first to a brilliant yellow, then to a blinding white. The stone radiated a mesmerizing blue-violet, from the extreme heat. Each stage of color seemed to pulse with otherworldly energy, illuminating the surroundings.

The stone was discolored. Fissures appeared on the surface. As the marble melted, it flowed, and the molten material took on a glassy, semiliquid appearance. In the final stage, the rock became a viscous, luminous substance that created an ethereal visual effect.

An opening appeared almost at once. Ursa waited for the stone to cool. With care, she stepped through the hole, first with one leg, then the other. The opening revealed a staircase lit by wil-o'-wisp trapped in jars attached to the walls. And yet the stairs ascended into darkness. Though it seemed illogical, she disregarded the tower's design.

As Ursa started up the stairs, she tapped the glass of the jars, shattering them to free the wil-o'-wisp. Instead of leaving, the wil-o'-wisp gathered at her feet, glowing to continue to supply light as Ursa climbed.

When she reached the landing, Ursa saw three doors in front of her. The first door to her left creaked open to reveal a bedchamber. She could not open the door to her right.

Ursa faced the third door, cursing at the sight of iron. She approached as close as she dared. There was a stench like burning metal. A thin sliver of light escaped from underneath the door. Ursa inhaled deeply, hoisted the hammer, then smashed it onto the door. The force tore the door from its hinges, shattering wood and a swath of masonry; timber and stone detonated outward like a blasted cliff, splinters and jagged shards hurling in every direction.

Ursa took in the scene before her in an eye blink. Lucea sat in a chair with her wrists and ankles bound by glowing bands of magic that hummed with a sinister energy. In front of her stood another woman, swathed in robes. Samara. She had a shale knife in her hand, pointed at Lucea, but upon Ursa's entrance the woman halted. Her head whipped to the side in shock.

Ursa was about to attack when she witnessed once again the exceptional power of the chronomancer. Lucea encased her would-be attacker in a translucent bubble that shimmered and pulsed. Intricate lines of runes swirled around the surface, their glowing symbols creating a mesmerizing dance of light. Samara's skin paled and wrinkled. Her hair turned silver and then white as she aged before Ursa's eyes.

Ursa shook herself out of her own fugue and rushed to Lucea, who struggled to push herself out of the chair. The bands of magic faded as she did so.

"Ursa," Lucea whispered.

"I have you." Ursa draped one arm underneath Lucea's shoulders while keeping a grip on the hammer with the other.

A scream wrenched their attention back to Samara. The scene that played before them was one of torturous horror. Ursa was disbelieving what she was seeing.

Lucea grabbed Ursa by the wrist. "We have to go, now!"

Together, they descended the stairs, the sounds of violence and the screams of agony fading behind them.

"Where to?" Once they were outside in the cool night air, Lucea turned to Ursa. Even in the semi-darkness, Ursa saw the panic in Lucea's expression.

"We're escaping from here," Ursa said. "Ionneld is helping us."

"But— Will she—?"

"Leaving now might prevent them from discovering her." Ursa took her hand and led her down the side streets and alleyways. "We need to get to the West Gate."

"Why there?"

"We need to leave before they close. We have a…companion waiting there."

"A companion? But who?"

"Lucea," Ursa said, "I'll explain everything later. Trust me."

"I do."

Ursa discovered not only the expected horses at the Rose but also laden saddlebags containing their possessions. Ionneld had also fastened a leather thong to Ursa's saddle to hold the hammer.

Wasting no time, Ursa and Lucea mounted the horses and fled into the night. Hooves pounded as they galloped through the cobbled street, ignoring anything or anyone in their path. They reached the town's edge and reined their horses in. Callen was waiting for them as planned.

"Thank the Vine!" Callen said. "Are you all right, Lady Lucea?"

"Yes," Lucea said.

"I'm Callen," he said, saving Ursa the trouble. "I am a friend."

Lucea didn't respond but continued to look at the faun with suspicion. From somewhere within the town there came a tolling bell.

"We must make haste!" Callen said. Ursa was taken aback by the sight of the wolf that stood waiting with the horses, who seemed unbothered by its presence. Callen vaulted onto its furry back and was off before Ursa could examine it. She and Lucea followed in his wake. The gates were closing, and Ursa spurred her horse faster, slipping through with moments to spare. They galloped their horses, guided by the full moon, until the horses were winded and foaming.

They slowed their pace, and as the moon disappeared behind clouds, the darkness enveloped them like a cloak.

"We can't continue like this," Ursa said. They had risked the welfare of the horses by galloping even in the moonlight.

"What is that behind us?" Lucea said.

A faint light appeared in the distance, growing brighter as it approached, which condensed into dozens of will-o'-wisps, their ghostly glow lighting the path ahead.

"Where, by the Vine—" Callen began.

Lucea giggled like a schoolgirl and slid off her mount. The wil-o'-wisp, seeming to know of her kind heart, gathered around her, brushing against her.

"They tickle!" Lucea laughed.

Ursa smiled as she watched Lucea interact with the ethereal beings, their soft light reflecting in her eyes. Amid the chaos, unexpected beauty blossomed. Ursa was quite content to allow Lucea this precious time of peace.

"I wonder why they followed us," Callen said.

"I freed them," Ursa responded. "Or at least a few of them." She didn't want to remind Lucea of Samara's tower. "I don't know where the rest came from."

"Samara—" There was a catch in Lucea's voice. "She killed one. And made me—"

Ursa slipped off her horse and within a few steps, pulled Lucea into her arms. "You don't have to talk about it now unless you wish to."

Lucea drew in a ragged breath, then released it. "No. We have to keep moving."

"We're not too far from my village," Callen said. "We should reach it by daybreak."

"Your village?" Lucea said.

Ursa was embarrassed about making such a decision without Lucea's consent. "It's another one of those things—"

"That you need to explain?" Lucea said, annoyed.

"It's my fault," Callen said.

"Lucea," Ursa said, "you said you trusted me. Do you still?"

Lucea glanced at Callen, suspicion still in her expression. “Again, yes.”

“Follow me.” Callen turned his horse and started down the road.

Ursa followed Callen, keeping a careful distance between their horses. The rhythmic pounding of hooves filled the air as they rode in tense silence. Despite her inability to see Lucea’s face, Ursa sensed her doubt. A tangible presence, like a burning brand on her neck, prickled with each imagined glance from Lucea.

CHAPTER ELEVEN

The storm intensified as it battered them with icy rain, soaking through Lucea's coat and clothes, sending numbing cold through her body. The wil-o'-wisp that had guided their way through the forest dispersed, their light flickering out as they vanished into the woods, leaving them in total darkness. The rain and howling wind created a wall of noise that swallowed any sound beyond their immediate vicinity. The only consolation was that the miserable weather deterred other travelers too, and the muddy road would obscure their tracks from any pursuers, if not stop them altogether.

Lucea squinted through the relentless downpour, her vision blurred by the sheets of rain. Each wind gust was like icy needles on her skin, and she could not remain stable in the saddle. Fatigue caused her shoulders to droop, and a shiver coursed through her, resulting in chattering teeth.

The darkness and the ferocity of the storm added to her sense of isolation and vulnerability. Ursa's nearby presence offered scant comfort against the intense cold and her consuming questions. Lucea was so deep in thought that she didn't notice at first Ursa and Callen had halted their mounts.

"Stop, Lucea!" Ursa shouted over the wind. "Dismount!"

It took a few moments for Lucea to understand what Ursa said.

Ursa guided her horse closer. "You can't continue like this."

Lucea looked at her, wide-eyed and confused, but obeyed. She slid off her horse, her legs unsteady from exhaustion and the cold. Ursa joined her and removed her cloak and wrapped it around Lucea, shielding her from the worst of the rain.

"Get on behind me," Ursa instructed, firmly but gently. She secured Lucea's horse to her saddle.

With Ursa's help, Lucea climbed on her horse. Then Ursa remounted. Lucea clung to her as Ursa urged the animal forward. The warmth of their combined bodies seeped through the cold, wet fabric of their clothes and brought a measure of comfort amidst the storm's fury. Lucea trembled against Ursa's back, but relaxed.

The storm continued, its icy fingers clawing at Lucea and Ursa as they rode through the darkness. The rain lashed against them, and the wind howled with a malevolent intensity. Lucea clung to Ursa, seeking solace in the comfort of her body. The world around her changed.

An otherworldly chill that seeped into her bones replaced the cold of the storm. The sounds of rain and wind faded into an eerie silence. Lucea's vision blurred, and she found herself standing in a shadowy, twisted landscape. The air was thick with the stench of decay, and dark thorn vines snaked across the ground, pulsating with sinister energy.

From the shadows, a figure appeared. Samara. But this was not the true giantess. Her once-pale skin was now marred by black thorn vines, which twisted and writhed beneath her flesh. Nettles sprouted from underneath her skin, breaking through in a grotesque display. Her eyes shone with an unsettling, otherworldly luminescence, locking onto Lucea.

"You cannot elude me, Lucea." Samara spoke in a chilling whisper that made Lucea shiver. "The Rot awaits you. And I have permission to take you myself."

"No!" Lucea cried, defiantly. "I will not become part of your wickedness."

Desperation fueled her as she tried to summon her power, to break free from the vision that ensnared her. But before she could gather her strength, Samara's mouth twisted into a cruel smile.

"You are mine, Lucea." Samara raised a hand wreathed in black vines. With a swift, forceful motion, she reached out and pushed her open palm forward. The vision shattered like glass, and the storm thrust Lucea back. She gasped, her breath ragged as the icy rain pelted her skin once more. She clung to Ursa, trembling – not just from the cold, but from the lingering terror of Samara's haunting presence.

Ursa's muscular form was her anchor in the storm's chaos, but

Lucea couldn't shake the fear that had taken root in her heart. She understood Samara's threat, and determined to protect herself and those she cherished from the approaching darkness.

★ ★ ★

Lucea awoke with a start, her heart pounding in her chest. She blinked in the dim light, trying to make sense of her surroundings. The bed beneath her was unfamiliar, and she was conscious of a nightshirt against her skin. Panic surged through her as she struggled to remember how she got here. She swept the room with her eyes before settling on a known face.

Across from her, seated at a wooden table, was Ursa. Relief flooded Lucea's senses as she recognized her friend. Ursa talked in hushed tones to an elderly faun. Brown and silver fur covered the faun, and flowers and beads decorated her braided hair. The sight soothed.

Lucea considered asking about their location and recent events, yet slumber beckoned. She didn't resist and let the comforting presence of Ursa lull her back to sleep.

When Lucea woke again, the room was silent. She lay still for a moment, listening to the soft rustling of leaves outside and the distant chirping of birds. With an effort, she came to a sitting position and noticed she was alone. The table where Ursa and the elderly faun had been sitting was now empty.

Curiosity sparked, Lucea examined her surroundings more closely. The room's circular shape and roughhewn walls indicated a rustic haven carved from the heart of an ancient tree. The circular bed, crafted from the same wood that made up the walls, gleamed. Luxurious quilts covered the bed, adding to the cozy, natural warmth of the space.

To her left stood a charming dressing table, its surface scattered with an array of delicate bottles, a water pitcher, and a ceramic bowl. Nearby, an open doorway led to a washroom. The rocking chair, next to a modest writing desk to her left, was hand-carved and draped with a colorful quilt that invited one to sit and relax. A round window allowed sunlight to pour into the room, casting gentle, golden beams on the wooden floor.

A closed wooden door marked the room's exit, shaped in a perfect half-circle, harmonizing with the room's organic, flowing lines. The entire room exuded a sense of timeless tranquility and natural beauty.

A soft knock interrupted the silence. Ursa entered and brought an immediate sense of reassurance.

"Good morning." Ursa greeted her with a warm smile. "How are you feeling?"

Lucea stretched and yawned, still somewhat sleepy. "Better, I think. Where are we?"

"We're in the faun village of Everfall," Ursa explained. "You've been asleep for a while. I hope you're comfortable."

Memories of their recent journey flooded back, and Lucea couldn't help but blush as she recalled how comforting it had been to be pressed against Ursa's body during their ride. She dismissed the thought and focused on the present.

If Ursa noticed her blush, she didn't comment. Instead, she said, "Why don't you get dressed and meet me outside for breakfast? The village eats as a community."

"All right." When Lucea was alone again, she rose from the bed, grateful for the fresh clothes folded on a nearby chair. Once dressed, she stepped outside with a mix of anticipation and curiosity.

Lucea paused, marveling at the enchanting scene before her. Ancient trees nestled the village in a semicircle, opening into a wide, sunlit clearing. The trees themselves bore huts crafted from branches and straw, some perched high among the boughs, while others rested on the forest floor. Each blended with its natural surroundings, as if grown from the trees themselves. Lucea glanced back and realized that her room was in one of these huts, part of a line of seven massive trees with dwellings carved into their trunks.

In the heart of the clearing were benches carved from smooth, gray stone, where some faun citizens relaxed while others entertained with the melodic tunes of flutes and harps. Children playing tag and hide-and-seek filled the air with joyous laughter, their lively games weaving through the clusters of wildflowers and patches of soft grass. Two elderly fauns, their fur streaked with gray, sat at a stone table engrossed in a game of draughts. Nearby, mothers tended to laundry in large washbasins, while others hung clothes on flax lines that crisscrossed between the trees, the garments fluttering like colorful flags in the gentle breeze. Some fauns worked in small gardens, their hands nurturing the earth.

Lucea walked on the plush, emerald grass, experiencing its softness underfoot as she passed by citizens who waved and called to her with cheerful greetings. She responded with smiles and waves, heartened by the sense of community and happiness that radiated from every corner of the village. She hoped this serene and joyful atmosphere would endure.

The sight of several long tables, each polished to a fine sheen, surprised her as she left the trees and entered a larger clearing. Faun groups dined and conversed at tables, constantly expanding. The communal spirit was palpable, a testament to the harmony of their woodland life.

At the gathering, Lucea spotted Ursa sitting at the end of one table, in discussion with the young faun. As the memory returned from last night, Lucea recalled the faun. What was his name again? Callen. When Ursa caught sight of her, she beckoned Lucea to join her.

Lucea approached and took a seat beside Ursa. A variety of vegetables, fruits, and freshly baked bread ladened the table. While the food looked appetizing, Lucea couldn't help but feel a pang of unease.

Ursa noticed her discomfort and leaned into whisper, "Is something wrong?"

Lucea hesitated before responding, "I appreciate the food, but I need meat to sustain my energy. As a cat shifter, it's a necessity for me."

Understanding dawned in Ursa's eyes. "I see. Let's find a solution."

Callen asked, "Is the food not to your liking?"

"No, that isn't the issue," Lucea said. "Maybe it would help you understand if I showed you."

Lucea started by shifting into half-form, her body elongating and fur sprouting along her limbs, which caused quite a few of the fauns gathered to cry out in surprise. Her features became more feline, her eyes glowing with an eerie yellow hue, and her movements fluid and predatory.

Lucea always appreciated how she, unlike the lycans, could fold away her garments into the hidden pocket she kept for such things, waiting for her when she returned. It was a simple and handy spell that needed no words or gestures.

As Lucea completed her transformation, she stood as a large black cat, sleek and powerful. The expressions of those gathered ranged from fear to shock, their eyes wide as they beheld the magnificent creature before them. Ursa, however, viewed Lucea's impressive metamorphosis with amazement and admiration.

"Of course! I see now," Callen said. "Please accept our apologies, Miss Lucea."

To respond, Lucea changed to her half-human form. "No need to apologize. You were unaware."

"Oh dear." Callen pinched his bottom lip, his expression perplexed. "I'm uncertain how we can deal with this situation."

"I'm assuming you have no hunting weapons?" Ursa inquired.

"No. The Vine tasked us as protectors," Callen said.

"Well," Ursa offered, "if you are not averse to the idea, you and I can hunt together."

Lucea's eyes brightened at the suggestion. "Yes. Let's hunt."

CHAPTER TWELVE

Lucea detested hunting, especially by herself. It hadn't presented a problem back home, where meat was abundant for their species. Hunters needed to avoid sentient creatures, though Lucea doubted their existence in this area.

Once she was back in her second animal shape, she easily kept pace with Ursa's extensive stride. Ursa fetched the hammer, leaving Lucea waiting at the clearing's edge.

Lucea still had questions about the hammer. Yes, she understood the Steel Driver had sent Ursa on her quest, but why her? She couldn't be the only descendant the Steel Driver had, not to mention the Rot's reign of terror over the Isles was of an unspecified duration. Lucea's initial knowledge of the Rot came during the quest for Reynard the Fox to bring him back to Vale to face justice. That's when she met the diviner Harper.

"You seem contemplative."

Ursa's statement drew her back from the past. "Yes. I have questions, but I don't want to make you uncomfortable."

"I believe we are past that," Ursa said.

"Truly?" Did Ursa trust her? The least she could do was return the kindness. "I suppose you may have some questions for me too?"

Ursa pondered for a short time. "I assumed you didn't prefer the vegetables because of your cat nature."

"It's less a preference," Lucea said. "Contrary to belief, being in our human form does not stop our bodies from the reactions to certain foods. Although shifters like my uncles Isengrim and Reynard can eat whatever they want, His Majesty is in the same situation as I."

"Reynard the Fox?"

"Yes. You know the story?"

Ursa replied, "To some extent. However, that's for later."

Lucea giggled. "What else would you like to know?"

Instead of asking another question, Ursa said, "You are so beautiful that way. In any of your forms, in fact."

The unexpected compliment had Lucea wrapping her arms around her torso. She ducked her head and smiled, aware of the heat in her face.

"Why are you embarrassed? Do compliments disturb you?"

Lucea drew up straight. "No – I mean—"

Ursa laughed aloud. That deep timbre that sent shivers across Lucea's flesh. "Stop being so modest." Ursa tipped up her chin with one finger.

"You don't—"

"Understand?" Ursa smiled gently. "You held steadfast against leaving the shadows, as many desired your strength."

"How did you—?"

"And unlike myself, you did not hide that fear behind a cloak of arrogance. That isn't in your nature."

Lucea finally saw Ursa. "Who are you?"

An expression of regret briefly crossed Ursa's features. "We should continue."

"So, you don't trust me," Lucea said.

"I did not say that." Ursa looked away. "It is a – humiliating tale."

Lucea noticed the memory wounded Ursa deeply. The events of the past had left grave scars on her, etching a profound sadness into her eyes. Lucea took her hands. "I'm sorry. You don't have to tell me."

"Stop apologizing!" Ursa's curt tone surprised her. "Take your animal form. There is much prey here, likely because the fauns protect the forest. Chase them and if I can, I will bring them down."

Lucea blew out a breath and without another word took on her cat form.

⋆ ⋆ ⋆

Ursa's assessment proved correct. This section of the forest teemed with game. Lucea doubted whether a lack of predators explained it. Lucea detected no protective spell, despite the possibility of faun magic.

As she prowled, she tried not to think about Ursa and that hurtful tone. She had to concentrate lest she starved or risked eating something that would make her deathly ill. When a noise made her ears twitch, she approached with her natural stealth. A tall, muscular buck came into view. Lucea sighed inwardly.

Despite her true animal form sharing the same proportions as her other forms, Lucea was unable to overcome a full-grown buck alone. Likely it wouldn't be an issue for Isengrim or Leonine, but one slash or stab from those antlers would spell her end. Besides, the animal's size far exceeded Lucea's capacity for a single meal, and she objected to the idea of squandering the rest.

Lucea hadn't seen Ursa since their split, so she hoped the dokkalfar would understand the buck wasn't the proper prey.

Soon, she encountered feral pigs, likely escaped farm animals. Lucea crouched low in the tall grass, focusing on the smallest, who seemed oblivious to Lucea's presence. In an instant, Lucea sprang forward, using her powerful hind legs. She pounced before the pig could react and sank her teeth deep into its throat. Its blood filled her mouth, hot and sweet.

The entire experience reiterated in her mind how much she hated this. Many years ago, her father had advised Isengrim to teach her about the hunt, though Lucea found no need and told him, "But Uncle, we have hunters who bring us meat."

"Yes, we do," Isengrim stated. "Still, you must sometimes trust your animal instincts. It is that or starve."

Now she understood.

The pig wouldn't surrender that easily and struggled to shake Lucea off. Its blood continued draining, making the effort futile. Then Ursa appeared. She swung the hammer and smashed it into the pig's skull, barely missing Lucea. A bone crunched audibly as the pig fell. Ursa retreated, nodded, then hid behind a tree, shielding herself from Lucea's sight. Did Ursa understand that sometimes, her people's animal forms unleashed overwhelming instincts, eclipsing their humanity? They became a true animal. It had happened to Reynard and his mother. Reynard had come back, but his mother lost herself to the beast.

Lucea ate her fill, then took her time cleaning herself up. Now what to do about the remains? Lucea didn't want some faun child stumbling on it by accident. Nor did she want the smell of blood to draw other predators.

Ursa approached just as Lucea reached her half-animal form. Although Ursa's tone still hurt and angered her, Lucea had important tasks to complete. "I don't want to leave the carcass here."

"I'll take care of it." Ursa grasped the hammer.

Lucea was awestruck as the runes on the hammer glowed with an otherworldly light. Ursa muttered the word *Forgeheart*, and the carcass burst into flames. Lucea took a few steps back, gasping in shock. Earlier, upon reading the runes, it was clear to her that the hammer was enchanted, yet this went beyond what she predicted. Her mind raced with curiosity, wondering what other powerful secrets the hammer held.

The flames consumed only the carcass, a fact unsurprising to Lucea. The flames didn't stop burning until they had reduced the carcass to ash.

"Amazing," Lucea whispered. Lucea still had questions, but felt uneasy about voicing them. She wondered if they would ever regain their burgeoning sense of trust.

★ ★ ★

They walked back to the village in complete silence. It devastated her. Still, Lucea put on a brave face as Callen approached.

"I'm glad you're back." Callen carried two wooden cups, which he handed to them. Lucea identified the juice as dragon fruit. "I figured that suited you, Lady Lucea."

"Just Lucea," she said. This Callen appeared pleasant.

"My mother is waiting to see you both," Callen said. "Please follow me."

"Your mother?" Lucea said, puzzled.

"Oh," Callen said. He looked at Ursa. "You haven't told her?"

"Not yet," Ursa said.

"Well, if you don't mind," Callen continued, "my mother has future-sight. She foresaw you two in a vision, being chased by the archbishop."

Lucea had forgotten about that lunatic zealot. And what was Callen implying about their pursuit? What reason might he have—?

"He wants the hammer." Lucea kept her eyes on Callen. Ursa didn't comment.

"That you will have to ask my mother," Callen said. "She noticed Barnabas spurred his people to arm themselves and follow the trail. They did not pack any provisions."

"That would slow them down," Ursa said. "There is an old saying. An army marches on its stomach. However, these people are not soldiers. He'll push them to exhaustion."

It made sense. Lucea had read stories and heard about commanders of armies leading their troops into impossible situations. Leaders attacked nations with brutally cold winters, winters only the residents understood, yet the leaders felt sure they could manage the severe snow and ice storms. Or marching them across deserts or swamps with little supplies. Often placing troops at a disadvantage because they lacked strategic understanding.

Lucea knew she should pity them, but their attack on her and her family created a problem. Callen led them through the heart of the village, past the hut where Lucea had slept, to the opposite end of the clearing. There, a gnarled and ancient tree stood alone. The sight was overwhelming. The tree reached so high into the heavens that its summit was invisible. It predated the Vine's fall.

Like others in the village, the entrance was a carved wooden door. Callen knocked a few times before opening it and motioning for them to step inside. The interior's size surpassed Lucea's hut threefold, featuring a grand, open area both inviting and mysterious. Woven rugs decorated the floors and ceiling, adding warmth and texture to the room.

Shelves lined the rounded walls, brimming with an eclectic assortment of bottles, jars, and various knickknacks that hinted at a life filled with curiosity and wonder. Strange and intriguing objects hung from the ceiling, casting unusual shadows in the dim light. A low table in the center of the room had large, plush pillows around it, inviting guests to relax.

To the right, in a crafted cage, two lovebirds cooed, their feathers a vibrant splash of color. On the opposite side, a large, exotic bird with a curved beak and vicious talons perched with regal indifference, its plumage a riot of bright hues. Lucea had never seen anything similar and was captivated.

An elder faun sat at the table, her resemblance to Callen unmistakable, though silver streaks highlighted her curly brown fur. Her hair had delicate flowers and beads woven throughout, adding a touch of elegance to her simple appearance. She wore a plain green shift that complemented the natural beauty of her surroundings. Several sheaths of paper, an ink bottle, and a few open books sat on the table before her. Callen's mother was engrossed in writing in one of them, her focus undisturbed by the surrounding activity.

"Afternoon, Mother."

She raised a finger, her attention never leaving the page she was scribbling on. Callen remained standing and silent. Lucea guessed they both should as well. Callen's mother set the pen down, looked up, and smiled in welcome. "Darling boy!"

Callen approached her and sat on one of the nearby pillows. He squeezed her hands. "I've brought the Ladies Ursa and Lucea."

"So I see. Please," the female faun waved them forward, "sit. Make yourselves comfortable."

Ursa sat opposite Lucea. Once everyone was settled, the faun said, "I am Damae. Elder of our village. It's a pleasure to meet you at last."

Ursa didn't respond, so Lucea assumed she wanted her to do the talking. "The pleasure is ours. Thank you for having us."

"I'm sure my son told you my reasoning?"

"I know a little of it." Lucea looked right at Ursa. Ursa met her gaze, her expression impassive. It infuriated her.

Damae glanced at Lucea, then at Ursa. If she judged, she didn't say so. "Each of you give me your hand."

Lucea did. She sensed no malice from the faun. Lucea had no experience with future-sight. Yes, she was familiar with divination, thanks to Harper. The divergence involved Harper's use of tarot cards to illustrate a potential future. Those who possessed future-sight understood the actual future. Reports indicated it couldn't be altered, despite any effort. Lucea was uncertain of what awaited. Damae's eyes remained open, though unfocused. Her breathing stayed steady. After a few moments, she blinked and released their hands. Her expression hardened.

"Who is Samara?"

Lucea hadn't expected that. "Did you see her?"

"I observed her and Barnabas together. And a wall of thorns between them, but they conversed despite its presence."

"Samara." Lucea had hoped to never hear the name again. "She held me captive."

"Why?"

"I—" Lucea began. She couldn't. Her memory of meeting Barnabas proved quite unsettling, yet Samara—

A chill touched her in the cozy warmth of the hut.

"This is still difficult for her," Ursa spoke. "You need to give her time."

Damae shook her head. "You may not have it. Neither of your enemies knows where you are. The protection around the village should hide you, but it's a possibility the sorceress at least may circumvent it."

"We don't want to cause you any trouble," Ursa said. "We can leave."

"No," Damae said. "There is likely more that I can perceive. Rest and we will try again."

Ursa finally spoke to Lucea. "What do you think?"

A snide remark lingered on Lucea's lips, but she kept it to herself. "We can stay," she said, "if you are certain, Elder Damae."

"I am," Damae said. "You can be quite useful during your time here. Callen, dear, bring them back here after evening meal."

"Yes, Mother." Callen rose; Lucea did so as well.

"Then we will visit again," Lucea said. They both followed Callen out.

"Let's put you both to work." Callen planted his hands on his hips. He exhibited a bit too much joy.

They were assigned various tasks for the next several hours. Raised wealthy and now living in the royal residence, Lucea had never been expected to do chores, and the thought made her flush with embarrassment. But one of the faun matrons reassured Lucea that she would learn quickly, and once she found her rhythm, Lucea performed the tasks flawlessly. Ursa had no trouble doing the arduous chores. Lucea figured solo travel needs such knowledge.

When the evening arrived and everyone assembled for supper, Lucea found, to her astonishment, that someone had fished and prepared the catch. Shortly, Lucea saw Ursa and tried to get her attention, but she remained engrossed in conversation with Damae. Well, she would not let that spoil her time. While she ate, Lucea befriended the other townsfolk gathered around her and enjoyed dragon fruit wine, though she stayed mindful of her intake.

Both Lucea and Ursa offered to help with the cleanup, but Damae's request that they rejoin her in her hut gave them a reprieve. As they sat, Damae served them a cold drink that appeared to be chocolate. A luxury even in the manors of Vale. With a sip, the richness immediately enveloped Lucea. The subtle warmth of cinnamon, a hint of honey, and the fiery kick of hot peppers registered with her. Lucea savored each swallow.

"Please have as much as you like." Damae set the pitcher on the table. "Now, shall we continue?"

Her mouth dry, Lucea emptied her cup and poured a second before taking Damae's hand. The faun took a few moments to gather herself until the glassy-eyed gaze returned. Again came the uncomfortable silence.

Damae's hand closed around Lucea's until the chronomancer gave a surprised cry. Ursa freed herself from Damae's grip just as the faun came to herself again, at the same time releasing Lucea's hand.

"What did you see?" Ursa demanded.

Damae spoke calmly. "I beheld the dark fey marching across the land, spreading misery and destruction. And at their lead existed – something."

"Something?" Lucea said. "Don't you mean someone?"

"No," Damae said. "This thing remained a shadow without true form or substance. It was two parts in constant battle."

"That doesn't tell us much," Ursa said. "You saw nothing of Samara and Barnabas?"

"No. Which is quite disturbing," Damae said. "I sensed it was a distant time. I can't say why I didn't see Samara or Barnabas. I found them together. Those thorn vines truly disturbed me."

"That was the Rot," Lucea said. "It often takes that form. That of a construct of evil. A mockery of the Celestial Vine."

"Can you tell us any more of what you witnessed?" Ursa said.

"I am sorry," Damae said. "I will say that with certainty it calls itself Amalgam."

CHAPTER THIRTEEN

"Amalgam?" Ursa inquired with evident concern. "If it's not like Samara or Barnabas, then what are we dealing with?"

Damae took a deep breath, her eyes distant as she tried to piece together her vision. "I've faced nothing similar. It's more like a fusion of multiple dark forces. Imagine a shadow consuming light, not lacking it. This constant internal struggle makes it unpredictable and powerful."

"This is not something we are prepared for," Ursa said. "Nor do I wish to face this thing."

Lucea rested a finger under her bottom lip. Her brow creased. "Two parts in constant battle. Does that mean it has weaknesses? Can we exploit the conflict within it?"

"Wait." Ursa raised one finger. "What are you saying? Should we fight this?"

"No. Of course not," Lucea said. "But we must consider our options. We are unaware of this item's location or its potential to hinder our goal. If it's also a Rot construct, we may have to confront it. And," Lucea continued, "we still have the danger of Barnabas and Samara."

Damae nodded. "If I may venture a guess, it is possible that Amalgam has a weakness; however, and again I'm speculating, its instability may mean it can adapt, shifting forms and strategies faster than we can expect, but of course without further study..."

Ursa clenched her fists. "Then we need to understand it better. How do we learn more about Amalgam? There must be some way to gain information."

"I would recommend continuing on your journey," Damae said.

"I understand that Jack-In-Irons' libraries and learning centers hold a great deal of knowledge."

"I don't feel comfortable leaving without being certain you and your village are safe," Ursa said. "What of your barrier? Would it be strong enough to keep this Amalgam out?"

Damae sighed and shook her head. "I'm unsure. Likely not. Unless my Gift shows me, I couldn't guess."

"I could work through the Vine to strengthen the spell. I'll just need you to instruct me," Ursa offered. "For what it's worth, at the very least, it may prevent Barnabas and Samara from harassing you."

"As a fellow Child of the Vine, I will be happy to instruct you," Damae said. "I will come for you at daybreak. The sooner we continue, the safer we'll be."

"Very well."

"We need a plan beyond that," Lucea said. "We are still unaware of their whereabouts. If they've passed already, they may double back and ambush us. Or catch up with us if they're behind. Either way, we're putting Everfall in a difficult position."

"What do you recommend?" Damae said.

"We should remain here until we are certain they will not find the village," Lucea said. "How far does the barrier extend?"

"Here." Damae pushed back her chair and stood. She splayed her hands on the tabletop.

Ursa sensed the subtle, yet powerful, calling of the Vine. It began as a gentle warmth that spread through her body, enveloping her in a comforting embrace. The aroma of tilled earth and fresh greenery filled her senses, grounding her in the natural world. With strengthening connection, she sensed the life force, a pulsing power echoing in her soul.

Never had she noticed the true depth of calling on the Vine. The experience differed here, amidst the serene beauty and surrounded by so many others brought forth by the Vine's creation. The vibrant greenery around her seemed to amplify the connection. Each leaf and blade of grass was a testament to the Vine's omnipresence. The shared bond intensified the sensation, as if the Vine's collective energy magnified in this sacred space.

Light bloomed like a delicate flower of multicolored gems on the table surface. Ursa leaned forward at the sight, as did Lucea. As the petals unfurled, they revealed a hand-drawn map – no, a village vista. They saw people and animals in motion. Ursa heard Lucea draw in a deep breath.

When the flower reached full bloom, they had a view of the entire village and the surrounding forest on the edge of the barrier.

"I see the road." Ursa lifted a tentative finger and pointed toward the winding strip of white. She didn't want to touch it for fear of disrupting the spell. "What do you figure the distance is? Possibly a mile and a half?"

"Closer to two, so we've measured," Damae said.

"Lady Damae?" Lucea asked. "What are those?" She pointed to a glowing circular spot. Ursa realized the pattern of their placement around the barrier was familiar.

"The monoliths."

"Yes, I see," Lucea said. "They position them at each point of a witches' circle."

"They hold the spell in place," Ursa said.

"Yes," Lucea said. "I can exact repairs on the stones. If they are seeing signs of deteriorating, I can remove them."

"It's a sound plan. However," Damae said, "we don't know how your power would interact with our spells. It would take research."

Ursa saw Lucea flush. "I don't understand. My Gift is from the Vine. Why would my magic be any more destructive than Ursa's?"

"Because her magic is familiar to me," Damae said. "I have never in my lifetime met a chronomancer. I'd rather not take a chance."

Lucea opened her mouth to protest further, then closed it. Ursa noticed Lucea's blush deepen and realized her embarrassment. She recalled how Lucea had said her Gift often put her in uncomfortable or dangerous situations. "We will carry on with the original plan. Lady Damae, I understand it's past the dinner hour, but would you be willing to start your research tonight?"

"Hmm… I'll see what I can find."

Ursa rose and bowed. "Thank you."

Lucea stood too. "Thank you. Good night." But she forced the words. If Damae detected the tone, she ignored it.

"I'd appreciate your help with chores."

"Of course," Ursa said. Lucea didn't respond. Ursa considered it ideal.

★ ★ ★

After the meeting, Ursa worked late; the faun village was always active. Exhausted, she crawled to her hut. She shed her clothes and underwear. Like Lucea's room, there was a fireplace, which Ursa had found odd, considering. Forest fire risk appeared nonexistent. Though one or two villagers may have known hearth craft, a simple spell may have stopped it.

Someone showed Ursa one of seven communal wells earlier, and they suggested then that she draw water for washing because none of the huts had rooms for that. Ursa was used to sleeping in such places and preparing her own bath. She was thankful for the simplicity of the task ahead.

Although a true bath would have been nice, pouring the hot water into the standing tub would suffice for now. She received soap powder with an unusual scent, but it created a fine lather when mixed with water. It made sense that they wouldn't use animal fats to make cakes of soap.

Ursa turned down the light and slid under the fur blankets, reveling in her nakedness, ignoring the nightshirt they'd provided, because it didn't fit. This seemed too wonderful to worry about. It was the first time she'd slept in a proper bed since— Though she had to curl up her legs to keep them from sticking out from underneath the covers.

A gentle knock roused Ursa. She was ready to shout, "Go away!" but she figured it might be urgent. Grumbling, Ursa pulled back the covers and took a moment to light the lamp. She took two steps toward the door before deciding to grab a quilt and wind it around her.

"Who's there?" she demanded at the door. She was certain her night caller couldn't hear her through the door, so she was shocked when she heard a response.

"Lucea."

Ursa pulled the door open, puzzled.

"What in the nether-realms—?"

Lucea looked terrified. She'd not bothered to cover herself and stood there in her nightshirt with her arms wrapped around her and shivering. "I-I'm sorry—"

"Come inside." Ursa didn't wait for her to move, but guided Lucea in with a hand on her shoulder. "And didn't I tell you to stop apologizing?"

Another shock when Lucea said, "I was only trying to be kind. Did you have to be so dismissive?" She was obviously speaking of their earlier conversation in the woods.

"I am aware you were. And I am sorry," Ursa said. "I hope you'll forgive me."

"I just wish you trusted me, like I trust you."

Ursa smiled. "I never said I didn't trust you."

"Then why?"

"It's a humiliating situation," Ursa said. "It is a part of my past I don't enjoy speaking about."

"What did you expect me to do? Curse the day you were born?" Lucea's voice was gaining strength.

Ursa realized if she admitted that it was her thought, it would be like saying she didn't trust Lucea. "All right," Ursa said. "I will tell you all. Is that why you came here?"

"No." Lucea whispered. "I – it was—"

Ursa sighed. "Do you want to stay here tonight?"

Lucea's expression went terrified again. "If— I mean, yes, but I'd rather not fall asleep."

"Did you have a nightmare?"

"Yes." Ursa didn't expect a straightforward answer.

"All right then. Get into bed." Ursa motioned with a nod. "You don't have to sleep, and I'll tell you anything you desire."

Lucea crawled underneath the furs. Ursa removed the one she'd used to cover herself. Lucea gave a squeak.

"What?" Ursa said.

"You're naked!"

Ursa arched a brow. "You've seen me like this before."

There came that telltale flush of hers, which never failed to make Ursa smile. *By the Vine, she is so adorable.* "I promise I won't accost you unless you ask me to."

Lucea growled in frustration, then spun from Ursa, pulling the furs over her head. Ursa turned down the lantern. Lucea still had her back turned when Ursa joined her under the furs. "Come here," Ursa gave the gentle command.

Lucea initially remained motionless, then turned.

"Come here," Ursa repeated.

Ursa wrapped her arms around the chronomancer, and Lucea pulled against her. "Is this all right?"

Lucea sighed. "Yes."

Ursa shuddered, her inner turmoil manifesting, though she denied her fear. Since Lucea seemed content, Ursa kept her word. "I am Princess Ursa, born in branch Ilve Belanore of Underneath."

"You're a princess?" Lucea raised her eyes to meet Ursa's direct stare.

Finally, hearing her title from her own lips felt as foreign to her as far-off lands. "They banished me from my home because—"

She blamed humans long after her troubles began. It had taken little time to realize how wrong she had been. She had considered finding those humans who survived the village attack and killing them. But she lacked the nerve. She initially wandered, then left the islands, recognizing the inherent peril.

It proved to be a sound decision. She studied extensively overseas. She'd planned on spending the rest of her life there if it hadn't been for her damnable ancestor. Ursa continued, telling Lucea about the humans requesting help and how she'd dismissed their fears, leaving them to be destroyed. She even mentioned Tantia and how her faun companion had turned away from her.

Ursa didn't pressure Lucea for sympathy, despite her hardships. Doubtless, others aided and comforted her. It had taken her many decades to trust again.

"Oh, Ursa." Lucea cupped her hands on Ursa's face. "I wish I had known you then. I would have welcomed you into Vale."

"Truly?" Ursa said.

"Everyone deserves a chance at redemption," Lucea said. "The old King Leonine was vain and shortsighted. It gave my Uncle Reynard many opportunities to talk his way out of whatever trouble he got into. However, when the old king died, his son vowed to bring Reynard to justice. But circumstances allowed Reynard to atone for his sins, and he gained the trust of the king."

Lucea yawned and rested her head against Ursa's breasts. "I believe your mother was mistaken. Yes, you deserved punishment, but to cast you out with no chance of earning redemption… That, I believe, was the height of arrogance."

"Lucea." In an almost unconscious action, Ursa kissed her on the forehead and nuzzled her chin in Lucea's hair. "Thank you."

"Thank you for giving me your trust," Lucea said. "Now I shall keep my word and tell you all."

As Ursa listened, anger started as a slow burn that increased to blood-boiling anger as Lucea began speaking of what had brought her to Ursa's hut.

"My nightmare," Lucea said as her grip tightened on Ursa's forearms, "that Samara had taken me and forced me to succumb to the Rot. I was at its mercy, and I was unable to fight it. They had me carry out such inhuman acts." She ended with a sob.

"Shh," Ursa said. "It wasn't real. And I promise I won't let anything happen to you."

Ursa was surprised by the pain threaded through Lucea's words. "For how long? Once we arrive at Jack-In-Irons, what do you plan to do?"

The question was valid. "My ancestor mentioned a looming evil requiring combat, though specifics were absent." Ursa said.

"The Rot," Lucea said.

"Someone tasked you with this journey to warn the leader of Jack-In-Irons," Ursa said.

"My king said we must band together, all the Riven Isles, to force the Rot back to Deep Earth," Lucea said. "And I believe that is the task the Steel Driver set for you."

Ursa didn't respond, although she had a strong feeling Lucea was right. No other reason made sense. "I'll stay with you. We'll face this challenge together, and afterward..."

Lucea's breathing was steady, telling Ursa she had fallen asleep.

Ursa kissed her temple. "Good night."

CHAPTER FOURTEEN

Ursa awoke, with Lucea still asleep in her arms. She stared lovingly at the beautiful chronomancer, not wanting to leave her. After a time, she disengaged herself as Lucea muttered a sleepy protest. Ursa tried to be as quiet as possible as she pulled on her clothes and boots, and took great care retrieving the hammer from under the bed. Ursa slipped out of the hut. Evenfall was just waking up, and Ursa caught the scent of breakfast being prepared. She wondered if anyone here ever slept in. Well, she would ensure Lucea rested.

Ursa realized Damae hadn't said where they should meet, so she visited her home. Both Damae and Callen were talking, and Callen especially radiated happiness. The young faun turned and caught sight of Ursa.

"Lady Ursa!" Callen jogged over to her. "Morning! I've informed others Lucea sleeps; she's not to be awakened."

Ursa reeled back and studied him. "How did you—?" Then she realized. "You received your Gift!"

"Yes!" His enthusiasm was infectious. "I have the future-sight!"

"Many good wishes to you." Ursa looked at Damae. "You must be very proud."

"That I am." Damae approached her son and draped an arm around him, giving his shoulder a squeeze. "He needs further training."

"Oh, of course!" Callen said. "But Mother will teach me."

Ursa found she was growing fond of the two fauns. She made another silent promise: she wouldn't allow anyone to ruin their happiness.

"Let's walk to the first monolith." Damae reminded them of their task. Villagers greeted them; some approached Damae with issues only their elder could solve.

When they reached the edge of the village, the first monolith came into view. It wasn't imposing, standing around six feet tall. The stone was rough and gray, with an ancient, weathered texture that spoke of countless years exposed to the elements. Etched on its surface were intricate runes, their lines delicate yet precise. The runes emitted a soft, rosy glow, casting a gentle light that seemed to dance across the monolith's rugged face. Despite its modest size, muted power and mystery emanated from it, hinting at concealed secrets.

"Lay your weapon aside," Damae said.

Ursa realized neither faun had asked her about the hammer or where she might have gotten it. She considered thanking Ionneld for the extra supplies and the thong but decided against it. If anyone got their hands on it, it would implicate her friends in their escape. She wondered: Could a sheath carry her hammer?

Both fauns approached the monolith and laid hands against the stone. They chanted in a language both foreign and familiar. She'd studied Fauni all those decades ago. However, with the passage of time, she'd forgotten quite a bit, which Ursa couldn't help but find annoying.

The runes were glowing. The fauns stepped back. "Please come forward and lay your hands on the monolith."

Ursa complied, though a sense of unease gnawed at her.

"Open your mind to the truth. Bring forth the connection."

Simple enough. Ursa did so.

"Now, share your quintessence with the Vine."

Wait, now she was confused. "My quintessence? I have no way to—"

"You do. I assume no one ever taught you that."

"How can I learn something that seems impossible?"

"It's not impossible," Damae said.

"Then why can't you do it?" Ursa hesitated to disrupt her life force – her essence as a sentient being.

"Ours is not durable enough." Impatience edged Damae's tone. Which was only a portent of trouble. Perhaps their safety was questionable.

"I won't pressure you," Damae said. "It is your choice."

"Fine." Ursa hadn't meant to sound so terse. "What do I need to do?"

Damae instructed Ursa to close her eyes and imagine herself merging with the Vine. "In your mind's eye, spread your arms and accept the Vine into your embrace. The Vine's essence flows."

Ursa took a deep breath, allowing the scents of earth and greenery to ground her. She envisioned the Vine's life force, a vibrant essence that intertwined with her own being.

"Now, imagine your quintessence is visible to your eyes. Call upon it in silence and it will occur."

Ursa felt the pulse of her own energy. "Like my aura?" she breathed.

"Exactly," Damae replied. "Now, reach for that light and shape a piece. Balls work. Something about the smoothness, I suppose. Now present that to the Vine."

In summoning her quintessence, Ursa saw a soft glow emanating from within her. She shaped a small orb of light, feeling a strange emptiness, as though something vital was missing.

"There is a part of me that is gone!" Ursa exclaimed.

"No!" Damae said. "The Vine will replace what you have given. Ask."

Ursa steadied herself and asked for the Vine's essence. The brilliant green of the Vine infused her aura, filling her with renewed strength and connection.

"Now gather your Gift and focus it into the monolith while repeating this chant," Damae said, leaning close to Ursa. *"Grow and wind, leaf and line, take our Gift, make your sign; whisper, weave, and clasp us tight; light the dark, give shape and sight."*

Ursa put her hands on the monolith and chanted. As her words resonated through the stone, she felt something touch her fingers at first, then entwine. Her eyes snapped open to see fissures appearing in the stone, supple vines sprouting and wrapping around the monolith, pinning her hands in place. She almost stopped chanting, but Damae's distant, urging words cut through the fog of her thoughts.

"Continue! Concentrate!"

Ursa's perspective changed. She could see the entire barrier as if she were viewing it from above. It glowed, veins of energy pulsing like living blood.

"There," Damae said. "You may stop."

Ursa ceased her chant, but her hands remained bound by the Vines. Damae reached out and touched one stem, and they untangled, freeing Ursa. She blew out a breath and stepped back.

"Thank you, Lady Ursa," Damae said. She went to her knees, and Callen followed suit. "Thank you for giving of yourself to protect our home."

"Now, then," Ursa said, "please get up. There is no need for that. Callen helped us. It's the least I can do."

Callen sprang to his feet and helped his mother up. Something behind Ursa caught their attention. As she turned, she found Lucea changed into her cat form. Lucea lay flat on the ground, her paws stretched out in front of her and her legs curled up against her body in a perfect feline pose. Ursa had to resist the powerful urge to stroke her fur, which shimmered in the light.

Instead, Ursa composed herself and said, "I'm glad you're here. Did you sleep well?"

Lucea responded by rising to her feet, stretching with an elegant arch of her back and an outstretch of her paws. She then approached Ursa, who kneeled and encircled her arms around Lucea's shoulders, feeling the warmth and softness of her fur.

"You were worried, weren't you? Don't. Everything is fine," Ursa assured her. Lucea purred in response. "Let's get some breakfast."

Once Lucea had taken her full human form, they walked together to the communal table. The fauns' thoughtful gesture – a simple offering of dried fish and sweet potatoes – warmed Lucea's heart.

Damae and Callen, to her right, presided at the table. Lucea sat to Ursa's left. They carried on with their conversation without disturbing the others. They agreed that once they had eaten their fill, they would take care of the other monolith. Damae told Ursa it should be easier since she had already accepted that piece of the Vine into her quintessence. Ursa remained uncertain. The Vine lived in her mind's farthest reaches.

However, she kept her misgivings to herself. Since her return to the Isles, the Vine had heeded her calls for help. Despite traveling far from the Isles, had she ever stopped feeling its influence? Even amidst companions, Ursa felt the Vine's enduring presence. She'd refused to acknowledge it for so long. Now she had to.

Upon reinforcement of the barrier, Damae would station sentries along the barrier and road. She nodded to her son. "Callen, as you may have surmised, is our best tracker. He'll see if he can catch the scent of your enemies."

"Mother!" Callen smiled with embarrassed delight.

The sight of Damae and Callen together made Ursa feel an intense sadness and loneliness. A catch formed in her throat, and a tightness gripped her chest as a vivid memory surfaced. She recalled her home, now lost to her, and her mother's look of disgust, the shame in her eyes. The memory of being seized and dragged from her bed to be thrown like a commoner at her mother's feet hit her with such intensity that her heart hammered against her ribcage. Her throat dried as the ache in her chest intensified. She had never experienced this before. What was this feeling?

"Ursa?" Lucea's words cut through the fog. "Are you well?" Lucea had taken Ursa's hand in hers and Ursa realized she was gripping it in desperation. Lucea's eyes betrayed it. Further realization came, and she saw everyone staring at her with a mixture of fear and concern.

"I'm sorry." Ursa released Lucea's hand and fought to still the thunderous beating in her chest and draw air into her lungs. "It was nothing."

"I can summon our healer," Callen said. He and Damae shared a worried glance.

"No, no," Ursa said. She needed to get away. "I apologize for the interruption." As she walked, her long, powerful legs eating up the distance, she said aloud to herself, "What's wrong with you?"

It was the mother and son, showing such love and affection for each other…

"It's not like you haven't seen such displays before!" Every time she did, she turned away. And whenever someone tried to get close to her, she ran away. How could she not? She was in exile and didn't deserve happiness.

"Come to your senses! You said you would let no one ruin their happiness. You said you were going to protect Lucea. It's the least you can do."

Ursa discovered she'd traveled extensively and found herself within their hunting grounds.

Lucea, what am I doing?

Years of homelessness and wandering had left Ursa exhausted, collapsing under their weight. On the woodland floor, muted rustling of the trees surrounded her but offered no comfort. Tears welled up in her eyes, and she tried to hold them back, but the floodgates had opened. Hot tears streamed down her cheeks, mingling with the dirt on her face.

Ursa hugged her knees to her chest; her body racked with silent sobs. The deep ache in her heart felt like it would consume her. She lay down on the forest floor, her cheek pressed against the cold earth. A sob escaped her lips, and she slammed her fist into the ground in frustration and despair, feeling the sting of pain shoot up her arm. The forest seemed to echo her sorrow but offered no reprieve from the overwhelming tide of emotions.

Ursa's breathing steadied as the intensity of her sobs waned. She lay there among the trees, listening to the rhythmic sounds of the natural world around her. The rustling leaves and distant bird calls seemed to offer a quiet, unspoken comfort, a reminder that life continued, indifferent to her pain.

Ursa pushed herself up to a sitting position, wiping the remnants of tears from her cheeks with the back of her hand. The cold earth beneath her was a grounding presence, helping her regain a sense of stability. She took a full breath, letting the crisp air fill her lungs and clear her mind.

Movement in her peripheral vision had her turning to look, although she already knew what she would find. Lucea, in her cat form, padded through the underbrush. She approached Ursa with a muted grace, her eyes full of understanding. Lucea's beauty again struck Ursa. Lucea sat beside her, a silent companion in her moment of grief. Ursa felt a calm wash over her, knowing she wasn't alone.

Ursa rose to her feet, brushing the dirt and leaves from her clothes. She took another deep breath, feeling the weight on her chest lift. The memory of Damae and Callen's heartfelt moment still lingered, but instead of allowing it to deepen her sorrow, she let it fuel her purpose. She fought for loved ones, including herself.

They walked back together in companionable silence. When they were within sight of the communal table, Ursa saw Damae and Callen waiting for them. They'd already cleared the table so Ursa wouldn't have to face the group of villagers.

Callen reached them first, his face filled with concern. "Is everything all right?"

Ursa smiled at him. "Everything is fine now. Thank you."

"Do you feel up to finishing with the monoliths?" Damae asked.

"Yes," Ursa said, satisfied with her newfound purpose.

CHAPTER FIFTEEN

Because they saw no sign of their enemies or Amalgam, Lucea and Ursa departed the village later that day. Callen, using his abilities, spent a week in the faun village searching for Barnabas and Samara. Damae again envisioned them intertwined, bound by black thorns.

Lucea found no solace in this. She was worried about their new friends, not wishing them to suffer at the hands of their enemies. Lucea wanted more time, but their mission mandated departure, regardless of how she felt.

As usual, they sat around the communal table enjoying lunch. Ursa had gone fishing again, and Lucea was enjoying crisp fried herring in a bed of leafy greens. Ursa broached the subject of their leaving.

"It is not surprising," Damae said.

"My apologies," Callen said. "I could find no trace—"

"Don't you dare apologize," Lucea said. "You and your mother – all of your people have done so much for us."

"We appreciate it," Ursa said.

"We are all Children of the Vine," Damae said. "We will always lend our help."

An idea occurred to Lucea. "Elder Damae, I have one further request. When I reach Jack-In-Irons, I will send a message to my king in Vale, letting them know what you have done and to consider you allies of Vale. So, if you ever need help…?"

"Thank you," Damae said. "Callen will escort you to the barrier, then wait for safe passage."

They enjoyed the meal and each other's company, then made their farewells to the village. They received their horses, overladen with supplies. Since it still got cold, the fauns provided them with warm coats and oilskin jackets for the rain. And there was something else that neither one was expecting.

"Lady Ursa, I hope you don't mind." Callen had a cloth-wrapped bundle with him. "I had a special vision, and I made this for you."

Ursa peeled back the cloth. "Well, I'll be damned!" She grinned in delight.

The scabbard wasn't intended for a sword. Someone designed it with practicality and elegance in mind. Lucea's first thought was, *That's not leather?* But she was wrong. The scabbard featured reinforced stitching to ensure durability. It was long and sleek, fitting the extended handle of the war hammer.

Subtle, intricate patterns adorning its surface hinted at its craftsmanship, while a soft material lined the interior to protect the hammer's handle from scratches. The top of the scabbard had a secure, adjustable strap that wrapped around the hammer's head, keeping it in place while allowing for easy access when needed.

Attached to the scabbard was a sturdy belt loop, designed to fit on the hip. Its width and reinforcement ensured the loop distributed the hammer's weight, providing stability and comfortable wear while moving.

Overall, the scabbard combined functionality with a touch of artistry, making it a practical yet stylish accessory for any warrior.

"It's exquisite." Ursa knelt and hugged the young faun. "Thank you!" When she regained her feet, Ursa said, "You saw this in a vision?"

"Yes." Callen grinned. "Many skilled artisans – a touch of magic, and there you are."

Ursa belted the scabbard around her waist. The hammer rested in the thong on her saddle. When Ursa embraced the two fauns again, Damae said, "Safe journey to you both."

They took to their mounts and started off, with the goodbyes following them. As promised, Callen escorted them as far as the road beyond the barrier. When they arrived, Callen sat under a tree. From within his shirt, he drew a flute.

"Farewell for now, Callen," Lucea said. "When all is well, we will return."

"I look forward to it." Callen raised the flute to his lips and played.

Lucea perceived an ethereal aura, palpable magic. Shimmering notes formed a celestial symphony, each tone glowing with its own luminescent hue and painting the clearing in color. The melody, both serene and powerful, washed over them and filled their souls with a sudden surge of energy.

As Callen's music continued to weave its spell, a delicate fragrance mingled with the music, a scent of blooming flowers and ancient forests. The harmonious blend of notes and fragrance twined around the nearby trees, caressing their bark and leaves with invisible fingers, creating a path of light and sound behind them.

Callen nodded, and Lucea and Ursa began their journey, the music trailing behind them like an ethereal memory. The melody lingered in the air, a gentle reminder of the magic that had graced their moment, filling their hearts with a profound sense of wonder and peace.

★ ★ ★

For a time, their journey was uneventful. They met only farmers and merchants going about their business. They passed with a wave, a greeting, or a touch to the brim of their hats.

"Everything seems so calm. Normal," Lucea commented.

"We know the truth, so we must take care," Ursa replied.

"Many are familiar with the Rot's evil, yet many ignore it."

"What choice do they have?" Ursa said. "Those lacking Gifts, military rank, or royal blood have no choice but to persevere. We cannot expect them to fight and face the Rot."

"You mentioned someone named Harper earlier," Ursa said, "and she possesses the Gift."

"Yes."

"Are you aware of anyone else who has knowledge of the Rot?"

"There is a witch named Isbet," Lucea said. "She came to Vale to speak with Harper. The Vine marked them as Beholden."

"That is a term I haven't heard for many a year."

Lucea said, "From what I understand, when a Gifted calls on the Vine and takes of its power, the Vine tasks them to be their champion."

"That's right," Ursa said.

"I know of Harper and Isbet," Lucea continued, "and more recently, a princess from Brigantia. Faith."

"Brigantia," Ursa said. "The name does sound familiar."

"Have you heard the Heroine's story?"

"Yes, if I recall. A woman, originating from a realm unknown to Above Ground, performed heroic feats in Brigantia, thus earning her title. But wait, her name wasn't Faith?"

"No," Lucea said. "Faith, born in The Heroine's world, found refuge in Brigantia."

"I believe I know—" Ursa went silent mid-sentence, and moments later, Lucea knew why. The sound of thundering horses' hooves, at first far away but drawing nearer. They appeared from around a bend in the road, soldiers clad in armor galloping toward them. Lucea and Ursa saw the relentless advance and moved their horses to safety.

The soldiers rode by so fast it was difficult to tell what kingdom they stood for, ignoring the pair. Lucea realized if they hadn't got out of the way, it would have resulted in their deaths.

Ursa pondered the meaning behind the chaos.

"I couldn't guess. But it's disturbing," Lucea replied.

It wasn't the only instance of soldiers riding by. Another group appeared unhurried yet ignored them.

"I don't recognize the livery," Ursa said. "But then I have been away. Kingdoms change, laws change, and the fickle royals change."

"I wonder," Lucea said, "are we riding into more trouble?"

"We could use Damae's future-sight," Ursa said. "But it is getting late. Let's search for a campsite away from the road."

As they continued, they approached the edge of the woods. It opened out onto an immense clearing on either side, and farms dotted the landscape. The scent of tilled earth and manure permeated the air. Spring was coming, and the farmers would start their planting soon. Homesickness struck Lucea. One thing she loved doing was visiting Vale's farmers' market. They knew her and understood her requirements. Besides food, a shopper could explore clothes, jewelry, and perfumes.

"Are you well?" Ursa asked.

"Yes," Lucea said. "I mean no – I just want to finish this and go home." Lucea amended, "Not that I'm in a hurry to leave you!"

Ursa smiled. "That is good to hear."

"I mean to say," Lucea said, "if you have no plans for the future, would you like to come home with me?" *Oh, dear Vine, what did I just say?* "I – I mean—" Her face was aflame.

"I will consider it," Ursa said with a slight smile.

"You're teasing me."

Ursa grinned. "No, I am not."

Lucea smiled to herself, shyly. *What a remarkable woman you are.* She realized she wanted Ursa in her life, despite the short time she'd known the dokkalfar.

As they came upon a farm, they saw a young woman scrubbing laundry in a weathered metal tub, her movements rhythmic and purposeful. The sun cast a warm glow over the scene, making the white linens she hung to dry almost luminescent against the blue sky. They halted their mounts, and Ursa said, "Give me a moment."

Ursa dismounted and approached the woman, who straightened from her task, wiping her hands on a stained and threadbare apron. Her eyes, sharp and curious, followed Ursa's movements. After a thorough assessment, the woman looked at Ursa and then gave a nod. With a swirl of her skirts, she turned and disappeared into the farmhouse.

Moments later, she re-emerged, followed by a burly man clad in overalls, his bare chest covered in a thick mat of black hair. He loomed large, drawing himself up to his full height, but Ursa matched his stance without flinching.

He scrutinized Ursa, then asked if she'd exchange work for lodging. "Ya seem strong, but what of her?" He waved a dismissive hand toward Lucea. "Don't look like she can pick ticks off a dog."

"She is quite capable," Ursa replied, her tone edged with annoyance, which Lucea caught.

Despite her reluctance, Lucea called on her Gift. The air shimmered with magic circles that danced across the clean laundry, causing it to billow as if caught in an unseen breeze. Within moments, the garments were dry.

"Well, I'll be damned!" the woman exclaimed, her eyes wide with astonishment. "They're bone dry!"

The man's eyebrows shot up. "Well, that's a neat trick. How much more can ya do?"

After much negotiation, the farmer agreed to let them sleep in the barn. If they cleared out the stalls, their horses could also rest there. The farmer explained he had more horses coming soon, and their help would save him some trouble. Ursa agreed to chop firewood, and Lucea couldn't help but wonder when Ursa had picked up that skill during her travels.

"Name's Marcus." He shook Ursa's hand. "We have a plan."

The wife, who introduced herself as Violet, led Lucea into the farmhouse. The cozy interior smelled of fresh bread and herbs. As Lucea helped cook and clean, she noticed two small children, a boy and a girl, watching her from the upstairs loft railing. She smiled and winked at them, and the girl smiled back and waved. The simple gesture brought warmth to Lucea's heart, a fleeting moment of happiness in their tumultuous journey.

Their meal was two plump grouses, baked until the skin was golden and crispy and juices flowed. Violet added stewing vegetables – potatoes, carrots, onions, and celery. The dish overwhelmed Lucea with its spices, and proved hearty and filling. Along with the meal, Lucea had prepared and baked a blackberry pie for dessert. Sherry was available afterward. Ursa accepted a glass, but Lucea refused as a precaution. She accepted a cup of cold well water.

Marcus leaned forward and rested his elbows on the table, entwining his fingers. A mischievous grin spread across his face as he watched Lucea sip. "What's the matter, little lady? Too dainty to handle a proper drink?" he teased, swirling his glass of sherry for emphasis.

Lucea regarded him, attempting to conceal her irritation. "It's not about being dainty, sir. As a magic-user, I can't afford to get drunk. Our powers become unpredictable and dangerous when we're intoxicated." She took a deliberate sip of her water, letting the weight of her words sink in.

Marcus raised an eyebrow, intrigued. "So, it's not just a party trick then, is it?"

Lucea shook her head, the seriousness of her expression leaving no room for doubt. "Magic is no laughing matter. It's a responsibility."

Marcus laughed deep in his chest. "Don't know nothin' about that. But I s'pose you wouldn't want a drunk witch."

"Indeed," Lucea said, wishing he would drop the subject.

"Tell me, Sir Marcus," Ursa said. "Did you or your lovely wife notice groups of soldiers riding by?"

"Aye, that we did."

Violet spoke to the children. "Are you finished? Do your lessons."

The children obeyed. Violet didn't want them to hear anyone discussing soldiers. The girl smiled and waved at Lucea again, and she returned the gesture.

Violet topped off the sherry, then sat at the table again, next to Marcus.

"There have been strange things goin' on. I ain't seen anything personal, but there's talk of dark fey slithering around and coming from the woods."

"We don't get much out here," said Violet. "Too far from the capital, we s'pose."

"Ya best get there as fast as you can," Marcus said. "Safer behind the city walls."

"We are on our way there," Ursa said.

"If ya come back by here, will ya bring us news?" Violet said.

"Yes." Ursa turned and nodded at her for approval. Lucea returned the nod.

Since the couple didn't have any other information, Ursa suggested they prepare to bed down. Lucea helped Violet once more with the dishes, scrubbing and rinsing while the steam rose from the basin. Ursa drew water from the well, her powerful arms making light work of the task, and set it to heat over the crackling fire. Marcus sank into the only comfortable chair in the modest home, his pipe sending tendrils of smoke curling toward the ceiling.

The children, clad in their nightshirts, padded down the stairs, their bare feet on the wooden floor. Violet scrubbed their faces with a damp washcloth, her touch tender and loving. The two children then sat at their father's knee, their eyes wide, reflecting on the firelight as he told a story. A loving family scene.

Lucea felt a pang of longing but also a sense of contentment seeing such a serene tableau. As they stepped into the cool night air, Lucea felt a quiet determination settle over her, ready for whatever challenges lay ahead.

As they approached the barn, the cool night air filled with the earthy scent of hay. Ursa said, "Ever slept in a hayloft before?"

"Yes," Lucea replied with a smile as Ursa swung the wooden door open, revealing the dim interior.

"You have?"

"Don't look so surprised." Lucea stepped inside, her boots crunching on the straw-covered floor. A single lantern cast a warm glow by the door. "When I was a child, my friends and I would spend nights together in our hay lofts." Fond memories warmed her expression. "Usually, we were indulging in unladylike books and scandal sheets."

Ursa drew in a breath in mock surprise, her eyes wide with feigned shock. "You naughty young woman!"

"Oh stop!" Lucea laughed, the sound echoing in the spacious barn. They had reached the ladder leading up to the hayloft, and Lucea climbed. "We would buy them in the human village. Sometimes, we'd pinch a bottle of wine from our parents' cellar."

Ursa placed the back of her hand dramatically on her forehead. "I believe I'm going to faint!"

Lucea giggled as they reached the top of the ladder, and the loft filled with hay that smelled of clover. Violet had placed blankets there for their use. Ursa spread them out close together. Lucea sat down and removed her boots. She yawned, surprised she was sleepy.

"We have been through much," Ursa said. "It's not surprising we're exhausted."

Lucea wrapped herself in the blanket. She watched as Ursa did the same, moving close to her. Lucea drifted off with Ursa watching her.

★ ★ ★

Deep within her animal self, her instincts roared for her to wake. Something was very wrong. Lucea struggled to awaken, fighting against the demanding pull of sleep. Her throat burned, and her lungs filled with an acrid scent, making her cough. She felt disoriented, her body sluggish and unresponsive.

"Lucea!" Ursa's urgent cry cut through the haze, accompanied by vigorous shaking. Lucea snapped awake, her eyes widening in alarm. A strange, dancing light surrounded them, casting flickering shadows on the walls. The intense searing heat filled the air with a deafening roar and the groaning of collapsing timbers.

The barn was on fire.

CHAPTER SIXTEEN

Ursa watched Lucea for a short time after she fell asleep, then the faint rustling of hay and the gentle stamping and blowing of the horses below soothed her. While drifting off, she initially ignored a sound, caught between wakefulness and deep sleep.

The tranquility shattered as flames erupted, casting a sinister glow and a suffocating heat that jolted Ursa awake. The fire consumed the wood and straw, sending tendrils of black smoke curling upward, reaching for the loft.

"Lucea, wake up!"

Lucea didn't respond at first, although her face showed some internal struggle, as if she were amid a nightmare. Ursa grabbed her and shook her awake. "Lucea!"

Her eyes snapped open, first without focus, and Ursa noted pure terror in Lucea's eyes. The usually composed chronomancer was now wide-eyed with fear. As the fire licked at the barn, this unfamiliar expression puzzled Ursa until she realized: the primal, animal part of Lucea was awakening. Fire was the ultimate fear for any creature, and the frantic, panicked screams of the horses only amplified that terror.

"We have to escape!"

Lucea's eyes regained focus, and she gasped, "Dear Vine!"

Ursa lunged for the loft window and forced it open with a grunt. They cleared the opening despite the fall's bone-breaking potential. Through the inferno's core, only the ladder offered escape.

"We can't leave the horses!" The crackling flames drowned out Lucea's scream. Ursa saw Lucea invoke her Gift. Glowing blue spell circles materialized in midair, shimmering like protective barriers against the fire. They descended the ladder, crossed the stables, and then exited the barn.

The flames that met the spell circles slowed their frenzied dance, but the rest continued their relentless advance. Lucea turned to Ursa, her tone steady amid the turmoil. "Ursa, we will burn, but I can keep us in an unending circle of time. Prepare yourself."

Ursa nodded and crawled across the loft toward the ladder. The wood snapped and splintered beneath her, each sound sending a spike of fear through her, but almost miraculously, the rungs held firm as she descended. The scorching heat felt like a brand, searing itself into her flesh. She looked up, ensuring Lucea was following close behind.

Upon reaching the spell circles, the heat persisted, an unyielding force seeking to break free. Reaching the stalls proved arduous. The horses, unaware of Lucea's protective magic, only saw their greatest fear and bucked.

As a dokkalfar, Ursa could communicate with animals, but she lacked the power to make them obey. For a tense moment, the horses refused to budge, but then more spell circles appeared, forming a barrier that obscured the flames from the horses' view. Ursa tugged on the reins, and the horses responded. Lucea followed, guiding them all toward safety. Once outside, the cool night air was a blessing. Ursa had left the hammer in the thong on her saddle. She pulled it out and then released her horse, allowing it to flee. She knew it would return. Right now, she was concentrating on Lucea. She was lethargic, and Ursa had to take great care as she lifted Lucea into her arms. She whimpered, experiencing the hurt from her burns on some level. Ursa saw in the firelight that Lucea's exposed skin was red and blistered.

"Damn it to the nether-realms," Ursa muttered. She carried Lucea over to the well, laying her down with the greatest care. Ursa set about filling the bucket and brought up water. She poured it over Lucea, bathing her exposed skin. No doubt she needed a healer.

Hysterical screaming caught Ursa's attention. Violet stood there, her stare fixed on the burning barn. Marcus came out, struggling with the full washtub. Upon noticing him, Ursa knew his actions would be futile. However, she was unable to remain and observe. Ursa didn't recall seizing the hammer; however, it rested in her hand. The runes glowed, and the spell, as the others had, came to her – *Mountain's Resolve.* Like the flames on kindling, her fatigue burned away, replaced by an infinite strength, or so it seemed. She locked the hammer in its sheath and dashed to where Marcus was struggling. She grabbed the tub at the other end.

"What in the nether-hells—" His eyes went wide with realization. They rushed the tub to the barn entrance. Ursa hefted it across her shoulders and splashed it across the barn floor and everything within her reach. It did little to quell the inferno.

"Tend to the children!" Marcus yelled to his wife.

The barn's distance from the homestead ensured safety, except during high winds. Excessive heat forced their retreat to the well. Ursa knelt at Lucea's side and settled her head in her lap. She stayed unconscious, perhaps too asleep for her to be aware of the pain. She would sleep for hours and need food.

"What in the nether-hells happened?" Marcus loomed, fury raw in his voice.

Ursa kept still, unwilling to disturb Lucea. "We were in the loft asleep," she said.

"They— some soldiers came—"

"Hush," Marcus barked.

"What soldiers?" Ursa demanded.

Marcus crossed his arms. The fire had sunk to embers and hid his face in shadow. "I coulda lost everythin' because of you."

"You're blaming us for this?"

"They came for you."

"These soldiers said they came for us?"

"They said a witch and a— whatever that word they call ya by."

Ursa said nothing. "And you told them we were in the barn?"

"O'course I told 'em. They said yer wanted criminals." Marcus spat the words. "I thought they'd just take ya, not burn ya out."

"Please," Violet said, voice small, "we want no trouble."

"We are not criminals." Ursa's tone was low and dangerous.

Marcus's anger didn't waver, but Ursa's eyes were on Lucea – skin blistered, breath thin. She set Lucea more comfortably in her lap and met Marcus's glare with steady calm. "She's badly burned," Ursa said. "She needs bandages and rest. If you turn us out now, she'll die on the road."

Marcus's face flickered. "I don't want soldiers back here."

"Neither do we," Ursa said. "We'll leave at first light but tonight, she needs shelter."

Violet stepped forward. "Please. I can help. I know how to dress burns."

Marcus looked from Violet to Lucea to Ursa. He swallowed. "You'll be gone at dawn," he said finally. "And you keep quiet. If any soldiers come askin', I didn't see nothin'."

Ursa inclined her head. "We leave at first light."

Marcus spat once, then turned away. "Fine. You sleep on the hearth. Don't make me regret it."

Violet lit two lamps and set them on the table. "Iris, get Mama a blanket," she said. "Thom, clear the table." The children moved without question.

Violet worked with practiced hands – cutting cloth, drawing water, dabbing a bitter, herbal salve onto Lucea's skin. Ursa watched, grateful and wary. When the wounds were wrapped, Violet produced a cloak from a chest and handed it to Ursa. "Take it," she said. "And there's bread in the pantry. You go at dawn."

Ursa laid Lucea on the rug by the hearth and draped the cloak over her shoulders. She sat down beside her, arm across Lucea's chest, listening to the shallow breaths. Outside, Marcus paced once, then shut the door.

They would leave at first light. For now, Lucea's burns were dressed, and the farmer's grudging mercy bought them a few hours of safety.

★ ★ ★

"Ursa?"

Ursa awoke, poised to strike, until Lucea's hand silenced her. A soft glow of a rune bubble surrounded her.

"Lucea! You're—?"

Lucea put a finger to her lips. She closed her eyes, and the runes passed over her skin. Ursa noticed someone had removed the bandages, and she watched the blisters disappear one by one.

"You shouldn't," Ursa whispered.

As the light faded, Lucea said, "What about you? Do you need—?"

"No," Ursa said. "I'm well."

She heard Lucea sigh with relief. "Let's leave this place."

Ursa couldn't help but grin, even in the semi-darkness. "And I thought to wake you first. They wanted us gone by dawn." Ursa pulled back the blanket and climbed to her feet.

"I left some gold pieces on the table," Lucea said. "Perhaps that will placate them."

They crossed the room then departed.

"Hold on," Ursa said. Again, she scanned their surroundings. The first false dawn eased the earlier difficulty, illuminating the tree line. Creatures and fey were returning to their dens, to re-emerge during the daylight hours or to wait until nightfall to go about their impish business. "Can you follow me?"

"Yes, my eyes are becoming accustomed."

Ursa moved toward the well, and even as they reached it, Ursa did not feel relief. It was only after they rode away at a walk that they entered the woods at daybreak.

"What happened? Who treated my burns?"

"Violet."

"She did?"

"She was quite skilled. I wonder if someone trained her in the healing arts."

"It's possible," Lucea said. "I hope the children fare well."

"So do I," Ursa said. "When we complete our mission, we can return and ensure their safety if necessary."

"I would appreciate that."

"I'll leave the trail to consult my map. I don't want to be on the road any longer than we must be."

Ursa kept her eye on the road as several wagons and horses passed. These citizens appeared quite rushed. They didn't notice the women, which suited Ursa just fine, but she sensed Lucea was as curious as she was.

"Ursa." Lucea looked up from the map, grinning. "We're not far off. We should be there soon."

"Thank the Vine." Ursa blew out a breath. She could get this damnable task over with. They continued their journey until the forest ended, and upon reaching the next hilltop, for the first time they saw the end of their journey.

The majestic panorama stretching before them, viewed from their vantage point atop the hill, glowed in the light of the setting sun. Towers and spires ascended, creating an enchanting yet imposing skyline. They noted sections of the city where each group of houses was a certain color. Reds, blues, greens, and purples mixed and merged, creating a living mosaic. The city's defensive wall stood as a testament to both architectural prowess and the formidable magic of Jack-In-Irons. The tall stone wall surrounded the city, its smooth surface gleaming with a faint, unearthly light that hinted at potent enchantments woven into its structure. Many turrets punctuated the wall, each one a small fortress unto itself, offering vantage points for vigilant sentinels to watch over the surrounding landscape. These rose at regular intervals; their tops crowned with crenellations and fluttering banners. Parapets connected them, where guards in gleaming armor patrolled, their silhouettes stark against the evening sky. The turrets were not only functional but also designed with intricate carvings and inlaid gemstones that caught and reflected the light.

Ursa felt excitement, and she knew from her expression that Lucea shared her feelings. This brought immense relief. "Let's be off before something else happens."

They spurred their horses on, and for once nothing accosted them. They noted people gathered at the main gate, a line of wagons, horses, and foot traffic.

The gate itself – immense, made from ancient wood – stood tall. Bands of metal reinforced the doors, etched with runes of protection and strength. The city's crest marked each of the twin towers that flanked the gates, their peaks touching the sky.

As they approached, they saw something strange.

A wide moat encircled the wall, filled with crystal-clear water that glistened in the light. A simple bridge spanned the expanse, yet travelers froze upon it, staying immobile until gate attendants signaled passage.

"Hmm, how odd," Ursa said. "Are those bridge runes a spell?"

"It's called a recognition spell," Lucea said. "It can help determine if the person crossing the bridge is friend or foe."

This was completely new to Ursa. "Couldn't an enemy just force their way through?"

"Not unless they are a powerful magic worker." Lucea nodded toward the bridge. "Notice how something is hindering their progress? The spell keeps them stationary. Anyone trying to break through, in my opinion, would likely be seen as an enemy."

"I understand." It made sense. They joined the line of people. Ursa hoped they would succeed.

A scream echoed from the crowd. Ursa initially thought someone was breaching the bridge, but Lucea called, "Ursa, look!"

In the distance, groups of soldiers rode toward the gates. Even from the distance, Ursa knew they were the same ones they'd seen before, who had likely tried to kill them. Their once-bright armor was now dull and corroded, tainted by the vile influence of the Rot. Their eyes, once sharp and determined, now burned with an unsettling, unnatural light. Their movements were jerky and uncoordinated, like puppets manipulated by unseen hands.

Among them, dark fey creatures bounded and crawled, a grotesque and fearsome entourage. The twisted beings, born from shadows and nightmares, reveled in the chaos and corruption they spread. Fey with tattered, bat-like wings soared above, their eyes glowing with malevolent glee. On the ground, twisted sprites with gnarled limbs skittered and leaped; their laughter echoed with a sinister resonance.

Panic ensued. The people, as they realized the horde was approaching, erupted into a chaotic wave of bodies, pushing and shoving. Some fell as others crushed them in their rush to flee. As the possessed soldiers and their dark companions neared the gates, the guards atop the turrets sounded alarm bells, and magical barriers shimmered into existence.

This failed for those outside.

Ursa exchanged a look with Lucea. Ursa drew Iron Reaver. "Stay here and protect the people."

Lucea nodded once, firmly, and Ursa spurred her horse forward, leading the charge directly at the enemy.

CHAPTER SEVENTEEN

Ursa stormed up the hill at a gallop with unyielding determination, her horse's hooves kicking up clods of dirt as the powerful beast pushed forward. Her eyes were fixed on the horizon, where the enemy soldiers and dark fey gathered, a storm of battle brewing in the dusk.

Ursa was no stranger to battle. Sometimes she joined in minor battles and skirmishes for money. She'd had many years to learn the different weapons and how to wield them. But never in her life had she faced so many dark fey. The soldiers Ursa didn't consider as much of a threat as the fey. Ursa guessed they were being controlled by the Rot. To end their lives would be an act of mercy.

As she approached her end, Iron Reaver was warm in her hand. A section of runes glowed.

Ursa.

That voice! She knew it but couldn't place the owner.

Earthshaker.

Fey Bane.

Time slowed, but she found no sign of Lucea's chronomancy. This was something else. More protection magic from the city. As Ursa pulled her steed to a halt, she dismounted and ordered it to flee back to the gates. Before her stood goblins, creatures that did nothing but fight, eat, and spawn. A creature she'd heard of, but had never seen, followed; taller, stronger, and far less attractive than its smaller relatives. Hobgoblins goaded the smaller goblins with threats and physical punishments. They intermixed with lamia and Cù-Sìth, large, shaggy black dogs with matted fur and burning red eyes. Unlike the Cat Sith, they were pure evil. None of these creatures concerned her much. It was the Basilisks, Red Caps, and Vine-be-damned – a manticore – that worried her.

Ursa swung Iron Reaver in a circle, stirring the surrounding air. The runes glowed, forming a luminescent circle as she chanted the incantation. The hum of magic pulsed through the air, resonating with an eerie, rhythmic beat. With a decisive shout, she brought Iron Reaver down and struck it against the rocky soil. A shock wave rippled from the point of impact, and cracks snaked outward in a fan pattern, creeping up the hill and threading through the mob of dark fey. They seemed oblivious, their malevolent focus on the impending battle.

Then a deafening rumble echoed through the valley, and the fissure exploded open, hurling chunks of dirt and rock skyward. Some of the debris was larger than the hobgoblins themselves. The cries of battle changed to screams of surprise and terror as the ground beneath the dark fey gave way. The earthen rain cascaded down upon them, smashing into their ranks with devastating force. It shattered bones, crushed bodies, and created blood-soaked chaos.

As Ursa watched the spectacle, a thunderous roar caught her attention. Colorful fireballs arced across the sky. These brilliant orbs of light painted the night with vibrant hues, leaving trails of sparkling embers in their wake. Upon impact, they exploded into blazing infernos, illuminating the battlefield with bursts of fire. Ursa realized the fireballs were being launched from the many turrets lining the walls. Next, the thunder of hoofbeats followed as soldiers stormed up the hill to engage the remaining defenders. Ursa chose to return to the bridge.

It didn't take her long to run back down the hill, taking care to avoid the groups of soldiers.

As she approached, she noticed Lucea slumped against the bridge railing, clearly exhausted from using her power. Lucea had ensured the citizens' safety by keeping the bridge untouched and clearing the crowds. Lucea had tied Ursa's horse to the railing next to hers. Ursa approached and knelt beside her. The chronomancer was asleep.

Ursa noticed some dark fey had bypassed the soldiers and were heading toward the bridge. "Lucea, I will return."

Ursa placed herself between the bridge and the advancing dark fey. Despite their scarcity, the ranks included Red Caps, lamia, and some stray goblins. Ursa brandished Iron Reaver like a shield before her and uttered, "Fey Bane." A sweet scent like wildflowers on a spring day permeated the air. The fey recoiled in disgust. As Ursa walked, they continued their retreat. One goblin made a play as though he would attack, and Ursa brought Iron Reaver down and crushed his skull. That satisfied the others. They turned to escape, only to meet the soldiers who dispatched them with ease, with a cleric dealing with the Red Caps.

Ursa turned away and strode back to where Lucea lay sleeping. Ursa sheathed the hammer, then as before pulled Lucea to her. More soldiers poured out of the gates, thundering past her. Ursa was glad they did not trample the two of them.

A dramatic scene unfolded as the soldiers returned, seizing credit for the victory. Ursa experienced a twinge of annoyance, then dismissed it. She thought the soldiers would continue to ignore them as they rode past, until a soldier stopped their horse right next to them. Ursa was not familiar with the rank insignia of Jack-In-Irons.

Someone had dressed the soldier in full armor, unlike any Ursa had seen in a long time. It appeared to be pure light, though Ursa recognized the illusion. A glistening silver that mirrored everything around it. A flowing white cape, etched around its edges with arcane symbols, covered everything, including his horse's haunches. All traces of dirt and blood vanished. The soldier reached for his helmet and lifted the faceplate.

Ursa cursed. *It's a damned ljósálfar. What in the nether-hells is he doing here?*

"You there, dokkalfar." He nodded at her. "What is your business here?"

It was the same as always. Condescending and arrogant. Most people hated dealing with them, and they never ventured into the cities of humans.

"Unless you are the praesidere, it's none of your concern."

That got to him. His expression darkened. "I'd advise against mocking me."

Ursa had had enough. "Do you not see my friend? She protected the people of this city and now needs food and rest to replenish her Gift. If you are not offering to assist, be on your damned way."

Several soldiers, reining their mounts, curiously watched the trio. One soldier, a younger ljósálfar, turned his horse and neared. "Captain Balric?"

So, at least Ursa had a name.

"Place this woman under arrest," Balric said. "And confiscate her weapon."

"I suppose you will not tell me what I'm being accused of?" Ursa stated, maintaining a steady tone.

"Reasonable suspicion."

"That's irrelevant, we both know it." When Ursa moved, Balric grabbed for his sword. Ursa snorted. "Is this resentment because I did better than you in battle?"

Balric grunted, causing his horse to backstep, and drew his sword.

"Captain!" the younger soldier said.

Balric glared at him. "Have a litter brought for the human woman." His attention returned to Ursa. "You will hand over that weapon."

"You can have it," Ursa said. "I didn't want the damnable thing."

Balric sheathed his sword and dismounted. "So why have it? Who gave it—" he said as he reached for it.

As Ursa suspected, the runes glowed red. Balric stopped, his fingers inches from the handle. His expression changed, at first confused and then annoyed. "I see."

Ursa picked up and sheathed Iron Reaver. Balric straightened away, still glaring at her with suspicion until two blue-clad young men walked up, holding the handles of a litter. Their uniforms were deep azure, crisp, starched cotton. The tunics featured elegant tailoring, a high collar, long sleeves, and intricate silver embroidery in the shape of healing symbols. Their tunics had flared hems that fell just below the hips. To complete the uniform were knee-high leather boots dyed in matching azure blue. Silver plating reinforced the toes and heels of the boots for protection.

"She isn't injured. She depleted her Gift and needs a place to recover."

As the pair lifted Lucea onto the litter, Ursa untied her horse while silently summoning her own. She didn't sense its presence. Hopefully, it would find its way back.

"Please follow us," they said in unison. After getting a better look at them, Ursa realized they were twins.

They continued across the bridge toward massive doors, which were open enough for them to slip through. It had been many years since Ursa had entered a big city. Although she'd always been aware of Jack-In-Irons, she had never traveled there.

Ursa ignored the surrounding wonders, but she noted a wooden board bearing a hand-painted map, brightly colored regions segmented into hexagonal cells, each marked with tiny symbols and routes. Their destination was near enough to the entrance gates, and it took only several minutes to arrive. A humble white-brick house was there. Double doors opened wide in welcome. Every so often, there was a tiny spark at different intervals at the opening. Ursa heard a slight hum as she crossed the threshold. She recognized the spell, having cast it herself as one to keep insects and vermin out.

The interior reminded Ursa of one clinic she had often seen on her travels. Several individuals, similarly, uniformed in white, azure, and light blue, helped those needing aid. They deposited the litter onto the nearest cot. With silent commands, they coordinated lifting Lucea onto the bed. Ursa claimed the chair beside it. Despite the surrounding bustle, Ursa's attention stayed on Lucea.

"Hello, miss."

A young human woman, dressed in the light blue uniform, her hair tied up under a tall cap, smiled at her. "Your companion needs replenishment?"

"Yes, thank you."

She nodded and walked away, returning only moments later with a bright red silk ribbon tied around her right arm. A line of runes was embroidered down its surface.

"What are you going to do?" Ursa asked.

The girl looked confused. "The replenishing."

Ursa surmised this was commonplace.

Ursa watched as the woman measured out a length of the ribbon, her movements precise and deliberate. The ribbon shimmered, with its intricate runes glowing with a soft, ethereal light. The woman measured the desired length and wrapped it around Lucea's arm.

The woman closed her eyes as her lips moved. The ribbon constricted, seemingly self-animated. The runes on the ribbon began to shift and dance, cascading down the length like liquid fire. As they reached Lucea's arm, the runes transferred from the ribbon to her bare flesh, etching themselves into her skin.

The transformation was mesmerizing. The runes glowed brighter against Lucea's skin before fading into a delicate pattern and vanishing. Ursa looked at the woman. She was pale and trembling, and she drew the ribbon back, wrapping it around her arm again. Her smile was tired. "I'll have a meal prepared."

"T-thank you." Ursa was confused, still uncertain about what had happened.

"Ursa?"

Ursa turned; relief washed over her. "Lucea!" Ursa took her hands and squeezed them.

"Where are we?" Lucea sat up.

"Well, I know for certain we're in Jack-In-Irons." Ursa grinned.

Lucea drew in a breath. "Thank the Vine!" Her brow creased, and she looked around the room. "What is this place?"

"Some kind of clinic, I believe." Ursa told her about the ritual the woman had performed. "Are you all right?"

"Yes. I am well." Lucea's eyes widened. "Where is my horse? The introduction letters—"

"I tied your horse right outside," Ursa reassured her.

"Right then!" Lucea swung her legs around and planted her feet on the floor. She stood and stretched. "No time to waste."

"They are supposed to be bringing you food."

"No need," Lucea said. "We must be away to the palace." She placed her hands on her hips, turning her body left and right. "Excuse me!" Lucea called out to a nearby worker. "We must leave with haste, what is the fee for this service?"

"Miss?" It was the young woman who had helped Lucea. She carried a covered tray.

"Are you the young lady who helped me?"

"Oh, yes."

"What do I owe you?"

"One gryphon."

Lucea removed her pouch and pulled out a coin. "There you are."

"Thank you," the woman said.

"Mistress dokkalfar."

They both turned. Lucea, her expression confused, looked at the ljósálfar soldier. Again, Ursa felt annoyed.

"I believe I have your mount. It returned by itself." Balric turned to Lucea. "I see your companion is awake."

"And you are, sir?" Lucea asked.

"Captain Elduin Balric." He nodded.

"Good," Lucea said. "Might you be able to escort us to the royal residency? I have an urgent message from His Majesty King Leonine of Vale for the praesidere."

Again came that haughty look. "No."

If he expected Lucea to accept that, he was mistaken. "And why is that?"

"Do you believe I would let two strangers anywhere near our praesidere?"

"As I said, this message is urgent. Surely you don't wish to be the one that prevented the praesidere from receiving it?"

Ursa smiled at the beautiful chronomancer in admiration. Her tenacity was impressive.

"The praesidere receives visitors at the noon hour each day," Balric said. "You are free to visit then. However, there is a curfew established because of the attack for the eleventh hour. Do not let me find you walking the streets or I will ensure your imprisonment, despite your help."

Ursa was about to give him a scathing retort, but Lucea said, "Thank you, sir."

He grunted and nodded again. "Just remember what I've said." He turned to go, making a show of twirling his cape. Then without looking at them, he said, "Welcome, travelers, to Jack-In-Irons."

CHAPTER EIGHTEEN

As Lucea watched Ursa gallop away, the first seed of fear blossomed in her stomach, spreading its roots into her chest. The sound of Ursa's horse's hooves pounding against the earth echoed in her ears, a stark reminder of the danger that lay ahead. It became clear to her that Ursa proved to be a formidable warrior, her skills unmatched by any other. But seeing her ride off to face the enemy alone, Lucea experienced a pang of helplessness.

The evening sun cast long shadows across the battlefield, creating an eerie landscape of light and dark. Lucea's heart ached as she yearned to follow Ursa, to fight by her side and share the burden of the impending battle. The distant cries of the enemy reached her ears, fueling the growing sense of urgency within her.

With a sigh, Lucea steeled herself, determination mingling with the fear in her gut. She wouldn't let Ursa face this alone. The moment for hesitation had passed. The chaos at the bridge surrounded her. A cacophony of sounds and smells, of panic and bloodlust. The people wanting to flee, compared with the soldiers eager for battle and bloodshed.

An impossible task lay before her. Lucea knew what she needed to do, however…

Lucea called upon her Gift, aware of the familiar warmth of magic welling up inside her. First, she needed quiet, a way to silence the terrified screams and shouted orders that filled the air. She closed her eyes and focused, raising her index finger and beginning to write in the air. Runes formed at her fingertip, floating in midair and pulsing with a soft, blue light. "Separate," she whispered.

The runes responded, illuminating the chaotic scene before her. She saw two distinct groups: fleeing refugees and Ursa's fighters. She crafted individual lines of runes for each refugee first, then their allies next. The lines wrapped around their bodies like strands of glowing silk.

The groups became motionless. Time itself had halted around them. An eerie stillness replaced the chaos. Lucea whispered, freeing the soldiers; however, their movement remained controlled to prevent harm to the frightened populace. She kept the citizens immobilized for their own safety.

Lucea disliked such manipulation. Harper once described using tarot – the Pied Piper card – to control a crowd, like puppets on a string, preventing panic. As she led the crowd to safety, Harper's guilt had festered, a raw wound in her heart. Lucea could understand that burden now.

With the soldiers set apart, Lucea turned her concentration back to the refugees. She was fast losing consciousness, the edges of her vision darkening. She released the people, allowing them to move at half-speed. It was all she could manage.

Then Lucea was done. She didn't see whether the citizens made it inside the city walls. Her vision faded to black as exhaustion overtook her.

★ ★ ★

"Well, he was all out of sorts." Lucea crossed her arms and shook her head.

"That's a ljósálfar for you," Ursa replied.

Lucea turned to her, grinning. She wrapped her arms around Ursa in a hug. "I'm so glad you're safe. I was worried sick."

"Were you?" Ursa smiled.

"Oh, don't give me that haughty look."

"I worried about you, too. I'm glad you're safe."

Lucea's heart swelled at Ursa's words. Overcome with a profound sense of connection and warmth, she leaned in and pressed her lips against Ursa's, a spontaneous gesture that seemed as natural as breathing. Their giggling filled the room. The young women who had gathered there exchanged knowing glances, their eyes sparkling with delight as they smiled behind their hands, the atmosphere brimming with a shared sense of camaraderie and joy.

Lucea recoiled as one of the young women approached.

"Mistress, should you require lodgings, I am aware of a respectable place." Her face flushed pink, and she kept her eyes lowered.

"We would appreciate that," Ursa said.

The inn lacked size, and it seemed incongruous among the nearby structures, which were made of striking blue stone. Its reddish stone façade bore a striking resemblance to an ancient, petrified tree trunk, gnarled with multiple roots winding their way into the earth. Rectangular windows were carved into the front, and inviting arched doors beckoned visitors. Lamps flanked either side of the door, casting a warm and welcoming glow. A weathered plaque hung beside the door, inscribed with characters in a language that Lucea didn't recognize, adding an air of mystery to the unique establishment.

They dismounted and tied their horses to the railing. "Do you recognize the language?" Lucea asked as they examined it.

It took a few moments while Ursa peered at it, but she said, "It looks like ogreish."

"By the Vine," Lucea said. "I've never seen an ogre, have you?"

"Plenty of times," Ursa said. "One stayed at the Grayfort tavern. It sat across from a dhampir. It was the oddest pairing I've ever seen."

Lucea drew in a sharp breath, and a shiver ran along her flesh. She'd almost completely forgotten about Grayfort and—

"Oh no," Ursa said. "Lucea, I'm so sorry! I didn't mean to—"

"It's all right." Lucea grasped Ursa's hands and squeezed.

"It's not."

"I will have to face her. Better not to be surprised."

Ursa stated firmly, "We will confront her."

They entered the inn. Lucea asked, "A dhampir, isn't that a half human, half vampire?"

"That's what they say."

"I thought vampires had died out."

"That's what they claim, but who really knows…"

She fell silent. Lucea knew she would discuss the Rot but reconsidered. An ogress staffed the desk. A fierce-looking she-beast with bright red skin and hair, curved horns and monstrous fangs. Lucea had to fight not to stare. Despite the ogress's gruff demeanor, she waited on them, offering them a large room with two beds. Much cheaper, she said, than two separate rooms. Lucea paid extra to stable their horses. The ogress promised excellent care and delivery back to the inn upon their departure. A human boy brought them their packs.

The ogress then called over a little girl who, Lucea thought, belonged to her. She had the same fiery skin and hair. Her horns were just coming in, and fangs were beginning to peek from underneath her top lip. She lifted both their packs as if they weighed nothing and bade them follow her. Once in their rooms, Ursa asked the girl where the showers were. Lucea realized she'd been anticipating it.

Two other women shared the shower room. One was another ogress, with blue skin and long, dark hair, and another dokkalfar. When Ursa saw her fellow dokkalfar, she paused. Lucea turned, puzzled initially, then understood the tension. Ursa returned her greeting. However, it was only after the other dokkalfar departed that Ursa seemed to relax.

"She is the first dokkalfar I've seen in a while," Ursa said quietly.

"You should be aware that, no matter the outcome, I will always defend you," Lucea said.

Ursa smiled.

"This time, you undress first." Lucea grinned wickedly.

As they showered, the ogress burst into a bawdy tune, which had Lucea blushing, but Ursa joined in, much to the delight of the ogress, who sauntered over and wrapped an arm around Ursa's shoulders, and they sang on.

Lucea laughed and applauded, but a strange sensation bothered her as she watched the ogress touch Ursa. An inexplicable sensation twisted in her chest. One she couldn't name. The sight unsettled her. She felt a rush of emotions unknown to her. Possessiveness clouded her mind. She felt envious – another new sensation. What other unfamiliar feelings swirled within her?

When they finished showering, they dressed and descended to the still-open common room. The ogress stayed, tearing at the broiled leg of some large and unfortunate animal. Among those present, Ursa noted humans, dwarves, and a collection of small, catlike creatures known as Cat Sith.

As they sat down, Lucea looked at the blue ogress, and the she-beast winked at her. Lucea's brow creased in confusion. If anything, Lucea would have expected the ogress to wink at Ursa. She tried to glare a warning, but the ogress had already turned away.

They had a delicious shepherd's pie, and Ursa drank her fill of ale. Afterward, while they were changing in their room, Lucea asked Ursa, "I've read of various ogres. What determines their color?"

"It's geographical. I'm surprised that blue ogress found herself so far inland. You find them around the Piper's Keys or the oceans."

"You two seemed to get along well." Lucea flinched. Why did that come out so sullenly?

Ursa looked at her, one brow raised. And then there came that damnable blush.

"Let's get to bed," Lucea said for want of anything else to end the awkward situation. "I plan to be at the palace gates early." Before Ursa responded, Lucea doused the nearby lanterns, which cast the room into semi-darkness, and hopped into bed. She pulled the covers up to her chin with her back turned. *You're acting like a jealous lover.*

Then Lucea heard Ursa moving again, though she couldn't tell what exactly Ursa was doing. But approaching footsteps clearly announced her arrival at Lucea's bed. Lucea's eyes became wide, and her breath caught when Ursa lifted the covers and slid underneath them. A profound sense of anticipation permeated the quiet surroundings.

"You're angry with me."

"No," Lucea responded.

"You are. You can't lie to me. Is it because of that ogress?"

Lucea opened her mouth to protest but said, "Yes."

"You think I'm interested in her? I don't know her at all. Just because we shared a song means nothing."

"I understand. It's strange. She winked at me in the common room."

"Did she?" Ursa sounded amused. "Do you understand the reason?"

Lucea thought she did but didn't respond.

"Come here," Ursa said.

Lucea turned to face her, and Ursa held out her arms. Lucea moved into her embrace and breathed a sigh. She found solace and contentment in the warmth of Ursa's body.

Lucea tipped her head up. The kiss seemed timid, tentative – a brush of lips more than anything. The air between them crackled with unspoken tension. Ursa pulled back, her eyes twinkling with delight. "Do I need to teach you how to kiss?" she asked, a playful smirk curving her lips.

Lucea huffed in annoyance. Lost in thought, she recalled a boy, a balcony, a name she'd forgotten. His kiss had been clumsy and aggressive, his hands roaming where they shouldn't. She'd pushed him away, her skin crawling.

She was brought back to the present by the warmth of Ursa's hand supporting her chin. Ursa firmly yet tenderly guided Lucea's face upward. Lips and breath executed a masterful dance.

When Ursa pulled away, her eyes searched Lucea's face. "What are your thoughts on that?"

Lucea's heart raced, her lips tingling. She met Ursa's gaze, a shy smile spreading across her face. "I liked it," she admitted.

Ursa smiled, her eyes filled with a mix of pride and affection. "Good," she murmured, her thumb brushing over Lucea's cheek. "You deserve to feel good."

They stayed like that for a moment, their foreheads touching. A comforting silence, the kind that spoke volumes without uttering a single word, filled the room. A newfound sense of calm washed over Lucea, a tranquility she hadn't realized she lacked.

Ursa's hand traced a delicate line down Lucea's arm, causing a cascade of shivers to ripple through her body. Ursa said in a melodic tone, "There is no need to rush."

Lucea nodded, appreciating the patience and understanding in Ursa's words. The profound fondness she felt transcended the physical, extending into areas of trust and emotional bonding. Lucea experienced understanding and appreciation for the first time in years.

"Thank you," Lucea murmured. "For everything."

Ursa's smile widened. "Always, Lucea. I'm here for you, no matter what." She pressed a gentle kiss to Lucea's forehead, sealing her promise with a tender touch. "May I continue?"

Lucea drew in a sharp breath. "I don't – I don't know."

"I won't do anything that makes you uncomfortable, I promise," Ursa said. "And if you don't like something, tell me to stop."

"All right."

Ursa's expression softened, and she cradled Lucea's face in her hands. "You're safe with me," Ursa's tone was sincere and warm. She leaned in; her lips brushed Lucea's in a feather-light kiss that promised everything without a word. Lucea's heart fluttered, excitement and nervousness bubbling within her.

Ursa closed her mouth around Lucea's right breast and suckled through her nightshirt. Lucea's nipples hardened. She drew in a sharp breath and whimpered, and bit down on her lower lip.

Ursa withdrew, and Lucea was disappointed, but this quickly faded when Ursa gently nudged Lucea's shoulder and turned her onto her back before similarly attending to her left breast.

A series of moans escaped Lucea's lips. Liquid heat pooled below her stomach while fire spread through her veins. She felt feverish. And she wanted this flame to continue to consume her.

"Ursa?"

"Yes, love?"

The word caused her heart to swell. "You can take off my nightshirt."

"Are you certain?"

"Yes."

Lucea raised her arms to allow Ursa to work. The dokkalfar pulled the nightshirt over Lucea's head, exposing her naked body. Lucea realized it shouldn't matter, but she was glad for the semi-darkness. "Ursa – I've never—"

Ursa laughed. "I understand you haven't."

"I just wanted to let you understand. I've heard men prefer—"

"I don't give a damn what men prefer. I want you, my beautiful chronomancer."

They kissed again. Ursa deepened the kiss, probing Lucea's mouth with her tongue, as Ursa plunged her hands into Lucea's hair. Ursa ended the kiss, and Lucea didn't wait long for Ursa's next move.

"I'm going to do something now," Ursa said. "And I want you to pay attention, so you'll be able to do it as well."

Before Lucea could ask what, Ursa lowered her hand between Lucea's legs, where her maidenhead rested. Her mind clouded, and she cried out when Ursa probed inside until her fingers rested on—

Lucea grasped the coverlet underneath her and her back arched, accepting Ursa's touch.

"Ursa! Ursa!"

Ursa responded only with ragged, rapid breathing, mirroring Lucea's. Lucea moved almost involuntarily as the heat within her quickly became an inferno where Ursa touched her. Even when it culminated in a burst of pleasure unknown to Lucea, the experience didn't end. It happened again and again as Lucea's hips bucked, and she cried out every time.

Then she fell, dropping into a warm cocoon of satiation, as she sensed a pulse that matched her heartbeat. Lucea hadn't known this was possible. Yes, she'd received instruction on how to please a lover, but she'd never expected this – experience.

Lucea lay there, enjoying the sensation. Ursa moved on top of her, and they kissed again. Lucea caressed up and down Ursa's back. She wanted to give Ursa the same pleasure. But for now—

"How are you feeling?" Ursa asked.

"I want more," Lucea said.

Ursa laughed. "Very well."

CHAPTER NINETEEN

The deepening night made the room feel smaller, a private space where time stretched. They talked about their hopes and fears, sharing stories that were tucked away in the recesses of their minds. Each word, each gesture, brought them closer, weaving an invisible thread of connection between their hearts.

Ursa opened in ways she had never imagined, revealing pieces of her soul that she had long kept hidden. Lucea listened with unwavering attention, a steady anchor in the sea of emotions. Lucea shared her own vulnerabilities, her dreams, and the scars that had shaped her.

The night stretched on, filled with whispered conversations and shared dreams, as they lay entwined, finding solace in each other's presence. They slept for a time. Ursa awoke, sensing the early morning. She had no desire to leave this bed. Memories of their night and the sensations behind it lingered. Ursa chuckled with satisfaction.

"Ursa?"

"I'm sorry, did I wake you?"

"No." A smile touched her words. "I wondered if I might—?"

Ursa chuckled, then rolled onto her back. Lucea bent to kiss her breasts; Ursa's nipples hardened almost at once.

Lucea pulled back. The pre-dawn light in the room revealed her worried expression. "Am I doing it right?"

"Yes, you are," Ursa said. "Don't stop." Ursa lay still while Lucea planted soft kisses on her abdomen, then did something unexpected, and fluttered her tongue in Ursa's navel.

"Where did you learn that?" Ursa asked.

"You're ticklish!" Lucea's tone was mischievous.

"I am not!"

Lucea resumed her fluttering.

"Stop it, you little vixen!"

"I believe you mean kitten?" Her amusement was obvious. "All right." She was silent for a moment as she caressed Ursa's thigh with gentle fingertips. "How should I—?"

"Here." Ursa took her hand, arranged Lucea's fingers and guided her.

"Like this?"

"Yes. Yes!"

Ursa surrendered to pleasure. She lay there, breathing through her mouth and moaning. Her hips rose and fell. When she reached completion, its power had Ursa crying out through gritted teeth. Once her heart stopped hammering and her breathing slowed, Ursa gasped, "You're a quick learner."

Lucea laughed in happiness and almost threw herself on top of Ursa. "I am so glad we met! You are wonderful, Ursa." Then they kissed until the first light of dawn invaded the room.

* * *

Ursa frowned at the immense map mounted on a rectangular signpost, protected by a pane of glass. The colored sections marked different regions. The labels on each section used a variety of languages, but comprehension was still difficult. She turned to Lucea, her brow furrowing deeper. "Are any other languages known to you?"

Lucea nodded, scanning the map with curiosity. "I am familiar with some Dwarven and Kobold." She traced her finger along one label written in the angular script of the Dwarves.

Ursa echoed, relieved, "I am also familiar with some Nagese, Druidic, and Faunese." Her eyes flicked over the map. She recognized a few words written in the flowing script of the Druidic language and the sharp, pictographic Nagese characters. Between the two of them, Ursa and Lucea were able to gain some understanding of the diverse regions. Each region formed a decagon shape that snugly fit next to its neighbor. The largest was in the center. They believed this to be their destination.

"It appears the various races separate the city." Ursa noticed Lucea squinting. "Is that – proper? Dividing along racial lines in that manner?" She was having difficulty putting her thoughts into words.

"Insular?" Ursa volunteered.

"Maybe more than that."

"I wish I had an answer for you," Ursa said. "But it's up to the people of this city to change the situation if they wish. It's not our place to tell them otherwise."

"I know." Lucea cast her eyes down. She drew herself up. "For now, I – we try to complete our tasks."

"Of course," Ursa said. "We have a few hours. Should we start for the palace now? Or perhaps we should breakfast first."

"I would rather start for the palace now," Lucea said. "Perhaps we may stop along the way." She revisited the map and highlighted something. "A bakery is on the same street."

"Good idea," Ursa said.

Navigating the overcrowded streets of Jack-In-Irons was no easy feat. Most in the city chose to walk; however, some horseback riders and carriages navigated the crowds. The air buzzed with the vibrant energy of the bustling crowd.

They found the bakery. Its enticing aroma drew a steady stream of customers. Some lounged in front of the store, savoring fresh pastries, while others had secured one of the wrought-iron tables and chairs. However, the seating allowed only humans to be comfortable. The furniture's craftsmanship barred those of Gifted or fey descent in an unspoken declaration of exclusion. The mix of tantalizing scents and the underlying tension of segregation created a unique, if bittersweet, atmosphere around the bakery.

Ursa sensed Lucea's distress, aware of Lucea's ability to sit at the tables, unlike herself. Although it didn't seem to upset anyone. Had everyone come to accept this as the norm? She saw no anger or sadness.

The bakery overflowed, both inside and out. People were calling out orders as the frantic employees worked to accommodate them. Upon reaching the counter, Ursa and Lucea stared at the neatly arranged sweets, their stomachs rumbling. The sweets had fanciful names like Fairy Honey Cake, Pixieberry Pie, and Goblin Ginger Snaps.

"Everything looks delicious!" Lucea said.

They decided on the honey cakes, which were handed over wrapped in parchment paper. Delicate edible flowers adorned the soft, flaky cakes, adding a whimsical touch. Each bite was like tasting pure sunshine, with a subtle floral hint that danced on the tongue and left a lingering sweetness.

They continued making their way through the diverse crowd. They fought to remain together.

"I wonder..." Lucea said. Despite the crowds, Ursa heard her. "Imagine if everyone knew what lay just beyond the gate. What awaited them in the darkness. Would they be so carefree?"

"Likely not," Ursa said.

Lucea ate more cake, chewing thoughtfully. "I wonder if I should keep silent. Let the people go on with their lives."

Ursa took her by both shoulders and turned Lucea to face her. Alone for a few moments, they created their own world, with Ursa locking eyes with Lucea amidst the crowd.

"No," Ursa said. "You were given a task. We were both given a task. Can you live with yourself if we ignore this and the Rot destroys everything?"

"No, of course not." Lucea smiled. "Let's continue."

As they emerged onto a wide thoroughfare, the grandeur of the palace lay ahead. On either side of it, near-identical buildings, all adorned in the same white and gold theme, stood tall. Polished wooden signposts hung from decorative brass rods to mark them as businesses.

The sight at the end of the thoroughfare, however, broke from the uniformity. Surprisingly, the architecture of the palace differed greatly from the shops. In fact, the palace looked more like an immense living inn. A colossal tree dwarfed all others Ursa had ever seen. Tangled roots twisted in every direction, adding to the organic chaos.

As they drew closer, they noticed windows carved into the colossal trunk, peeking out even from the interwoven branches. At the top, the tree appeared shorn off, its severed end now growing anew, curving downward. Despite the distance, Ursa spotted movement atop the tree.

Ursa took Lucea's hand and quickened her pace, feeling an inexplicable pull toward this marvel of nature. Lucea made no complaint, likely using her powers to match Ursa's stride as she had done in the forest.

The crowd parted as if by magic, and they stood before the magnificent structure. Immense arched doors, taller than several men, stood open. The façade bore the cracks of age, some revealing the soft green of fresh growth. Nearby, they saw the tree's bent section re-rooting.

Both Ursa and Lucea gaped in awe, realizing the honor of standing before such a sight. They'd known it existed, but experiencing it with their own eyes was beyond words, a privilege for the chosen few. "This is—" Lucea began. "Is it really?"

"Yes," Ursa said. "The heart of the Celestial Vine."

"This is where it began," Lucea said. "The Farm Boy, the Woodsman's Axe. His desire for gold and adventure stranded numerous giants."

"I just realized," Ursa said, "have we seen any giants at all?"

Lucea's eyes went wide, and she placed her hand over her mouth, drawing in a breath. "No, we haven't."

"You would think they would all be here, at the very center of the city," Ursa mused. "Perhaps, seeing the Vine and realizing their sole route home is blocked could be too painful for them to handle."

No one knew what the Farm Boy had seen when he climbed the Vine. More accurately, variations of the story existed. Ask the giants and they would tell you of the floating kingdom of Brobdingnag. Study and learning thrived there. Each member contributed his or her unique skills to advance their society. The Vine's appearance sparked their curiosity, prompting them to investigate its origin. Many decades ago, Jack-In-Irons consisted of only farms and a small, unnamed town. Yet they came right before the wars between the humans and dark fey began.

Ask the humans – particularly the descendants of the Farm Boy – and they would tell you that giants were enormous but dull-witted and violent, which is why he had to escape back down the Vine to stop the giant from pursuing and he used the legendary Woodsman's Axe. With one swing, the entire Vine tore from its base, falling to the earth, splitting the entire continent asunder.

"Why do we look at him as a hero?" Lucea asked.

"Well," Ursa said, "would we exist? We were all born from the Vine, even the dark fey."

"I know." Lucea worried her lower lip in that adorable way of hers.

Ursa gave her a quick peck on the lips. "We could debate endlessly. However, we have work to do."

"Yes, of course."

Guards, with military precision, inspected identifications and packages at the gate. Ursa saw a ljósálfar conversing with a woman in a matching uniform.

"There's that captain," Ursa said. "What was his name again?"

"Balric," Lucea said. "Captain Elduin Balric."

"Well, I'm glad you recalled it."

"Felines have long memories." Lucea smiled.

Naturally, Balric saw them when they stepped before the guards. He sniffed, then whispered a comment to his neighbor. She looked at them. Ursa maintained eye contact. The woman walked toward them. The most noticeable thing about her was her red hair and green eyes. Which meant the person was part fairy, likely a descendant of Robin Goodfellow, and of course she had the Gift.

"Good afternoon," she said. "I am Captain Iris Greenstone."

Ursa thought it would be best if Lucea took the lead.

"It's a pleasure to meet you, Captain Greenstone." Lucea extended her hand, which Greenstone shook. "I am Lady Lucea of Vale, here with a message from His Royal Majesty King Leonine the Third."

Greenstone looked at Ursa or, more accurately, at Iron Reaver. "That's quite a formidable-looking weapon. Tell me, you are…?"

"Ursa. As my companion says, it's a pleasure."

"We searched for you both," Greenstone said. "Word arrived of talented women who fought the encroaching evil."

"That is why we are here. Please, may we see your praesidere?" Lucea said.

"You may have to wait. There are people before you." Greenstone looked at Ursa again. "I trust you will keep your weapon sheathed?"

"Of course." Perhaps the woman knew that asking her to check the hammer was pointless. It wouldn't be hard for the fairy part of her to see the aura of the runes and understand their meaning.

"Follow me." They walked down the hall on thick carpeting the same color as Greenstone's uniform.

Glances to their left and right revealed nothing. Instead, it appeared as though ethereal sheets of fog hung between towering columns of white marble. They rippled and glimmered with an otherworldly life, shifting and shimmering as if whispering secrets from beyond. The fog wasn't mere mist; it had a luminescent quality, with tiny, sparkling lights moving within it like stars embedded in a tapestry. As they moved, they seemed to react, swaying and parting, hinting at the hidden realms just beyond the reach of their current reality.

"What in the nether-hells," Ursa muttered.

"Dear Vine," Lucea said, "are those – veils?"

Greenstone glanced back at them and said matter-of-factly, "Yes."

"But how?" Lucea's breath hitched, the fear clear in every syllable. Ursa didn't blame her.

"It's safe," Greenstone said.

"She didn't ask if it was safe," Ursa said. "She asked how."

"The praesidere alone possesses this secret," Greenstone continued.

A tremor ran through Lucea as she walked beside Ursa. "Don't fret. I'll protect you."

She expected Lucea to say she didn't need protecting. Instead, Lucea nodded.

Did anyone see the deadly threat? These shimmering veils weren't just beautiful; they were vital, keeping the loyal creatures of darkness – beings that dwelled in the nether-hells and worlds unknown – out of the living realm. Gifted individuals, focusing their abilities, conceived these magical barriers. The task required precision. One misstep, one mistaken twist of power, and something horrid from beyond might slip through, unleashing chaos and destruction. The thought of such a cataclysmic breach sent shivers down Ursa's spine, a chilling reminder of the unending vigilance needed to guard against the darkness lurking just beyond the veils.

This praesidere was arrogant or just insane. Either way, Ursa couldn't envision a single being possessing the ability to achieve this, at least not among anyone she'd encountered. The praesidere jeopardized countless lives throughout the city, potentially the entire Isles.

Ursa refused to trust her.

Greenstone noted six individuals gathering in a small alcove. Two small tables held food. Just sweet treats like they'd had earlier.

Greenstone said, "Help yourselves. When your time comes, I will invite you in." Greenstone nodded again and walked away.

Two more white-clad guards stood before another set of arched doors. Somewhere above, a bell rang, yet looking upward they could only see shadows. The two guards opened the door.

A finely dressed man, accompanied by a group of beautiful women, emerged looking displeased. They allowed the next group in. Ursa got a glimpse of the immensely decorated room before the doors closed.

"Did you see the praesidere?" Lucea asked.

"Just what seemed to be the usual overlarge attendance hall."

Lucea clung to Ursa as the next exchange of visitors occurred. Lucea occasionally gasped, noticing movement behind the veils. When their turn arrived and Greenstone approached again, she motioned them forward with a bow. "Walk forward, please."

The guards unbarred the doors and as they pulled them open, a flash of light erupted, compelling them to shield their eyes.

"Come forward, please." The words rolled out, rich with the resonance of old wisdom. In that instance, the light faded. It took them several moments for their eyes to adjust. Instead of a glamorous hall, the audience area resembled a cozy haven, like a faun village within a giant tree. Dozens of bookshelves, circular, lined the walls; each brimmed with books of all kinds, some old and leather-bound, others newer with vibrant covers. Between the shelves, rounded windows let in soft, natural light, blending with the warm glow of a wooden chandelier hanging from the ceiling. But the chandelier's lights weren't ordinary candles or bulbs. Instead, they were glowing balls, much like the wil-o'-wisps; however, these turned out to be magic, casting a gentle, otherworldly illumination throughout the space.

At the back end of the room, an immense fireplace stood ready, though unlit, its hearth prepared for a cozy fire. A mix of family photos and art adorned the mantel above, hinting at personal history and cherished memories.

A polished, low round table dominated the room's center. Six crafted wooden chairs surrounded the table, but the largest and most ornate chair clearly awaited the kobold leader. Intricate carvings on this seat of honor reflected the authority and respect commanded by its occupant.

Warmth, welcome, wood scent, and leaf rustle charmed the space.

"Princess Ursa of Ilve Belanore and Lady Lucea of Vale, please come sit with me."

CHAPTER TWENTY

Lucea despised these feelings of helplessness and fear.

The veils and inhuman shadows unsettled her. She had never seen the veils. Her Gift didn't have such power. The only person Lucea knew who could manipulate the veils was Harper. And even she was cautious in her manipulations.

This kobold showed no hesitation in using the veils. What was her endgame? Safe spells guaranteed privacy if she desired it. This was just madness.

And now, while the kobold spoke of things she couldn't know, Lucea watched Ursa tear the hammer from its sheath. "What in the nether-hells are you about?" Ursa's grip tightened around the haft, and the runes began their soft glow.

Lucea reached out, aching to take Ursa by the arm, but she was fearful of how her lover would react.

"You may have heard our names," Ursa continued, "but how in the nether-hells did you know who I was? How did you know where we are from?"

Lucea noticed that Ursa's rage did not affect the kobold. Her expression was impassive. She seemed to wait for Ursa's ire to fade.

"I've lived since before they felled the Vine. There is little I don't know," the kobold said.

"That's impossible," Ursa said. "That would mean—"

The kobold laughed. "I am Dhidihn Farstride. And I have held my position since the first. I was present when the Farm Boy felled the Vine."

Somehow, Lucea believed her. "That is your true name?"

"Yes."

"That does not concern you? I'm sure you know what it means."

Farstride laughed. "I am powerful."

"And modest," Ursa muttered.

"How are you so long-lived?" Lucea asked.

"The Celestial Vine speaks through me. Whatever happens in this world, the Vine allows me the knowledge." Farstride motioned with her hand. "Please, Your Highness, will you sit?"

"Don't call me Your Highness," Ursa grumbled. "Your extensive knowledge of me should confirm I haven't held that position for many years."

Farstride inclined her head. "As you wish."

Ursa sat. Lucea laid her hand on Ursa's forearm. Ursa still held on to the Iron Reaver. Lucea supposed she couldn't blame her.

"To begin," Farstride said, "thank you for how you protected my city and people. I am in your debt. Anything you desire shall be yours."

"We saw many soldiers while we traveled," Lucea said. "They were with the attackers, under the influence of the Rot."

"They tried to kill us," Ursa said. "We took refuge with a farmer, and they set his barn on fire where we slept."

"The Rot is influencing the smaller and weak-minded leaders of the outlying villages and drawing them into the darkness. And there is more. I'm afraid we may have brought more trouble to your gates," Lucea continued. "We are being pursued by a being."

"Amalgam."

"Then you know of it, too," Lucea said.

"Yes. But do you know what it is?"

"A construct of the Rot," Ursa said.

"Indeed." Farstride nodded. "It is two evils, bonded by the Rot but fighting for supremacy, although they have the same goal."

A sudden realization hit Lucea. "It's them." She looked at Ursa, chilled.

"You know?" Farstride said.

"Barnabas and Samara," Ursa said. "They have joined in some unholy alliance."

"Perhaps not an alliance," Lucea said. "Remember Damae said they were fighting as well. I'll wager the Rot consumed them both and they each wish to be the dominant one."

"It's a competition between two children for their parents' affection," Ursa said.

"They will find their way here," Lucea said.

"How do you plan on protecting the people?" Ursa asked.

"That is my worry," she said, "although I am quite capable for now of keeping the enemy at bay. My soldiers are great and loyal."

"I will give you that you have power," Lucea said. "But I must beg your pardon. You are being reckless with those veils."

If Farstride was offended, she didn't show it in her expression. "I am confident of my abilities. Perhaps—"

"No," Ursa said. "We will not remain in this city."

"Ursa—"

"Your king should understand," Ursa continued. "You must return to Vale and warn him."

Lucea frowned at Ursa's words. Despite her fear, Lucea knew she still had the king's task before her. "Milady, knowing the world, you understand the danger." Lucea withdrew the papers from her jacket and laid them on the table. She inhaled deeply, beginning to speak, then Farstride held the papers.

"King Leonine Noble the Third of Vale has tasked me with seeking your help in our battle against the entity known as the Rot. It threatens to destroy the Riven Isles. We are confident that, with your aid in engaging the other provinces, it will be possible to achieve a mutually acceptable agreement."

Lucea had practiced her request many times before leaving Vale, and now the words came to her. When Farstride didn't respond, Lucea went on. "May we have your cooperation?"

Farstride lowered her head, her eyes closed. "We must wait for the others."

"Others?" Lucea said.

Farstride's head snapped up, and she caught Lucea in her silver gaze. She believed the woman could see into her soul. "I arranged a private waiting area for you both."

"Wait for what?" Ursa demanded. "These others, whoever in the nether-hells are they?"

"It is essential that they be here before we can continue. After they arrive, we can form a plan—"

"Are you not listening?" Ursa pushed back her chair and stood. "We lack time and patience for puzzles. We're not waiting here for others, that's for certain."

"Ursa!" Lucea admonished. Ursa turned to glare at her. It hurt. They'd been making love just last night, and now Ursa seemed furious with her. In the next moment, Lucea understood why. *You're terrified, aren't you? Of even more than the Rot.*

Of course, Ursa would never admit that aloud. She knew Lucea felt the same way. The possibility of a veil breach horrified her.

"You must understand," Lucea continued, "we aren't doubting your abilities—"

Ursa snorted.

"But we don't feel safe here. Would you be willing to, at least temporarily, hide the veils?"

"I have a task for you," Farstride said, ignoring Lucea's fears.

Her patience waning, Lucea asked, "What task?"

Farstride explained that a single method exists to help the Vine repel the Rot. "The Farm Boy's tale you know, yet how he obtained the Vine seeds remains a mystery, does it not?"

"Yes," Lucea said. "That became lost to history."

"I suppose you know," Ursa said.

Farstride's eyes gleamed with secret knowledge. She made several intricate motions with her hands, and a book materialized in a sudden cloud of smoke, dropping to the tabletop with a resounding thump.

The book was a hefty tome, its cover made of weathered, crackling leather that bore the marks of countless years of use. Deep, intricate patterns embossed the leather, hinting at ancient, forgotten symbols and runes. Tarnished brass reinforced the corners. The spine bulged with multiple ridges, each one stitched with faded, but sturdy, thread.

Lucea lifted the ancient book. Its weight was reassuring in her hands. When she opened it, she found the pages filled with stories written in a multitude of languages, each one more captivating than the last. Elegant, flowing script characterized some texts, while others were scrawled in a more hurried, jagged hand. Newer additions stood out with their crisp, bold lettering, written in vibrant ink that seemed almost to glow on the aged parchment. Turning the pages felt like uncovering stories and languages from many ages, all bound within the book's aged covers.

As Lucea turned the pages, what she saw made her smile. Her parents' bedtime stories and her schooling shaped her familiarity with these narratives. Some were true; others were fanciful tales. Detailed maps also showed the locations of legendary weapons, including Iron Reaver. However, maps pinpointed several dangerous items, including the Bottle Imp, the Witch Mirror, and the Apples of Immortality.

Lucea was no longer smiling. "Please tell me no one is aware of the locations of these items?"

"They are well hidden," Farstride said. "Do not concern yourself with those." She waved her hand, and the pages moved by themselves. They opened to the story of the Farm Boy.

"Go on," Farstride encouraged.

The story started as everyone knew. The Farm Boy was to sell his cow at the market, but on his way, a stranger traded him seeds for the cow. His mother was not pleased. Lucea's expression became more troubled as she kept reading. The storyline shifted in an unforeseen direction.

"Wait, this is wrong—"

Her protest piqued Ursa's curiosity. The dokkalfar moved her chair closer so she could read over Lucea's shoulder.

"Keep reading."

Ursa muttered something very unladylike behind her, having trouble understanding this new information as Lucea was. "Wait, this is saying that the parents of the Farm Boy were the true rulers of Brobdingnag, and a giant named Gogmagog killed the father and stole the throne. The mother escaped."

"I've never heard of such!" Ursa said what Lucea was thinking.

Despite her disbelief, Lucea continued to read, her brow furrowed in deep concentration as she worried her lower lip. "No, no, this isn't right."

"Why are you so disbelieving?"

"Given this scenario, how do you account for the remaining giants after the Vine's collapse?"

"Also," Ursa said, "how did the Farm Boy's mother escape to Above Ground from the flying island with an infant?"

Farstride folded her hands. "I heard this story thus."

"Didn't you think to ask these questions?" Ursa said.

"I did not. Does it matter?"

"Who is privy to this information?" Lucea said.

"A few descendants of the Farm Boy," Farstride said. "And now you, of course."

"And they've kept this secret?" Lucea asked.

"Of course," Farstride replied. "They know what would happen if this ever became common knowledge."

Lucea was uncertain whether she wanted to read further. Yet she continued. "The stranger that gave him the beans was a giant."

"In disguise, yes," Farstride said. "A fairy disguised him with a glamour and gifted him the seeds for the Farm Boy to reach Brobdingnag."

"The Farm Boy relinquished his throne, choosing instead his mother's company."

"Had he not, our great city would not exist."

Lucea wondered how someone chose Farstride and who that person was. The Farm Boy?

Ursa reached over and turned a few pages, her eyes scanning. "It's unclear how he obtained additional seeds, or their current whereabouts." She straightened, her eyes locked on Farstride. "We are leaving."

"Oh?" The kobold raised a furry eyebrow.

"Ursa—"

"You said yourself we are not safe. Let's return to Vale together. I am your witness to your king. Not to mention this—" Ursa dismissed the book with a wave.

"Move along." Farstride leaned against the chairback as she laid her hands on her lap and closed her eyes. She seemed ready for sleep.

"There is nothing further on these pages," Ursa said.

Just as Ursa was about to close the book, the letters on the page shifted, forming strange patterns and symbols. Golden smoke swirled up from the pages, wrapping around her hand. The letters seemed to come alive, rearing up and latching on to Ursa's wrist. She gasped as the words glowed, burning into her skin before fading away.

Lucea watched in shock, unable to move. "Ursa, are you all right?" she asked.

Ursa stared at her wrist, where the faint outline of the words stayed, pulsing with a gentle light. "I think so." Her tone was uncertain. Ursa looked to Farstride. "What does this mean?"

Farstride opened her eyes and sat up, examining Ursa's wrist with a keen interest. "They made the book from the Vine itself. You have everything you need now."

"Puzzles, always puzzles!" Ursa said. "Be straight with us, old woman."

"I don't know what you wish for me to say. The Vine has given you what you need."

"It's instructions on where to find the seeds?" Lucea asked.

"I would say so. If the Vine wishes for you to find them."

Lucea turned to Ursa to inquire if she understood the runes, but Ursa, appearing confused, was rubbing at them as if trying to remove them. "Ursa?"

"Yes," Ursa said. Her eyes never left the glowing runes on her flesh.

"Are you…?" Lucea wasn't certain what to ask.

"Stop resisting," Farstride demanded. "You won't hear the message if you ignore the Vine."

"Damn you," Ursa muttered. "Lucea, we should make haste."

Lucea had the sense she did not mean finding the seeds. "I know you are fearful. I am too." She thought Ursa would protest, but she didn't.

"Then we should leave before this entire city's destruction," Ursa said.

Lucea's eyes stung with tears. "No, I'm sorry, I can't." Lucea pushed back from the chair and stood, wrapping her arms around Ursa's waist. "We have to do this together." She lifted her chin and fixed her eyes on Ursa's. "Please."

"No," Ursa said. "I will keep my promise to you and protect you, but not here. I'll return to the inn for a time, and wait for you. But I will not stay there forever."

Lucea dropped her arms to her sides. Her throat constricted, and she had to force down a swallow. She let the tears flow.

"And you," Ursa pointed at Farstride, "if you live and Lucea dies, I will spend the rest of my life making you suffer. I don't give a damn how powerful you may be."

Ursa turned, then stopped abruptly. Lucea turned and saw it too. The door was gone, replaced by a solid wall.

"Let me out!" Ursa demanded.

"That way." Farstride gestured to their left, where a smaller, unadorned door of standard height and width appeared.

Ursa stormed out. A new light enveloped her as she opened the door, which then closed mysteriously.

CHAPTER TWENTY-ONE

Why did I leave?

Ursa went ahead through the doorway; a rose garden unexpectedly unfolded before her. The trimmed hedges formed a waist-high maze with carved benches in closed-off passages. A fountain sat where two paths converged. White marble, its smoothness shone in the soft light. Statues of fauns adorned it, their playful forms frozen in mid-dance. They circled a central column, a station of the Celestial Vine, its delicate tendrils carved with a grace that mirrored nature's own handiwork.

Ursa found herself impressed by her surroundings. The consistent sound of the water and the fragrances emanating from the roses created an ideal setting for a romantic meeting. Ursa immediately quelled those thoughts.

She resumed her walk, circling the fountain to find the path that led to a postern gate made of wrought iron. However, that did not seem workable. Ursa surveyed her surroundings. The tall stone wall presented the garden's only exit. As she approached, the gate swung inward by itself. Ursa passed through. As she stepped outside of the palace grounds, two nagas greeted her, standing guard, holding the weapons favored by their people, the halberd.

They did not appear surprised to see her. "Afternoon, miss," the one on her left spoke. "Leaving for the day?"

"Yes," Ursa said, still cautious.

"Very well then," the naga continued. "Please hold out your left hand."

"Why?"

"For your badge, of course." As though Ursa should know what that meant.

"It will make it possible for you to reenter the palace," the second said.

Ursa was about to protest. She had no plans to revisit the palace, yet...

"Yes, palm down. Thank you." He took out an oblong device only a few inches long. Ursa identified it as a stamp. She'd seen such before in her travels. She waited while the naga pressed it to the back of her hand. It left what Ursa assumed was the crest of the royal family of Jack-In-Irons. It glowed blue for a moment and then resembled a normal tattoo.

"Safe travels," they said together.

Safe travels indeed. Jack-In-Irons was a city teetering on the edge of chaos.

As she made her way through the bustling streets, Ursa couldn't help but notice the obliviousness of the townsfolk. Children played, vendors hawked their wares, and life continued as though nothing was amiss. She sighed, knowing the calm was a façade, a thin veneer over the storm brewing just beneath the surface.

Despite what she'd said to Lucea, Ursa did not return to the inn. Instead, she was directionless. The runes under her skin were pulsating, not uncomfortably, but the sensation was disturbing. Ursa continued to walk as she rubbed them again, as if she could scrub them away, though she knew it wasn't possible. Tantalizing scents made her pause, and her stomach rumbled. It came to her that she had eaten nothing since...

As she walked, memories filled her. Memories of Lucea. Those catlike eyes, smooth skin, and her dark silk hair. Her smile and the way she responded to...

Ursa shook off the memories and kept walking, muttering to herself as passersby gave her curious looks. She banished all thoughts of Lucea.

Ursa's anger, though still present, waned as she walked through the streets. With each step, it seemed to dissolve, granting her a newfound clarity of thought she had been missing for days.

The scenery changed. The buildings became familiar, the faces more recognizable. Ursa's heart ached when she realized she had wandered into the quarter where her fellow dokkalfar lived. Jack-In-Irons prided itself on being a city of progress, a melting pot of cultures and ideas. However, beneath this progressive veneer, old prejudices and divisions still lingered, casting long shadows over the city's attempted unity.

Ursa sighed. The place saw the forging of new alliances and the collapse of ancient barriers; it also bore the crushing weight of history. Jack-In-Irons was a city both ahead of its time and anchored in the past.

As she stood there, the runes under her skin ceased their pulsating, and she felt a strange calm settle over her. Instead of anger, a sense of stubbornness remained. Ursa realized her path was fraught with challenges, but she also knew that in this city of contradictions, she would find her way.

Ursa saw another illustrated map and noted that it labeled the dokkalfar region Lylethyr. Ursa wondered why this group had lived Above Ground. Thinking of the tranquil dim light, the glowing plants, and the comforting smell of earth always calmed Ursa.

Somehow, they had mimicked the profound connection her people had with Underneath. To transplant such a culture to the surface world required a delicate blend of adaptation and reverence for its subterranean origins.

The architecture of Lylethyr reflected a harmonious blend of surface and underground elements. Tall, slender structures rose, mimicking the stalagmites and stalactites of their traditional homes. Intricate carvings, telling the stories and legends of the dokkalfar, adorned the dark stone buildings.

Windows were fewer and smaller, preserving an interior dimness while allowing for strategic glimpses of the outside world. Bioluminescent plants, transplanted from their underground habitats, being nurtured in hanging gardens and terrariums, cast a gentle, ethereal glow.

Lylethyr integrated into the surrounding natural environment. The dokkalfar's deep respect for nature was clear in the town's design.

Laborers constructed buildings around large trees, preserving and incorporating roots and branches into the architecture. Bioluminescent flora thrived in rooftop gardens, showcasing beauty and heritage.

An ache gripped her heart, one she had carried since her exile. She had kept it at bay until now, but all the memories resurfaced: loneliness, homesickness, and taken-for-granted comforts. Fear followed, that she would be exposed as exiled and deposed. Yet, it didn't matter – they had banished her from her kingdom, not the Riven Isles. Even her mother lacked that power.

She nearly fell into the avenue but recovered her balance. Ursa noticed a tiny green space nestled between two structures, a small flowering tree in its center. Three benches were available, and Ursa slumped onto one.

Don't you dare weep like a miserable child.

Ursa slowed her breathing, drawing air in to fill her lungs and then releasing it. She wrapped her arms around her stomach and leaned forward, until she regained her calm. When she straightened, she realized that she was in a part of the section where people of wealth lived. It wasn't difficult to tell. The décor was ostentatious. Her people normally shunned such displays, yet some flaunted their wealth to assert superiority over lesser fey. Although any ljósálfar were likely to turn up their noses.

Displeased by the tasteless display, Ursa left. Nightfall held no appeal; the city's late hours did not entice her. Besides, Lucea was likely worried sick. And of course, Ursa owed the lovely chronomancer an apology.

Ursa's jaw dropped in astonishment at the distance she'd covered. She reached an area called Castleford, inhabited by humans. The residences, while unpretentious, were well-maintained, as evidenced by the manicured lawns and freshly painted façades.

Tree-lined avenues crisscrossed the neighborhood, their branches meeting overhead to form a natural canopy that provided shade and privacy. Ursa noticed how the air here was tinged with the scent of blooming flowers and cut grass, a stark contrast to the earthy aroma of her beloved Underneath. There was a sense of tranquility that pervaded the area, akin to the serene semi-darkness she remembered from her underground home.

As she wandered further, Ursa couldn't help but admire the way they had shaped their environment, creating a haven of beauty and comfort. Despite that, she yearned for her kin and their distinct culture.

Had she gotten turned around? Ursa knew the runes on her hand were pulsing again when she began rubbing. Call it instinct or some supernatural force that guided her further into the human enclave. Of course, she received very furtive glances and expressions of disapproval or confusion. At one point she heard someone whisper, "Doesn't she know where she is?"

Despite all of that, Ursa kept walking.

Somewhere beyond the derisive looks and whispers, Ursa found herself walking down a tree-lined trail, lit by tall lamps of wizard light. Ursa knew people used imprisoned wil-o'-wisps to do so. She smiled at the notion that some poor human laborer would have had a time replacing shattered lamps.

An opening in the trees before her revealed a clearing. Her stride quickened, although she didn't know why. Ursa urgently needed that open space, seeking something crucial.

What she saw spread out before her was a well-tended graveyard.

Obviously this place was meant for humans, considering the fey either cremated their dead or, if of a particular race, the being would be consumed by their own magic upon death. Ursa saw this once with an ancient fairy emissary. People rumored him to be several thousand years old. During this process, their aura became visible and continued to brighten, emitting various rainbow colors until it disappeared, leaving nothing behind.

Humans, however, built monuments using stone, granite, and marble. Unless you were a laborer who could only afford modest tombstones or simple crosses to mark their graves, assuming they were permitted burial there. As dusk fell, Ursa pressed on; her path led her through the cemetery. Ahead of her stood an enormous mausoleum.

The architect had designed the structure like a small castle, featuring four turrets at each corner of a steep roof. Two circular columns adorned with what appeared to be an offshoot of the Celestial Vine were also present. The front had two barred windows with darkened glass. The access point was a solid wooden door, fortified by iron bands and rivets, and further secured by a locked iron gate. Even in the dim light, the description was visible:

SPRIGGINS
HERE HE LIES

Ursa lifted her arm to stare at the runes, which were glowing so brightly they made her skin burn. "So, this is what you wanted me to find," Ursa said aloud. "What do you expect me to do? I can't touch the iron."

The glow of Iron Reaver accompanied the light from the runes. Without hesitation, Ursa grasped the weapon. Could this succeed? She would soon discover as the words formed on her lips. *Forgeheart*. She lifted the hammer and brought it down on the iron lock.

CHAPTER TWENTY-TWO

The lock shattered in a rain of sparks.

The intense heat separated the metal, melting it into searing hot blobs that dripped to the ground. Ursa pushed the gate open with her foot. Well, that was one problem solved. She didn't want to further damage the scared place any further.

Ursa sheathed Iron Reaver and slipped off her jacket. She wrapped it around the door handle, noticing the worn and rusty sections. If even a tiny flake of iron touched her skin, she wouldn't have to worry about the beasts behind the veils, the Rot, or anything else anymore.

The unlocked inner door surprised her. As she pulled it open, the hinges creaked, echoing through the silent chamber. A damp, musty smell wafted out, carrying with it the stench of decay and neglect. The air was thick, making it hard to breathe. She wrinkled her nose and sneezed, the sound startling in the oppressive quiet. Flickering lights sparsely illuminated the chamber, throwing eerie shadows. Dust motes danced in the air, disturbed by her presence. Each step she took echoed off the stone walls, amplifying the sense of isolation and unease.

A diminishing light streamed down from a stained-glass window in the ceiling that appeared to depict the flying island of the giants. Because she had never seen it before, Ursa could only assume.

A narrow corridor led to the chamber where the dead lay, its floor littered with withering reeds that whispered underfoot. Six iron sconces clung to the walls, each holding a torch that guttered low; Ursa hoped the caretaker would not come to check them. Two benches flanked the room. Rectangular plaques lined the walls in neat rows, each one marking the burial place of six family members; beneath every plaque a slim shelf held small, cherished mementos and knickknacks. Tokens of lives now quiet. It might have been morbid curiosity that made her read a few of the inscriptions.

PLEASANCE SPRIGGINS-UNDERHILL
BORN 1000 – DIED 1080
AGE 80

TOBIAS UNDERHILL
BORN 990 – DIED 1060
AGE 70

TEDRIC RAYNSFORD
BORN 1011 – DIED 1078
AGE 67

MATHILDE UNDERHILL-RAYNSFORD
BORN 1011 – DIED 1096
AGE 85

CORNELIA RAYNSFORD-BETTS
BORN 1027 – DIED 1114
AGE 87

ALDEAN BETTS
BORN 1031 – DIED 1112
AGE 81

GODFREY RAYNSFORD
BORN 1027 – DIED 1116
AGE 89

The family was long-lived for humans. "I could never imagine dying alone." Ursa spoke aloud while noting Godfrey's wife was absent from the list. Of course, she had expected just that to happen to her. Until…

"Rest well, Godfrey Raynsford." Another thought occurred. Tobias was Pleasance's second husband. What had happened to her first?

She'd been so angry at the palace that she only heard part of the story. Yes, now she recalled. The Farm Boy's father was the true ruler of Brobdingnag, and a giant had stolen his throne. Or at least according to the Farm Boy's descendants, which if she also recalled, made no sense and left unanswered questions.

Ursa entered the adjacent room, where lamps hung from the ceiling, casting a warm, ethereal glow with wizard light. The magical illumination danced on the ancient stone walls, creating shadows that seemed to come alive. She spotted a large, ornate plaque on the wall, carved with the family name. The plaque, framed with gilded edges, bore an air of solemn reverence, telling tales of generations past.

Etched on its face were two sets of dates:

BORN 1017 - DIED 1170
BORN 1015 - DIED 1103

Ursa scrutinized the first set. After some quick mental math, she thought, *Impossible!* Such longevity defies human possibility. Only fey had such extended lifespans. Was it a mistake? The Farm Boy's behavior was purely human.

Ursa went back to her examination. Two granite sarcophagi, finely carved with images of the deceased, occupied the room's center. Almost as if in a trance, Ursa approached them and traced her finger over one.

Shelves lined the walls. Tiny figurines, toys, jewels, and gold. Dusty old tomes shared the space. Ursa was loath to touch those in case they were fragile. Underneath the family plaque, placed on a low shelf, were four urns of solid gold, each adorned with a different type of gem. Ursa examined the metal urn labels.

PLEASANCE
HONOR
FORTUNE
COMFORT

The children. Ursa guessed Pleasance was the oldest. Opals adorned her urn, garnets for Honor, pearls for Fortune, and jade for Comfort. She saw the murals on each wall, which depicted the Farm Boy's journey. The artwork, despite its clear antiquity, kept vibrant colors and seemed animated, giving the appearance of movement. Ursa was startled by a wall-mounted weapon. The Woodsman's Axe.

The magical double-edged weapon gleamed, razor-sharp blades shimmering with a faint, otherworldly glow. The sturdy leather wrapped around the handle provided a secure grip. Ancient runes, like those of Iron Reaver, pulsed with mystical energy along the blades.

People knew this legendary instrument for its role in destroying the Celestial Vine. The story of the Farm Boy's acquisition of the axe stayed a mystery. It belonged to an unidentified Woodsman who wielded it to rescue a young woman from a witch intending to transform her into a lycanthrope and make her a slave. Despite killing the witch, the Woodsman had to kill the young woman before the full moon. Although killing a lycanthrope freed the victim's soul, it was still an arduous task.

Other tales recounted his defiance against an evil sorceress-queen who commanded him to kill her princess. Instead, he allowed the princess to escape and killed the sorceress-queen. After that, the Woodsman disappeared. He reportedly aided global travelers.

With such a formidable weapon, I would be invincible.

Ursa couldn't help but look down to where Iron Reaver rested on her hip. Despite denying her ancestors' wishes, she was proud to be heir to such an impressive weapon. Ursa resumed her scrutiny. A long, wooden cabinet with sixteen doors occupied the far side. Fortunately, someone had made the tiny handles of gold. Ursa pulled one open and frowned. Stacked rectangular packages in paper wrappings filled the space. Ursa removed the paper only to find a clay brick. The brick, Ursa guessed, was used to preserve something important. She knew what they were for, but she wasn't about to crack it open to verify her suspicions. Ursa re-wrapped it, put it back and closed the cupboard door.

Where are those damnable things? The second cupboard contained wrapped gold coins; the third, silver. The fourth had boxes containing smooth fire opals, the next sapphires, then black pearls, so rare that they took years to cultivate. It went on like that. Each cupboard hid a well-kept, priceless gem or metal. The story had always said the Farm Boy had brought riches from the giant's lair. The only thing missing was the renowned magic harp, which was said to have abilities such as stopping wars, promoting crop growth, and influencing weather patterns through its singing.

"That could prove useful in battling the Rot," Ursa mumbled as she remained focused on her quest.

When the last drawer yielded nothing but stacks of wax-sealed scrolls, Ursa straightened, stretching the kinks out as her gaze fell on the sarcophagi. "Damn it to the nether-hells." It appeared this would be her second time robbing a grave. This made her wonder why no one else had cleaned out the tomb. Maybe the Farm Boy commanded such reverence; it felt unthinkable to disrespect him.

Ursa examined the first sarcophagus, sliding a finger beneath the stone lid for leverage, but it would only budge a hair. When the carved runes at her touch flared with a faint light, a memory of the old unlocking spell surfaced. An incantation she had learned long ago. She traced the pattern with her fingertip and whispered the words; the runes pulsed in answer, the seal grinding loose.

"Yes," she murmured, then pressed and heaved. The lid shifted and, with a powerful strain, Ursa lifted it.

She didn't know what to expect once she peered inside. She'd seen corpses in various stages of decomposition, but this one was well-preserved.

"So, there you lie, old man."

Jack Spriggins' remains had reached their mummified state, the skin devoid of moisture, with the expected leathery, gray appearance. The sarcophagus – a cold, stone enclosure – had collected layers of dust and ancient grime over the centuries. Inside, his eyeless stare unnerved. His skin, pulled back to expose the remains of jagged teeth, gave a ghastly grin. Strips of cloth, what remained of a shirt and trousers, had long since fallen apart. Instead, thick strands of cobwebs draped over his form, creating a natural shroud.

The dim light illuminated the eerie sight of Jack's hands folded across his chest. Clutched in his grasp was an ornate metal box; its intricate designs had not worn down over the passage of time. The box seemed to glow, a stark contrast to the decayed remnants of the one called the Farm Boy, as if it held secrets of its own.

"Please forgive me." Ursa reached for the skeletal hands and worked them apart, prying the fingers until the box came free. A tiny padlock hung at its clasp – clearly the work of talented artisans – but it was no match for Ursa. She snapped the hasp and tossed the broken lock aside. Ursa paused, hand on the lid, weighing the condition of the remains – whether they were fragile or preserved by fey magic – and the thought of their fairy heritage made her hope the contents would be intact. Satisfied, she lifted the lid.

Four beans rested in a red velvet bed. Ursa wasn't certain what she'd expected. Some unusual coloring or shape? Shining with the force of fairy magic? No, they looked like ordinary beans.

"Well, this is disappointing." Ursa closed the lid and set the box on the floor. Then, using her might once again, she lowered the granite slab down onto the sarcophagus, sealing Jack Spriggins in again to continue his rest.

"Thank you." Ursa inclined her head. She didn't know why, but she had the sense that she should show respect.

Ursa retrieved the box and walked toward the exit, feeling relieved that she had finished her task. However, as she approached the door to the other room, she gasped in shock. She was no longer alone.

"Lucea?"

She opened her mouth as though to speak; a hand reached out. But as Ursa took a step forward, a sudden excruciating pain like daggers plunged into her and halted her. Ursa threw her head back and a scream exploded from her chest. She could feel her blood flowing down her arms and hands as it dripped crimson off her fingers.

"Ursa!" Lucea screamed. She moved toward her, but the way Ursa saw it, she was coming from a great distance.

As Ursa's arms went up, thorns pushed up through her skin, horrifying her. Her gorge rose, then she collapsed into welcome darkness.

CHAPTER TWENTY-THREE

"I must follow her."

Lucea placed both palms flat on the table, pushed the chair back and stood all in one motion.

"Here." Farstride produced, it seemed from nothing, a bracelet crafted from interwoven sticks. "Her whereabouts will be clear to you."

"Thank you," Lucea said. She slipped the bracelet on, amazed by its smoothness.

"Take the side exit and come back the same way," Farstride said. "Two naga guards will escort you and show you how to return. Let them give you my stamp."

"I will." Lucea bowed before leaving.

The maze garden was a brief interest to her, her attention on finding Ursa. Two nagas guarded the gate, as Farstride said. They seemed pleasant enough, and she tried not to seem impatient as one of them stamped a tattoo on her hand. The bracelet heated around her wrist. Lucea saw a spark of light that traveled along the bracelet, moving around each curve until it returned to its point of origin.

Lucea's vision blurred and then sharpened with an eerie clarity as the light settled. She saw Ursa moving through the intricate pathways of the garden, yet she could still see the people around her. Two worlds, past and present, intertwined before her.

Ursa, confident and determined, seemed to float through the maze, her steps sure and purposeful. Around her, shadows of the gardens' past inhabitants flickered – ghostly figures dressed in ancient attire, going about their lives as if unaware of Lucea's watchful presence.

Lucea marveled at this newfound ability. She saw a laughing young woman, elegantly gowned, alongside a man wearing a floral crown. Nearby, a group of children played a game, their joyous cries ringing in her ears. Now and then, the scene would shift, revealing Ursa's precise location and the path she took.

As Lucea walked, her surroundings seemed to pulse with life. The naga guards reappeared; their forms seemed to blend with past sentinels who had protected this place. She sensed Ursa was drawing closer; her presence was growing stronger with each step.

The bracelet on Lucea's wrist pulled, guiding her like a beacon. With every action, she became more aware of the bracelet's inherent power.

She continued through the maze, her senses heightened, ready to face whatever lay ahead.

A bizarre sensation overcame her as she walked, seeing the past and present merge in a continuous film. Amidst the chaos, she missed Ursa several times. Lucea thought maybe this was time travel. She sensed the bracelet was draining her power. It took little, just enough to show Lucea where Ursa had traveled. Lucea had never used her power that way. Yes, she had, so she might refresh her body, but she'd never found a reason to go beyond healing herself and others.

Was it possible to classify this as time travel? With no mentors, necessity forced Lucea to learn about her Gift with minimal help. Leonine extensively searched Underneath for a chronomancer to tutor her, unsuccessfully. She consulted numerous books and scrolls on the topic. Those were especially lonely times for her. Lucea thought perhaps another chronomancer might be in Jack-In-Irons. She quickened her pace. Ursa's wraith was getting too far ahead of her. She wanted to find her and return to the palace to question Farstride.

She was losing focus again. She turned her attention back to Ursa, wondering whether her lover knew where she was going, or if the rune tattoo dictated her path. Lucea was walking through an avenue lined with opulent homes, where humans dwelled. Ursa turned off the main avenue and continued to walk down a narrow path until she came upon a cemetery. Ursa entered a huge mausoleum after forcing it open.

When Lucea noticed Ursa didn't exit, she was worried. Lucea placed her hand on the bracelet, to withdraw her Gift and return to the present world. This left her dizzy, and she collapsed near the cemetery gate. It took a few moments for her to recover.

Lucea stood on shaky legs as she took a few deep breaths and waited for her head to clear. Then she strode toward the imposing structure. The words carved into the stone took her aback.

SPRIGGINS
HERE HE LIES

"So, this is where you rest." Now the identity of the visitor and Ursa's purpose were clear.

Lucea cautiously handled the iron gate and noticed the cloak wrapped around the door handle. Lucea entered the first room. As curious as she was to examine the room, Lucea continued forward.

She encountered Ursa outside the second chamber.

Lucea's face brightened with relief. She didn't remember when she had been so happy to see another person. Lucea noticed Ursa held a small and bejeweled metal chest. Lucea stepped forward. "Ursa?"

"Lucea?"

The box slipped from Ursa's fingers as her back arched in spasms and her head fell back with a scream, which continued and echoed through the chamber.

Lucea screamed as well, shocked. Unable to act, she put her hands in her hair. Thorns pushed from underneath Ursa's skin. This horror propelled Lucea forward; she summoned her Gift, and the rune ribbons animated, encircling Ursa as time stilled. Now what? It was clear to her that Ursa was still in excruciating pain.

With steady hands, Lucea manipulated the threads of time. This was a complex task. Each instance of turning back time for rejuvenation required a significant amount of power. Healing someone demanded even more of her Gift. However, dealing with this trap, which was likely designed to activate if someone exited the burial chamber with the box, caused both reversing the clock and setting off the trap. The individual masterfully cast it. If they were nearby, as they must be, they were on their way. It would have been illogical to have set such a trap otherwise.

"I won't let you go, Ursa," she vowed. As the surrounding air shimmered and bent, moments rewound like an unraveling tapestry, each second bringing her beloved Ursa one step closer to the present. Reality warped, memories flickered; Lucea fiercely held on to hope, defying time's flow.

When Lucea severed the thread between past and present, Ursa fell toward her. Heart pounding, Lucea lunged forward, catching Ursa just in time. She dragged Ursa's limp body over the threshold and grasped the box, drawing it closer. Horror coursed through her veins when she saw the violent spasms racking Ursa's body.

Lucea crawled over and cradled Ursa's head in her lap. An overwhelming wave of dizziness hit her, threatening to pull her into oblivion.

"No, no, no!" she cried, panic shaking her. She couldn't afford to lose consciousness now. With the final spark of her Gift, she was about to revive Ursa when a booming command shattered the quiet. "What are you doing here?"

Lucea looked up abruptly to see an enormous giantess, whose height was at least nine feet, her head nearly touching the ceiling. The giantess stood like an enraged deity, muscles rippling beneath her skin, her hands planted on her hips. Adorned in a side-split tunic, her throat, wrists, and ankles gleamed with intricate jewelry. Fury radiated from her as she bellowed, "How dare you enter this sacred—"

"Shut *up*!" Lucea screamed, throwing out a hand. Threads of shimmering light snaked around the intruder, cocooning her in a ribbon of slow-moving time. The shimmering light made the giantess almost motionless, despite her struggle. Lucea's heart sank, realizing she had spent the last of her Gift on this momentary distraction. Her strength waned, her vision darkening as her Gift ignored her desperate pleas. She examined her hands, once smooth but now withered, bluish veins prominent beneath the fragile skin. How many years had slipped away this time?

With nothing left to give, she collapsed, falling over Ursa's trembling body as the oppressive darkness surged to engulf her.

★ ★ ★

As consciousness returned, the world around her shifted into a slow, surreal panorama. Firm arms cradled her; people carried her away from the cemetery. Through hazy vision, Lucea tried to see who her savior was.

"Ursa?" she whispered before darkness claimed her once more.

★ ★ ★

Whispers woke her.

Instead of opening her eyes, Lucea waited and listened. Her body lay on something soft.

"Keep an eye on them. We must understand their intentions before deciding their fate," the giantess spoke, calmer now than earlier.

"Yes, mistress. They are quite an odd pair, aren't they?"

"Perhaps."

"The small one. She grows young again. You said she has a special Gift?"

"I believe she is a chronomancer."

Relief filled Lucea. It hadn't taken as long for her youth to renew as before.

"Shall I prepare the binding charms, just in case?"

"Yes, but we don't want to alarm them if they wake."

Silence fell. "A human and a dokkalfar. Not too odd a pair for thieves."

Lucea bristled at being called a thief. She readily pictured Ursa's response. She waited as time passed.

"I have the charms ready."

Damn it to the nether-hells! As Lucea lay there, continuing to feign unconsciousness, the surrounding air carried the unmistakable scent of burning iron. The sharp, metallic odor filled her nostrils. An acrid tang stung her nose. She recognized the power that had brought such a horrible device to life. Necromancy. However, they called these charms soul catchers, regardless of their construction.

Lucea opened her eyes and forced herself upright, calling on her Gift. Her reserves weren't fully restored, but they were enough to repeat the mausoleum spell and slow time to a near standstill.

She found herself on a couch piled with pillows and, after a panicked moment, saw Ursa on a similar heap on the floor, too long for the second couch set catty-corner to hers. The room was plainly human. Moonlight cut through small leaded panes and laid a silver pattern across the worn boards, and a low hearth anchored the space with steady heat and a soft, amber light.

A stout oak table cluttered with a hand-carved figurine, scandal sheets, and a scatter of polished stones sat between the couches. Shelves crowded the walls with books, scrolls, and odd trinkets; a modest writing desk in the corner held parchment, inkpots, and a quill. Oil lamps added a muted glow, and the scent of burning wood mixed with dried lavender and rosemary.

Ursa looked whole enough, though Lucea still felt uncertain. Her stomach tightened when she noticed Iron Reaver was missing from its sheath. She knelt and shook Ursa's shoulder. "Ursa!"

Ursa's eyes snapped open, unfocused; as recognition hit, she swung with a balled fist. Lucea, ready for it, dodged and called again, "Ursa!"

"Lucea." Her words came out a dry croak. "Where in the nether-hells are we?"

"I don't know," Lucea said. "I recall you carrying me."

"Yes," Ursa said. "That woman – the giantess. When I woke, she was there. The spent magic permeated the air."

"That was me," Lucea said. "Do you remember what happened in the burial chamber?"

"Yes, somewhat." Ursa's brows creased. "I have a memory of – pain – it was agony. And thorns?"

"It was an egress snare," Lucea explained. "You're familiar with them?"

"Yes." Ursa pursed her lips into a thin line. "I didn't even consider—"

"Likely it is because you had the chest. Otherwise, entry to the chamber to pay respects was impossible for anyone."

"The chest! That damnable chest! I had it right in my hands!" Then she glanced down at her empty sheath. "And where is Iron Reaver?"

"Please, you must calm yourself." Lucea framed Ursa's face with her hands. "Tell me you're well."

Ursa's expression softened. She realized how upset Lucea was. "I'm fine, don't worry. You saved me, love."

Lucea's cheeks warmed at the word love. "Can you rise?"

Ursa sat up, and her eyes tracked to their motionless captors. "Did they tell you anything?"

"I had to act fast," Lucea said. "The girl was going to imprison us in iron charms."

"Well done," Ursa said.

They shared a brief embrace, and Lucea kissed her. "Now." Lucea stood once again, facing their captors. "I know you can hear me. I'm going to release the spell but not so much that you can attack us."

She nodded toward the second figure, a petite human girl who appeared no older than twelve. Her dark-brown hair was in two braids, and she wore the brown shirt and trousers of a servant. Her heart-shaped face kept a touch of baby fat. She possessed the Gift, but being human rather than fey, she handled the two plain collars of brass with flecks of dark gray. Methods approaching torture were needed to make the girl give them up.

"Collars?" Ursa asked from behind her.

"Have you heard of soul catchers?"

"Son of a whore," Ursa muttered. Her tone was a mixture of disgust and outrage.

"Why were we brought here?" Lucea was surprised that they hadn't given them to the authorities. She lessened the potency of the spell on the girl. Lucea understood she needed to work.

The girl blinked several times before responding. "You. Stole."

"Then your mistress is keeper of the mausoleum?"

"Yes."

"We weren't stealing anything. Praesidere Farstride sent us."

Lucea noticed the giantess struggling against the spell. "You, giantess. Have you something to say?" She drew back a bit of her power as with the girl.

"You. Are. Thieves! You. Lie. About. Why. You. Entered."

"To the nether-hells with you!" Ursa stepped forward to stand beside Lucea. "Where is my hammer?"

Maintaining the spell proved difficult. The giantess continued to struggle.

"Will. Not. Tell."

Lucea blew out an exasperated breath. She tugged at her bottom lip as she considered her next course of action.

Ursa spoke. "My friend is a chronomancer, as I'm sure you've realized. You can share the information we look for, or she will hurl your bodies through time until nothing remains of you but dust."

Lucea understood Ursa's intentions but disliked her tone. Yes, Lucea could kill them, her initial plan for the girl; however, this was cruel and inhumane. Such use of her Gift might cause Lucea to be dragged down a dark path.

"Cruel. To. Child?" the giantess responded to Ursa.

This was getting them nowhere. She glanced back at Ursa, mirroring her own acceptance. "Listen, we will talk but may we have your word you won't try to force us into those collars?"

The giantess said, "I. Will. Give. My. Word."

Lucea nodded once and released the girl. Lucea hadn't enjoyed holding one so young in that state. She turned and looked at the girl's mistress. "Please have her put those away."

"Put. Them. Away."

The girl quickly left the room. Lucea then released the giantess. Her anger flared, but she kept her promise and didn't attack them.

"Thank you, Mistress Giantess. Please forgive my insolence."

That seemed to placate her. The girl returned, although she wouldn't approach them. She looked fragile and scared, as though not wanting to get anywhere near the evil magic worker.

The giantess motioned to the couch where Ursa had lain. "Please sit." They did. "Rebecca, please fix coffee and snacks."

"Yes, mistress." Rebecca bobbed a quick curtsy and escaped into another room.

Lucea started without a preamble. "My name is Lucea of the Kingdom of Vale, Underneath." Lucea motioned to Ursa. "And this is my companion, Ursa." She would not give her any other information about Ursa without her permission.

"I am Tiriana Naefir."

"Thank you, Mistress Naefir."

"Now then," Naefir said, "you had better explain yourself. Although you entrapped me, I will warn you not to underestimate me again. I am not without power."

"I am certain." Lucea did not hesitate. "However, it will mean nothing if the Rot destroys all."

CHAPTER TWENTY-FOUR

Something delicate shattered.

"Rebecca!"

The girl, red-faced, entered. Her eyes downward, she wrung her hands. "I'm sorry, mistress. When I heard—"

Lucea was about to come to Rebecca's defense if the giantess punished her.

"Come here." Naefir reached out a hand and took Rebecca's. "It's all right. There is no need to be frightened."

"Thank you, mistress. I'll go clean up and prepare repast."

"Very good."

"She has reason to be afraid," Lucea said.

"Explain yourself."

"Would you return my companion's weapon first?"

"Fine," Naefir said. "We couldn't touch it anyway. The spirit's removal required Rebecca's summoning, yet the hammer responded. It told Rebecca not to touch it. There is another spirit attached to it?"

"If you would show me where it is," Ursa said, evading the question.

"Rebecca, would you show our guest where her weapon is?"

"Yes, mistress."

Ursa smiled at Lucea and then left with Rebecca.

"Your servant is a necromancer," Lucea commented.

"Yes," Naefir said. "Her parents cast her out when they discovered her Gift. I rescued her from the streets."

"That was kind of you," Lucea said. She avoided wondering what egocentric motives might have been behind her decision. Ursa returned, with the hammer on her hip. She sat down next to Lucea.

Rebecca reappeared, balancing a coffee pot, three cups, cream, sugar, and a small plate of chocolate scones on a tray. She arranged them on the coffee table. Rebecca served her mistress first, preparing her coffee how she preferred it, no doubt. Ursa laid a hand on Lucea's wrist, her expression questioning. Lucea shook her head.

"How would you like yours, miss?"

"None for me, thank you," Lucea said.

Confusion crossed Rebecca's face; then, Ursa also refused.

"Is the repast not to your liking?" Naefir asked. Her words were soft, but her face reflected a momentary irritation.

"I cannot consume many things as a cat shifter."

"Oh!" Naefir said. "Why didn't you say so? Rebecca?"

"Please don't go through any trouble," Lucea said, glad she didn't have to provide further explanation.

"It's no trouble at all, miss." Rebecca gave a quick bow and disappeared into the kitchen again.

"I am curious about that hammer of yours." Naefir addressed Ursa. "After what Rebecca told me."

Ursa shook her head. "I wasn't aware there was a spirit."

"If you like, when Rebecca returns, she may supply more information."

"We have more important matters," Ursa said. "I saw what was inside the chest."

"So you did," Naefir whispered.

"Then may we have the chest, please?" Lucea asked. "If you are still unsure, you can send a message to the praesidere estate."

Naefir appeared reluctant. When Rebecca entered the room, she said, "Rebecca, I need for you to summon a spirit to send a message."

"Yes, mistress." Rebecca set down a second tray. This time it had a tea set and sandwiches. The scent was familiar – peppermint. Rebecca left the room again.

"I believe these will be more to your taste and constitution." Naefir took one sandwich. "It is the meat of a shellfish from the Stormbringer Sea."

They chopped the shellfish into chunks and blended it with a creamy white sauce that was unfamiliar to Lucea, smooth and spiced. The crunch of chopped celery complemented the dish. "This is delicious! What is this sauce?"

"It's called mahonnaise."

"Yummy! May I have the recipe?"

"I purchase it from a local hearth witch who can place a protection on the container in case you want to take some upon your return," Naefir said. "I doubt she'll part with the recipe."

"I would love that." Lucea took another bite and held her hand over her mouth as she chewed. "Thank you."

"Mistress?" Rebecca returned. She shook and wrung her hands.

"Yes?"

"I – I'm having difficulties."

"What do you mean?"

"The veils are in turmoil." Fear filled her eyes. "A disquieting presence affects the inhabitants."

"Do you know what?"

"Damn it all." Ursa pushed off the sofa. "Naefir, are you aware that Farstride has exposed veils in the estate?"

"Yes. Everyone knows about those."

"And you find no cause for concern?" Ursa demanded.

"You aren't aware of Farstride's power."

Ursa clenched her fists, her jaw tightening with rage as fury blazed across her face. "No one is that powerful. Your leader is being ruled by her arrogance."

"Mistress!" she cried, the strength in her words belying her flushed face.

"Continue, Rebecca."

Lucea stood and took Ursa by her elbow and laid her head against her shoulder. Ursa relaxed a bit, but not enough to ease Lucea's worry.

"I caught a spirit who will carry a message for a price."

"Which is?"

"He wants us to find the man who murdered him and bring him to justice."

Naefir huffed in exasperation. "Tell him we accept, but there is no guarantee he will see justice."

"Yes, mistress."

"You appear accustomed to dealing with spirits," Lucea said.

"One would believe after death they would be more cooperative," Naefir replied. "Their impulsiveness and demands rival those of the living." She slumped back into her chair, clutching the armrests, and closed her eyes, as though dealing with all the troubles in the world. "Rebecca taught much of it to me. Our relationship is one of mutual learning."

"She is fortunate to have a mentor and friend like you," Lucea said.

"We are both fortunate."

When Rebecca returned, she said, "I sent the message."

"What do you see of the veils?"

"They are still very—"

A distant horn's call pierced the silence, growing louder and more urgent. Additional horns created a vibrant, pulsing, resonant cacophony.

"What is that?" Ursa asked.

"A warning," Naefir said. "People are being advised to return to their homes and businesses must provide temporary shelter."

"They expect the citizens to do that?" Ursa said.

"All citizens of our city have practiced the command of the horns."

"And what about visitors to your city?" Lucea crossed her arms.

"It's up to them to look for instruction. It shouldn't be too difficult."

"Do we know what the horns mean? Is the city under attack?"

"No," Naefir said as the horns continued their message. "It is a precaution."

"But there is something that bears investigating," Lucea said.

"The guards will see to it. I suppose the scandal sheets will be raving tomorrow."

"A better path to the truth exists, I hope," Ursa said.

"There are several in fact. By morning, we will know."

"And in the meantime?"

"I would recommend you stay here as our guests."

"Thank you," Lucea said.

"Rebecca, please prepare the guest room," Naefir said by way of response. "I hope you two are agreeable to sharing?"

"Of course," Ursa said. "When do you suppose that spirit will return?"

"It's impossible to say. It may not, if some creature beyond the veils catches it," Naefir said. "It will have to navigate them. The request stemmed from this."

"I can understand that," Ursa said.

"Now, I hate for food to go to waste, please finish your meal." Naefir stood and without another word exited the room.

* * *

"I don't like it." Ursa sat on the bed. It surpassed all earlier beds in size, consuming most of the room. Silk sheets and a down comforter provided luxurious comfort. A wardrobe and vanity also decorated the room. Rebecca had told them where the bathing room was and, being a near-perfect servant, she had prepared fresh basins of hot soapy water, washcloths and two sets of combs and brushes.

Rebecca took responsibility for their clothes, promising to have them clean by morning. She arranged two nightgowns on the bed, both of which belonged to the giantess; Ursa's, even after washing, proved too large. On Lucea, the hem dusted the floor, not to mention swallowing her arms and dipping down her front almost to the point of exposing her breasts. Ursa chuckled, readjusted her dress, and met Lucea's glare.

"What's to stop us from just tearing this house apart until we find that damn chest?" Ursa continued. "You can immobilize them both, can't you?"

Lucea sat at the vanity and brushed her hair. "Yes. But I won't."

Ursa snorted and climbed onto the bed. There was a single window there, with latches that pushed outward. Ursa opened them and peered out. A single lamp enabled Ursa to see the street below.

"See anything curious?"

Ursa mentioned several people lurked nearby. "This isn't typical for such a large city. I would wager the citizens are still nervous or downright afraid."

"Do you blame them?" Lucea said.

When Ursa didn't respond, Lucea turned to her. Sitting on the bed, the dokkalfar looked at Lucea with desire in her eyes.

"May I brush your hair?"

"Of course." Ursa approached, smiling. Lucea handed her the brush. Ursa lifted a section of Lucea's hair and smoothed it down.

"I want to apologize," Ursa said.

Lucea looked at Ursa's reflection. "For what?"

"Leaving like I did. I was wrong."

Lucea's heart melted at the simple, straightforward apology. "Ursa." Lucea stood and turned to her, encircling her shoulders with her arms. Lucea placed light kisses over Ursa's face. She eased Ursa onto the bed. Ursa needed no instructions. Having shed their borrowed nightdresses, they both relished the feel of their smooth, warm skin together. Play melded into lovemaking in a matter of moments.

★ ★ ★

They were coming. Lucea stood on the battlements, watching a wave of darkness crest the hill. Though not alone, an icy loneliness carried on the chill wind. People were all around her, but they appeared only as shadows and smoke, streaks of black and gray light flashing.

The ground split and broke apart, and from the dark earth, thorn vines appeared. They reached out, wrapping the oncoming hordes in a deadly embrace. Even from her distance, Lucea saw bursts of light travel down the thorn vines and into the ground as they drew from their prey.

From the vine-shrouded horde, a shadowy figure appeared. And she found its source. Their presence, although still far away, brought a foreboding message, which Lucea heard.

"I knew I would find you. You belong to me."

Words breathed against the back of her neck. With it came an awful familiarity. Everything around her shifted, and Lucea found herself wrapped in thorn vines. They wanted to take her identity, demanding she succumb to darkness. Lucea awoke, stifling a scream as she wrenched herself from the nightmare.

"Lucea?"

Startled by her name being unexpectedly spoken, Lucea instinctively struck out, but someone quickly grabbed her wrists.

"Lucea!"

Her breathing ragged, Lucea fought to calm herself. When she closed her eyes, she felt herself pulled back into the dream.

"Ursa!" Lucea cried. "Don't let me fall back asleep!"

"All right."

Lucea was thankful for Ursa's discretion. She pulled Lucea from the bed and walked her around the room. And at one point she poured the rest of the water into the washbasin and coaxed Lucea to splash some on her face.

Ursa led her back to the bed, where Lucea sat down. The lamp was lit soon afterward. Ursa walked over and sat beside her.

"What happened? What did you see?"

"It's – they – it's coming. The Rot. They have servants in their wake. I know who they are." Lucea swallowed, her throat raw. "Samara spoke to me. She said she's coming for me. But she wasn't alone. I sensed Barnabas. They are Amalgam."

CHAPTER TWENTY-FIVE

"Take her. Come with me."

Ursa mistrusted the giantess, but she figured she didn't have a choice. The memory of her raw agony enveloped her, as if her flesh were on fire. Ursa had fought her way back from the darkness to find Lucea's unconscious body draped over hers.

When Ursa saw her lover's face, her heart sank. Lucea's once vibrant features were now darkened and wrinkled, her hair gray and stringy like an old, tattered curtain. Her vibrant eyes now held only a faint spark. Ursa realized then that Lucea had overused her Gift.

And a woman – no, a giantess – stood between her and freedom with the fading remnants of what she guessed was Lucea's spell. Now freed, what did the giantess plan? Then, the giantess, body racked with pain, addressed them. Ursa gathered her remaining strength and lifted Lucea into her arms. Matching the giantess's long strides proved difficult for Ursa.

The giantess had to stop and wait several times for Ursa to catch up. The giantess guided them away from Ursa's former path, bypassing the human settlement. Ursa felt her strength waning. Before darkness fell, she remembered the giantess pausing in front of a modest home.

Now they were – guests? Despite their understanding of sorts, Ursa still didn't trust the giantess or her servant. Not after they'd tried to put those collars on them. As always, Ursa's primary concern was Lucea's safety.

When Lucea cried out as they lay in bed together, only Ursa's alertness enabled her to stop Lucea from pummeling her. Ursa didn't need to ask for an explanation. Something terrible had invaded her dreams, and when Lucea told Ursa the reason behind it, Ursa knew they had to leave.

A distant bell chiming five times clarified the time for her. The house shifted. Someone crept to their door, paused, then continued.

"Wait," Ursa said to Lucea. She approached the door and opened it a crack. Their clothes were lying there folded. "Well, look at this." Ursa grabbed the clothes and closed the door. "It appears Rebecca left us a gift."

They dressed and hurried down the stairs to the parlor.

Rebecca stood in the middle of the room, facing an apparition. He appeared to be a young man, floating a few inches above the floor, his whole body immersed in blue and golden fire. The strangest thing was that the apparition seemed out of phase with everything else, duplicating and showing fuzzy images of various colors. He inhabited multiple dimensions, each with a distinct shade and hue.

He was speaking. Ursa didn't understand his words, but Rebecca was nodding and responding, which Ursa was also unable to understand. She looked at Lucea. "Can you understand them?"

"This is the first time I've seen a true apparition," Lucea responded. "I am having a general impression of what they are saying. He is shifting through places outside of time and the nether-realms."

"Would you use your Gift to translate?"

"I don't know how and I'm afraid it may disrupt Rebecca's Gift."

Nevertheless, Ursa saw the eagerness in her eyes. When they had first met, Ursa recalled Lucea saying something to the effect that she was a scholar. Ursa was about to comment, perhaps when this is all over—

Ursa chose not to guess what Lucea really understood from the apparition's words.

Ursa hadn't noticed Naefir entering the room, but she was there, standing to Ursa's left. The spirit reached out a hand, and Rebecca grasped it. Lucea gasped. Rebecca was consumed by flames. That moment freed her spirit, which then vanished. Rebecca fell back in a faint, but Naefir was there to catch her. She carried Rebecca to the small couch.

"Is she all right?" Ursa asked.

"It takes time for her to regain her strength," Naefir replied.

"May I?" Lucea asked. Ursa knew what Lucea was about to do as she summoned her own Gift. Rebecca opened her eyes and sat up, confused.

"What – how am I—?"

"I returned what you lost," Lucea said. "I shifted time to give you back the strength you started with."

"Thank you," Rebecca said.

"Now," Naefir said, "what message did the spirit deliver?"

Rebecca turned to Lucea. "She knows." Her tone was not accusatory. Still, Ursa didn't appreciate the implication.

"What do you mean?" Ursa demanded.

"My nightmare," Lucea said.

"Impossible," Ursa objected. "How did the spirit manage to see—?"

"The veils." Lucea laid her hand on Ursa's shoulder. "Spirits can pass between them if they are strong enough. The veils construct dreams. The spirit's closeness implied its ability to see through."

"I demand an explanation!" Naefir said.

Lucea nodded at Rebecca, who took a deep breath before she spoke. As the tale unfolded, Naefir's face lost its color. She raised a trembling hand to her forehead; her steps faltered as she crossed the room. She sat down on the large couch, appearing burdened by the news she had received.

"Mistress?' Rebecca approached her. She kneeled at her feet and laid a hand on Naefir's knee. To Rebecca's shock, tears fell from beneath Naefir's hand. "Mistress!"

"I was home." Naefir began with measured pride, then faltered. "An instructor at a prestigious university. Until that damnable child severed me from my people."

Ursa hesitated, words eluding her grasp. She glanced at Lucea, whose face mirrored her own bewilderment.

Naefir steadied herself. She wiped away her tears, and the sorrow in her eyes transformed into a resolution. "Rebecca, please fetch the chest."

"Yes, mistress."

"Can you guarantee your success? That you can defeat this thing?"

"No." Ursa refused to make false promises. "If you wish to flee the city—"

"No." Naefir responded at the same moment that Rebecca returned, clutching the chest.

"Here you are, miss." Rebecca handed the chest to Ursa.

"Thank you." Ursa acknowledged her with a nod.

"This is my home," Naefir continued, "and if I have to fight for it, I will."

"We will need you very much," Ursa said. "Thank you, Lady Naefir."

"You are welcome," Naefir said. "Return to the royal house. Tell Praesidere Farstride that I will gather what remains of my people and we will fight."

"Naefir," Lucea said, "please excuse my curiosity, but you seem to have bitterness toward the Farm Boy. Why should you fight? What led you to guard his crypt?"

"Jack-In-Irons has become my home while I dwell Above Ground, until I may return to Brobdingnag," Naefir replied. "I will not lose faith that I will someday be home."

"You shouldn't," Lucea said. "Your faith, I know, sustains you. But I will say, I hope you do someday find your way home."

Naefir's expression softened in appreciation, and Ursa's pride in her chronomancer knew no bounds.

"Concerning your second question," Naefir continued, "that's a longer story. You must complete your mission. It will be dawn soon. You will go then."

"Thank you." Ursa inclined her head. Then she smiled. "Perhaps we will meet later on the battlefield."

Naefir returned the smile. "Perhaps."

Naefir's words lingered in the still air, her muted strength settling over them like a protective cloak. As dawn's first light filtered through the windows, painting the room in hues of gold and amber, Ursa and Lucea prepared to leave.

The streets were silent as they stepped outside; the world around them was caught in the fragile stillness of early morning. Ursa glanced back at Naefir's house, both a beacon of hope and a reminder of the weight of their mission. With a determined nod to Lucea, she began the journey back to the palace, the faint warmth of the rising sun urging them forward.

★ ★ ★

At the postern gate, two female nagas met Ursa and Lucea. They still had their stamps and presented them. The naga attendants escorted them into the same receiving room, their serpentine tails gliding across the floor. With a courteous bow, the attendants excused themselves and their scaled forms disappeared through the doorway. Moments later, a young human servant entered, her demeanor cheerful, carrying a tray laden with fresh coffee and pastries that caught the eye.

The pastries, called olykoeks, had a whimsical charm – fluffy and golden, their round shapes adorned with a glistening glaze that shimmered like morning dew. The puzzling hole in the center added to their intrigue, making them appear almost too perfect to eat. The servant, smiling, suggested dipping the olykoeks into the steaming coffee, as though she shared a cherished tradition.

Ursa had no choice but to try it; she reached for an olykoek and dipped it in the coffee. She took a tentative bite before succumbing to its sugary allure. Lucea followed suit, devouring the pastries with equal enthusiasm, her eyes closing as she savored the perfect harmony of sweet glaze and fluffy interior. The coffee added a warm, bitter contrast to the indulgent treat.

At Praesidere Farstride's arrival, the room's atmosphere changed. A faint ripple of energy, like the hush before a storm, heralded her arrival. She moved with a grace that defied explanation, her presence both commanding and otherworldly. The light from the windows dimmed as though bending to her will, casting her silhouette into sharp relief. She scrutinized both Ursa and Lucea, lingering on the pair as if amused by the comforts they indulged in.

"Welcome back to my home," Praesidere Farstride hummed, melodic and warm. "Delighted you're here."

Ursa licked the sticky glaze from her fingers, then reached for one of the cloth napkins with deliberate movements. "Thank you," she replied, her tone clipped but polite. "Though I must admit, despite our enjoyment of these confections, I can't say we are happy."

Ursa took the chest out of her pack and placed it on the table.

Farstride glided to her usual seat, her movements as fluid as the energy that seemed to hum around her. By a slight movement and a muttered spell, her tea instantly came into being, the steam coiling elaborately. Alongside it appeared a fresh batch of olykoeks, their tops covered with rich chocolate frosting. The aroma of cocoa mingled with the subtle spices of her tea. She crooked her finger as though telling the box to come hither, and it did, sliding across the table to her.

Farstride's expression was one of profound relief. Carefully, she opened the chest, and, despite her calm expression, she inhaled sharply. To Ursa's surprise, tears welled in the kobold's eyes. "Thank you."

"Tiriana Naefir sends her regards," Ursa said. "She wanted us to let you know she will gather her people to assist you in fighting against the coming darkness."

Farstride smiled. "I figured she would come and fight, despite everything."

"Now tell us," Lucea said, "what threatens the towering wall of Jack-In-Irons?"

Farstride took a deliberate sip of tea, her eyes shifting from the cup to the distant windows. "I needn't tell you."

"Perhaps you should," Ursa warned, her tone carrying steel beneath the calm.

At that, Farstride set her cup aside and lifted a hand. Almost imperceptibly at first, delicate tendrils of green stirred along the base of the table. With an air of practiced command, she extended her fingers, and the vines took heed – twining and curling in a graceful, deliberate dance. Their emerald ribbons stretched upward, coiling into a bowl-like structure right before their eyes. It was a serene, unreal transformation; the Vine yielded.

As the bowl formed, cool water rippled in, filling the vine-crafted cradle. Tiny glowing seeds – each a spark of pure magic – drifted on the surface, pulsing as they ascended. Their light played across the room, mingling with the subtle fragrance of jasmine and fresh earth that now filled the air. The seeds' glow sharpened into a vivid projection that spanned the expanse of the bowl.

Details emerged. The forest gave way to the open field, and a trail of exasperated figures materialized. Refugees, desperate and haggard, appeared from the forest's edge. Their forms blurred into hurried movement as they crossed the field toward the city walls. The dark shapes of an enemy army advanced relentlessly not far behind with precise coordination.

Ursa's face hardened as she studied the unfolding vision. "They're exposed out there," she murmured, as she absorbed every detail – the ragged cloaks, the trembling hands clutching tattered bundles, and the encroaching hostile forces closing in step by step.

Beside her, Lucea's eyes, calm and discerning, narrowed with mounting concern. "Farstride, can you adjust the focus? I must decide whether hope remains."

Farstride's brows knitted in concentration and beads of sweat gathered at her temples as she coaxed the magic to intensify. The glowing seeds danced faster, their light contracting and expanding until the projection zoomed in on a narrow stretch of the field. In that moment, Ursa glimpsed the advancing enemy – a disciplined, shadowy vanguard whose arrival promised little mercy.

The atmosphere in the room grew thick with tension. Ursa pushed back from the table, her warrior instincts igniting. An unmistakable perseverance pulsed in every heartbeat. "They must not reach the wall before we act," she declared, leaving no room for compromise.

The sound of the wind, far-off shouts, and Farstride's spells combined, making a musical sign that trouble was brewing. Their understanding became clear: what they did now would decide if the refugees survived and if the city was safe.

Refugees fled the forest toward city walls; the room held lingering echoes of the projection, the enemy watching nearby. Ursa's pulse quickened. She exchanged a final look with Lucea, and without waiting for another moment, she rose from her chair.

"We can't just stand here," she said, urgency sharpening every word. "These people need us – now."

Lucea's eyes burned with the muted intensity of someone born to negotiate the fate of others. "We must go, Ursa. Their safety is at stake. We'll deal with the Rot when the others arrive; for now, our duty is to help these frightened souls."

Before they could leave, Farstride's next words pierced the fading murmurs of magic. "No, you must stay! When the others come, we're to hold the line against the Rot. Leaving now risks our goals."

Ursa regarded Farstride and spoke in an unwavering but sympathetic manner. "Farstride, we cannot remain behind. Innocent civilians, your own, suffer amidst the turmoil. We know the risks – and we are ready to face them."

Lucea nodded, adding, "Protection sometimes demands sacrifice. We'll confront the Rot when it's our turn. These refugees need help immediately."

Prolonged silence filled the room, broken only by Farstride's magic humming softly. The vines that had just moments prior held the shimmering bowl of visions now lay still, as if holding their breath. Farstride's determination faltered, her sigh accompanied by a knowing, yet unwilling look. "Then go. I cannot stop you. But be cautious out there, take every measure to ensure your safe return."

Ursa and Lucea exchanged one last determined look before stepping away from the table. The lingering scent of jasmine mingled with the aroma of earth and impending rain as they moved to exit.

Beyond the palace walls, where the first light of dawn wrestled with lingering shadows, desperate refugees clustered together in fear while the enemy's steady march advanced on the horizon.

CHAPTER TWENTY-SIX

Lucea's heart pounded as she tightened her grip on the reins. The city wall loomed ahead, once a bastion of strength amidst the chaos. Now she wondered if it would be any defense against the onslaught. The refugees needed her, and she would not let them down.

The sight of Elduin Balric waiting with two horses surprised them.

"Ladies," he said, "these horses will do better in battle. I will meet you out there."

So Farstride's command had reached him, telling him Ursa and Lucea were there to fight.

"I won't let the Rot destroy us," Lucea vowed fiercely. Beside her, Ursa nodded, her own sense of purpose mirroring Lucea's. The horses snorted, sensing the urgency in their riders' movements.

With a swift motion, they mounted their steeds, and in an instant, they departed. The world blurred around them as they raced through the streets, the rhythmic thundering of hooves a testament to their unyielding spirit. The wind whipped against their faces, but their focus remained unbroken.

As they approached the city wall, Lucea noticed the frightened refugees huddling together, finding comfort in each other's presence. This intensified her determination.

We will protect them, Lucea reflected, urging her horse forward. They just kept coming, these people with nothing, hoping to find safety inside the city walls.

Ursa rode beside her, a silent pillar of strength, ready to fight alongside her in the coming battle. Together, they would be unstoppable. Together, they would lead the charge and defend their home against the encroaching darkness.

As they reached the wall, Lucea and Ursa slowed their horses. Their eyes met in silent understanding. The surrounding world buzzed with activity – the shouts of guards and the murmurs of refugees blending into an anxious hum. Lucea exhaled, her grip steady on the reins as she brought her horse to a halt. Ursa, astride her steed, nodded once, as commanding as the towering gates behind them.

A steward hurried forward and took the reins of both horses, his movements brisk but careful. "I'll attend to them," he said, gruff but respectful. Lucea slid from the saddle, her boots hitting the dry earth with a muted thud. She patted her horse's neck, whispering a quiet thank you. Beside her, Ursa dismounted with practiced ease, her tall frame radiating a calm authority. She handed the reins over to the steward without a word, her focus already shifting to the throng of refugees pressing close to the gates.

With the horses led away, Lucea stole a glance at Ursa. Her friend's eyes blazed with a strength that reassured Lucea even as the alarm bell's mournful toll echoed through the air.

The midday sun scorched down, its heat unyielding, yet Lucea's attention remained on the people near her – the fatigued, the fearful, the hurt. The city gates stood wide open, their sturdy iron seeming almost fragile in the face of the tide of humanity seeking refuge.

"Hello!" The booming voice caught their attention. The blue ogress they'd met at the inn came closer, her imposing form made larger by an overflowing bag across each shoulder.

The ogress offered Ursa and Lucea her hand after dropping the sacks. "Assistance?"

"Yes," Ursa responded, "and to fight."

"Well, I'll help here, but I'm no fighter."

Lucea found that difficult to accept. Ursa's doubtful look showed she agreed.

"I know, I know." The ogress grinned, sharp teeth flashing. "I'm a troubadour."

"That is a surprise!" Lucea said.

"If we get through this, maybe my troupe and I will entertain you." She nodded toward troops distributing bread to refugees. "Let me get you some satchels."

"Wait," Lucea said. "We haven't introduced ourselves. I'm Lucea, and you've met Ursa."

"You've got a set of pipes on you!" the ogress replied with a hearty laugh. "I'm Dazreal Ashfire. Call me Ash."

"Right then," Lucea said, managing a smile despite the tension.

"Wait right here," Ash instructed, striding away.

"She's quite an interesting person," Lucea remarked.

"I suppose." Ursa turned to her with a mischievous grin. "But you understand I'm yours."

"Of course!" Even with chaos erupting all around them, Ursa's words filled Lucea with joy.

Ash returned with two satchels filled with small crusty loaves, waterskins, and an assortment of other supplies, including clean cloths and small containers of milk. "Look for me when you run out," she said with a wink.

"We will, thank you," Lucea replied.

Lucea moved through the crowd with purpose, her satchel slung over one shoulder. She handed out pieces of bread, her movements steady. The lack of cups prompted people to drink out of their hands. Gentle words, warm and steady, eased the fear that had rooted them. "Here, eat," she whispered to the young boy clutching his mother's skirt. "Your health will improve soon." Her calm demeanor seemed to quiet the storm raging in their hearts.

For some time, Lucea remained engrossed in her task, failing to see Ursa. When Lucea saw her again, Ursa had completed her distribution of bread and water. Now she carried a crate filled with supplies, distributing blankets and bandages with the same quiet strength that Lucea so admired. Lucea saw Ursa kneel to aid a man with a leg injury, her broad hands gentle as she readjusted a makeshift splint.

A baby wailed somewhere in the crowd, and Lucea's heart clenched. Lucea saw the mother – a young woman whose pale face was grime-streaked. Without hesitation, Lucea knelt beside her and opened her satchel, retrieving a clean cloth and a small container of milk. "It's okay," she murmured, handing over the items, "you're not alone."

The refugees were a sea of faces, each carrying their own burdens, their own stories. Lucea moved among them, her steps determined, her words steady. "Stay close to one another," she urged. "We'll help you."

And then came the alarm, the deep, resonant clang of the bell, cutting through the heat and noise. Lucea froze for a moment, her breath catching. The alarm hushed the crowd, as if the air itself had been evacuated.

Lucea looked at Ursa and called, "We must get the rest of them inside the walls!" Her eyes scanned the horizon, where the initial sign of movement indicated the enemy's arrival.

She straightened, her heart pounding as she turned back to the refugees. "Follow us!" Despite her words being a command, the fear bubbled beneath the surface. Lucea knew that even the smallest crack in her composure might unravel the fragile thread of hope holding these people together.

With insistent but steady commands, Lucea and Ursa guided the remaining refugees behind the gates, helping them to avoid stumbling or trampling in the frantic rush.

The last few stragglers slipped through just as a flood of soldiers and militia surged past the gates, their movements swift and precise.

Lucea and Ursa followed close behind, quickening as the sound of the approaching enemy grew louder. The air was thick with tension. A sudden metallic clang reverberated through the air, sharp and final. Both women turned to see the iron portcullis slam down with a deafening crash. The gates groaned, their unseen mechanisms grinding, as they sealed the city with an almost ominous efficiency. The portcullis cut off the outside world, leaving only the defenders and encroaching darkness.

At the head of the line stood Captain Balric, his ljósálfar features sharp and commanding. He radiated authority, and the surrounding soldiers mirrored his strength and purpose. The soldiers arranged themselves in disciplined rows, interlinking shields to form a barrier, with archers positioned behind and magicians scattered throughout. Lucea and Ursa joined the line, their hearts pounding as they prepared for the inevitable clash.

From the forest's edge, the enemy emerged – writhing, pulsing lines of oily darkness that seemed almost alive. As it advanced, the darkness took grotesque shapes, their forms twisted and warped. They resembled humans, but their bodies bore the marks of mutation and decay, their movements unnatural and jerky. Lucea's stomach churned at the sight.

Balric's command rang out. "Archers, magicians, be at the ready!"

Lucea turned to Ursa, steady despite the fear clawing at her chest. "I'm going to join them."

Ursa's jaw tightened, her displeasure clear, but she nodded. Lucea felt sure she would accomplish more among the Gifted. She wove her way through the lines, her movements quick and determined, until she reached the forefront. Her breath caught when she spotted Rebecca among the magicians. Lucea opened her mouth to protest but hesitated, swallowing her words.

"Chronomancer!" Balric's call cut through the din. "Send them back to the nether-hell from which they came!" he commanded.

Lucea's determination grew as she nodded. Her ability allowed her to send them back so far in time that they would cease to exist – if her strength held. She focused. Her Gift surged within her as she prepared to act.

"Archers, fire!"

A flurry of movement followed Balric's order. A cloud of arrows soared through the air in a graceful yet deadly arc. Many struck true, felling some of the enemy, but others seemed impervious, pulling the arrows from their bodies or absorbing them into their hideous forms. The stench of decay and mire grew stronger as the enemy advanced, the rank odor causing some soldiers to retch. Lucea's heart ached for them, but she forced herself to focus on her task.

"Gifted!" Balric's call acted as a rallying cry.

Lucea summoned her Gift, homing in on the nearest creature. She undid its creation, removing the Rot's effect to show the person's true form. Those not succumbing to the Rot collapsed, their bodies limp and faint. Lucea's chest tightened with remorse, knowing they might still be alive but injured in the chaos. She pushed the guilt aside, her focus unwavering.

Rebecca's spirits filled the air, their ethereal forms darting through the battlefield. They possessed the enemy, forcing the darkness out with relentless precision. The air was heavy with their presence, a luminous mist against the growing shadows.

Lucea saw two groups of giants flanking her, their immense size a stark contrast to the surrounding turmoil. Somehow, they arrived despite the closed gates and portcullis. She didn't question it. Their arrival was of great help, and they threw themselves into the fray with unyielding force.

The enemy's numbers dwindled, but Lucea was relieved only for a short time. From the rear, something even larger rose – a towering figure that sent a chill down her spine. Recognition struck her like a blow. Her heart sank as the figure crossed the field with unnatural speed. It stood before her, its grotesque form shifting as two faces fought for dominance. Samara's emerged first, her grin twisted and lascivious, but Barnabas's grim countenance soon pushed it aside.

"Give yourself to the Enclave!" Barnabas proclaimed, the words ringing like an invocation.

A hand shot out, grasping Lucea's wrist with a vise-like grip. "To the nether-hells with you! She is mine!" Samara let out a snarl.

The two quarreled, their grotesque forms writhing as they fought. Lucea froze, her mind racing but her body unable to move. Samara reached for her again, so focused on Lucea that she missed what came.

Ursa rushed forward, Iron Reaver gleaming in the dim light. "Fey Bane!" she roared, bringing the weapon down with deadly precision. The Amalgam's head split into two, collapsing into an oily blob that crawled away.

"Get back here, you son of a whore!" Ursa shouted. She moved to pursue, but thorns erupted from the ground, halting her advance. Ursa cried out and stumbled, the sharp thorns tearing into her flesh.

"Ursa!" Lucea frantically rushed to her friend's side. Ursa spewed a string of expletives that would make a sailor blush, her frustration palpable even as she knelt, bleeding from several wounds.

"Oh, Ursa!" Lucea's tears spilled over, her emotions overwhelming her.

"I'm fine," Ursa said, steady despite the pain. "Don't worry, Lucea, love, this is nothing."

The enemy retreated, their movements calculated. Both women understood this signified no victory – merely a regrouping, a preparation for the next assault. The battle remained unfinished.

CHAPTER TWENTY-SEVEN

"We must destroy Amalgam."

Farstride tapped a clawed finger on the surface of the table. "It is not the true enemy."

"It will be difficult to complete our task if I have to watch out for them," Lucea responded.

"They will continue to harass her!" Ursa struck the table with her fist.

They were not in the comfortable room that Farstride had hosted them in earlier. Now, a genuine War Room surrounded them. Lucea and Ursa arrived first, and Balric soon joined them. Four others entered the room; three were unfamiliar to Lucea, called when she and Ursa recovered in their assigned quarters. Lucea had used the last of her power to reverse Ursa's wounds, and they helped each other off the battlefield, instructing anyone who came to assist to take care of others with graver injuries than Ursa's.

"Welcome," Farstride greeted them. "Please take your seats."

Lucea knew the lineage of the initial pair. The rest remained a mystery.

"You may be familiar with our two guests," Farstride nodded at Lucea and Ursa, "but I will introduce them. Lucea of Vale and her companion Ursa."

They exchanged greetings. Farstride went on. "You are familiar with Captain Balric. And this fine woman is Captain—"

"Iris Greenstone." Lucea smiled at the woman. "I would say it's a pleasure, but considering the circumstances—"

"Understood." Greenstone grinned, and her emerald eyes shone with a dim light. Her Gift was at its peak.

Farstride was about to continue when a sharp, persistent knock shattered the moment. The sound echoed through the room, jarring and relentless. Lucea's gaze went to Farstride, and for the first time, she glimpsed something other than calm composure. The faintest look of annoyance crossed her face. A crack in the serene façade that Lucea associated with her.

Farstride's fingers tightened around the edge of the table, and her eyes narrowed. The subtle change escaped no one as observant as Lucea. A tension, fleeting but palpable, filled the room, before Farstride straightened and allowed the mask of calm to slip back into place.

"Enter."

A naga soldier moved into the room, his posture rigid with formality. "I apologize, Madame Praesidere, a woman awaits with a message."

A voice outside roared, "Let me in!" The sound was raw and commanding. Lucea missed what followed, "I represent…" when Ursa's sharp intake of breath filled the unexpected silence. Ursa's composure shattered, replaced by a turbulent mix of guilt and fear.

Ursa extended her hand and seized Lucea's. Her hold was painful and shaking. It seemed to her that Ursa gripped her last lifeline in the rising tide.

"Ursa, what is it?" Lucea spoke softly but with conviction, and her heart was pounding.

Ursa didn't reply. Her lips parted, but no sound came out. Instead, her features tightened further. With a fragile tone, she whispered the words, barely audible over the hush, Ursa said, "I'm sorry."

Farstride spoke. "Allow her in."

"No!" Lucea cried.

The door burst open and an elder faun woman strode in, brushing past the naga without hesitation. Farstride was the first to experience her intense stare. "Are you the—?"

She froze mid-sentence, her eyes narrowing as her head turned. When she saw Ursa, her features twisted into pure hatred. "You!" She spat the word.

Before anyone could react, the faun moved with lightning speed, drawing a gleaming dagger as she leaped onto the table. She raised the blade high above her head, poised to strike.

The room erupted in chaos. Lucea's Gift flared in response, the magic coiling through the air like an iridescent ribbon. It caught the faun mid-leap, freezing her in place. The nagas surrounded the table, forming a shield on either side of Farstride. Balric extended his hand, and a brilliant flash of light enveloped the faun. The two spells intertwined, holding her captive in shimmering strands of power. Lucea's stomach tightened – too many spells might disrupt each other. She prayed the balance would hold.

"Get the praesidere away!" Balric ordered.

"No," Farstride countered.

"But Madame—"

"This woman wasn't after me," Farstride said. Her icy, unwavering gaze fell upon Ursa, who stood rooted to the spot, her trembling fists clenched tight. "Correct, Ursa?"

Ursa's lips moved. Lucea's chest tightened seeing her love appear so different from the strong, unyielding dokkalfar she was familiar with.

"Lady Lucea," Balric said, "I have her."

With a cautious motion, Lucea withdrew her spell and the ribbons of magic faded into the air. "Madame Praesidere," she said, "please excuse us."

Farstride inclined her head. "For now, but of course, we will need to discuss this. Take care of your Ursa."

Lucea turned to Ursa, whose hand still gripped hers with bruising intensity. She pulled, and Ursa rose without protest, as though in a trance. Her steps were mechanical, and her eyes distant, as if held captive by a memory from which she couldn't escape. When Ursa's eyes flicked back toward the faun, her expression dark with raw hatred, Lucea intervened, seizing her arm. "Don't."

A hidden side door appeared, and Lucea led Ursa through it. The path brought them to their chambers, as Lucea had suspected. She guided Ursa to the bed, coaxing her to sit and then lie down. She removed Ursa's boots. Her movements were deliberate and soothing, but Ursa's eyes remained unfocused, her features stiff with unspoken pain. Something haunting her had a connection with the faun.

Lucea pulled the cord in the ceiling that summoned attendants. Moments later, a young servant arrived, her eyes wide with concern. Lucea requested tea kindly but firmly. The girl returned with a silver tray holding a teapot and two delicate cups. Lucea recognized the medicinal scent. She murmured her thanks, brought the tray to the bedside and set it down.

Lucea uttered, "Ursa," her tone quiet but persistent.

Ursa didn't respond. "Here, sit up," Lucea coaxed. "Drink this."

Ursa obeyed, cradling the cup in trembling fingers. Lucea placed her hand over Ursa's, steadying the dokkalfar as she took tentative sips. "Careful, it's hot."

To Lucea's surprise, tears slid down Ursa's cheeks, pooling at her chin. Lucea choked out, "Ursa." She guided Ursa's hands, helping her take sip after sip until the cup was empty. Then she laid Ursa back down. Sleep claimed Ursa almost instantly, though her expression remained haunted even in rest.

A soft knocking at the door stirred Lucea from her thoughts. Annoyance flickered, but she answered it. Iris stood there, her eyes filled with concern.

"I won't stay long," Iris said. "I just want to know how she is."

"I gave her medicinal tea," Lucea replied. "She's asleep now."

"They've detained the faun. Do you recognize her?"

"No," Lucea said. "But I intend to find out who in the nether-hells she is and why she tried to kill Ursa."

"It may not be easy. She's refusing to speak to anyone but Farstride, and Balric isn't allowing that," Iris explained.

Lucea didn't blame the captain. "I'm sure I can persuade her to divulge the necessary information."

Iris hesitated, then nodded. "I'll take you to her. In the meantime, I'll have a guard placed at the door."

"Thank you," Lucea said. She had always promised herself she would never abuse her power, but this was different. This surpassed a crisis; this was Ursa. Vine-be-damned, Lucea would have answers.

★ ★ ★

Iris led the way, her steps brisk yet muted, the echo of her boots a faint rhythm against the cold stone floors. The halls they passed through were lit by flickering wall sconces, their shadows stretching long across the ancient masonry. Lucea followed, her heart pounding with anticipation as the narrow corridors twisted and turned, each intersection appearing more labyrinthine than the last.

At the far end of the last corridor, a stairway dropped into shadow, its worn edges a record of centuries. Iris glanced back at Lucea – solemn, steady – then began the careful descent. The air cooled with every step, carrying the dry tang of stone and the faint sweetness of old wine. At the bottom, an iron-banded door, scarred and darkened by time, blocked the way; Iris rested her palm on the rough wood, then pushed it open to the room below.

The cellar was lit by a single oil lantern swinging from a rusted hook in the low beams, its light pooling in the center and leaving the corners in deep relief. The stone walls bore the marks of hand tools and age; the air smelled of damp rock, wine, and a whisper of dried herbs.

One wall was taken up by racks of bottles, glass catching the lantern's gleam, each cork sealed with wax and labeled in a looping, faded hand. Opposite neat stacks of burlap sacks and wooden crates held dried fruit, grains, salted meat, and tied bundles of herbs, their earthy scent sharpening the room's character.

A heavy wooden table stood at the heart of the space, its surface nicked and stained from long use; a squat chair sat uneven on the cracked flagstones. Nearby a thin cot with a single woolen blanket and a clay pitcher with a tin cup on the floor were the only nods to comfort in an otherwise practical storehouse.

The faun sat at the table, her presence an uneasy contrast to the quiet stillness of the room. Her hands were bound with glowing rope, enchanted, its light casting eerie shadows on her weathered face. The sharp scent of magic lingered in the air. She sat, watching the lone guard at the doorway and the staircase that climbed to a thick, reinforced door – the only barrier between her and freedom.

The room appeared small, mixing old stone, confined space, and stored supplies, giving it a claustrophobic atmosphere. Yet the faint flicker of the lantern and the rich scent of wine provided an odd, almost deceptive sense of warmth and history – a stark juxtaposition to the tension crackling in the air.

The guard snapped to attention as Iris and Lucea entered the room, the echo of his boots sharp against the cold stone floor. Iris waved him off with a dismissive gesture. "As you were. We need time with the prisoner. Have you had supper yet? Tell the cook I sent you."

The guard paused momentarily before acknowledging the request and exiting; his leaving created a silence in the room. As the door clicked shut, Iris turned to Lucea and motioned toward the table where the faun sat, her presence radiating defiance.

"Look at me," Lucea commanded.

The faun looked at her. Eyes ablaze with raw, unyielding hatred. Not merely emotion, but a tangible, hostile force crackled around her.

"Why did you try to kill Ursa?" Lucea demanded.

The faun's response came in a language foreign to Lucea, its lilting syllables harsh and biting. Despite Lucea's inability to understand the words, their sharp intent resonated with an unmistakable menace.

"I know you speak common," Lucea countered. "Answer me!"

The faun spoke again; her words were unfamiliar but laden with venom. They cut through the room, a blade of sound that resonated with tension. Lucea held her ground, refusing to let the faun's defiance unnerve her. She rounded the table and lowered herself into the seat opposite her.

"Could you at least tell me your name?" Lucea asked with frustration.

The faun lifted her chin, silent and unyielding, her expression daring Lucea to press further.

"You said you needed to see the praesidere," Lucea fought for calm. "Perhaps we can arrange that, if you answer my question."

Still, the faun refused to speak, her defiance unwavering. Lucea exhaled, her frustration mounting. "Very well," she said, turning to Iris. "Would you excuse us for a few moments?"

Iris hesitated, her brow furrowing with uncertainty, but after a moment's pause, she nodded and stepped out, closing the door behind her. Alone now, the tension between Lucea and the faun thickened.

Lucea closed her eyes, a silent prayer for forgiveness echoing through her thoughts as she summoned her Gift. The ribbons of light coiled around her, glowing as runes formed. But there was a wrongness to the magic – an aching nausea that clawed at Lucea's chest and twisted her stomach. Yet she pushed forward, determined.

"What – what are you doing?" the faun stammered with a rare tremor of fear.

Despite the faun's inability to see the changes overtaking her body, she felt the effects of Lucea's spell. As her strength waned, her speech faltered and her breathing grew uneven. Wrinkles etched themselves onto her face, her once-sturdy hands becoming frail and emaciated.

"Stop! What are you doing to me?"

Lucea halted, not out of mercy, but because her own body betrayed her. A wave of nausea surged, followed by a sharp, pulsing pain in her head. Clutching the edge of the table for support, she fought to steady herself.

"How dare you assault me!" The faun's breath hitched with fury, the tremor in her words unmistakable.

"How dare I?" Lucea shot back. "I'll discover why you tried to kill Ursa. If you don't want me to age you into dust, then answer my damn question!"

The faun's lips curled into a humorless smile as she regarded Lucea with bitter disdain. "How long have you known Ursa?"

"Answer my question!"

The faun's laughter was devoid of warmth. "You don't know her at all, do you?"

"I suppose it's safe to assume you are someone from her past?" Lucea countered.

The faun sneered, her eyes gleaming with derision. "Which I'll wager she's told you nothing about."

"She told me everything."

The statement hit its mark. Her eyes widened, surprise breaking through her veil of hatred. "Well, that is unexpected," she admitted, clearly intrigued.

"Well?" Lucea pressed.

"I will only speak with Farstride."

"You'll speak to me first," Lucea retorted.

"And who in the nether-hells are you?" the faun shot back. "If Ursa revealed everything, then you should understand."

"From what I understand," Lucea said steadily, "her mother exiled her. Are you saying someone intended to assassinate her?"

"How ignorant are you?" the faun sneered. She tried to rise from her seat, but the spell on her binds held her firm. "Ursa gave up her life by returning to the Riven Isles! It is my right—"

"How ignorant are *you*?" Lucea countered. "You're aware that your queen has no power outside of her kingdom. What you were about to do amounted to cold-blooded murder."

"She deserved it!" the faun snarled, tears welling in her eyes as she mumbled, "Why wasn't she able to—" The words faded, choked by the intense emotion welling inside her.

"Who are you?" Lucea softened her tone.

The faun hesitated before speaking. "Tantia." She scrubbed the tears from her face, her expression hardening once more. "It no longer matters. I am here by request of my queen."

Another question lingered on Lucea's lips, but she bit it back. Taking a steady breath, she met the faun's gaze. "You're right, my behavior toward you was unjustified. Please forgive me." Lucea hesitated, overcome by remorse. "I'll see what I can do about arranging for you to meet the queen."

The weight of shame settled on Lucea's shoulders as she pushed her chair back and stood. She left quickly, her decisive steps belying a breaking heart.

CHAPTER TWENTY-EIGHT

In a surreal and haunting nightmare, Ursa wielded Iron Reaver to drive spikes into unyielding stones. Each strike ignited a shower of sparks, resonating throughout her being and intensifying the loss and guilt that troubled her. As she labored, memories of her exile resurfaced, tormenting her with the consequences of her actions.

She swung until her arms trembled and the iron would not yield. The spike bit the stone and held, stubborn as guilt, and every failed blow sent a fresh wave of shame through her chest.

Heat licked at her face. The ground split with a deafening crack; molten light gaped like a wound and sulfur choked the air. For a heartbeat the pit's heat was real on her skin, and she tasted ash. Then the world folded back on itself, and the hammer was only a memory of weight in her hands – still heavy, still accusing.

★ ★ ★

They hauled her from the hearth like a thing to be discarded. Rough hands tore at her sleeves and shoved her into the mud; the council's livery flashed in the dim light as they laughed and joked about warm beds and hot drinks, as if she were already a story they'd finished telling.

Ropes bit into the soft skin of her wrists, cords cutting bright crescents that flared with every struggle. Her breath came ragged and sharp, each inhale tasting of damp wood and old smoke. The men's boots thudded against the path, a steady, indifferent drum that matched the pounding in her temples. When one of them spat the word exile, it landed like a stone and stayed there, heavy and final. They shoved her forward to the border and left her face-down in the loam, the world narrowing to the scrape of dirt against her cheek and the echo of footsteps receding.

Shame arrived as a physical thing – hot and crawling under her skin. She tried to rise and found her limbs slow and uncooperative, as if the mud itself wanted to keep her. The silence that followed their departure was not empty; it was a verdict, deliberate and absolute.

★ ★ ★

Tantia stood at the edge of the clearing, older now, silver threading through her fur. The lines at the corners of her eyes deepened the steadiness there, as if time had carved patience into her face. She wore the comforts Ursa had lost: a cloak that smelled faintly of cedar and warm hearth smoke, the quiet ease of someone who had never been forced to count the hours by hunger.

Ursa remembered the promise. Tantia's hand had been warm on her shoulder, the grip of someone who meant to stay. I trust you to always be by my side, Ursa had said. Of course, Tantia had replied, and the words had settled into Ursa like a vow.

In the nightmare the memory curdled. The same steady eyes became an accusation – calm, unblinking, as if the promise had been a bargain she'd broken. Small details that once comforted now cut like a dagger. The way Tantia's laugh had softened into polite conversation, the way she accepted hospitality without looking back. Those gestures stacked into a ledger of absence. Ursa could see Tantia in the warmth of the home Ursa had been forced from, and the sight sharpened the ache until it felt like the spike itself.

Betrayal arrived not as a single blow, but as a slow, accumulating cold. The promise remained a bright, impossible thing. The world had rearranged itself to prove the promise meaningless. The contrast between Tantia's steady presence and Ursa's sudden exile made the wound feel deliberate.

★ ★ ★

She crawled through a narrow tunnel and found a wooden door. Hope flared; she knocked with trembling fingers and rasped a plea. The door creaked open a crack and a shadow filled the gap – a figure half-hidden in gloom, a single cold eye fixed on her.

"Who are you?" the voice demanded, harsh and small.

"My name is Ursa," she said, voice raw. "I am… exiled. I need sanctuary."

"Princess Ursa?" the man interrupted, disdain curling his tone.

She flinched. "No more. They cast me out— no food, no water—"

He slammed the door before she finished. She pounded until her knuckles bled. "Please! I just need food and water!" Silence answered, thick and indifferent.

An elderly brownie later told her the truth: her mother had sent the decree through the Vine. The throne had made her disgrace public. No shelter, no aid – every denizen of Underneath had been warned away. Greater and lesser fey alike turned their backs to avoid offending the crown. Alone, she learned what exile meant in practice.

★ ★ ★

She stopped fighting, her strength sapped, and stumbled upon an exit to Above Ground. The narrow tunnel before her, slick with mud and stinking of decay, permeated the air with the smell of rotting wood with every breath she took. She dropped to her hands and knees, dragging herself forward as the walls closed in around her. Insects skittered across her arms and legs, their sharp bites raising angry welts on her once unblemished skin. She grimaced but didn't swat them away. She had no more will to resist.

When she emerged into the sunlight, she squinted, taking in the sparse copse of trees that surrounded her like silent witnesses. Nearby, a tiny stream glimmered, beckoning her with the promise of relief. At the water's edge, she plunged her hands into the cool water, splashing it over her skin to rid herself of the clinging insects. As she tumbled, her body ended up partially in the water, her face against the muddy bank. She remained still, barely breathing, with a vacant stare. The world she knew vanished.

* * *

The hammer crashed down, the spike biting deep into the stone. A deafening crack split the air as the ground ruptured beneath her, and shards of rock detonated outward in a glittering spray. A jagged maw opened – a churning inferno of molten rock that hurled waves of heat across her skin. Sulfur stung her throat, each ragged breath tasting of ash and acid. Before she could steady her grip, a violent wrench yanked the hammer free; she lost her footing and, with a raw, piercing scream, pitched forward as the fiery abyss lunged up to meet her.

* * *

Ursa awakened with a sharp intake of breath. Sweat clung to her skin, soaking through her shirt, and her heart pounded against her ribs like a war drum. The remnants of the nightmare, filled with pain, rejection, and isolation, churned within her, a relentless storm.

She sat frozen for a moment, her gaze fixed on the surrounding room. Despite its size and opulent furnishing, it was suffocating, walls closing in as her anguish clawed at her throat. Then the storm within her broke. She lunged for the nearest object – a chair – and hurled it against the far wall with a guttural scream. Splinters scattered across the floor like pieces of her shattered pride.

Her hands seized whatever was nearby – a tiny table, an empty pitcher – and her fury consumed each thing, raw and uncontrolled. The room bore the scars of her anguish. She collapsed to her knees amid the debris, her hands clutching at her hair as the sobs overtook her.

Tears flowed freely, showing the sorrow, fury, and disgrace she'd suppressed. At first, the crying engulfed her like a tempest. Hers was a strange combination of emptiness and darkness, but also... a sense of freedom. For the first time, the unbearable weight on her shoulders seemed to loosen.

As the room settled into stillness, so did Ursa. The surrounding mess showed her breakdown, but it didn't matter. Let them deem her a wanderer. Let them whisper of her disgrace. She wiped her face with the back of her hand, steadying her breath. Lacking a home, she would build one. One broken piece at a time.

Ursa stirred when the sharp rhythm of boot heels striking stone echoed through the hallway outside. The sound grew louder and unrelenting, until the door burst open with a force that made her flinch. Lucea stood there.

"Ursa?" Panic and confusion warred on Lucea's face, her wide eyes taking in the room's disarray and the fragile figure before her. "Dear Vine, what happened?"

Ursa managed a wan smile, her lips trembling as she tried to find the words. "I—"

Lucea didn't wait. She closed the door behind her and crossed the room in an instant. She knelt, enfolding Ursa's shoulders in her arms with a tenderness that stole the breath from Ursa's lungs. The warmth of Lucea's embrace cut through the lingering chill in her heart, and Ursa leaned into her, allowing herself to collapse into the moment.

Ursa caught the familiar scent of Lucea's blend of herbs and soft florals: lavender from her hair, a sweet cologne clinging to her skin, and a faint note of lilies-of-the-valley. It was hers. Her beautiful chronomancer – the one constant in a world unmoored.

★ ★ ★

"I did something unconscionable."

They lay together naked after lovemaking. The room was still in shambles, but neither one cared. Lucea had cast a spell that placed them out of time with everyone and everything else. Therefore, no one interrupted them.

"Hard to believe," Ursa said.

Lucea buried her face in Ursa's shoulder. "The faun, Tantia. I demanded an explanation for her attempt on your life."

"Did she tell you anything?"

"Not what I wanted, so I—"

Ursa smoothed a hand over Lucea's hair. "Continue."

Speaking softly, Lucea told Ursa about her progress. The weight of her deeds was palpable, filled with silent implications. Her words trembled as she recounted Tantia's confession. Though it remained unsaid, Lucea suspected Tantia's pain stemmed from a deeper connection to Ursa than mere loyalty. The truth of it glimmered just beneath the surface, unspoken but unmistakable.

Ursa murmured, the burden of past grievances intoned, "It was devastating when she did not advocate for me or offer her support. In time, I came to understand – it wasn't her responsibility. I was not entitled to demand that she sacrifice everything for me." She shifted closer to Lucea, her chin resting atop her companion's head, her breath catching the soothing freshness of her hair.

"You asked nothing of her," Lucea said softly, with muted conviction. "But if she genuinely loved you, she wouldn't have hesitated. Instead, she faltered – perhaps out of fear, perhaps out of weakness. When she tried to kill you, guilt, not hatred, motivated her actions."

"I can't ease her pain, not anymore," Ursa said. "Whatever feelings I once held for her have disappeared, leaving only traces of what existed. My only recourse is hoping she perceives the Isles' danger and temporarily relinquishes her anger."

The knock came, sharp and insistent, breaking the quiet stillness of the room. Moments later, an envelope slid beneath the door, its edges catching the faint light. "What might this be?" Lucea rose, but Ursa stilled her with a gentle touch.

"Let me," she whispered. Though she loathed to pull away from the warmth of Lucea's embrace, she slipped from under the sheets, the cool air brushing her skin. She retrieved the envelope. The paper was smooth and luxurious beneath her fingertips, a stark contrast to the roughness of her own calloused hands. The complex design of the wax seal on the flap caught her attention, immediately signaling its importance.

Ursa broke the seal and unfolded the letter, scanning it. "The praesidere has summoned us."

"I'll go by myself if you prefer."

"I'm fine now," Ursa said. "We'll go together."

After taking time to wash up and change into fresh clothes, Ursa followed Lucea to Farstride's receiving room. Balric and Greenstone stood ready, but Ursa focused on Tantia. She stood rigid at the doorway, flanked by two imposing nagas.

They moved toward their seats, but Ursa hesitated, remaining on her feet. Instead, she stepped closer to Tantia. All eyes followed her.

"I forgive you," Ursa spoke calmly.

Tantia froze, her expression hardening into stone. Ursa waited, ready for a tirade or the curses the faun would unleash. But none came.

Their gazes locked, stretching the moment into eternity. Tantia's shoulders eased. No, it exceeded that. The anger seemed to seep out of her, leaving a hollow exhaustion in its wake. Her anger toward Ursa seemed pointless.

Ursa walked away from Tantia, leaving the unpleasantness behind. Without another glance, she sat, her focus shifting to what lay ahead.

CHAPTER TWENTY–NINE

Farstride held a sheath of papers in her clawed hand. The queen impressed her seal onto the top. Ursa remained ignorant of the details until Farstride handed the papers across the table.

"It's from Queen Asphira," Farstride said, as neutral as ever. "She's planning to join the fight against the Rot. Will that bother you?" She directed the question at Ursa.

Ursa's fingers curled around the edge of the table. She breathed out, letting her pulse settle before responding. "No," she said, meeting Farstride's gaze. "I have buried my past with her. She can fight, or she can vanish – it makes no difference to me."

Ursa handed the sheath to Balric without hesitation. Her words may have been cutting, but she no longer cared. Though a part of her would always hold love and respect for her mother, that bond had unraveled. Asphira was a stranger.

After a brief pause, Farstride acknowledged her with a nod. "Good," she replied. "Because you'll need a clear head for what comes next. As for you," Farstride turned her attention back to Tantia, "did your queen require a response? What command did she give you to obey after you delivered the message?"

"I am to wait here for her arrival and obey your instructions until then," Tantia responded.

"Very well," Farstride said. She briefly considered, lightly pressing her index finger against her chin before continuing. "You've delivered your message. You're no longer needed here," her tone was sharp and final, "and I don't want you in my home."

Tantia had fulfilled her duty, delivering the queen's message as instructed. But Ursa could tell Tantia had believed Farstride would allow her to stay in the manor in comfort. It was clear now she'd assumed too much.

"Madame—" Ursa began.

"No." Farstride lifted a single finger. "I know you have no fear of her, but I do not trust her, so Tantia, you are free to stay in the central hub of the city, or you can stay in the faun province."

Balric spoke up. "Madame, it would be more convenient if she stayed in the hub, I think."

"Agreed." Farstride nodded once. "Can you afford to stay at an inn?"

Tantia's eyes widened, but the flash of surprise hardened into anger. "How dare you dismiss me like this!" she spat. "I came here because my queen trusted me, and I felt this fight to be important. You don't appreciate—"

"This fight's important, however not at the cost of trust. Your presence is a distraction, and your history with Ursa is a liability I can't afford."

The naga shifted, their movements deliberate and subtle, as if to silently reinforce Farstride's words.

Tantia laughed bitterly. "So that's it? Cast me out like some wandering rogue? Fine. But don't expect me to come running when the Rot reaches this door!"

Mother will order you here regardless of what you say, Ursa thought.

Tantia spun, her hooves striking the stone floor with each purposeful step as she approached the guards. Her stiff movements showed her wounded pride. A final backward glance, anger mixed with mystery, marked her pause before the doorway.

"Enjoy your false sense of security, Farstride," she hissed, before disappearing into the corridor beyond.

"Since we've concluded this unpleasantness," Farstride gestured to the trio seated across the table, "let me introduce our other guests."

Ursa had forgotten the others. During the Tantia incident, Balric remained the sole voice of dissent. A dwarf, a selkie, and—

"Chirana Thunderforge of the Ironclad Quarter." The female dwarf inclined her head, her braids tinkling with metal clasps as if echoing her name.

"Maris of the Silken Reefs." Farstride nodded to the selkie woman in human form. Her sea-green eyes held a light that seemed to shift and shimmer like the tides. The situation must be dire to make a selkie leave the ocean to venture inland, to a city, no less.

"If you don't mind." Farstride gave a small bow to the third and final guest. And she differed from any creature Ursa knew. Ursa turned to Lucea with a questioning look. Lucea gave a subtle, almost imperceptible shake of her head.

Her angular features resembled sculpted stone. Lizard-like eyes glinted in the light – vertical pupils narrowing as they surveyed the room with an eerie, unblinking intensity. Her hair shimmered not with strands but with fine scales that cascaded down, catching faint glimmers of silver and green as she shifted.

The folds of the robe obscured their form, leaving the details of their body shrouded in mystery. Hidden power and untamed force were implied by the fabric's movement.

"This is Phasa of Crimson Spire." Farstride noticed their confusion and said, "She is of the Dracaena."

"Dracaena!" Lucea said in a surprised breath.

"We are distant kin to the naga." Despite her fierce appearance, her voice was soft, almost musical.

"I-I know," Lucea said. "It's just that—"

"You believed we didn't exist?" Phasa smiled with pointed teeth much like the naga.

"No – I mean – there was no definitive—"

"I've never heard of your kind." Ursa didn't appreciate this Phasa upsetting Lucea.

"Many haven't," Phasa said. "Those who remain, and the other winged ones, live in Crimson Spire."

"Winged ones?" Ursa raised an eyebrow.

Phasa pushed back her chair and stood. She reached up and shed the garment in one fluid motion. The truth became clear.

Wings, vast and sinewy, unfurled with a grace that seemed both regal and predatory. Their membranous surface gleamed, etched with veins that pulsed like molten rivers under the skin. A tail coiled out behind her, tapering to a lethal point, its movements fluid as a serpent. They projected a controlled fierceness, an atmosphere of immense age and might held in check.

She wore leather armor and a long skirt. Her legs were covered in scales, like those of a naga, yet they ended in avian limbs. Her clawed, talon-like feet clicked against the ground with each step.

"Magnificent," Lucea said, awed.

Ursa agreed.

"Thank you." Phasa bowed low before taking her seat. "Should you wish, we may extensively discuss my team, given a chance."

Lucea's eyes lit up. The scholarly part of her was eager at the notion. Ursa smiled, finding herself warming up to the dracaena. Not to mention, Ursa figured she would be quite formidable in battle.

Farstride extended her hands in precise, practiced arcs as soft whispers of an incantation flowed from her lips. Threads of light wove through the air, tracing intricate patterns that shimmered like threads of spun glass. With a final sharp motion, she brought her hands together, and the glowing lines coalesced into a vibrant map suspended midair.

The map pulsed with life, the city of Jack-In-Irons stretching out in breathtaking detail. Streets and alleyways glimmered like silver veins, while districts glowed in soft hues to distinguish them. Beyond the city walls, the surrounding terrain unraveled – rolling hills, dense forests, and rivers flowing like ribbons of sapphire. Tiny moving specks dotted the landscape: caravans winding their way to the gates, sentries patrolling the outer boundaries, and even the faint, ominous flickers of something stirring in the distant woods.

The air around the map vibrated, as if the magic itself lived, murmuring secrets of the land. Farstride stood back, her gaze focused, as if the entire world lay within her grasp.

Ursa caught a fleeting crack in Farstride's calm façade, a subtle tremor that vanished as soon as it appeared. Yet in that fleeting instant, she understood. This remained Farstride's home, her people. The mere idea of their suffering tore at her heart like claws rending fabric.

Empathy stirred within Ursa. She couldn't ignore the burden etched into the kobold's features, no matter how well hidden. Leading was a difficult challenge.

Farstride leaned over the glowing map, her sharp claws tracing the outline of the city's rear walls. "I will station the soldiers here," she began, her voice steady, every word deliberate. "They'll hold the line at the rear barricades, where the stone is weakest."

Ursa's brow furrowed. "And what if they breach it?" she asked, her tone edged with worry.

Farstride straightened, the faint shimmer of magic glinting in her scaled hands as she spoke. "They won't." She was calm, unyielding. "I've conjured a veil – a barrier strong enough to encircle half the city. It will hold."

Ursa's concern deepened. "A veil that size? That's too much power, Farstride. What remains when the enemy attacks with greater intensity?"

Farstride met her gaze, her expression unreadable but firm. "It won't come to that. The veil is stable. I've measured every thread of magic to ensure it." Her words carried no hint of doubt, though the room seemed to hold its breath.

Discussion moved to the woods and possible enemy attacks from the dense trees. Farstride waved a hand and the map shifted to focus on the looming forest. "It's probable they'll come from here," she said, her finger tracing the approach. "We'll deploy formations – blocking groups here, here, and here."

Ursa turned her eyes toward Lucea, who stood next to her, as they began to form a shared, unspoken decision. Before Ursa spoke, Farstride continued. "You and Lucea will stay in the manor," she declared, leaving little room for argument.

Lucea's voice cut in like the snap of a bowstring. "No. We fight with everyone else."

Ursa nodded, her jaw set. "You're not leaving us behind, Farstride."

Farstride sighed, seeming to recognize the pointlessness of continued argument. Her attention returned to the map, but her shoulders slackened, and her gaze was somewhat unfocused.

Ursa noticed first the odd stillness that crept over her. "Farstride?" she said, yet the kobold remained silent.

Farstride's hands hovered over the map, her claws trembling. "The First has come."

"The First?" Lucea asked. Her face mirrored the curiosity of the others.

"The witch," Farstride said, still entranced. "Isbet."

The room again buzzed with questions and comments. The words echoed within Ursa, although she didn't understand why. She glanced at Lucea, saw the faint flicker of recognition that crossed her face. Ursa's sharp eye caught Lucea's almost invisible reaction.

"Are you familiar with her?" Ursa's voice remained low, so she wouldn't attract attention from those at the table.

"Somewhat," Lucea replied. "She's a friend of Harper the diviner. She visited Vale a few times in the past to assist her teacher. She seemed pleasant enough."

"She is a warrior?"

"Warrior and witch," Lucea said. "I can say she will be invaluable to us."

The kobold continued to address the group. "I've spoken to a few of you concerning the three," Farstride said, her voice stronger as she straightened. "Certain women, bound to the Vine, combat the Rot's return."

"Madame, I beg your pardon," Balric asked, "but are you certain you can trust them?"

"Don't fret, my friend. These are likely the most trustworthy women in all the Isles." Her gaze settled on Ursa and Lucea. "The two of you will soon join them. You summoned the Vine. Expect repayment when you repeat the action."

The implication in those words displeased Ursa. She looked at Lucea, whose face showed acceptance. *I wish I had your unerring devotion.* Ursa used the Vine. She invoked power to rescue Lucea and others, though Farstride implied she should serve.

Ursa missed the following words.

"Madame, how shall we distinguish them?" Balric inquired.

"I'm acquainted with two of them," Lucea said.

"It's doubtful we'll have time on the battlefield for you to point them out to us, I'm afraid."

"You will recognize them," Farstride said.

Balric seemed to accept this. He inclined his head. "Yes, Madame."

For several minutes, Farstride issued commands about where they should station. Ursa and Lucea would lead one group to find Isbet while the rest would wait for the enemy to advance. The enemy remained unseen, but Farstride predicted their movements would reveal them. That all made sense.

Farstride concluded, and they left. However, despite the rush, preparations were neither swift nor simple. The soldiers busied themselves carefully gathering supplies, sharpening blades, and saddling horses for the long journey ahead. Tension buzzed in the air. Each movement was charged with purpose as Ursa oversaw the last details. She caught sight of Lucea standing apart from the others, her hands moving as if feeling the flow of time itself. Though she stood unarmed, unlike the soldiers, she was prepared – Lucea's strength required no weapon.

Farstride, meanwhile, remained behind at the manor. But her earlier instructions lingered in Ursa's mind, etched clearly. "You'll need every capable hand," she said, her tone steady but carrying an unmistakable urgency.

As darkness fell, the group gathered at the city gates. A scorched landscape stretched before them, shadows lengthening ominously.

The journey began. The hill stretched before them, its grass charred and lifeless, as though fire had ravaged the land in a rage that spared nothing. Every step closer revealed more unsettling details – puddles of black goo pooled among the cracks in the scorched earth, their surfaces shimmering with an unnatural, oil-slick gleam. The smell of rancid meat hung thick in the air, a nauseating stench that clawed at their senses and refused to be ignored.

Ursa tightened her grip on the reins, scanning the horizon for any sign of movement. The group pressed on, the forest looming closer with every step.

The trees swallowed them whole, their twisted branches forming a canopy. Shadows danced across the ground, and the faint sound of a skirmish reached their ears – clashes of steel and guttural cries.

Ursa's heart quickened. "There's someone ahead," she said, her voice sharp with urgency.

They urged their horses forward, the sounds growing louder until they broke through the underbrush.

A woman stood in the clearing, her movements fluid and precise as she fought off a group of goblins. Her old wooden staff whirled through the air, striking with the force of a hammer. Magic crackled at her fingertips. Bursts of light and energy sent her attackers reeling.

Ursa's breath caught. The woman commanded attention. Her skill went unquestioned. This wasn't your average fighter.

A green aura, a mark only the Children of the Vine and the Gifted could perceive, identified the woman. She triumphed against the enemy because goblins fought. Still, Ursa dismounted and charged forward with a cry and the radiant light of Lucea's power. A moment's observation revealed no suspicion or malice in the woman's gaze. She knew they helped.

With the final goblin defeated, some by blade and others by spell, Ursa approached the stranger just as, from the rear, Lucea called out.

"Lady Isbet!" Lucea reached her the same time Ursa did.

"Well, if it isn't Duchess Lucea." The woman grinned. "I received information that you would be present." They embraced. "And you must be Princess Ursa." Isbet offered her hand, which Ursa took with a firm grip.

"Just Ursa—"

"I'm starved!"

Everyone froze, all eyes on the staff Isbet held in her hand. Some were shocked; others, without the Gift, confused.

"Oh, hush up!" Isbet admonished.

Ursa could see it. A tortured soul trapped in something surpassing any prison.

"I suppose I don't deserve any introduction." If that staff didn't pout.

"You've met Lucea before," Isbet said. "This is Ursa."

Ursa bowed, questioning her actions. "A pleasure, sir—?"

"Gaemyr," he said, appearing happy. Ursa had addressed him as such.

Balric moved toward them. "You are the one that Madame Farstride spoke of?"

"I am Isbet." She neither bowed nor showed respect. "Advisor to Prince Bram Greyward. I preceded him here by command of the Vine. He will arrive soon with the might of his soldiers."

"Then we shouldn't tarry here. That was a scouting party; their absence after we killed them all would draw attention." Balric turned away, then looked back. "As for that—" he motioned to Gaemyr, "—abomination, you will need to leave it somewhere."

"How dare you!" Ursa sensed that Isbet seldom lost her temper; however, insulting her familiar was not something witches tolerated. "Had you not been a Child of the Vine, I would have Gaemyr rip your precious soul from your body."

Balric drew his sword to challenge Isbet, but Ursa stepped between them. "We don't have time for this!" She spread her arms, acting as a shield between the two. "You said it yourself, Balric. We must return to safety. And she is the one Farstride expected."

"Would you disobey the commands of your praesidere?" Lucea offered.

Balric snorted and turned away. He whispered something un-ljósálfar-like before mounting and signaling them to follow.

"That proved unnecessary," Isbet spoke. "But you have my gratitude." Then the witch's eyes went wide. Ursa saw clearly, despite encroaching darkness, that her gaze was focused on Iron Reaver.

"Is that—?"

"The Steel Driver's Hammer? Yes."

To her surprise, Isbet bowed low. "It is an honor."

"As you said, that is unnecessary," Ursa said. "We should depart before more problems appear."

Isbet and Gaemyr chuckled. They mounted Ursa's fore, Ursa first, then Isbet. Gaemyr rested in a sheath across Isbet's back.

"I trust you're prepared for what lies ahead," Isbet murmured, her breath warm against Ursa's ear.

Ursa responded, "To the best of my ability."

CHAPTER THIRTY

"We were fortunate," Lucea said, her voice steady but tinged with weariness. "The enemy lacked numbers and strength. I am not saying it wasn't difficult."

They had lost people in the first skirmish, lives cut short before the tide of battle shifted in their favor. Though Lucea was relieved to see Lady Isbet again, the burden of her knowledge remained. Because of her, they now understood that the Rot was aware of their presence.

"There was something there," Isbet began, her words deliberate as she gestured to the circular table around which they sat, and to the conjured map on it. Lucea watched it shift, the magic alive. She guessed Farstride had created it with her Gift, as she had with so many other vital tools. Two empty seats flanked Isbet, their absence conspicuous. Lucea occasionally worried about Farstride's potential for overexertion, a common concern with the Gifted. However, the kobold displayed seemingly endless energy.

This was a true War Room, humming with activity. Servants, messengers, and scouts brought vital updates from the city walls to the manor. The atmosphere outside these walls was no less frantic. With Farstride manipulating the veils, those viewing the map could see the actions of the noncombatants. Civilians shepherded the vulnerable – children, older adults, and the ill – into deep chambers beneath the city. Tradesfolk raced to stockpile supplies, their hands busy with sewing, baking, and hammering. In one part of the map, a healer prepared tinctures, stooped over a workbench. Another showed smiths carrying weaponry to reinforce the soldiers. The veils shimmered and rippled, parting like gossamer curtains to reveal these glimpses of desperate resilience.

They served food at the table, but few paid it any mind. Someone had pushed aside the simple, used plates. A smoky brandy gleamed in Balric's hands, its scent mingling with the faint tang of wine from goblets of others. Lucea, Ursa, and Iris abstained, unable to understand how the others would even consider drinking when the enemy was at their gates. The dark wooden walls around them bore scars of age and conflict, and thick logs spaced around the room created a fortress-like enclosure. Lanterns hung. Their glow intertwined with the soft, flickering light of wil-o'-wisps. These ethereal beings hovered near Farstride, as if drawn to her magic or looking for some kind of reassurance.

"It was two," Isbet continued, breaking the tension. She leaned forward and her gaze fixed on the map. "Beings of pure malice that fought for supremacy."

"The Amalgam." Lucea's voice was quiet but bitter. The name evoked a powerful sense of recollection.

"You know of this thing?" Isbet's tone was sharp with curiosity and concern.

"All too well." Lucea shivered, as if her memories had cast a shadow over her. Samara's venomous words still whispered in her mind, entwined with the searing rage of Barnabas. The two clung to her psyche like the stench of a decaying swamp. But then, as if sensing the storm within her, Ursa laid a gentle hand on her thigh. The warmth of the touch revived her, the dark emotions subsiding enough for her to take a steady breath.

"It has dogged our steps for most of the journey," Ursa said. "However, it did not control us. I believe it is because of their inner turmoil."

"We must devise a plan to use this against them," Farstride said. "They must fight to the death."

"As loathe as I am to admit it," Lucea began, "Samara—"

Ursa cut in. "No."

"Ursa—"

"I won't allow it." Her voice was firm, but beneath it lay something unspoken.

Lucea inhaled, steadying herself.

"If I am understanding," Iris spoke, "this Samara wants to – make something of you?"

"She has said so many times." Lucea spoke in a measured tone, but the weight of her words lingered.

"So, what you are proposing," Balric said, eyes flicking between them, "if I may be so bold, is that we use you as bait to lure this Samara out of the Amalgam."

Lucea turned to Ursa. "Tell me true, would Barnabas have any interest in me at all?"

Ursa hesitated. When she spoke, frustration edged her voice. "Not likely." A slow breath. "But he will have a vested interest in me. He looks upon me as some sort of infidel who dares oppose him." Her hand came to rest on the head of Iron Reaver. "And for this."

"I've been wanting to ask," Balric said, "is that the Steel Driver's Hammer?"

Ursa's gaze met his. "Yes."

Balric whispered something in ljósálfar – words too hushed for Lucea to decipher. Suspicion ignited in his gaze. "The hiding place of the Steel Driver's Hammer remains unknown."

"All of this is irrelevant," Farstride interjected, cutting through the moment. "We can answer these questions later. Lady Ursa and Lucea, would you be willing to act as decoys to divide the Amalgam for now?"

Lucea turned to Ursa again, her heart thudding. Ursa held her look, uncertainty wavering for a moment. She nodded. "Yes."

"They will still need protection," Iris said.

She pushed back from the table, graceful as ever, and circled behind them. With deliberate care, she leaned down, pressing a kiss to Ursa's forehead, then Lucea's.

Heat bloomed at the touch – something unseen yet unmistakable.

"That should protect you somewhat," Iris murmured, eyes dancing with mischief. A wink – green eyes glimmering with untold years of fairy power, ancient yet impetuous, the very smile of Robin Goodfellow himself. It was breathtaking.

"Thank you," Lucea breathed. "Lady Goodfellow."

Ursa gave a slow nod. "Indeed."

Iris laughed, delighted. "My pleasure."

★ ★ ★

The air in the War Room was thick with unspoken dread. Reports had streamed in from scouts and spies – whispers of movement in the forest, shadows threading between trees like ghosts. The most harrowing came from a scout who had dragged himself to the manor's threshold, his body broken, breath shallow. He had fought to deliver his warning – on three fronts. The enemy was gathering. Then, Death took him.

Lucea's stomach twisted. She was able to bend time, but not Death. Even the necromancers, despite their mastery over the veils, were unable to bargain with it. It was absolute.

"Then we have set the strategy," Balric said, fingers tapping against the wooden table in restless agitation. "We divide their forces. We make them believe they hold the advantage."

"Deception is key," Iris murmured. "If they suspect we know their true numbers, they will adjust."

Farstride nodded, her amber eyes glinting in the candlelight. "Agreed." A slow exhale. "We bait them. Lucea, Ursa – you will draw a faction to the north flank."

Lucea heard her. But her mind was still on the dying scout. So young. So desperate. She clenched tightly the edge of the table. Unable to prevent the inevitable, she decided to make his warning meaningful.

Tiny sparks of magic pulsed at her fingertips – small threads of time's fabric. She wove them into the surrounding bodies, a silent fortification. Not like Iris's fey magic, no. But there was a barrier, a faint delay between their bodies and Death's grasp. It would not save them, but perhaps it would grant them a moment longer to fight.

Farstride's gaze swept the room. "We all know what must be done." Even with her determination, her voice took on a gentle quality. "Dismissed."

The group dispersed with grim readiness.

Lucea lingered for a moment, her heart weighty with the knowledge of what lay ahead. She wished for another night with Ursa. A deep ache settled within her. When she stepped into the cool night, the manor appeared still, as if it held its breath.

In the garden, Ursa swung Iron Reaver in practiced arcs. The hammer resonated in the dimness, with her actions being exact and calculated. Her posture reflected a somber realization, which reinforced her unwavering determination.

Lucea watched from the shadows, her chest tightening. She knew she should eat and rest. But when she brought food to her room, the taste was ash in her mouth. And when she lay down, sleep avoided her, leaving her tossing and turning.

Frustrated, she sighed, then went to the window, gazing out into the night. The stars, cold and unfeeling, seemed unaware of the weight pressing down on her. Somewhere beyond the manor gates, the enemy stirred.

Night deepened, seemingly without end.

⋆ ⋆ ⋆

It was the blaring cacophony of horns that dragged Lucea from her fitful slumber. She didn't recall falling asleep, yet somehow, Ursa had joined her in bed, her warmth a faint comfort in the night.

Now they were both awake. Ursa sprang up, her instincts sharp and unwavering, but Lucea's sleep-deprived body kept her in a fog, struggling to catch up. Precious moments slipped past.

"Stay here," Ursa said, already heading toward the door.

Lucea blinked as her mind cleared. "Wait—" she started, her voice cracking with grogginess.

"I know you didn't sleep well," Ursa interrupted, her tone gentle but firm. "I'll investigate this and return promptly."

"Wait—" Lucea tried again. But Ursa was already gone, the door slamming shut behind her.

Frustration surged, dispelling the last vestiges of fog in her mind. "Damn it to the nether-realms," she muttered, calling on her Gift. The familiar rush of magic coursed through her veins, snapping her body into full wakefulness. Without hesitation, she threw on a shirt and trousers and bolted out of the room, her bare feet slapping against the cold stone floors.

The horns echoed through the castle, accompanied by the chaotic din of running feet and shouted orders. Servants and guards alike rushed past her in all directions – some with panic in their eyes, others with grim determination. Lucea's heart sank as dread coiled in her stomach.

Had the enemy attacked? Broken through their defenses? The surrounding chaos made it impossible to tell.

She dodged a sprinting guard but was shoved aside by another figure. A startled servant paused momentarily to bow before hurrying off again. The urgency of their movements only deepened Lucea's unease.

She hurried forward, weaving through the mêlée, her mind racing. She needed answers. The castle was alive with fear and purpose.

When Lucea stepped outside, the crowd had already gathered before the gates. Their eyes were all locked on a cloud racing across the sky, bridging the distance between the far-off gates and the manor. Somewhere amidst the din, a sharp voice rang out: "Archers, to the ready!"

Lucea hesitated, torn. Should she save her Gift for a genuine threat, or unleash it on something that might fall to mere arrows? The archers loosed their volley, a dense curtain of projectiles soaring skyward and dimming the warm glow of the sun as it crept over the horizon. To her shock, the cloud fragmented, breaking apart into smaller, agile forms that twisted and dodged the arrows with uncanny grace.

Then, one shape plummeted toward them at an incredible speed, its descent heralded by startled screams as the crowd scattered. Lucea's breath caught. Not a cloud. A gryphon. Its sleek black feathers gleamed like polished obsidian, and its muscular frame exuded power. Emerald eyes, sharp and fearless, locked with hers for a heartbeat as it landed with a grace that belied its immense strength.

The rider astride the gryphon was a sight to behold. Dressed in a striking red and white suit coat paired with a split skirt, the woman's light skin seemed to glow in the early morning light. Her green eyes, reminiscent of Ursa's, scanned the crowd with quiet authority. Yet what captured Lucea's attention most was her hat: an immaculate white top hat adorned with two jeweled hearts, connected by a golden bow. The hat's side bore a pattern of tiny fireworks, a detail that seemed both whimsical and focused, like everything about her.

Who was this woman, and why had she come?

The gryphon extended its front legs and lowered its shoulders, easing the woman's dismount. Their eyes met, and Lucea felt a sense of familiarity that she struggled to understand. The sounds of the approaching guards, who were now surrounding them, seemed subdued, even though Lucea recognized their lethal weapons aimed at the distinguished visitor. The woman appeared indifferent. Then, with a grand gesture, she removed her hat and bowed at the waist, toward Lucea.

"Greetings," she said. "I am Faith Carter, Princess of Hearts and Daughter of Theophilus Carter, known by all as the Mad Hatter." She set the hat back on her head, tipped at a jaunty angle. "My Queen Belladonna of Brigantia sends her salutations. Could you escort me to Praesidere Dhidihn Farstride?" She looked to Lucea's right, and knew without having to turn that Ursa had approached to stand next to her.

Lucea stepped before Faith and held out both hands in greeting. Faith took them in her warm grasp. "Yes, of course," Lucea said. "They expect you. On behalf of Praesidere Farstride, I welcome you to Jack-In-Irons."

CHAPTER THIRTY-ONE

She knew.

Upon noticing the woman, Ursa immediately assumed she was among their four visitors. No one with evil intentions could command such beautiful creatures without unleashing them to destroy everything in their path.

Not wanting to appear threatening, Ursa sheathed Iron Reaver. The alarm had sounded when she rushed down the hall, her powerful strides eating up the distance. Soldiers and civilians fled before her.

A majestic display of power and grace filled the sky with the gryphons' flight.

Stepping forward, Ursa extended her hand. Princess Faith gripped it, her handshake strong and confident. "I am called Ursa," she said, nodding toward the woman's companions. "As my comrade mentioned, welcome to Jack-In-Irons."

"Please follow us," Lucea said as she turned, glancing at the armed soldiers still standing at the ready. "It's fine; she's a friend."

The soldiers did not move, their vigilance unbroken. Ursa hesitated, unsure of what should come next. Balric and Iris approached, taking the decision out of her hands. Balric dismounted first and strode toward them with his familiar haughty air.

"Do you know this girl?" Balric's tone was sharp. His gaze pointed.

"This girl," Ursa replied, placing severe emphasis on the word, "is Princess Faith of Brigantia – one of Farstride's honored guests."

"And how can you be certain she is who she claims to be?" Balric challenged. The suspicion and anger in his demeanor drew Ursa's brows together in a frown. Rarely did she see someone of Balric's race so distrustful.

"I would think that is obvious," Ursa countered evenly.

Princess Faith stepped forward. "I carry letters of introduction," she said, retrieving them from her satchel. "They bear the seals of both my Queen Belladonna and the Spinner Queen of Tidaholm."

Ursa exchanged a glance with Lucea, noting the recognition on her face. Few could forget the story of the Spinner Queen, the thaumaturge whose father claimed she could spin straw into gold for a greedy king. By a twist of fate, the monarch fell in love with the Miller's Daughter and made her his queen.

Iris dismounted, approached and bowed. "Your Highness, it is an honor to meet you. Please, follow me." She gestured for the princess to walk ahead of her, much to Balric's visible dismay.

"Fine," Balric conceded reluctantly. "Soldiers, stand down."

The princess turned to her gryphon and whispered something. Then, with quiet resolve, she took hold of its harness and led him forward as she followed Iris.

"Your gryphon is magnificent," Ursa said.

Rather than the princess replying, the gryphon himself spoke. "Thank you."

Ursa's shock lasted only a moment. She'd seen gryphons from afar but never close enough to talk.

"I am called Argestes." He spread his wings, his presence radiating both strength and dignity. "Thank you for welcoming us."

"I wish it were under better circumstances," she admitted.

"As do I." The subtle shift in his tone caught Ursa's attention – there was sorrow in it.

"Are you unwell, Sir Argestes?" Lucea asked.

"I am, in body," he said, hesitating. "However—" He fell silent, unable to continue.

"He started a family," Faith supplied.

Lucea's eyes lit up with joy. "That's wonderful! Congratulations."

Of course, his concern was for his mate and kits. Ursa considered suggesting he stay within the city's safety, but the thought faded. It was clear why he had come – he wanted to protect those he loved.

The soldiers, stiff and formal, formed an aisle. Faith and Argestes walked between them toward the manor entrance. As they neared, Faith whispered to the gryphon again, and he peeled away toward a nearby patch of grass and wildflowers, to curl up in the sunlight.

Inside, as they traversed that damnable hallway, they came upon Isbet. She stood before one veil, eyeing it. Beyond the delicate fabric, something shadow-like shifted – moving as though aware of her presence, stalking unseen prey.

Her staff spoke aloud. "This is not her power, although she may believe it is."

"Surely you do not wish to anger her again."

Again? Ursa thought.

"What more could she do to punish me?" Gaemyr grumbled. "I am just relieved she bonded me with someone of good nature and character."

Isbet stayed stoic, yet her cheeks flushed. "Join with the Vine. Refresh yourself and tell me of the goings-on around the city."

"As you wish."

Isbet stepped toward one offshoot growing in the hall's corner, nestled beside the double doors. Ursa hadn't noticed it before.

Without hesitation, Isbet pressed Gaemyr against the verdant growth. The Vine absorbed the staff, astonishing them.

They watched in silent awe as the foliage shifted, accepting the weapon as if it had always belonged.

"I see you are worried about these veils too," Ursa said to Isbet.

"I am, but there is little that can be done."

To fill the sudden awkward silence, Lucea said, "Princess Faith of Brigantia, this is Isbet of Rhyvirand."

They exchanged greetings before entering. Servants continued their duties with careful precision, their tasks uninterrupted but their gazes wary. Some glanced at the newcomer with curiosity, while others avoided looking, shoulders stiff, lips pressed into tight lines as they carried trays of maps, documents, and steaming cups of tea.

Farstride sat in her usual place, unmoving, her gaze distant. The look of one entranced.

Ursa studied her, curious.

She saw Faith hesitate as she stepped through the doorway. Unlike Ursa and Lucea, Faith was new to these people, new to their conflicts, and it showed in her posture, her measured stiffness, the quiet evaluation of a strategist unsure where she fits into this play.

Chirana Thunderforge, Maris, and Phasa sat in silence, their presence grounding despite their unreadable expressions. Faith slipped into the chair next to Isbet with Chirana to her left. As Ursa's group settled in, their gazes lingered on the lone empty chair – its absence unspoken yet undeniable.

Ursa hesitated. Should she suggest a search party? But where would they begin? Did anyone even know this person's face, their name? The questions churned in her mind, unanswered and unsettling, like whispers in the dark.

Maris adjusted in her seat, fingers tapping against the wood, eyes locked on the map before her. Phasa's arms remained crossed, her expression tense, though she stole occasional glances at Farstride, as if willing her to speak. Chirana was the only one who seemed relaxed despite their situation. She leaned back in her chair, with her hands behind her head. Ursa was surprised the dwarf captain refrained from putting her feet on the tabletop.

Farstride inhaled, her eyes widening as if she caught sight of something just beyond reach. The room reacted with everyone leaning forward, waiting. Even the servants seemed to pause, trays hovering midair, listening to the charged silence that filled the space.

Farstride held the breath for a long moment before releasing it in a slow, measured exhale. A few rapid blinks, and her gaze sharpened.

Then the questions came. A barrage from every side, voices overlapping in urgent waves. Farstride couldn't reply before the next inquiry crashed against the last.

Ursa noticed Princess Faith examining those seated at the table, her expression a mixture of confusion and worry, while Lady Isbet sat, seemingly indifferent to it. Her arms crossed at her chest much like Phasa's.

Maris spoke, low but firm. "What did you see?"

Farstride exhaled, tension rolling from her shoulders. "The enemy is coming from both fronts."

That much, they already knew.

"And?" Phasa pressed.

Ursa and Lucea became the focus of Farstride's attention. "The Amalgam was split in two."

"By us?" Lucea inquired.

"That I could not see."

The weight of her words settled; silence stretched.

Ursa slammed her palms flat against the table, breaking the quiet. "If we lose control above, it won't matter what happens in Underneath – the Amalgam will overrun everything." She traced the battle lines on the map. "The Vine must hold, but the battlefield is our best chance to dictate the fight."

Lucea shook her head. "No. If Underneath collapses, the Vine falls before the battle begins. This fight—" she gestured to the war unfolding beyond the manor walls, "—only exists because the foundation stands." Her voice was unyielding, though urgency burned behind her measured tone.

"You just want to save your friend," Balric accused.

Ursa bristled. "What the fuck did you just say?"

Lucea placed a calming hand on her forearm. Ursa still seethed but swallowed the words.

"Yes, I want to save my friend," Lucea admitted. "But that doesn't mean I'm willing to let everyone else perish."

Pride tempered Ursa's anger. Where she might have gone for Balric's throat, Lucea remained unshaken. Ursa smiled. They made a perfect match.

A murmur spread through the council – some nodding, agreeing with Ursa. Others scowled at the risk of neglecting the fight above.

Farstride was positioned at the head of the table, her regard alternating between her strategists. "We stick to the original plan."

The declaration landed like a hammer.

Balric squared off against Chirana. Heated words flew like sparks from a forge – accusations, counterpoints, the weight of countless battles pressing into their voices.

Servants moved around the room, keeping their distance from the heated exchanges. One near the corner of the chamber poured wine with deliberate care, eyes flicking up once before returning to his task.

Balric scoffed, arms crossed tight. "This choice is foolhardy. Separating our forces weakens both the city and Underneath. If we gamble like this, we risk losing everything."

Chirana's voice was ice. "It ensures that both are defended. Neglecting Underneath guarantees its destruction – what happens when the Amalgam swarms the tunnels and emerges beneath us?"

"Tunnel skirmishes and drunken brawls aren't war," Balric countered, tone edged with condescension.

Chirana leaned forward, eyes narrowing. "We hold the tunnels with blood and steel, Balric. We do not falter – not even when the ground itself turns against us."

Balric's nostrils flared. "Arrogance. You dwarves dig holes and call it defense."

"And you ljósálfar stand in the sun, blinded by your own brilliance."

A few chuckles, barely audible, spread. Balric stiffened, fingers curling against his belt. His glare swept across the table. "Cowards, the lot of you. You'd gamble with survival rather than stand firm."

Chirana crossed her arms. "And you would bury yourself in arrogance rather than see reason."

"If Underneath crumbles, don't come begging for rescue." He turned, cloak snapping behind him as he strode toward the chamber doors. The wood groaned as he shoved them open, leaving tense silence in his wake.

"Madame Praesidere?" Iris asked.

The stakes had only grown higher. Ursa and Lucea's mission –

to lure the Amalgam away – had been dangerous enough. But now, protecting the Vine's roots added another layer of complexity.

Stick to the original plan, and the battlefield stayed contained. But Underneath remained vulnerable, and Lucea's friend might not last.

Shift focus to Underneath, and the Amalgam remained unchecked chaos brewing above.

Farstride exhaled, tension rolling from her shoulders. Her sharp eyes flicked from Ursa and Lucea to the dwarven captain, who was still bristling from Balric's insult.

"We stay the course," Farstride said, voice steady.

The captain sneered after Balric – though he was already gone. "Light dwellers always think they know better."

Ursa met the dwarf's glare with quiet intensity. "Then prove them wrong."

Chirana's lip curled, but instead of replying, she squared her shoulders and let out a quiet breath. "Dwarves don't retreat," she said, voice steady, conviction sharpening each syllable. "We stand. We endure."

Farstride reiterated their plans: Ursa and Lucea would take position on the ramparts, luring the Amalgam into the open, while the dwarves secured Underneath. The rest would guard the rear and the city's interior. As murmurs faded and they made last checks, Farstride's voice cut through the lingering noise.

"The plan is set."

Ursa turned to Lucea. No words were necessary. Their resolve was absolute. They stood firm against the Amalgam.

Farstride called her. "Ursa?"

"Yes, Madame?"

"Balric's doubts don't come from nowhere," she said. "We're gambling everything on this."

"We are," Ursa acknowledged. "But hesitation won't serve us now."

The battlefield awaited.

CHAPTER THIRTY-TWO

The ramparts were a cold, unwelcome relic of winter clinging on despite spring's arrival, unwilling to yield, gripping the air with icy fingers.

Lucea drew the folds of her jacket tighter, shielding herself against the night's chill. The thought of shifting into her cat form crossed her mind, but with her magic suppressed, it would serve only one purpose – battle. Brutal. Instinctive. She might resort to that, but she knew her magic had a greater purpose.

The sun dipped below the horizon, and the full moon began its ascent. Lucea had a terrifying premonition deep inside. She shuddered at the thought of lycanthropes among the enemy ranks, as inevitable as the rising moon.

As if summoned, distant howls echoed.

They built Jack-In-Irons like a fortress, although it housed a diverse population. A towering wall encircled it, while the river – redirected through ingenious engineering – formed a natural moat around the city's perimeter. Even if an enemy dared to swim across, whispers of the creatures lurking in its depths ensured few risked the attempt. No one who tried ever reached the far wall.

Not that it mattered. Maris and her selkie troops patrolled the waters, supported by Phasa and the aerial forces, who commanded the skies with effortless precision. Lucea longed to see the emerging beings.

Below, Iris and the other captains prepared to lead the charge. To the west, Faith and her gryphons stood ready, while Isbet and a contingent of magic wielders took position to the east. Their arrangement formed a wedge meant to force the enemy into the open, leaving them surrounded. As planned, reinforcements would close the trap from behind. And if fortune favored them, Faith and Isbet's reinforcements would arrive just in time to tip the scales.

If they did not…

Four gates required defending. Cardinal points marked each person's position. Should any enemy reach the bridge, they would meet the soldiers on the ramparts, masters of their weapons and seasoned in battle.

Though the forest stretched for miles, the dark fey had so far attacked head-on, advancing toward the South Gate by the main road – the same path Lucea and Ursa had traveled. Someone would spot their attempt to cross the river long before they reached the city walls.

A blast of horns tore through the air, their echoes rippling like a wave down either flank, carrying the grim warning – the battle was upon them.

Unsettled silence gripped the battlefield, a calm before the storm. It showed in how those around her braced themselves. Bowstrings pulled tight; swords unsheathed; white-knuckle-tight hands around the grip. Lucea glanced at Ursa and found she held Iron Reaver the same way. Lucea was about to touch her arm; would that calm her? Then she decided against it. Nothing should distract Ursa; nor her, for that matter. Lucea focused her attention on the scene below.

Then, just as the moon crested the tree line, the dark fey surged forward like a living tide. Their grotesque forms twisted in the cold moonlight; their shadows elongated across the hillside. The wind carried a foul stench long before the dark fey arrived, a stench so foul that some of the less hardened soldiers retched. The first wave surged, a stampede of creatures clawing and trampling into a writhing mass of snapping jaws. Then came the command. Arrows whistled through the air, their flight swift and deadly.

At the heart of the defenses stood Iris and other magicians, including Isbet. With hands raised, their fingers wove through the air, and a shimmering veil shuddered into existence. Only Lucea and the Gifted could see them, hence the ground troops' readiness. The battlefield bent beneath their magic – figures wavered then vanished. Within seconds, soldiers materialized in new positions, blinking through the veil's illusion to flank the unsuspecting wave of dark fey.

Confusion rippled through the enemy ranks. Some beasts hesitated, growling at the empty air where prey had once stood.

The line of trebuchets unleashed a volley of destruction. A deep, resonant thunk sounded as the counterweight dropped, followed by the whomp of air displaced by the swinging arms. Immense tension caused the ropes to groan; a silent moment preceded the projectiles' whooshing, roaring flight.

Lucea watched as they released their payloads, fire-streaked projectiles arcing through the night sky before crashing onto the hillside. The moment they struck, the ground became a seething inferno – flames licking across earth and bodies with an unnatural hunger. It didn't burn out like typical oil-fed fires; it clung, ravenous, consuming everything in its reach with a heat that defied logic. She had seen something like this before, whispered among alchemists and war strategists – a concoction rumored to be born of pitch, resin, and something more volatile, perhaps lime or sulfur, twisted together to create an inextinguishable blaze. Whatever its composition, she knew one thing: water would do nothing. It would incinerate all remaining fuel.

After dozens of shadows glided across the sky, mere silhouettes against the full moon, they came careening down to snatch up whatever enemy was nearby. Faith and her gryphon army. Bones were crushed by strong talons and flesh rent with their razor beaks. Gryphon tears doomed any basilisk they touched.

Those dark fey who broke through the lines with their bodies aflame hoped to find relief in the icy waters of the rushing river. Lucea was helpless to relieve their suffering.

Lucea saw a group of defenders of the Silken Reef waiting near the riverbank, prepared to ambush any dark fey that tried to cross. The water held a dangerous edge that night. As the moonlight glinted across the surface, something stirred beneath – the river itself had become a battleground.

A Cù-Sìth leaped into the water, claws churning as it fought to reach the far side. But the moment it plunged deep, the unseen current dragged it below. More creatures tried the crossing, some swimming, others plunging into unseen depths. The river, sentient, didn't merely absorb; it resisted, possibly because of selkie magic. Manipulating the waves to their desire came naturally to the selkie. A spectral wraith rose from the water's surface, its form half-flesh, half-liquid, pulling anything too slow into its grasp.

Smoke rose from the battlefield, the flaming trebuchets casting flickering shadows against the fortress walls. The Amalgam hadn't appeared, which Lucea found strange, and sensed Ursa mirrored her feelings. Chemical and magical fires, combined with the full moon, illuminated the battlefield, making enemy concealment improbable.

A drumming sound, seemingly from above, relentlessly echoed. Massive waves of trees fell, groaning under unseen forces. The air shivered with the impact, dust and splintered bark thrown skyward as the forest itself bowed to the greater dark fey.

The battlefield fell silent – an eerie pause, as if the world held its breath.

Then, the horizon tore.

A presence rose, twisting like spilled ink across water. Darkness bled from it in waves, and with each pulse came a rancid breath: burning rot, wet ash, and the metallic tang of things long dead.

Someone whispered, "What… What moves like that?"

It stepped into view.

Skinless, sinews glistening, a centaur-nightmare welded from spite and agony. A single red eye smoldered in its skull, bright as a kiln, hungry as a star. Every hoof-fall corrupted the ground: grass crisped, soil curdled, and fresh blossoms shriveled black.

"What by the Vine is that abomination?" a soldier cried.

"Nuckelavee," Ursa spat before Lucea could respond. In her studies, Lucea had seen charcoal sketches – ink so hesitant it almost flinched from the parchment – but nothing prepared her for the living horror. Cold slammed through her ribs; her heartbeat sounded tiny in her ears.

Brave fools loosed arrows.

Shafts vanished into the flayed muscle without a ripple. Swords struck and vanished, devoured by living raw flesh. The beast did not bleed. It absorbed. Soldiers recoiled, horror blooming into madness. One vaulted the battlements, choosing a clean death on the rocks over this Rot-lord.

The Nuckelavee was not alone.

Behind it lumbered two mountain-high shapes – behemoths, reluctant yet dreadful, their thunderous steps cracking battlements. At their flanks surged Fomorians – hunched, tusked giants who warped the earth beneath their feet – followed by towering Firbolgs, their bark-armored frames exuding a hatred for every green thing.

We are stories waiting to end, Lucea thought, numb.

The Nuckelavee's breath swept the parapet. Stone wept black tears. A dozen men screamed, throats bubbling as skin blistered. Panic spread like wildfire; discipline shattered. Even Ursa's arms – so often Lucea's refuge – appeared icy, drained by proximity to the thing.

"Come here!" Ursa hauled her close, yet her embrace held no warmth; the monster had stolen that, too.

Below, lines collapsed. Soldiers discarded shields, fled, or fell to their knees, hope gone. The enemy pressed in. The city's last hour peaked.

And then – something answered.

From the riverbed beyond the eastern gate rose a hush, soft as a lullaby, clear as a chime. Mist coiled over ruined fields, pearlescent and cool. Where it drifted, Rot recoiled; blackened roots brightened, if only for a heartbeat.

A selkie – skin still glistening with brine – stood atop the shattered ford, arms lifted to the crescent moon. Her voice was surf and storm as she called upon an older name.

The River Wraith appeared.

At first a translucent silhouette, it gathered substance from every droplet, becoming a figure of rippling water shaped by moonlight. Its eyes shone like twin pearls; its robes were swirling currents that never soaked the ground. With each step, fresh water pooled, steaming where it met corruption, carving quicksilver channels through the blight.

The battlefield froze between two extremes.

Nuckelavee embodied heatless decay, a furnace of sickness, darkness so dense it felt harsh on the tongue. On the other, River Wraith – living fresh water, luminous and clean, the scent of rain after drought.

Rot hissed at purity; purity hissed back.

Nuckelavee charged, with a shriek of rusted iron. The River Wraith swept an arm – no, a wave. Water whipped forward, crashing against flayed flesh. Steam exploded; the monster reeled, its sinews smoking where droplets clung. For the first time, it bled. Not red blood, but black ichor that fizzed away under the Wraith's touch.

Lucea's heart stuttered with stunned hope. "Fresh water," she breathed. "Yes, I recall. It can hurt it!"

Around them, the despairing host looked up. The silver mist kissed their cheeks, cooling terror, quenching the creeping madness. Banners lifted anew. Archers dipped arrowheads into conjured pools that shimmered like liquid moonstone. Those with the elemental Gifts whispered cantrips of tide and torrent.

The River Wraith advanced, each stride birthing rivulets that braided through trenches, turning killing fields into reflective moats. The Nuckelavee hacked and writhed, hooves churning mud, yet every lunge brought more water, more searing purity.

Tonight, decay met the river.

Steam and starlight would reveal tonight's outcome.

Lucea stood transfixed, the spectacle holding her, so that she did not notice Balric's approach – only registering his presence when he strode into their space, breaking the moment like a blade through still water. "You will do better there." He enveloped the world in fog, his right hand a blur, before either Lucea or Ursa could object. There was a fleeting glimpse of movement – shadows shifting, figures writhing in the mist – before the veil lifted and they stood at the forefront of the battlefield.

"What in all the nether-hells—?" Ursa hissed, Iron Reaver already clenched white in her fist.

Through the half-lit murk, a lone rider burst from the gloom. Iris reined in her mare, which danced sideways. "How did you—?" She swallowed the rest, recognition flaring. "Balric."

The horse half-reared, reading the air. Iris pointed at the bridge. "Cross the span – warded stone. We'll hold them."

"No," Lucea said, planting her feet. "We fight."

Ursa's answering nod snapped like tempered steel.

War horns blared again, deeper, closer.

"Too late now," Iris muttered. "Both of you – on me. Match my pace."

"Yes, Captain," they answered together.

Shadows streaked overhead, then plunged: gryphons and riders, Faith at their head, talons ripping dark fey from the ranks like hawks shredding field mice.

Ursa powered forward, each sweep of Iron Reaver vaporizing armor and bone. When she slammed the hammer into the earth, a fissure yawned wide, coughing fire that swallowed the fleeing.

Lucea raised her hands. Time thickened. She aged marrow inside her foes until weapons clattered from brittle fingers and bodies sagged to ash that the wind hurried away.

The defenders rallied – until the largest dark fey drew together for a thunderous charge that shattered the line.

A new horn, not from their leaders, answered from the tree line as Lucea again grasped for power.

Out of the shadows surged a new group of soldiers in gleaming scale. Behind their vanguard stormed three colossal hounds – bristle-backed, eyes too wide for their skulls – closing straight on the darkest leviathans. The dark fey recoiled; they knew the dogs.

The lead rider sat tall and unmoving, his gold-and-white robes marking him as a figure of authority rather than just a warrior. The pendant on his neck gleamed with intricate engravings, a silent declaration of power or faith. Behind him, the decorative frame caught the light, lending him an almost ethereal presence. Watching him, Lucea experienced a quiet unease – this man wasn't leading. He was delivering judgment.

Allied ranks roared and pressed forward.

Lucea jolted. Ursa was gone. Panic flared until she spotted her beside Isbet, hammer and staff in lethal duet.

A ribbon of frozen instants carried Lucea across the chaos; she re-formed at Ursa's side. Her lover grinned through blood spray, then stiffened.

Lucea followed her gaze.

Across a carpet of corpses, something vast crawled, drinking the spilled life – the Amalgam.

No hell-wrought artist imagined it. A knot of flesh at war with itself, birthing limbs only to devour them, an entire battlefield's agony given shape.

It reared – towering, hungry, impossible – and the night itself seemed to buckle around it.

CHAPTER THIRTY-THREE

The world fractured at the Amalgam's arrival – not into chaos, but revelation. Thick smoke suffocated the battlefield, once a cacophony of steel and cries, dense enough to drown thought. Now, only essentials remained, the rest shed like dead skin.

The Amalgam carved through reality's marrow, stripping it to the bone, and in that stark clarity, Ursa found something close to peace. No distractions. No doubts. This moment was always inevitable. She had nowhere left to run.

She tightened her grip on the hammer, its worn handle pressing into her calloused palms, grounding her against the whirlwind of everything else. Beside her, Lucea stood steady, an unshaken sharp contrast to the roiling storm of smoke and sorcery around them. Finally, the weapon fit snugly in her hand, extending her reach. She might have laughed without mirth if they weren't standing at the precipice of war. The pulse hammering in her throat, the sting of sweat cooling against her skin, the slow, measured exhale before battle – these were the only truths left.

The entity twisted, its form a grotesque struggle of two souls unwilling and unable to separate. Its movements jutted and lurched, each shift distorting as unseen hands molded tar into something more monstrous. A face pushed forward. Hands reached outward. Beside her, Lucea drew in a sharp breath – but she did not waver.

With careful steps, Lucea shifted, keeping the intricate weave of runes as if threading order through the unraveling world around them. Here, now, Ursa found herself captivated, not just by the magic, but by the woman herself. Lucea bore no armor and carried no weapon, yet nothing had touched her. No blood had been spilled.

"Ursa." Lucea's voice cut through the moment, snapping her attention back to the Amalgam. Its malformed limb stretched toward her – oily, grasping. The reach was too human, too familiar, as if remnants of Barnabas still lingered within the unnatural form.

She had let him catch her unawares.

As the limb inched closer, Ursa braced herself – and the moment Iron Reaver met the air between them, Fey Bane's spell ignited. A violent, searing force tore through the space, sending the Amalgam recoiling, its form twisting as though burned from within. The tar-like substance rippled, warping in protest as Barnabas fought to push past the pain. It wanted her. It wanted through.

The shriek that followed was neither human nor monstrous. A voice, edged with hatred and need. He was still in there.

Ursa steadied herself, pressing Iron Reaver tighter against her chest. As long as she held the weapon, as long as Fey Bane remained active, Barnabas couldn't reach her.

But that didn't mean he would stop trying.

Barnabas recoiled from Ursa with sudden violence, flinging himself toward his other half, dragging a wake of tar across the earth. From the spreading blackness, new figures appeared – humanoid, yet like their creator, formless. They wailed in eerie unison, their mouths gaping wide as gurgling cries bubbled from deep within.

Their elongated limbs didn't reach for her – they reached for him. Not through violence, but through a terrible, worshipful devotion. And Ursa knew then what they were.

The spawn. Twisted echoes of the Netherborne Enclave, once comrades, now consumed by Barnabas's madness and reborn in Rot. Their forms were faceless, but she recognized them all the same – in the way they staggered, the way they wept his name.

A ripple of sorrow cracked through her, sharp and immediate. These were people. Dreamers. Fighters. She remembered the old laughter around the fire, hands clapping shoulder to shoulder in the dark. Now they crawled for him like starving dogs, eyeless and lost.

Barnabas turned them loose with a roar. They flinched at it. And then came the language – wet and guttural, something ancient and wrong. At his command, the spawn crawled toward her.

Ursa did not flinch. Not this time.

Iron Reaver came down in a sweeping arc. The earth split open like a wound, fire surging from the depths. The spawn did not scream. They welcomed the flame.

She watched as something devoured them – formless wretches returning to ash – and she quietly breathed out.

"For your souls," she whispered, and bowed her head.

Then the Rot's vessel unraveled. Cursing with a voice half-remembered from better days, Barnabas melted into the mud.

A flash of unyielding light cleaved the midnight gloom as Lucea's ancient runes blazed across the open scar of the battlefield. The brilliant runes swept over Samara and the scattered remnants of Barnabas like a decree from an otherworldly tribunal. Outside the timeworn walls of Jack-In-Irons, Ursa watched with grim clarity as Lucea's deliberate magic eroded Samara's once-defiant spirit – each pulse aging and withering her even within the insidious grip of the Rot. Near collapse, both adversaries faced Lucea's attempt to destroy their corrupt power.

With the potent essence of Fey Bane, Ursa plunged her hammer deep into the soured earth. In that charged moment, Samara's features contorted. A deep rift cleaved her face into two conflicting visages – one set in steely defiance directed at Ursa, the other, desperate, straining in vain toward Lucea. With measured resolve, Lucea's voice broke through the chaos:

"You will never have me."

Those words shattered what remained of Samara's will. The defiant half of her faltered under Lucea's proclamation, its light dimming as the inexorable pull of the Rot reclaimed its hold. Samara's form unraveled into scattered motes of shadow – soon absorbed by the ancient decay. Barnabas, too, yielded to the relentless force, collapsing into a quiet void where fierce defiance had flickered.

As the tumult of battle ebbed away, a profound silence gathered around Lucea and Ursa. The chaotic clash dwindled into a fading murmur, leaving the scarred battlefield – soaked in the residue of hardened magic and shrouded by the encroaching gloom of the Rot – to bear witness to the final, faltering pulses of conflict. At the fringes, the remnants of the dark fey stirred with a restless unease, their spectral forms flickering in the twilight as if mourning the burdensome toll exacted by ancient power. The quiet aftermath showcased a land silently attesting not to triumph, but to a somber cost. Power exacted through sacrifice.

Without having to look, Ursa reached out her hand and felt Lucea's slip into her grasp, warm and firm. "Follow me. Our task is complete," Ursa said. She almost didn't recognize her own force; there was a maturity there. She had never felt such profound peace, not even during her days of luxury at home. This, to her, was right. Back then, things had never been right.

Death and destruction fueled her determination. With Lucea with her and her love, she knew which way to go, and with a silent promise she would stay by Ursa forever.

As they reached the bridge, a veil appeared. Without hesitation or fear, they passed through it. Twisted shapes moved around in those unfamiliar territories once more, things so horrifying that a person would prefer death over encountering them. But it meant nothing to either of them.

When the veil dissolved, they stood in the hallway outside the meeting room.

An unnerving silence reigned.

Soldiers were absent. No servants. The guards who were supposed to be at the door were nowhere to be found. However, a figure sat in the shadows, positioned to the left of the doorway, leaning against the aging branch where Isbet had infused her staff into the wood, nourishing the Vine's essence.

Ursa and Lucea's approach interrupted her posture of knees drawn to her chest, head resting on them.

The woman's head snapped up. Recognition didn't come at once. Surprise flickered across her face, and her eyes darted between them – then dropped to their clasped hands.

Tantia.

Her fury thickened the air, a searing wave of emotion visible to Ursa's eyes. She was certain Lucea saw it too. But the white-hot anger parted before them, washing around them like a flame around stone.

Lucea declared, "Ursa," with conviction.

Ursa turned and squeezed both her hands. She smiled. It felt so cliché. Years of conflict culminated in a face-to-face meeting with the manifested voice. A memory given flesh. Ursa almost laughed.

She released Lucea and stepped toward Tantia. As she did, the quintessence of fury intensified, but despite that, it couldn't burn her. She stood before her once-friend, once-love.

"I loved you!" Tantia screamed.

"I did too. Back then. I should've seen the truth."

Seeing Tantia's expression, Ursa believed the faun's disgust stemmed from her views on humanity. That was entirely untrue.

"You left me alone!"

"Yes. I know that now." Ursa inched closer. "I didn't see it then."

"I would've gone with you!"

"I know," she breathed. "I would've sent you back."

"Why? Didn't you think I could survive?"

"I knew you could." Ursa spoke with a reassuring steadiness. "But you'd done nothing wrong. This burden was mine."

"That didn't matter to me!" Tantia's face twisted, her eyes filled with darkness.

"So," Ursa said gently, "you gave yourself to it." Of course she had. Ursa understood, completely. She almost wished she didn't.

"I was supposed to wait. To enter the War Room and kill Farstride."

"What stopped you?"

"The Vine. Here, it's strongest."

"But you still got in."

"I was already in." Tantia's gaze drifted. "After Farstride sent me away, I found a place to hide – in the shadows. The Rot found me there. I cowered at first…but it showed me."

"Showed you what?"

"Why they did all of this. They just want to be free. To see sunlight again."

"I know," Ursa said. "Don't you see? The Vine drew us together to weaken the Rot on all fronts. Our destiny was always to finish it together."

Something stirred in the air, whispering, *You are correct.*

"But why?"

"Don't you know?" Ursa stepped closer. "Why were the dark fey cast out, do you even remember?"

Tantia flinched. Her fists clenched, and black blood dripped between her fingers.

She whispered, "Creation of a new world was their desire. A better one. Without humanity. They don't deserve this land. We were here first."

"What world would this create?" Ursa's voice rose. "You say they want sunlight – but most of them can't endure it. Not even before their banishment to Deep Earth. How could they possibly endure a world bathed in light? Think, Tantia!"

She didn't need to imagine. The Vine responded to Ursa's will, revealing the vision.

An obscuring presence eclipsed the sun here. Perhaps destroyed. A frozen world, cloaked in darkness. Life perished by degrees – plants first, then the insects, the birds, the animals. Rivers turned to poison, and the Vine itself twisted into something monstrous. The Gift no longer given. Only sustained darkness.

And the light fey?

Broken, hunted, turned – or exiled. Ursa could see it. No magic, no sanctuary. The Rot would spread unchecked through every valley, every pool. Not just the Riven Isles, but every world connected to it.

Even the witches, being human, would be considered unworthy. Gifted or not. They would die too.

The land wouldn't last – not truly. Even the dark fey would exhaust it. But they would cheer the slow death. Cheer the end of all things.

That was the nature of the Rot.

And Death would wander this place, futile, searching for quintessence – but finding none. Powerful Gifted ultimately destroyed the Riven Isles.

The vision faded, and with it the surge of emotion ebbed away. Now Tantia appeared defeated – her shoulders slumped, her head bowed as she murmured words that Ursa couldn't quite catch.

"What did you say?"

"Your mother – the queen sent me here to spy."

"She had no intention of sending troops?"

Tantia looked up, and as Ursa had expected, let out a dry, mirthless laugh. "The letters of introduction, the offer of help – everything was a lie." Despite the bitterness in her tone, faint amusement lingered. "I never expected to find you here. When I learned you would help, I assumed you'd lend both yourself and the hammer. It belonged to the Steel Driver, correct?"

"Yes," Ursa replied. All pretense ceased. Iron Reaver was hers.

"It will make a fine trophy – a gift for the queen," Tantia murmured, speaking more to herself than to Ursa.

Ursa remained unflinching. "Surely you don't intend to."

"No," Tantia said, moving forward with steps that carried both determination and despair. Her hands, clasped together, betrayed the desperation in her expression. "You know what the queen will do! She'll punish me. If I present her with this and say I took it from you, she might spare me."

For a moment, Ursa couldn't fathom why Tantia believed that. The messenger presented no reason for royal reprisal. Ursa said, "The queen has no cause to punish you. You obeyed orders."

"She will be told you are here," Tantia insisted, her tone urgent. "And she'll demand to know what I did about you. I won't lie to my queen."

"Is she so concerned about me?" Ursa scoffed. "Oh, I see – I'm nothing but an embarrassment to her." Cradling Iron Reaver close to her heart, she declared, "I swear on this sacred weapon, I will return, confess my faults, and accept full responsibility."

"She'll have you killed!" Tantia cried.

"Let her try," Ursa replied. "I will defend myself. Is that not enough?"

Tantia faltered, then turned toward the entrance. "But what about Farstride?"

"What about her? This has nothing to do with Farstride or Jack-In-Irons," Ursa retorted.

"Well..." The oily tears that had been streaming down her face ceased. Tantia scrubbed the grime away with her fingertips. "All right. But I will not be responsible—"

The air between them shifted.

Ursa watched in horror as the transformation gripped her friend. Before she could speak, Tantia's body jerked with a cruel animation, and without warning, she lunged. The Rot dictated her every spasm, forcing an attack on her former confidante. Ursa's heart clenched with grief and disbelief, the tender bond they'd once forged now shattered by this foul corruption.

Ursa called upon the ancient spells that had sustained her through darker hours. She channeled her inner strength and the blazing resolve of her spirit first with Forgeheart. Except this time, without even willing it, a searing flame erupted from within her, wrapping her in a protective aura that burned with both warmth and pain. At the same moment, Ursa invoked the Mountain's Resolve. The steadfast shield of energy, as unyielding as a peak of rock, swirled into being around her, halting a frenzied blow from Tantia's corrupted limbs.

The corridor itself seemed to tremble under the force of the magic. The strikes against the barrier reverberated like a melancholic echo from Tantia's past, when she was lively, promising, and kind. And yet, as the spells held firm, Ursa's eyes searched for a glimpse of the friend she once knew beneath the Rot's influence. For a fleeting heartbeat, amidst the fury and the roaring flames of Forgeheart, something soft stirred in Tantia's gaze. The faun's compassion whispered this must end.

But the Rot's corruption was beyond a simple cure. The malignant force propelled Tantia's assault, extinguishing the gentle soul that once smiled at Ursa. With a heart shattered by the cruel inevitability of fate, Ursa realized the only way to break the Rot's hold was to end this tragic possession forever.

With both regret and resolve, Ursa stepped forward. Her spells flared more fiercely as she raised her arm, summoning the searing energy of Forgeheart into a single, decisive blow. In that excruciating moment, she poured her desperate hope into each pulse of light and heat, praying for her former friend's liberation from the darkness – even through death.

The fatal strike landed. Tantia staggered, her corrupted form faltering. As she fell, the hideous mask of the Rot receded in patches, and for one brief second, Ursa saw the faint glimmer of the kind faun she had once known. That inner spirit, broken yet dignified, assented. The faun conceded that this painful sacrifice offered the only chance for redemption.

Silence fell oppressive like a funeral dirge. The acrid tang of burning magic and bitter despair filled the air. Ursa stood alone, the weight of her act pressing down upon her soul, as the Rot's echoes faded into a mournful stillness. In the lingering glow of Forgeheart and the unyielding support of Mountain's Resolve, the memory of Tantia – of a friend lost to corrupt destiny.

In the cooling aftermath of the confrontation, Ursa stood amid the lingering echoes of desperate magic. The corridor pulsed with the fading warmth of Forgeheart while the unyielding shield of the Mountain's Resolve receded. A profound silence descended, its weight mirroring the unspoken sorrows surrounding her. Lingering battle traces faded, but not the ruins – instead, her gaze fell upon the void left by her departed friend.

Tears, mingled with the bitter tang of smoke and loss, welled in her eyes. Briefly, grief almost shattered her hard-won resilience. The memory of Tantia's gentle features, visible beneath the corruption, served as a reminder of what the Rot had stolen away. And yet, as the sorrow deepened, something profound stirred within her smoldering anger that refused to be quenched.

From the deep reservoir of resolve that had guided her thus far, Ursa felt familiar heat rising within, kindled by a fierce, almost primal wrath against the corrupting force. Despite twisting the soul of someone cherished, the Rot wouldn't prevail while she lived. With steady hands, she pressed her calloused fingers against the old, weathered bark of the Vine at her feet and listened to its subtle murmur – a reminder of ancient strength and enduring purpose.

Her voice, though raspy, sounded determined, and it shattered the silence of that tense moment. "I will destroy you, Rot. To reclaim the light, I will rid these Isles of your corruption – for Tantia, for all that's lost."

Every syllable was a promise, forged anew in the crucible of her grief and tempered by hard-won experience. This vow signified not despair, but progress toward a higher purpose. Ursa would not allow her progress to be undone by the remnants of tragedy; instead, she transformed her sorrow into a blazing resolve that would guide her path forward.

And she would not be alone.

CHAPTER THIRTY-FOUR

Above her fallen friend, Ursa felt the solemn hush of the palace corridor wrapped around her. Cool air gently radiated from sconces, reflecting off polished stone. The veils shimmered as the ethereal creatures remained fleeting silhouettes. In the profound silence, Lucea's gentle hand found its way to Ursa's, a tender, grounding touch amid the weight of loss.

"I'm sorry," Lucea whispered, her voice tinged with regret and empathy.

Ursa pressed her hand over Lucea's. "Thank you," she murmured, anchoring herself in that shared moment of sorrow and resilience.

A resonant creak pierced their quiet communion. The War Room's weighty, embellished doors slowly opened, exposing the customary room illuminated by dim light. Within its depths, every detail, the elegant curves of ancient architecture and the vacant seats that once buzzed with purpose, spoke of bygone battles. And there, in her customary spot, sat Farstride. The kobold's intense gaze and commanding aura conveyed meaning without the need for speech.

They stepped forward through the massive carved doors and approached the silent figure, the leader of all Jack-In-Irons. Without a word, she raised her hands above a scarred, use-worn table. In response, a luminescent magic circle shuddered into being, its twin sets of runes spiraling in opposition. From its heart, the Seed Box ascended. With a single, deliberate nod from Farstride, Ursa opened it and removed the seeds, stuffing them into her bodice, and perceiving the heat against her skin.

Before long, measured footsteps echoed down the corridor. All eyes turned as Iris strode in. Despite her ravaged uniform, a testament to dark fey claws, her wounds closed, revealing uncanny resilience.

Farstride broke the silence. "Iris will lead you to Underneath and the Root."

Ursa's gaze sharpened as she glanced at the battered messenger. "No," she replied, "look at her. She needs rest – and real medical aid."

"I'm healing fine," Iris insisted, with a note of impatience. "We haven't a moment to lose on idle quarrels."

Isbet entered, followed by Princess Faith. Ursa first met these men. In the corridor's hush, their unspoken solidarity said everything.

"Have we won the battle?" Farstride ventured, though Ursa sensed a greater complexity to the situation.

"We've slain most of the dark fey," Iris explained, her voice low with solemn conviction. "Some were driven back into the forest. Balric now leads our troops, and Phasa's people are in close pursuit. But a few have slipped away."

"And they will—" Farstride paused when her expression shifted to deep distress. Her hands clutched her temples.

"Madame?" Iris cried, rushing to Farstride's side. "What is it?"

After a few agonizing moments, the kobold's tone turned grim. "They are coming. The Rot is forcing its way in."

"More dark fey?" Lucea asked, her eyes narrowing in concern.

"Yes – but they come in its wake," Farstride murmured.

"No one has ever seen the true face of the Rot," Ursa declared, her voice wavering between dread and defiance.

"We have seen it take form," Isbet offered. "As an almost human, misshapen visage—"

"So have we," Faith added.

"But that is not its true face," Lucea interjected. "I doubt it even possesses one of its own – it borrows and warps the faces of others to hide behind."

"I assume you did not see its face, did you, Madame?" Iris asked, her voice laced with worry as she peered at Farstride.

Farstride's eyes darkened. "I did not see it. I sensed only its presence. It stayed visible."

Ursa stated firmly, "We aren't afraid." She didn't need to search Lucea's eyes. The deep bond they shared proved that fear was absent from their hearts when facing the very essence of evil.

Ursa's voice rang out with unwavering determination: "We fight to protect the Celestial Vine – the force that birthed us all into this world."

★ ★ ★

They ran.

Through the winding corridors of the palace, Ursa and her companions pushed past startled servants and hurried healers tending to incoming wounds. At one point, Ursa glimpsed a mysterious figure in a nearby room: a woman with skin darker than night, draped in flowing black robes, bent over a motionless figure on a cot. In that fleeting moment, their eyes met. With a subtle nod, the ghostly woman hinted at a final goodbye, conveying a silent message from Death that this apparition and its significance would not trouble them for quite some time.

Ursa followed the curving passage upward and soon recognized that they had reached the grand arch connecting the palace to the base of the Vine. Instead of a door or a staircase waiting below, a dark tunnel yawned before them, its walls illuminated by drifting wil-o'-wisps. This proved no mere passage but a chute, carved by dwarven hands.

Her surprise deepened when Iris, without hesitation, lowered herself onto the chute and pushed off into the void. Lucea's face, alight with exhilaration, mirrored the same bold spirit as she followed suit, while Isbet's staff even emitted a playful whoop as she slid down in graceful abandon.

The ride constituted a straight, unyielding descent with no curves to soften the fall. Iris shot to her feet at the bottom, ensuring that none of them would collide in their frantic scrambling. Ursa paused to notice that even Faith and her prince – in their decorative armor – moved as if the metal and their bodies were a single unit.

And so, with hearts pounding and resolve unbroken, they plunged deeper into the unknown, each step charged with the promise of danger, destiny, and hope.

And the Riven Isles centered there.

Ursa stepped into the ancient cavern, her heart pounding with a mix of awe and determination. Before her lay the secret heart of the Vine – a mystical tableau alive with the spirit of ages past. A vast circular pool of still water mirrored the cavern's wonders in ghostly perfection, its surface disturbed only by colossal, gnarled roots that appeared from depths unseen. These massive roots twisted with raw, almost defiant power, as if guarding a magic older than memory.

A gigantic tree, resembling a monument, stood in the cavern's center. Its powerful trunk, cloaked in emerald moss and intertwined with delicate, whispering vines, spoke of millennia lost and reclaimed. The tree's sprawling branches reached upward toward a natural opening in the cavern's lofty ceiling, where soft beams of light filtered in, casting an ethereal glow that danced over every surface. In the interplay of light and shadow, Ursa found a profound mixture of hope and solemn duty stirring within her.

Her gaze wandered along the elegant arched walls, where magical veils hung like silken draperies. Through these translucent curtains, ethereal creatures drifted in a silent, otherworldly ballet, a constant reminder of realms beyond the tangible. The gentle illumination from distant torches revealed fine details in the weathered stone, each marking a testament to forgotten history and quiet power.

Amid the enchanted sanctuary, Ursa understood this cavern represented more than the resting place of the Vine's root, the living, enduring soul of a force that created her world. In that hushed, hallowed moment, she vowed she would protect this sacred ground from the encroaching darkness, even if it meant facing the core of her own resolve.

"The water."

Lucea's voice, trembling with horror, shattered the silence. Ursa's eyes drifted back to the pool encircling the sacred Vine

– it lay in a menacing sheen of oil-black, reminiscent of the Rot's insidious corruption.

"Are we too late?" Lucea whispered with dread.

Ursa responded with calm determination. "No. Do you hear it? The call of the Vine?"

In the flickering reflections on their companions' faces, they discerned not a gentle summons but a dire warning.

From the vast tunnel to their left erupted a cacophony – a savage chorus of guttural cries and roars punctured the darkness. As if summoned by some primordial fury, the sound of flesh being torn mingled with a distant, thunderous explosion that shook the cavern to its core, sending stones cascading from above. They dove for cover, pressing themselves against the cold, hard walls, as a writhing, twisted mass of dark fey spilled into the light – a macabre, tumbling horde of writhing bodies and spilled blood.

As if emerging from a nightmare, a beast unexpectedly appeared – its form so strange that Ursa momentarily questioned her vision. A colossal fox, its fur gleaming fiery red, bore ivory blades for claws, and its fierce golden eyes blazed. The dark fey – lesser creatures, mere goblins, lamia, Red Caps, and their ilk – sputtered in disarray. Some fled in terror, while others tried to resist, only to be torn asunder.

Beside her, Lucea inhaled before dashing forward. In a swirl of motion, she shifted shape mid-stride and joined the fox in the fray. That single act spoke volumes to Ursa. This gleaming guardian represented friendship. Together, Ursa and her companions pressed the assault – chasing the fleeing, engaging the stubborn – while Lucea and the magnificent fox carved a bloody path through their enemies.

Later, movement caught Ursa's eye. A young, dark-skinned woman appeared from the shadowed recesses of the same cavern. Intricate, shimmering squares spiraled across her skin like a living sigil, circling her in a mesmerizing pattern. Each time a dark fey neared, she would draw a card from a worn deck, and with it, an apparition would materialize – a warrior woman whose mere presence sent the fiends scattering into the dark. One specter emerged, then another, joining the chaos until the enigmatic woman withdrew, locking eyes with Ursa briefly. Her eyes widened, after which she hurried inside and sat. Her hands re-formed the deck.

Ursa's confusion ended when she noted the dark fey's distance. The woman lifted one card, the face to Ursa, who remained too distant to read it; however, something immense formed between them. A giant emerged from the swirling convergence; he towered like the Vine's sprawling root. His skin showed a deep, earthen tone. He wore overalls fashioned from a strange, unknown weave. As his form crystallized before Ursa's eyes, a flicker of recognition stirred within her – he constituted something other than a mere phantom. Over his broad shoulder, he carried Iron Reaver.

"You!" Ursa breathed, awe and a hint of accusation mingling in her tone.

He haunted her nightmares and fueled her relentless quest.

He met her gaze with a roguish grin, pride radiating in every line of his face. Ursa felt justified in her rage but recognized his intervention reignited her purpose. This pivotal meeting revealed a love that now sustained her.

Ursa knelt and held Iron Reaver aloft, as if offering it back in sacrifice. She waited, anticipating the restoration of his past achievements. When the silent moment stretched, she dared to raise her eyes. The Steel Driver – now in spirit – bent low, an immense finger first pointing at her, afterward at the hammer. With a final, solemn gesture, he straightened, and in that transformative instant, Ursa knew – the hammer belonged to her.

Without a word, the Steel Driver pointed to the cavern's entrance. Ursa noticed a lone figure – the card-wielding woman – step aside, and from deep within the cave, ominous sounds gathered once more.

In an astonishing moment, the Steel Driver shrank to Ursa's size. A surge of spectral energy preceded his merging with her essence, empowering her with his immense strength. With surging determination, Ursa advanced a few measured steps before leaping toward the cave entrance. Clutching Iron Reaver tight, she brought the mighty hammer down upon the ancient stones. The impact resonated with a deep, reverberating rumble; the stones crumbled, the cavern walls collapsed, and a dense plume of smoke billowed forth. In the ensuing chaos, Ursa saw the advancing dark fey become entombed beneath falling rubble – a grim, brutal retribution.

Breathless, she dropped back to the cavern floor. Then, from the incandescent swirl of her quintessence, her ancestor emerged – a spirit whose infectious smile lit his weathered features. Ursa couldn't help but grin as he offered a respectful salute before turning back to the mysterious woman, disappearing once more into the confines of her ethereal card.

"Harper!" Lucea's cry rang out, and she rushed to embrace the newcomer with open arms. As she clutched Harper, the magnificent fox padded near. Lucea turned and wrapped her arms around the fox's neck, burying her face in his warm, familiar fur. "Uncle Reynard, it's so good to see you!" Thus appeared the infamous Reynard the Fox, a cherished ally in their arduous journey.

The others gathered as the revelry stirred until a sudden noise – faint yet foreboding – echoed from behind the shattered stone wall.

"They're coming," Iris warned.

"Will the wall hold?" Isbet asked as Harper and Reynard joined their ranks.

Ursa's voice, steady and imbued with the urgency of fate, cut through the murmur. "Likely not." She'd already sensed this from the shared might of the Steel Driver within her.

"Then we must hurry."

They pressed onward toward the pond that encircled the Vine. There, a creeping darkness, a malignant, ravenous blackness – slithered through the earth, reaching for the root. The raw agony of the Vine's suffering struck them all like a physical blow; Ursa, Lucea, and the other women faltered, collapsing to their knees beneath the overwhelming pain.

"What's happening?" Iris demanded, panicked.

"We are Beholden," Isbet gasped, voice trembling as she realized, "this close to the Vine—"

"But we're not—?" Lucea began, only to be halted as Ursa's fierce hand tore at the shoulder of her robe. Encircling Lucea's shoulder, a tattoo of the Vine showed up – one that resembled Ursa's. Ursa pressed her shoulder against Lucea's, their kindred marks fusing with unspoken resolve.

"We can't let it stop us."

With renewed determination, Ursa seized Iron Reaver and plunged it into the pond. The moment the steel met stone and sacred water, the encroaching darkness recoiled, as if wounded. Winding her arm around Lucea's shoulders with gentle strength, Ursa hoisted her beloved upward. They hauled Iron Reaver in their wake. Ursa's focus on reaching the Vine Root was so intense that she did not notice the sound of the crumbling stone wall behind them.

At last, she extended a trembling hand and pressed it against the ancient Vine. To her astonishment, it yielded – her hand passed through as if the barrier itself was an illusory veil. In that heartbeat, the darkness swallowed both Ursa and Lucea, falling into the secret heart of the sacred root.

CHAPTER THIRTY-FIVE

"Hold on to me."

Ursa and Lucea tumbled from the ancient tree, landing in a vast realm, starlike in its expanse. They stood on a radiant pathway of pure, shimmering light suspended in a void studded with countless stars. Ursa's eyes took in the endless darkness, punctuated by brilliant portals that swirled with mesmerizing colors and intricate patterns. One portal shone with deep aquatic blues that evoked distant, forgotten seas. A second pulsed, its vibrant green a mystical forest giving life to the shadows. Still others flickered with fiery reds reminiscent of molten landscapes and softened into hues of enchanted purple, as if capturing the magic of twilight.

Every detail of this cosmic vista enraptured Ursa's senses – the interplay of light and color, the promise of unseen worlds shimmering just a step away. Boundless space stirred Ursa; wonder, adventure, and unimagined destinies beckoned from every portal.

"Ursa?" Lucea's voice was soft, but it echoed through the space they found themselves in.

"This is the Vine, where it reaches out to all other worlds," Ursa said.

"But why here?" Lucea was confused. "We were supposed to plant the seeds."

"And we will." Ursa reached into her bodice and drew out the seeds. They were shining like stars. A new hole appeared as Ursa prepared to drop them, but it was just a formless void. Emotions poured forth – desperation, anger, fear, sadness – it all came through as something and nothing appeared.

Lucea moved to Ursa's side. A fragment of darkness solidified into Tantia, but Ursa knew it wasn't real.

"You would rob me of happiness?" Tantia's voice merged with the fallen.

"I know you are not Tantia," Ursa said. "As for robbing you of happiness? Does a monster understand this?"

False Tantia opened her mouth, let out a scream born of frustration and melted away. A second and third figure stepped forward.

"Blasphemer!" Barnabas cried, pointing an accusing finger at Ursa. "Infidel!"

"Come to me," Samara spoke to Lucea. "I will show you desire and grant all of your wishes."

"You are both the spawn of a creature who would destroy everything. We have no interest in either of you."

They roared, spat and protested, but in the end they perished.

"What else do you have for us, creature?" Ursa challenged.

Another stepped out. It appeared as a dokkalfar unfamiliar to both of them.

"I am a prince of your realm," it said. "You will pledge fealty to me, and I will make you great."

"Who in the nether-hells are you?" Ursa demanded.

"His name is Serval." A familiar voice came from behind him. The others were there. Isbet, Faith, and Harper.

"How are you all here?" Ursa asked.

"We are not," Isbet replied. "What you see is a part of our quintessence, shaped by the Vine."

"But are you all right? Back there?" Lucea said.

"We are," Faith said. "We have rid our world of the rest of the dark fey or driven them back to Deep Earth."

"That was swift," Ursa said, bemused.

"Time flows differently here," Lucea said. Of course, she would know.

"He poorly imitates the man who threatened me," Isbet said.

"And mine," Faith added. "They exiled him, and he gave himself to the Rot. And I destroyed him. Do you recall, Serval?" Faith directed her words at the being. "You perished in water, your body transformed."

"I hate you!" Serval cried. "You took everything from me! My kingdom. My pride. You stole…him from me!"

"He never wanted you. He finds you reprehensible, as do we," Isbet said.

Serval plunged his hands into the writhing black and threw his head back and screamed aloud, the others echoing his pain. He succumbed as they did.

A woman elaborately dressed replaced Serval. Ursa and Lucea remained unaware of her identity. Harper spoke that time. "The ghost of a powerful woman who gave herself to the Rot and I tore her asunder. She asked me to read her victory in my cards, and I told her she would fail."

The woman stamped her foot like a belligerent child. "You lied to me!"

"I did not," Harper said.

The woman threw a tantrum, hemmed and hawed, and pulled out black strands of hair before she too vanished. The darkness was silent.

"We have a message for you," Isbet said. "The Vine has reached the realms visible beyond these gates, extending its presence to offer many Gifts to each of these places. Some embraced them, and magic flowed. Others have abandoned the Vine and its Gifts."

"Some places have destroyed the Vine," Harper said.

"It's these places where you must follow the Rot and wipe it away, let the Vine flourish."

Lucea questioned. "Why do it? Forsaking the Vine?"

"We couldn't say." Isbet inclined her head to her companions for agreement. The other women nodded in response. "Perhaps they do not understand the importance of the Vine."

"Or don't care," Ursa muttered.

"Those gates you must close against the Rot returning here," Isbet said.

"Is that right?" Lucea asked.

"Isolating these worlds from the Vine? No hope exists for these places?" Ursa inquired.

Faith urged, "Open your mind to the Vine. It will answer."

"What will happen next? Will we return after we have finished?" Ursa said.

It was the Vine who answered, its words heard by all.

"So, this is goodbye." Faith's voice faltered.

"No." Ursa smiled, her tone imbued with quiet resolve. "We'll return. Many destinations await. The Vine will guide us."

The four embraced, and they whispered farewells which became until the next life, perhaps the next time. They wept together but there was that bond between them that would never fade. An elegy to both hope and sorrow. It would lead them home and their sisterhood would be anew. The four stayed to see them off, before returning to their reality.

Together, Ursa and Lucea turned toward the encroaching darkness.

"Have you nothing more to say?" Ursa challenged the Rot. Without response, it surged from the portal in a violent, churning torrent, advancing against them. In a heartbeat, an overwhelming gloom swallowed both.

"Ursa!" Lucea screamed into the void.

"I have you!" Ursa cried as she drew Lucea close. "Go forward!"

For a dreadful moment, the Rot battered the two within its depths. Then, as if time itself bent to Lucea's inner Gift, a soft radiance appeared – reversing the destruction, healing their wounds. With renewed strength, they tore through the Rot from the inside out.

Following this struggle, they beheld the first gate shimmering in hues of vibrant green. Passing through, they entered a realm overflowing with life: endless stretches of lush foliage, oceans clear and deep blue, and freshwater ponds and lakes, and rivers that glittered like silver ribbons. Here, nature flourished unchallenged by human presence – for now. Yet, the promise of change hung in the air. Drawn by smelling the Vine, they soon found a scar upon the land: a blackened valley where the Rot had forced its way in, corrupting wildlife and warping flora. As the hostile darkness stirred to reclaim this defiled space, Ursa and Lucea, with the strength of iron will, and mastery over time's fleeting moments, drove it back into a realm beyond.

Ursa then planted the first seed, her will imbuing it with life. They watched, mesmerized, as the seed unfurled its tendrils of light, mending the wounded earth. Bolstered by this success, they pressed onward – each time the Rot lashed out with bitter fury, they countered in kind, unweaving its dark strands until nothing remained but limp, ashen remnants.

Their next destination glowed red – a realm of raging, fiery mountains, where molten rock cascaded like infernal waterfalls and toxic seas seethed with boiling despair. Humans survived here, their numbers dwindling in the merciless environment. Yet within this hellish tableau, a tiny village clung to life. In its heart, a little girl nurtured once-deadly plants, coaxing poison into blossoms of hope. Within this fragile sanctuary, Ursa placed the second seed. In that moment, a gentle smile struck her. The girl directed it at her silent benediction amid chaos.

The third world comprised an expansive realm of water. Here, scattered islands and drifting communities made their living on vast, rolling seas. Though the land was sparse, a quiet resilience reigned. The 'watchers' of this realm celebrated each small rebirth, their hearts buoyed by the Gift that rekindled hope with every rising tide.

Not all worlds were so generous. In one realm, a stark, silver light shrouded an urban expanse – a place not unlike our Earth in its modern, industrial garb. Imposing skyscrapers, clinging metal and glass, and relentless smokestacks belching black and gray plumes obscured any sign of nature's gentle protest. Here, the relentless pace of progress had erased the primal pulse of the Vine. Pollution marred the land; water was thick with sludge, and vibrant greens had been all but overwritten by the harsh neon of a modern decay. In this crucible of metal and smoke, petty conflicts tore through society like ragged scars, and the Rot laughed as it claimed every desolate alley and vacant field.

They felt despair for the first time.

"No," Lucea declared, voice trembling with anguish. "There must be some haven here?"

Ursa's reply was a bitter whisper. "With the true Gift denied, the Vine torn from Earth's heart, what hope remains?"

Tears fell as they contemplated sealing off this desperate, dying world to prevent the Rot from creeping back into the heart of the Vine. Was there no redemption here at all?

Then, from somewhere within that lamentable desolation, a soft murmur echoed – a call from the Vine itself, perceptible, and insistent. With hearts intertwined by love and emboldened by faith, they raced toward its faint promise. Even as the Rot surged, clawing at them with the last vestiges of its malevolence, their bond held firm.

They reached a secluded refuge with few inhabitants. Amid the ruins of ancient trees and the delicate regrowth of wildflowers, a young man drew water from a well. His gentle smile spoke of resilience. Instead of planting a seed on the barren soil, Ursa held it out in her palm. The young man accepted it with a grin, then strode toward a tilled patch of earth. When marauders tried to seize his humble harvest, he defended it with a fierce, unyielding spirit – proof that even amidst a world choked by toxic fumes and decaying metal, hope could still ignite. They departed, hearts hopeful, believing transformation possible despite pervasive modern decay.

Further on, they journeyed to lands less ravaged by industry – realms of modest villages and hamlets reminiscent of the bygone traditions seen in the Riven Isles. Here, the people clung to age-old ways yet still lacked the true Gift; the Vine's promising tendrils were scarce. Guided by its silent call, they pressed forward.

"Such sorrow," Lucea murmured, eyes lowered in contemplation. "What desolate lives these people must lead, bereft of the Gift."

"Oh, I do not know," Ursa replied as they approached a towering, ancient tree – once mighty, now succumbing to decay. With gentle deliberation, she planted another seed, her thoughts lingering on the mysterious gap within its vast root network.

Their odyssey carried them through realms with human clamor and those where nature reigned supreme. In some areas, sentient animals dominated, reminding them of a world where nature still ruled. In others, the familiar landscapes of the Riven Isles and distant coastal lands unfolded, each battle against the encroaching Rot inching toward victory.

They arrived at a terminal point – a void of pure darkness, interrupted only by the soft, persistent sound of water lapping against unseen shores. Here, the Rot launched one final, desperate assault. Its fury was overwhelming, and in one terrible moment, it tore at the bond between them.

"Ursa!" Lucea cried out in despair.

"I'm here!" Ursa fought her way through the torrent. "Come to me!"

As the Rot strained to keep them apart, a brilliant force surged forth – manifesting the Vine itself. It split the dark mass in two, and Ursa seized Lucea's hand, pulling her close. The Vine enveloped them both, drawing them into its luminous heart while cloaking them in a velvety darkness that promised renewal.

Well done. Sleep claimed Ursa after a whispered phrase.

★ ★ ★

Ursa stepped out of the copse of trees, unsure how she had arrived.

What was her final memory? Worlds, layered like dreams, unfurled before her: luminous, ravaged, divine. She and Lucea had crossed them all. Where others recoiled in fear, they had stepped forward together – hands clasped, hearts steady.

The task was done.

Although the Rot was indestructible, they pushed it back and buried it deep within the world's marrow. Beneath stone and myth. The Deep Earth held it now. Not vanquished, but contained.

For a period, their world – and several others – remained secure.

Ursa found herself in an unfamiliar world.

Perpetual twilight blanketed the land. To the east, a vast golden light touched the swaying grasslands, its source a glowing sphere not quite a sun – too immense, too knowing. It exuded the memory of warmth. In the west, velvet night bloomed wide, thick with stars. The forest stretched into it, silver-dusted and deep. A full moon – not theirs – hung low, glimmering like rippling silk in a phantom breeze.

Night sounds drifted through the stillness – crickets, an owl's song, and beneath them all, a whisper from below. Familiar. Faint. The Rot, acknowledging them one last time...and then silence.

Ahead, a grassy hill rose from the twilight. At its crown stood a great willow, its branches full with floating lights. Not lanterns – but fragments. A flower emerged, visible only during twin eclipses. A pearl shell from the singing sea. A cinder-marked leaf from the city that burned and healed. Echoes, all of them.

And beneath the branches, Lucea waited on an ornate iron bench, clothed in darkness.

Ursa glanced down. She wore white, as brilliant as the first snowfall – yet it comforted her. Not mourning. Just balance. They had seen too much to call either light or dark pure. They were complementary truths. Yin and Yang. Two parts of the same quintessence.

Lucea rose, smiling. She waved, love radiant across the dim air.

They knew this was not the end. Their world would call them back again. But time here was soft and slow, a hush between beats. Ursa stepped forward.

It was the last hill that Ursa had to climb.

Afterword

Dear readers,

Though *Steelbound* may mark the final chapter of *Tales from the Riven Isles*, it isn't the end of my stories – not by a long shot. The Isles will call me back someday, and when they do, I hope you'll walk those war-torn shores with me once again.

This journey was never mine alone. To my Big Brother, Lance Flemmings, and soul-sister, Kelli Riffle – thank you for standing behind me with love and grit. Your encouragement turned doubt into resolve.

To the indie bookstores and Barnes & Noble locations that opened their doors and treated me like I belonged – thank you for believing in the magic of these tales and the hands that penned them. You made the road feel less lonely.

To my stellar agent, Anne Tibbets, and the team at Flame Tree Publishing – your faith made this series real. I'm endlessly grateful for your support and vision.

And to you, dear reader, thank you for walking beside me through myth and mayhem. Whether you've been here since *Tinderbox* or discovered the Isles just now, I'm so honored to have shared this world with you. I can't wait to lead you into the next one.

And ladies – get those mammograms. No magic spell replaces self-care.

Peace,
W.A. Simpson

About the Author

W.A. Simpson has been writing since the age of five after a family friend gave her an old typewriter, when she saw that she enjoyed creating works of mystery and suspense that only a five-year-old could. She completed her first novel and started shopping it at fourteen. In later years, she figured out mystery wasn't her thing. It was a story by Ray Bradbury that she enjoyed that turned her toward fantasy.

On a more personal note, she likes to think she is the world's biggest bibliophile. When she's not writing, she indulges in her favorite pastimes, which include working in her garden, video gaming, and streaming. Come see her on Twitch as Runic Nightshade.

Her previous books with Flame Tree in the *Tales from the Riven Isles* series are *Tinderbox, Tarotmancer* and *The Hatter's Daughter.*

FLAME TREE PRESS
FICTION WITHOUT FRONTIERS
Award-Winning Authors & Original Voices

Flame Tree Press is the trade fiction imprint of Flame Tree Publishing, focusing on excellent writing in horror and the supernatural, crime and mystery, science fiction and fantasy. Our aim is to explore beyond the boundaries of the everyday, with tales from both award-winning authors and original voices.

•

Other titles in the *Tales from the Riven Isles* series by W.A. Simpson:
Tinderbox
Tarotmancer
The Hatter's Daughter

You may also enjoy:
The Sentient by Nadia Afifi
Junction by Daniel M. Bensen
Keeper of Sorrows by Rachel Fikes
Silent Key by Laurel Hightower
The Widening Gyre by Michael R. Johnston
The Heart of Winter by Shona Kinsella
The Sky Woman by J.D. Moyer
The Guardian by J.D. Moyer
Brittle by Beth Overmyer
Tempered Glass by Beth Overmyer
The Goblets Immortal by Beth Overmyer
One Eye Opened in That Other Place by Christi Nogle
The Last Feather by Shameez Patel Papathanasiou
The Eternal Shadow by Shameez Patel Papathanasiou
The First King by Shameez Patel Papathanasiou
A Killing Fire by Faye Snowden
A Killing Rain by Faye Snowden
A Sword of Bronze and Ashes by Anna Smith Spark
Idolatry by Aditya Sudarshan
The Roamers by Francesco Verso
Whisperwood by Alex Woodroe
Of Kings, Queens & Colonies by Johnny Worthen

•